PRAISE FOR

In the Arms of the Heiress

"*Downton Abbey* fans will fall in love with Maggie Robinson's Ladies Unlaced series. Sexy intrigue, sharp wit, tender romance . . . *In the Arms of the Heiress* delivers them all, and in grand style. A must read!"
—Tessa Dare, *USA Today* bestselling author

"Maggie Robinson has done it again. Her new Edwardian-set story is an openhearted romance that will sweep readers into the turbulent times at the turn of the century when manners and mores were changing as fast as hemlines. I was utterly charmed by the madcap, motor-driving heroine and the wounded war hero who finds more than he bargained for *In the Arms of the Heiress*. Full of witty dialogue and scorching romance, *In the Arms of the Heiress* kept me reading nonstop. I will read anything and everything Maggie Robinson writes—no matter what time period!"
—Elizabeth Essex, RITA Award–nominated author

PRAISE FOR THE NOVELS OF MAGGIE ROBINSON

"Robinson turns in an unusual Regency packed with drama. Despite the heavy secrets, the romance is unaffected and pure." —*Publishers Weekly*

"Robinson crafts an intelligent, powerful, emotional, highly sensual love story . . . Readers will become so invested in the characters that the fast pace and heated sexual tension only add to the delight. Fine storytelling." —*RT Book Reviews*

"A charming, extra-sexy tale."
—Eloisa James, *New York Times* bestselling author

"Sexy chemistry and the wry humor permeate the story. I really enjoy those books where the characters take real joy in their pleasure, and this is one of them." —*Dear Author*

In the Heart of the Highlander

Highlander

MAGGIE ROBINSON

♡

Maggie Robinson

B

BERKLEY SENSATION, NEW YORK

THE BERKLEY PUBLISHING GROUP
Published by the Penguin Group
Penguin Group (USA) LLC
375 Hudson Street, New York, New York 10014

USA • Canada • UK • Ireland • Australia • New Zealand • India • South Africa • China

penguin.com

A Penguin Random House Company

IN THE HEART OF THE HIGHLANDER

A Berkley Sensation Book / published by arrangement with the author

Berkley Sensation Books are published by The Berkley Publishing Group.
BERKLEY SENSATION® is a registered trademark of Penguin Group (USA) LLC.
The "B" design is a trademark of Penguin Group (USA) LLC.

For information, address: The Berkley Publishing Group,
a division of Penguin Group (USA) LLC,
375 Hudson Street, New York, New York 10014.

ISBN: 978-0-425-26580-2

PUBLISHING HISTORY
Berkley Sensation mass-market edition / October 2013

PRINTED IN THE UNITED STATES OF AMERICA

10 9 8 7 6 5 4 3 2 1

Cover art by Judy York.
Cover design by George Long.
Interior text design by Kelly Lipovich.

Chapter

1

Mount Street, London
May 31, 1904

$\mathcal{M}$ary Evensong was tired. Tired of wearing smoke-gray spectacles that covered her hazel eyes. Tired of wearing an itchy gray wig that covered her russet hair. Tired of the problems that came in by the sackloads every time the mailman rang her doorbell.

And most especially tired of her Aunt Mim, who was the original Mary Evensong and refused to stay *re*tired.

Every day when Mary locked up the Evensong Agency offices and trudged upstairs to the elegant apartments above, she had to face Aunt Mim's questions and Aunt Mim's gouty foot. It was the gouty foot that had been both their undoing. Mim had been running her employment agency and people's lives since 1888, after a successful career as housekeeper to a duke. Instead of relaxing in the handsome cottage the duke provided once she turned fifty-five after forty years of exceptional service to the family, Mim Evensong sold it, took her savings, and set up her business in London. She knew what great—and not so great—houses needed in the way of reliable servants.

She also knew what flighty young society girls needed—she'd had experience helping to marry off the duke's five difficult daughters, and had sat up with the girls more nights than she could count discussing the vagaries of young gentlemen. Her cleanliness, canniness, and common sense made her uniquely qualified to solve various domestic disasters.

But one morning in 1900, just in time to herald the new millennium, her big toe began to throb. Soon the other toes joined it. Her ankle, too. Now it was with the greatest difficulty that she rose from her chair and hobbled to the window to watch the traffic on Mount Street. There was no thinking of her going downstairs to her thriving business to interview footmen or meet with a mama in her private office to discuss her daughter's slide into scandal with an impoverished musician who insisted on playing ragtime instead of Richard Strauss.

So four years ago, Mim had invited her namesake niece, Mary, to make her home with her and learn the ropes of the Evensong Agency. Mary was a spinster, just as Mim was—the *Mrs.* was an honorific that had been granted to her as the duke's housekeeper as she rose up the ranks.

Mary really had nothing better to do—both her parents were dead, her brother married and running their grocery shop. She faced a dismal future of keying the cash register and unpaid babysitting for her hellacious little nephews.

Mary was a sensible young woman, and looked forward to a new life in London, without frogs in her bed and the constant chatter of her bossy sister-in-law at home. She would not miss the scents of overripe melon and problematic sausages at work, and hung up her spotless apron there with no regrets.

It was only when she arrived in Town that Mim's plan for her looked less than sterling. Mim was harboring the fond delusion that one day her foot would miraculously reduce in size and she could return to the massive mahogany desk in her corner office. The fact that she was in her seventies did not dissuade her from feeling the company could not function without her and her vaunted wisdom. It was imperative to continue its lucrative services, and imperative that her clients trust the dispenser of those services as they had these dozen years.

Young Mary did not look especially wise. True, she had a broad forehead and shrewd hazel eyes, but her hair was reddish and some people thought redheads were unbalanced. She was short of stature, too, though Aunt Mim was of a similar height and her lack of inches had never stopped her from being terrifying when the situation called for it. If the agency was to carry on and prosper, a disguise was necessary. Thus Mary was bewigged and bespectacled—just temporarily, Mim assured her, until she could get back on her feet, so to speak. No one would really *look* at her—older women in large black hats were a dime a dozen, nearly invisible in their ancient ubiquity, so Mary should have no fear of discovery.

An army of doctors had been discreetly consulted, and Mim was no closer to waltzing than she was before they mounted Mount Street's steps. And poor Mary never got a chance to waltz at all—she was too busy pretending to be an elderly woman, and growing into the part more perfectly every day.

Something must be done.

But not today. Today was . . . taken.

There was a rap on the frosted glass of her office door, and her secretary, Oliver Palmer, poked his head in. "Lord Raeburn is here to see you, Mrs. Evensong."

Oliver was a handsome young man with impeccable manners. He made an excellent impression at the reception desk, and was totally discreet. If he suspected Mary was not exactly who she purported to be, he never gave any indication of it. He had secrets of his own.

Oliver had been frank about his unfortunate situation—and hungry—when Mary interviewed him. Flat broke, he'd come about another job, but Mary claimed him for her own and he was now invaluable to her. Oliver's finger was firmly on the pulse of all society gossip. It was he who'd provided the newspaper clippings about Lord Raeburn, not that she'd needed reminding. She remembered the grainy scowling photographs on the front pages.

Accident, though there had been invisible quotation marks on the word. Open window. Insufficient evidence.

"Oh, dear. Do I look all right?" Mary could have bitten her tongue. She'd never asked Oliver such a thing no matter how noble her clients were, and he gave her an odd look. Lord Raeburn was only a baron, after all. And after what happened in Scotland, no decent woman should even give his good opinion a second thought.

"Very handsome, as always, Mrs. Evensong. Your hat is very becoming."

It was perhaps ridiculous to always wear her hat indoors, but with judicious pinning, it kept her wig on straight. "Send him in. We'll need a tea tray."

"If I were you, Mrs. E., I'd offer the fellow a whiskey."

"I'm sure you're right. See to it, would you, Oliver?" There was single-malt whiskey in a cabinet somewhere. The Evensong Agency always had everything at hand and *in* hand. In the past four years, Mary Evensong had found husbands for heiresses, valets for viscounts, and even a dairymaid for a marquess who kept a Hereford cow in his kitchen much to the consternation of his cook. The agency was famous for achieving the unusual—in fact, her aunt had hit upon "Performing the Impossible Before Breakfast Since 1888" as its motto.

Some members of the peerage, like that marquess, were known for their eccentricity. Lord Alec Raeburn was not one of them. What he *was* known for caused Mary's heart to beat a little faster.

If he had a simple staffing problem, he would never have bothered to come himself. So the nature of his visit must be personal. She doubted he was looking for a new wife—his old one had not been dead a year, and the scandal surrounding her death would take much longer to die down. Mary was not naïve enough to think he was celibate after all the rumors, but surely it was too soon to seek her matchmaking services.

Mary cleared her throat and drummed her gloved fingers on her desk. Her hands were nowhere near as wrinkled as they should be, so she wore her gloves at all times, too. And right now, her palms were damp with perspiration.

The clacking of the typewriter keys ceased in the outer office. Her girl stenographers were no doubt swooning— discreetly, she hoped—as Lord Raeburn made his way to her inner sanctum. It was with the greatest difficulty that Mary stopped herself from swooning along with them as Oliver opened the door to announce Lord Raeburn.

As if one wouldn't notice the man. A woman would have to be blind or dead not to respond to the man's physical presence.

For one thing, he was more or less a giant, but in the best possible way. Mary had been to a fair once that advertised "the tallest man in Britain," but the poor fellow had been the ugliest man in Britain as well. Lord Raeburn was not ugly, except perhaps for his attire. He wore a walking kilt in his family's tartan, an unfortunate combination of yellow and black that reminded Mary of angry bees. But his black jacket molded his massive shoulders and matched his longish hair and neatly trimmed beard. Mary was not at all fond of beards, but somehow she didn't think Lord Raeburn was hiding a weak chin. His eyes looked black as well, giving her and her office intense scrutiny while she stumbled to her feet and extended a hand.

"Good afternoon, Lord Raeburn," she said briskly, hoping she could trick herself into feeling as confident as she sounded. "Won't you sit down? Oliver, bring us in the refreshments we discussed, please." She needed a stiff drink herself—she was feeling like a giddy schoolgirl. He was gorgeous. No wonder women fell at his feet.

And out his windows.

Lord Raeburn tucked himself into one of the leather client chairs. It was a very tight fit. "Thank you for seeing me on such short notice. I'm bound for home in a few days, and I have to know I have your help before I go."

"What can the Evensong Agency do for you, my lord?"

"I'm not sure you can do anything. But I'd like you to try. I won't beat about the bush. Do you think I murdered my wife?"

Mary took a quick breath, then stalled for time with a question of her own. "Does it matter what I think?"

"It might. If you just take my money and pay me lip service, there's no point in me hiring you now, is there? We Scots don't like to waste our time. Or our gold."

Her spine stiffened. "I can assure you the Evensong Agency does not take on clients merely to humor them and pad our account books. If we can perform a legitimate service, we do our utmost to fulfill our obligations."

"So you won't say if I'm a killer or not."

"I'm afraid I'm not sufficiently acquainted with the particulars of the case," Mary lied. Oliver kept scrapbooks filled with the most interesting articles under his desk. Lord Raeburn had one all to himself.

Oliver chose that moment to step into the office with a silver tray. There was not only a decanter of whiskey but a pretty china teapot on it. They were silent as Oliver arranged and poured. Mary reconsidered her thirst and decided to keep her wits sharp, settling on a cup of oolong. To her surprise, Lord Raeburn did the same.

"Thank you, Oliver. That will be all."

"I'll be just outside if you need me, Mrs. Evensong. *Just* outside."

Lord Raeburn gave Oliver a wry smile. "Don't worry, lad, I won't ravish your employer. I may be a blackguard in the eyes of the world, but I do have some standards."

Well. Could the man be any more insulting? She shouldn't be offended—she was meant to look like an old trout—but the twenty-nine-year-old woman beneath the black hat was inexplicably annoyed. Mary set her tea down, causing the liquid to splash on its saucer.

"Perhaps you'd better tell me why you are here."

"I need a woman for a month."

Mary rose to her full height—not that there was much

of it—in umbrage. "We are not that sort of employment agency, Lord Raeburn. Good afternoon."

"Oh, get off your high horse and sit down. I didn't make myself clear. I need to hire a woman to infiltrate the guests of that new hydrotherapy spa. The Forsyth Palace Hotel. In the Highlands. Have you heard of it?"

Mary had. There had been full-page advertisements in all the London papers when it opened last year. It was built in the Scots baronial style, hosting two hundred guests and offering first-class accommodations for healthy visitors and various hydropathic treatments for those whose health was not so robust. Mary had even entertained the idea of sending her aunt there, but Aunt Mim would never leave the agency solely in Mary's hands.

To be fair, Mary had received amazingly astute advice from her aunt—Mim was sharp as a tack, especially when it came to the trickier clients. Lord Raeburn might be joining that list, if Mary could figure out what he wanted.

"You say 'infiltrate.' Why do you not employ an inquiry agent? I know several reputable agencies I can recommend."

"They're all men, Mrs. Evensong. I need a woman to lay a trap for the doctor who runs the place. The man responsible for my wife's death."

Mary turned her teacup, wishing she had the ability to read the dregs. "Why haven't you gone to the authorities with your suspicions?"

"Och, what's the point? They think I'm guilty—it's just they don't have enough proof. But I'll tell you this—my wife was seduced by that piece of sh—slime. Dr. Josef Bauer," he spat. "I have my wife's diary. Everything's in there. She paid him a fortune to keep it quiet."

Mary looked across her desk at the baron. His color was still vivid through the light gray of her lenses. Judging from the expression on his face, he was in a state of controlled fury. She wouldn't want to see him lose control. A man his size would frighten anyone with a modicum of sense. It was difficult to imagine his wife daring to be unfaithful. Surely she would know there would be consequences.

"What would you want this woman to do?"

"Pretend to be a patient. Toss around my money and attract Bauer's attention. Get cozy with him."

She shook her head. "As I said, we don't employ ladies to do that kind of work."

"She wouldn't have to fu—uh, fornicate with him. Just catch him doing something unethical. Like trying to kill her and pass it off as an accident after she made her will over to him."

"I doubt anyone of my job seekers would be willing to make themselves a possible murder victim, Lord Raeburn," Mary said dryly.

"It doesn't have to go that far, of course. If he's accused of carrying on romantically with one of his patients, that should be enough to ruin his reputation. What husband or father would trust him to cure his wife or daughter? And anyway, I'd be there to keep your woman safe."

Mary's mouth dropped open a second too long. Goodness, she must look like the veriest imbecile. "You?" she asked, when she gathered her scattered wits.

"I've booked a suite of rooms there. I'm having some renovations done to Raeburn Court now that Edith is—gone, and the hotel is not two miles away. It's only natural I stay close to supervise, and the hotel is the only decent place to stay in the area. The only place, period. We're a bit isolated from the world."

Yes, that was the spa's attraction—unspoiled countryside. Pure air, high altitude, fresh water. Enough wildlife and waterfalls to thrill any amateur photographer. Yet there was train service to Pitcarran, a charming little town close enough for a day trip in one of the hotel's horse-drawn wagonettes.

It seemed Mary had committed the advertisements to memory. She wondered if Oliver had saved any stories about it.

"Bauer knows me. I make him nervous," Lord Raeburn continued. "He may slip and make a mistake."

"He also may be on his best behavior," Mary said. "Does he know he has you for an enemy?"

"Oh, yes."

Mary shivered at the glitter in Lord Raeburn's black eyes.

"Let me see if I understand this. You wish Dr. Bauer to be discovered in a compromising position with a patient, even though he knows you will be watching him."

"The man's ego—you are familiar with that alienist fellow Freud?—knows no bounds. He's full of himself. I think because I will be there he'll flaunt his indiscretions in front of me, knowing there's not a damn thing I can do about it. Who will believe anything bad I have to say about him? Me, a man who killed his wife? I have no credibility." Lord Raeburn sat back in his chair, looking vulnerable for the first time. Mary decided she had to reread all the newspaper accounts of Lady Edith Raeburn's death.

"Let me think about this."

"I don't have time for you to dillydally, Mrs. Evensong. If you can't get someone to do it, I'll have to hire some actress. I do know a few."

Yes, Mary had heard that he did. Lord Raeburn and his wife had lived apart for most of their marriage. No wonder the poor woman sought comfort in the arms of a sympathetic Dr. Bauer.

"Why haven't you already?"

"The girls I know—let's just say they're more suited to the chorus line than playing an heiress. I need someone fresh. Innocent. Someone Bauer will think he can corrupt with no consequences. From what little I know, he only debauches virgins, who are then too mortified to confess their stupidity."

"Then why did Dr. Bauer target Lady Raeburn?" From the moment she asked the question, Mary knew she had made a mistake. She watched Lord Raeburn struggle to frame his answer.

Instead of the shout she expected, his words, when they came, were quiet. "My wife was very young when we married. Delicate. She had a disgust of the marital act. Or perhaps she just had a disgust of me. Josef Bauer somehow overcame her objections."

Despite her relative youth, Mary Evensong was rarely surprised by anything her trickier clients had to tell her. She was surprised now. Lord Raeburn had bared his heart. His pain. Somehow she knew he'd never told the truth to anyone before.

Edith Raeburn had been a virgin. And a fool.

Mary made her decision, and hoped she wouldn't be sorry. "I'll do it. That is, I'll find someone for you. When will she have to leave?"

"We wouldn't want to arrive at the hotel together—let's say, get your girl to come a week from Thursday. The sooner we can put a period to Bauer's villainy, the better. Do you have someone in mind?"

"Yes," Mary said, hoping Aunt Mim would approve of her madcap plan.

Mary wasn't madcap—she was steady. Sensible. Responsible. Boring. But that was about to change.

She pulled out a contract and discussed terms as if she didn't have black and yellow bees buzzing drunkenly in her head.

Chapter

2

Forsyth, Perthshire, Scotland
June 9, 1904

Alec Raeburn puffed on a cigar in one of the Forsyth Palace Hotel's turrets dedicated for just such manly activity. Across the slate roof, the ladies' turret held several young white-clad female guests who were oblivious to Ben-y-Vrackie looming blue in the distance and were plainly viewing him. They tried to catch his attention through prodigious handkerchief-waving and head-tossing, but Alec ignored them, gazing down at the hotel's circular drive.

The girls must not have heard about him and his wickedness yet—no doubt their mamas would be swooping in any minute to round them up and tell them everything they thought they knew. After nearly a year, Alec was almost used to the sudden silence when he entered a room, eyes sliding to distant corners, people remembering forgotten appointments. He'd always attracted attention—a man his size was not invisible—but now the attention was most unwelcome.

He was sick of it. After this was over, he'd hunker down here. Fleeing England would not be such a hardship, since Scotland was the home of his heart. However, Edith's death had cast a pall on his beloved Raeburn Court that would not really be changed by the addition of new drapes and furniture. It would be a wrench to remain in isolation, but Alec couldn't see the social climate changing for him any time soon.

He couldn't tell the truth. Even a man as black-hearted as he would not use Edith's folly to explain what happened. Her parents already loathed him for his shortcomings. Alec could live with their hate—had since almost the first days of his marriage—but not the fresh grief he would cause if they discovered the reason for their daughter's despair.

No matter what he'd done, he'd not been able to convince Edith to trust him. After a while, he'd given up and gone his own way, just like so many men of his class. He was no saint; no one was. Look at the king—"Kingie"—a man who'd had more than his share of extramarital adventures.

At least Alec hadn't taken anyone seriously to heart—his amours had been brief and bloodless. He'd fallen in love with Edith, for all the good it did him, and he would never do that again. So there was nothing for him but to find justice somehow, and his helpers were on their way.

He'd received a telegram from Mrs. Evensong yesterday. His two new employees—a male and a female—would be arriving on the afternoon train. Alec hadn't objected in her office when she explained that a proper lady would never travel to the wilds of Scotland alone, even to such a superior establishment as this, which provided personal maids and valets to the guests.

He didn't care how much this effort cost him—his reputation was ruined. He wouldn't marry again and have a son to pass his title and estate to. Alec's brother Evan would never miss a few thousand pounds when he inherited—Evan owned a successful distillery whose product was favored by King Edward himself and was richer than Alec to begin with.

Alec craned his neck as the hotel's shiny black horse-drawn omnibus came down the long lane below. Its passengers had been picked up at the railway station, and traveled the winding road that ran along the sparkling River Tummel, famous for its salmon. They'd passed the gentlemen guests who'd been dropped off earlier in the day, wading and casting, the hotel chef promising to cook their catch for their dinner, and were now driving by golfers who were chipping away on the hotel's own nine-hole course.

Bauer and his business partners had hit on a grand scheme with this enterprise, appealing to every taste— sportsmen, hypochondriacal dowagers, families with shy daughters they wished to accustom to society in the communal dining room. Alec had a grudging respect for the genius of it all. The late queen had made the Highlands fashionable decades ago, and there was no place more fashionable now than the Forsyth Palace Hotel.

Which one of the disembarking people was his Mary Arden? Who was her "brother"? All he saw was the tops of heads—straw boaters and fantastical hats so big they obscured the bodies of the women who wore them.

Alec ground out his cigar in a crystal ashtray. He would make his way to the reception area oh-so-casually and see if he could pick out the actress Mrs. Evensong had hired. He hoped she looked naïve and insecure—according to Edith's diary, Bauer had boasted he went after the weakest women, who were unfailingly flattered by his attention. He wheedled himself into their beds and out of their money. There was never a chance he would marry any of them—he had a wife and children hidden down in Edinburgh.

Alec could not understand why anyone would keep secret about Bauer's depredations, but then he was not a woman. Even though the world was changing rapidly, society's rules were intact. Scandal was still scandal. A woman was meant to be pure until marriage.

Sometimes pure after marriage, he thought sourly.

Eschewing the lift, Alec hurried down the stairs to the grand ground floor. Pillars and archways led to an enormous lobby, which in turn led to a glassed veranda that ran the whole length of the rear of the building. The scenery was spectacular. Even Alec, who'd been raised in the Highlands, could not take its perfection for granted. A good crowd was taking high tea in ornate wicker chairs at the moment, and he heard the subdued chatter over the clink of saucers and forks. A few people turned in his direction, then hastily turned away. As usual.

Porters were rolling loaded luggage carts toward the byzantine ramps that led from one floor to the other. The architect had been careful to provide as many escape routes as possible to accommodate the number of guests and staff. Fire was common to these large hotels, and every safety effort was in place. There was a bank of modern lifts, several sets of stairs, iron fire escapes at the rear of the hotel, as well as the service ramps that kept the maids' mops far from the customers.

The dozen or so new arrivals were being greeted by Josef Bauer himself, resplendent in his crisp white doctor's coat, his blond beard neatly trimmed. Alec had passed the hotel's barbershop this morning and seen Bauer relaxing in the leather chair.

How relaxed would he be if Alec held a razor to the man's throat? No, that's what Mary Arden was for. He didn't know what use he'd put her male companion to, but it never hurt to have an extra pair of eyes and ears and hands. What he wouldn't countenance was Miss Arden carrying on with the fellow she'd brought. She was meant to devote her sole effort in snaring Josef Bauer.

Alec had given them a week to accomplish the downfall of the doctor. The renovations to his home should take no longer than that. Mostly the workmen were removing all of Edith's spindly furniture and tearing down chintz curtains. He needed chairs to sit on that would not break, and he was certainly not a chintz sort of fellow. But at the beginning of their marriage, he'd given Edith carte blanche to change his ancestral home, and change it she had. A free hand with decorating had not led her to be any freer with her person, and Alec had been frustrated by both the coldness of his wife and the inadequate seating.

Good God. Alec ducked behind a pillar. Mrs. Evensong was here herself, dressed head to toe in black with her little gray spectacles, leaning heavily on a cane. A maid fussed over her and made her sit on a sofa in the lobby while the doctor gave his little spiel.

Surely she didn't expect Josef Bauer to seduce *her*? No, of course not. She must be here to keep an eye on the two actors. Alec was impressed—he never expected to get such attentive service when he'd signed the contract.

A few other guests followed Mrs. Evensong's example to the sofas. Left standing was a pale redhead in blue with a simple, elegant hat, and a devilishly handsome young man at her side. He was familiar-looking. The secretary? She must be Mary Arden. Everyone else in the party looked too old, though this woman was not in the first blush of youth.

She was not precisely beautiful, but beauty was not necessary to attract Bauer. Alec thought she was handsome enough in an unshowy way, her nose thin and straight, her lips full but not bee-stung. She had a wide forehead, which might bespeak some intelligence. He had never been immune to women's forms, and Miss Arden's was fine. She was on the short side, but very curvy. Her waist was ruthlessly nipped in by her corset, and her visible skin was so white it looked as if she hadn't been out in the sun in ages. There was a slight look of the sickroom about her, though it was probably due to the application of paint.

It was not enough that the woman he hired be a regular female guest, one who came to walk the manicured grounds and take photographs or play tennis. Regular guests did not fall under the purview of Dr. Bauer; there was an obsequious hotel manager, Mr. Prescott, for them. Dr. Bauer's patients took all the cures in the far wing of the hotel—the Turkish, peat, and Droitwich brine baths, massages, and body shampooing, which lasted at least twenty minutes. There were attendants to assist the patients, but sometimes Dr. Bauer performed those services himself, the better to take advantage of vulnerable—naked—young women.

Alec imagined Miss Arden would look quite lovely naked,

with all her white skin and pale red hair tumbling down her back. He hoped she wouldn't feel obligated to go that far—he had a feeling old Mrs. Evensong would object rather strenuously, even if Mary Arden was just an actress hired for the part. She clung now to the man who posed as her brother, and with a look of disgust, he shook her arm away. Miss Arden swayed backward, and it was all Alec could do not to race across the lobby and catch her before she fell.

She didn't topple over, but reached out to steady herself on the back of the sofa where Mrs. Evensong sat. The old woman looked up and said something to her, and Miss Arden nodded. She tottered gingerly around the sofa and collapsed into the cushion.

Josef Bauer noticed, and broke from his prepared speech to make sure she was all right. Clever girl for calling attention to herself from the get-go. She looked up at the doctor with limpid hazel eyes, and Alec suppressed a chuckle. She was the picture of sweet vulnerability—he could not have asked for a better performance.

He'd seen enough. True to her reputation, Mrs. Evensong had come through. Little Miss Arden was appealing enough to make any man notice her. Alec would try to steal a moment alone with her before dinner—he'd come up with what he hoped was a brilliant plan to speed the doctor's seduction along.

It was time to return to his rooms and brace himself for the evening with some of his brother Evan's finest. The Forsyth Palace Hotel was a temperance establishment, serving no alcohol for "health," but at least they didn't search the guests' bags and confiscate the forbidden. A great many guests fortified themselves discreetly during the course of their stay, ladies and gentlemen alike. Alec had taken a case of whiskey from Raeburn Court and was working his way through it methodically. Not too much, not too little. When Edith died, Alec had made an utter ass of himself, lending credence to the whispers. He had raged and stumbled in his drunkenness, and most of his servants had left him, fearful that he'd throw them out the window, too.

It hadn't taken long for the servants' gossip to sweep down to London. There was probably no place in the British Empire that hadn't heard of wicked Lord Raeburn. Alec hadn't helped himself any when he'd gone to his London townhouse and taken up with his loose women, but he was damned if he was going to live the rest of his life like a monk. He'd tried celibacy for Edith's sake, and it hadn't stuck.

His marriage had been a disaster. But revenge would be something to hold fast to on the empty nights that loomed ahead.

Alec entered his top-floor suite. His man Mackenzie was already arranging the drinks tray. Wordlessly, Alec downed the first bite of liquor and held his hand out for another. That would be all for today to take the edge off his anger. He'd take another bath, civilize himself beneath correct black and white evening clothes, and keep his secrets like bitter pills under his tongue.

Chapter

3

unt Mim put her foot up on a tufted hassock. "The view is tolerable."

"For heaven's sake, it's more than that. This must be the most gorgeous spot in the world." Mary opened the window and took a deep breath. She felt like she were tasting sunshine. What a change from the grubby streets of London. She could see mountains, woods, and water for miles in all directions in Aunt Mim's tower room. The spacious two-bedroom suite down the hall that she and Oliver were sharing paled in comparison.

"I can't but think I should not have come," Aunt Mim said. "Are you sure Miss Benson is competent to run the agency in my absence?"

Mary knew Aunt Mim thought she was barely qualified herself, even after four years of intervention and intrigue. Just recently she'd made her most satisfactory match yet, a marriage between the banking heiress Louisa Stratton and war hero Charles Cooper. She'd received a breezy letter from Louisa in New York a few weeks ago, and a handsome dividend from the Pegasus Motor Company in the same post, which had gone a long way to provide her with a suitable wardrobe for her current situation.

"We've gone over this a thousand times. This trip will do you good. No matter how wretched Dr. Bauer is, his treatments have proven very efficacious in many patients. And Harriet is a whiz at everything. Remember, you hired her, even before you fetched me down to London. If anything unusual occurs, she'll send a wire."

"Maybe Oliver should have stayed behind."

My, but her aunt was stubborn. "Nonsense. He's very good in social situations and enormous fun." Oliver had begged and begged to come once she'd confided in him, and Mary could not deny him a working holiday.

"But this doctor fellow might view him as an obstacle."

"Not he. Oliver will act as the aggrieved brother, saddled with a sickly sister and cranky aunt and bored to death with both of them. We plan to fight in public every chance we get. He'll be off playing golf and flirting with—" Here Mary paused. Who exactly would Oliver be flirting with? "—the other guests and will leave me to my own resources. There I'll be, wistful and alone, just ripe for the plucking."

"What about me? I'm supposed to be your guardian, am I not?"

"I'm much too old for you to be a real dragon. There's no hope for me. Almost thirty, remember, and firmly on the shelf. Besides, you're meant to be so self-absorbed with your own condition that you pay no attention to me. Just think, Aunt Mim, you can be as haughty as your old duchess and twice as rude. What fun you'll have scaring everyone! I declare, I am jealous." Mary thought her aunt would enjoy herself enormously getting out from being prim and proper Mrs. Evensong. Mim Arden would have much more leeway—as would she.

Mary Arden had a trunkful of fashionable dresses and all her own shining hair pinned up in the latest style. She wasn't saddled with wigs and gloves and crow-black clothes. She had hired enough people to pose as someone else for whatever reason her clients had, and now it was her turn. Truth to tell, Mary had a batch of gleeful butterflies struggling against the lacings of her long corset. She couldn't wait to begin to seduce—

Dr. Bauer.

"Where is Oliver anyhow?"

"Seeing about getting you a pushchair. Now, don't say no. You'll want to get around, spread a little gossip. We are depending upon you."

Aunt Mim made a face but said nothing. Privately, Mary was sure her aunt was excited about the whole escapade. It had been a long time since she'd been at the heart of an adventure.

"Hamblen will get you settled. I hope you don't mind that you're having dinner in your room tonight instead of at the communal tables. I don't want you so worn out from the trip to be tired when the curtain raises tomorrow."

"I suppose you're right. It has been a long day and my foot is on fire." Aunt Mim rarely complained. The trip north had been taxing to them all. But now they had a week ahead with every luxury.

The Forsyth Palace Hotel was famous for "mixing" its guests. No small private tables were to be found in the formal dining room. Rather, four long tables spread the length of the room and the guests filled in at random. Keeping the same seats night after night was frowned upon. Mothers brought their young daughters here to sharpen their conversational skills, and Mary was determined to make sure none of them fell victim to Dr. Bauer.

She gave her aunt a kiss on the cheek and hurried to her own room to ready herself for dinner. It had been years since she'd fussed over her own appearance, other than to bury herself in unattractive black to make herself less attractive. A very young Mary Evensong once had hopes of romance, but the deaths of her parents had curtailed those dreams. Her brother, Albert, had inherited their grocery store and put Mary to work after pulling her from Miss Ambrose's Academy for Young Ladies, not only there but at home, too, to mind his boys while he and his wife, Phyllis, expanded the shop. There were now three stores and five boys, and Mary knew she was better off in London even if she did have to disguise herself daily.

This sojourn in Scotland was her chance to shine—if ever so briefly—and she intended to make the most of it. Their maid Hamblen had already unpacked her things while she was talking to Aunt Mim, and Mary opened the wardrobe, admiring the snow-white shirtwaists and a mini-rainbow of evening dresses. Four hatboxes were stacked on the shelf, only one of them containing a black hat in case of emergency. Mary allowed herself a spin of delight, and then proceeded to make her first difficult decision—which silk faille dress should she wear this evening?

She might see Lord Raeburn again. This time, she might even be able to speak to him when they met. It had unnerved her to see him popping around a pillar in the lobby when they'd first arrived—it was not as though a Corinthian column could hide his bulk. He was not wearing his plaid this afternoon, but a well-cut Norfolk jacket and jodhpurs, a checkered cap upon his unruly raven hair. Though she pretended not to see him, his face was tanned from his time back in the mountains and his eyes were dark with distrust as Dr. Bauer gave his welcome speech. It had been difficult for Mary to concentrate with him lurking about—she'd have to tell him to keep a much lower profile, or the game would be up.

Of course, Alec Raeburn wouldn't know that they'd spoken before. He thought she was a strange woman hired to entrap Dr. Bauer.

Mary unfastened her blue traveling costume and stood before the mirrored doors of the wardrobe in her combination, s-corset and frillies. It was warm for a June day in Scotland and as she'd traveled most of it, she turned on the hot water tap and sponged herself, removing the layer of rice powder she'd applied to make herself look interestingly pale. It seemed a shame to start all over again with her powder puff, but she was slated to be "delicate." Mary gave an experimental wheeze and hoped when she had her private appointment with Dr. Bauer tomorrow she would pass muster as an invalid.

But being sickly did not mean she had to dress in rags. As arranged, Hamblen returned to lace her even tighter and help her with the pale peach dress she'd chosen. Rows of ruffles emphasized her bosom, and a jeweled cameo was placed in a strategic location to call attention to what the ruffles didn't. The pin was Mary's only true extravagance. There would be flashier jewels on display at the hotel, but between Oliver and Aunt Mim, she would be described as an heiress to entice Dr. Bauer.

It had been decided that the manufactured Ardens had made their money in wool. Oliver could draw from his knowledge of his family's own business, just in case anyone was too nosy and rude enough to ask. The Boer Wars had made his parvenu father unbearably rich, although wool was entirely unsuited for army uniforms on the hot plains of South Africa.

Mary adjusted a copper curl at her temple. "What do you think, Hamblen?"

"You look lovely, Miss Mary. Just as you should. But I think I can do more with your coiffeur."

Mary sat on the dressing table bench. "It makes for quite a change from my usual attire, doesn't it?"

"I don't see why your aunt makes you dress the way you do. 'Tisn't fair for a young woman. Four years of it. It wouldn't harm the agency if the truth was known after all you've done on your own."

Mary shook her head. "I'm not so sure. People trust Mrs. Evensong because of her years of experience. Four years isn't much. It's hard for a woman to be taken seriously."

The young maid sniffed. "You wouldn't think that way if you'd met my mam. Her word is *law*."

It was different in the lower classes—women were expected both to work and run their households. But the female guests at the Forsyth Palace Hotel were probably incapable of boiling water. They couldn't even dress—or undress—themselves in their seven layers of undergarments without assistance. Their men preferred them helpless, bound by corset strings and conventions. It was a very odd world, and Mary Evensong was expected to keep her balance and her place in it.

Oliver knocked on the connecting door, and entered before Mary had a chance to invite him in, just as an annoying younger brother might. He was in immaculate evening dress, his burnished head glistening with macassar oil. He really was much too pretty, and Mary told him so.

"You're not so bad yourself, sis." Oliver draped himself on the arm of a chair and fiddled with his watch fobs. "I'm not sure I can get used to my boss looking like a *woman*."

Mary opened a drawer and tucked an extra handkerchief in her petit point bag. "Don't worry. It's only for a week. Then we'll go back to business as usual."

"I don't know how I didn't guess. Your old-lady act has had me fooled for over a year."

"You and everyone else, I hope. Oliver, I must count on your discretion once this is all over. The Evensong Agency is a thriving concern, and any rumor about Mary Evensong is bound to affect business." She trusted Oliver, but he did love his gossip.

"I know which side my bread is buttered on, Mary. Lord, it sounds odd to call you by your Christian name. There are two of you, one up, one down. It defies belief. No wonder you wouldn't invite me to tea."

She shrugged. "You've met my aunt now. After the journey, you already know how headstrong she is. This secret is important to her. To the business. Until she can come downstairs and take her rightful place, I'll continue the masquerade."

"Seems a damn shame. You clean up rather nicely." Oliver gave her a cheeky grin.

"Thank you so much," Mary said dryly. "Now, no more compliments, little brother. You are peevish that you are stuck in Scotland with two female relatives when you could be enjoying the tail end of the London season or going to the country to shoot something. Complain long and loudly to anyone who will stand still long enough to listen."

"It shall be my pleasure to be a perfect boor. This place really is amazing, isn't it?"

"It certainly has every amenity."

Oliver gave her a knowing look. "Plus your Lord Raeburn. You saw his handsome wooly face in the lobby when we arrived, didn't you?"

So, he remembered how nervous she'd been the day Raeburn came into the office. Well, she wasn't an old lady and the baron was attractive enough to cause heart palpitations even if she was.

"He is not 'my' Lord Raeburn, just a client to whom we owe a fiduciary responsibility. So, let's get to it." She turned her head to the mirror, quite liking what she saw. "I think you've done about all you can do, Hamblen. Please keep an eye on Aunt Mim and make sure she takes her tonic after supper."

Mary and Oliver descended by way of the wide central staircase, as the lifts were full of guests on their way down to dinner. Quite a crowd had gathered on the plush couches and chairs in the lobby, waiting for the dining room doors to open. After a quick glance, Mary was satisfied she was younger than the average woman present, which boded well for their scheme. The hotel did not seem to be quite full at the moment, so Dr. Bauer would have fewer women to choose from. She coughed gently and Oliver drew his arm away.

"As we have no assigned seats, you won't mind if I find someone more interesting to sit with, do you, Mary? I've had enough of your sniffles and snorts," he said in a loud voice.

Mary fished out a handkerchief and dabbed at her eyes. "Oh, Oliver, how cruel you are!"

"You'll be perfectly safe. You're old as the hills. Who'll look twice at you?"

"I will."

Both Oliver and Mary startled at being interrupted in their scene. They turned to see Lord Raeburn in all his evening finery, a wicked twinkle in his dark eye.

"Bugger off, then. I'll take the lady in to dinner." He took

Mary's suddenly clammy hand into his. She hoped the perspiration wouldn't seep into her gloves. "I am Raeburn. Forgive my impertinence, but I hate to see a lovely lady such as yourself abused. I presume that young pup is your brother and not your husband?"

"Y-yes," Mary stuttered. Sitting with Lord Raeburn had not been part of her plan.

"Little brothers are damned worthless. I've got two myself, and they give me a devil of a headache. Come, Miss—?"

"Arden. Mary Arden," Mary whispered. It did not require much acting to feel faint and overwhelmed at the moment.

"They're opening the doors now. You won't be disappointed with the food or the company, I promise. I've been here a few days while my estate is being renovated and I wager I've gained half a stone."

"Do you think this is wise?" Mary asked in a low voice, as the people swarmed noisily around them.

"Bauer is a predatory fellow. If he thinks you're of interest to me, he'll be anxious to remove you from my side. Have I seen you before on the stage? You look familiar."

Even Oliver had not recognized her when she revealed herself, and he'd spent every day in her company for a year. "I doubt it. This is my f-first job."

"Fallen on tough times, eh? Well, I hope that old trout Mrs. Evensong is paying you well. She's charging me a fortune."

Mary bristled. "I assure you you'll have no complaints. Now, no more talk of business. If you're pretending to woo me, do it properly."

Lord Raeburn gave her an assessing look. "I shall do my utmost. You are a fetching little thing for all the sharpness of your tongue. Who's the boy with you? Isn't he that secretary at the agency?"

"What part of 'no more talk of business' did you fail to grasp, my lord? You'll ruin everything before the fish course."

Lord Raeburn threw back his head and laughed, causing

quite a few more people to glance in their direction. He led them to the end of one of the tables, and instead of sitting opposite, plunked himself down next to her.

The dining room was filling, yet it seemed the guests were reluctant to join Mary and Lord Raeburn. His reputation was with him always. If he hadn't intervened in the argument with Oliver and spirited her away, he'd probably be sitting alone. A group of sporting gentlemen took their seats several chairs away, but did not acknowledge them.

Mary wondered how Lord Raeburn had spent days here so far. She would have to warn him in no uncertain terms not to interfere.

Though perhaps he had a point. Men were territorial, and often coveted what was not theirs. As much as she didn't wish to be a bone tussled over by two handsome bearded men, Mary thought it would suit her purpose.

She wanted to laugh herself. *Two men.* Never in her life had she been as close to an attractive man as she was this evening. She could smell the cologne he wore—Blenheim Bouquet, her very favorite—and could count the threads of silver in his neat beard. His thigh brushed hers and she inched away.

Fleet-footed waiters emerged from the kitchen and began laying down white china platters. Meals were served family-style, though there was no one close enough to ask to pass the dish of glistening oysters.

Mary eyed the empty chairs separating them from the others. "Should we move down?" she asked.

"We should, just to make the bas—fellows nervous. But we won't." The baron raised his finger, and a freckled young waiter appeared instantly.

"We'll need our own platters, lad. See to it." Lord Raeburn slipped some coins into the boy's gloved hand. In a minute a plate was placed before them with more oysters than two people could possibly eat.

Or so Mary thought. Lord Raeburn served her and made quick work of the rest. His appetite was certainly unaffected by the snubs all around them. Mary craned her neck to look for Dr. Bauer. The senior hotel staff ate with the guests, and she spotted him making conversation with a gray-haired couple across the room.

Lord Raeburn noted where her eyes were straying, and wiped his mouth on a linen napkin. "He'll be around before coffee is served. He goes table to table greeting his patients, and he won't like it that you're sitting with me. In fact," he said with a cheerful grin, "he tried to have me barred from the hotel. But Prescott loves his pounds above all things, so my reservation stood."

More food arrived, but Mary felt too enervated to eat much. "This must be very awkward for you. Being . . . shunned."

"It will all be worth it if I can catch Bauer making love to you."

Mary's cheeks warmed. "It will not come to that, I hope. But your friends—has no one stood by you?"

"My brothers don't think I'm a villain. But then, they're so wild themselves their opinion doesn't matter. Enough about me and my nefarious plans. Tell me about yourself, Miss Arden."

Mary took a sip of water. The hotel did not serve spirits, although judging from their roar, the sporting gentlemen had indulged before dinner from flasks in their suitcases.

"There is not much to tell. My family owns a small chain of grocery stores in Oxfordshire. I worked in one of them until I came down to London." There was no point in trying to disguise her background—Mary wasn't ashamed of her parents, or even her aggravating, ambitious brother.

His dark brow raised. "A grocery store? That's a long way from the stage."

"I told you, I'm not an actress." Which was rather a fib when it came right down to it.

"How did you come to Mrs. Evensong's attention?"

"Shh. Don't even say the name. Many of these people will have heard of the agency. I wouldn't be surprised if we—um, they—hadn't placed servants in half their houses."

"The old girl is rather well-known. Why is she here?"

Mary stared at her fork. "She prides herself on personalized service. The situation intrigued her."

"And the secretary?"

"It's always easier to travel with a man."

"He's not sweet on you, is he?"

"Oliver?" Mary choked back her laughter. "Oh, no."

"That's all right then. I wouldn't want you to have to juggle three males, since this is, as you say, your first job."

"Well, I did help out in the store for years." Far too many of them. "One gets to know a lot about people when one is filling their shopping list." Mary wondered what would be on Lord Raeburn's—it would take a lot of food to fuel someone of his stature. He had to be almost six and a half feet tall. While he didn't seem to have an ounce of extra fat, he was broad where it counted, and the tailoring of his evening clothes showed his shoulders to great advantage. She had admired his muscular calves when he'd turned up in his kilt, but really—if she was going to get through this dinner, she would have to stop thinking about the various parts of the man's body.

That just might prove to be impossible.

Chapter

4

To his surprise, Alec was enjoying himself. Miss Arden was not like his usual flirts—in fact, he'd take her for an innocent virgin, just like the role she was playing. Her fair skin flushed when he teased her too far, and though she appeared to understand his every double entendre, she refused to acknowledge them.

Her primness was intriguing—however, he'd fallen for a prim woman before, and look where that had gotten him. Alec had been foolish enough to think he could thaw Edith out, but for four years he'd failed miserably.

Someone *had* succeeded, and he was on his way across the dining room. He covered Miss Arden's gloved hand with his. "Don't look up, but our prey is headed to our table."

"Let go of my hand, my lord." She would have hissed if any of the words had an *s* in them.

"Not a chance. He's been looking at us all night. Let him think you're easy to conquer."

"You have it all wrong. A man like Bauer wants to know he's the first one. It may amuse you to stir his jealousy, but it will doom our project if he thinks you've plowed the field first."

"Miss Arden! Such imagery! You shock me." Nevertheless, he released her hand.

Miss Arden immediately coughed into it, then picked up her water glass, her hand shaking.

"Good evening, Miss Arden. Are you quite well?"

"I—I—" The woman appeared quite breathless. Her bountiful bosom was heaving over the ruffles of her low-cut dress. Alec quelled the urge to tug the fabric up so Bauer wouldn't get such a show. "I am sure I'll feel better tomorrow."

"Perhaps your dinner companion has upset you."

Alec had to bite his tongue as Miss Arden cast her eyes down to her empty coffee cup. He waited for her to condemn him. "Oh, not at all. Lord Raeburn has been m-most k-k-kind. My brother—" She coughed again, managing to look adorable as she did so. "—abandoned me. I'm sure he found much more amusing company." She looked up at Bauer, her eyes wide and innocent.

"I'm sure no one could find a better dinner partner than you, Miss Arden," the doctor said in his damned oily voice. "Allow me to escort you in tomorrow evening. The hotel's clientele are usually la crème de la crème, but every once in a while, there are exceptions."

"You cannot mean Lord Raeburn, surely. He has been a complete gentleman." Her lashes fluttered.

Now Alec knew Miss Arden was an accomplished liar. He'd rubbed up against her skirts to feel her plump thighs and looked down her pastel dress enough to disabuse the most naïve woman of his honorable intentions. He told himself it was all part of his plan to anger Bauer, but he'd had more fun than he expected. She was a seductive little package, wrapped tight in silk and sweet innocence.

"Indeed, Bauer. I was about to ask Miss Arden to sit with me again," Alec said.

Miss Arden's eyelashes fluttered some more. "Oh, Lord Raeburn, you know that's against hotel rules. We're all meant to m-mingle. I find that to be very democratic, Dr. Bauer. I get to meet so few people at home. Oliver and Aunt Mim must be quite sick of m-me."

"I'm sure that's not possible, Miss Arden. You are a very charming girl." Bauer bowed, picked up her gloved hand and grazed her knuckles with his lips. She was hardly a girl, but Alec knew that pointing it out would not aid his cause. He imagined Miss Arden's sharp elbow piercing his ribs.

All that Continental folderol had made Bauer successful with the ladies. The slight Viennese accent, the golden hair, the bright blue eyes—Alec wanted to stab him with a fork.

"Th-thank you, Dr. Bauer." Miss Arden was blushing again. By God, could the woman blush at will? What an actress. She'd been wasted in the grocery store.

Suddenly Alec wanted to know where else she might make herself blush. He pictured flushed breasts and pink earlobes, then his mind's eyes traveled to its natural conclusion. Soft belly, fiery hair between her parted white thighs—

"Did you say something, Lord Raeburn?" He heard the warning in her voice.

Och, he must have grunted aloud. It was his turn to take a sip of water. Better that he dump it into his lap.

"Frog in my throat," he growled.

"I find Fisherman's Friend drops are very helpful for that," Miss Arden said. "I'm sure Dr. Bauer knows all the best medications."

"As we shall discuss tomorrow at your appointment, Miss Arden. I'll give you a thorough examination."

Alec would just bet he would. The thought of Miss Arden stripped and bare to Bauer made his stomach knot. He rose, happy to tower over his enemy. "Since Miss Arden needs her rest, I'll escort her back to her room."

"I c-can find my own way back."

"Nonsense," Alec said, not wanting to let her go off on her own. Who knew what could happen? "This hotel is like a rabbit warren."

"I say!" Bauer objected. "It is the finest hotel in the British Isles. In all of Europe!"

"Is it, now?" Alec sneered. "I wonder if your patients would agree."

"They have nothing to complain about," Bauer said,

smug. "They get first-class service. In *every* respect. Your late wife took the cures and was very grateful. I daresay she was as happy here as she'd ever been before her . . . unfortunate . . . demise."

Alec's fists bunched at his sides. He wasn't going to be goaded into pummeling Bauer in front of all these people. And what the doctor had said was damnably true—Edith's diary was proof of that—before she realized she was just another one of Josef Bauer's conquests.

"Oh! Lord Raeburn, I was not aware you were a widower. My condolences on your loss," Miss Arden said, standing up between the two men as if she anticipated trouble. She was a brave little thing.

"Miss Arden, I regret to inform you that Raeburn has the blackest of reputations. No decent woman—or man, for that matter—is seen in his company. As you have been so ill and isolated at home, you would not know. I'll make sure to exonerate you amongst the guests. But if you will take my advice, you will not allow him to escort you anywhere."

Miss Arden looked from one man to the other, rather like a trapped fawn between two hunters. She covered her mouth with a gloved hand and coughed, a noisy racking spasm that was not adorable at all. Alec felt every eye in the room focused on them.

"See what you've done, Bauer? You've frightened her and made her ill!"

"She should be frightened. Come, Miss Arden, I'll take you upstairs."

Alec opened his mouth to argue when Miss Arden's "brother" sprinted across the room.

"What mischief have you gotten into now, Mary? I can't leave you for an hour without you making a scene. Sorry, gentlemen, but my sister's completely clueless when it comes to men. Whatever she's said to upset you both, I'm sorry for it." He was towing Mary away, grumbling all the way to the dining room doors. Miss Arden looked chastened and stared down at her rapidly moving feet. She gave one desperate backward glance before young Mr. Arden propelled her out the door.

Bauer smirked at him. "Well. I'll make sure Miss Arden's brother knows all about you."

"What makes you think I won't do the same?" Alec asked.

"You can't, Raeburn. Your pride and honor will stop you from dragging out your wife's dirty laundry. And who would believe you anyway? After all, you pushed her out her bedroom window in a jealous rage."

Alec wished a window was handy now. "You know why she died."

"Do I? I'm a doctor, not a miracle worker. She was very unhappy. I did the best I could, but not every treatment is successful. You must know I offered to relieve her of her little problem, but she refused."

If Bauer had seemed the least bit penitent, Alec might have changed his course. But there was no true sorrow in Josef Bauer. He had dismissed Edith's death with a shrug and a few glib words.

"I don't care what you say about me. We both know the truth. If I were you, Bauer, I'd watch my step with any future patients. Like poor Miss Arden."

"She's rather sweet, isn't she? She'll do nicely for the next week or so—it's slim pickings yet. The best people come in August. What's today, Thursday? I estimate she'll be in my bed Sunday at the latest. You'd best not interfere."

There—that was what Alec had aimed for, wasn't it? But the thought of Bauer's hands anywhere on Mary Arden was sickening.

"Don't touch her," he growled.

"You can't stop me." Bauer gave him a wolfish smile. "Even if her brother finds out, I don't believe he'll care— there's no love lost there."

"She has an aunt."

"Who's so consumed with her own affliction she has no time for her niece. Yes, I'd say Mary Arden is just what the doctor ordered." Bauer chuckled at his own joke.

If Alec stayed in the dining room one more second, he would bloody Bauer's nose. The end result would be his ejection from the hotel, and he had promised Mrs. Evensong that he'd protect Mary Arden.

So he turned on his heel and left, hearing the whispers and sighs of relief as he quit the room. Sometimes retreat was necessary to win the war, though it galled him to leave Josef Bauer standing unscathed. He would have to warn Mrs. Evensong that his plan was succeeding all too well.

He'd inquired earlier—she was in one of the tower rooms a floor below his. Was it too late to call upon the old woman? He hoped not, for Mary's sake.

He bounded up the stairs, thinking he was getting more than his share of exercise here even if he didn't use the rooms designated for the purpose. Coming to the end of the corridor, he knocked gently on the door with his still-clenched fist.

Instead of a maid, it was Mary herself who answered the door. She grabbed his arm and dragged him inside.

"Are you insane? What the devil are you doing here?" she asked, clearly furious.

"Invite Lord Raeburn to sit down, dear," Mrs. Evensong said. "I was getting bored with your lack of details about dinner."

Miss Arden—Mary—turned scarlet. "There is nothing to tell, Aunt Mim."

"Ho, that's not what I'd say." Oliver was presiding over a decanter of brandy in a corner of the sitting room. "Care for a libation, my lord?"

"He is not staying," Mary said.

"I'd be delighted, Mr. Arden," Alec replied, earning daggers from her.

"Call me Oliver, please. I might not answer to the other."

"You'd better!" Both Mrs. Evensong and Mary admonished the boy in unison.

"All right, all right. Just teasing, y'know. All this havey-cavey stuff is a bit new to me." Oliver grinned and poured everyone a drink. "Cheers! I'd say we're off to a smashing success, what?"

Alec accepted his drink and sat down in a striped chair without being invited to by Mary. "I came up to tell you just that. Bauer is bragging that he'll have you in his clutches by Sunday."

Mary blanched. "Wh-what?"

"He has picked you to be his latest victim. I felt sure if he saw you with me, it would be like waving a red flag in front of a bull, and I was right."

"Sunday is just two days away. Surely I should not be quite so easy a conquest," Mary muttered.

"He's convinced you have no champions. But he shouldn't discount me."

"Lord Raeburn, if I may interrupt."

He turned to Mrs. Evensong, realizing suddenly that she was already in a figured robe, night rail, and lacy nightcap. One foot was wrapped in linen and raised upon a hassock. "Do forgive my intrusion at this hour," Alec apologized. "I just thought I should inform you."

"At this hour? The sun is still shining this far north, is it not? It will be hours yet before I can fall asleep. All this excitement. Quite like the old days. All you young people."

"Umm, yes." At thirty-five, Alec had not thought of himself being young for years.

There was something different about Mrs. Evensong, though Alec could not put his finger on it. She still wore her tinted spectacles, and gray curls peeped from under the fringe of lace. She seemed older, less brisk than she had the day he'd come to Mount Street. Not quite as businesslike, almost as if she were enjoying herself at his expense.

Which, by God, she was after what he'd paid her.

"May I make a point? If you become Mary's champion and deter Dr. Bauer, you will spoil your own scheme."

Alec took a measured sip of brandy. She was right, of course.

"You cannot keep following me," Mary added crossly. "It will ruin everything."

"I wasn't following you. I came to speak to Mrs. Evensong."

He'd been as surprised as she when she'd yanked him into the suite.

"Whatever you want to say to her you can say to me."

"Forgive me, Miss Arden, but you are merely the hired help."

Green fire flared in Mary's eyes, but vanished in an instant. "Yes, my lord."

Oliver snorted but wisely said nothing.

"So," Mrs. Evensong smiled, "tell me about tonight. I believe Mary omitted all the most interesting things."

Chapter

5

$\mathcal{M}$ ary sat fuming and drinking as Lord Raeburn told Aunt Mim about the evening and his encounter with Bauer. Well, not *all* about the evening—he did not mention how he ogled her bosom and said inappropriate things to her as if she were a Florodora Girl. It was obvious he thought she was no better than she should be, but Mary was damned how she could convince him otherwise. She was posing as a seductress, after all, although it didn't seem to take much to get in Josef Bauer's good graces. Sunday!

The smarmy, smirking lout.

Mary was not exactly sure to whom she referred. Bauer, she supposed. She could see where his courtly Viennese manners might sway a susceptible female, but he'd left her quite cold. Lord Raeburn, on the other hand, had made her feel itchy and warm. Those butterflies in her stomach had picked up speed and had battled and batted away through seven courses. If wine had been served, she would have tried to drown them.

No, she'd better keep her wits about her. She and Aunt Mim always shared a bedtime brandy as they discussed agency business, but she put the glass down and tried to relax without it. She looked out the window at the darkening mountains and counted a sprinkle of stars in the pearl-gray sky. She estimated the number of studded nails on the ottoman where Aunt Mim's foot rested. Mary looked everywhere around the room except where she wanted. She would not meet Oliver's eye, for that scamp must know exactly what she was thinking. Oliver was sensitive to changes in atmosphere after being the youngest of six brothers. He'd escaped many a beating with his good instincts.

Damn it all. Despite Lord Raeburn's warm language and untoward familiarity, she was . . . smitten. Under all his wickedness, she knew he was vulnerable. And much too handsome for his own good.

It was only because she lacked sufficient experience, she assured herself. The last time she'd worn a regular dress, it had been covered with a capacious grocer's apron. None of the customers—most of them women or servants—had noticed her femininity, and her brother, Albert, had discouraged her from walking out with any young gentlemen, not that there were many who had asked. It suited Albert to keep Mary occupied with the store or his household, and she had no choice, not having finished her education or having any money of her own. If she left her brother's employ, she'd only have to drudge for some stranger.

When Aunt Mim had written, Mary didn't have to think twice. But the freedom she had hoped for in London never materialized. It was remarkable how much time it took to solve other peoples' problems, and how little was left at the end of the day, brandy or not. Mary kept meaning to go to plays or concerts, but somehow the opportunity never presented itself. When she did leave Mount Street, it was always for business—to straighten out some domestic tangle, for which her Mrs. Evensong uniform was necessary.

She brushed her silk skirts with a fingertip. Her gloves had been discarded first thing, and the feel of the material was heavenly. How delightful it was to have bare hands, and how delicious it would be to bury them in Lord Raeburn's beard.

Where had such a thought come from? She didn't even *like* beards. Mary kicked herself, a real, true kick of right kid shoe to left stockinged ankle.

"What do you think, Mary?" Aunt Mim was looking at her sharply over her spectacles.

"I—I'm afraid I was appreciating the view and lost track of the conversation."

"It's for your own good, lass. Get in, get out, and then you'll be safe and can go about your business, whatever that is. Young Oliver and I will be hiding in his room, with anyone else we can round up."

"I beg your pardon?"

"Saturday night. Cards. Drinks," Oliver said, enunciating as if she were deaf.

"You are having a p-party?"

"What we'll be having are witnesses. You invite Bauer to your room, then scream a little and young Oliver here will burst in through the connecting door to save you."

"That's ridiculous," Mary said. "Surely Dr. Bauer wouldn't attempt a liaison with a roomful of gentlemen next door."

"Nothing would fuel his lust more, to have you helpless and at his mercy. He'd never think you'll raise your voice to object. The girls he victimizes are too cowed to cry rape," Lord Raeburn said with bitterness.

Mary faltered. "H-he's a *rapist*?"

Lord Raeburn flushed. "Nae. They're willing enough. Needy poor wee things. He sweet-talks them until they can't think straight, then turns around and asks for money so he won't talk anymore. All he has to do is threaten to diagnose them as hysterical—as nymphomaniacs—and their families will lock them up with no hope of hotels or anything else in their futures. He'll say *they* made advances to *him*. Either way, he makes money."

"Bastard," Oliver spat.

"Mind your language," Aunt Mim said, "though I quite agree. Mary, had I known the risks of all this, I would have put my foot down. This is no place for a sheltered young woman such as yourself."

Lord Raeburn's head turned, eyebrows raised. "I was under the impression Miss Arden had some experience."

"Nothing prepares one for these precise circumstances," Mary said quickly. She was not going to allow Aunt Mim to forbid her to go forward. It was only two days' work, after all, and a hefty, nonrefundable fee even if she wasn't successful. "I think we should coordinate the evening. It's very possible I won't be in any position to scream, you know." She pictured Bauer's long-fingered hands over her mouth and shuddered. "And if I do, you may not hear me if your new friends are drinking and playing cards with any sort of animation. The men we sat near tonight would not have heard a bomb go off at the next table, they were so foxed. We shall have to set a time for my ravishment."

"An excellent idea, Miss Arden. Though you will *not* be ravished." Lord Raeburn was scowling precisely as he had in all those newspaper photographs.

"My attempted ravishment, then. We will fix the hour amongst ourselves closer to Saturday evening—Dr. Bauer may not be available."

"Oh, trust me, he will cancel all engagements to ensure that he is and can best me. To seduce two of my women will be too tempting."

"I am not your woman, Lord Raeburn," Mary said, not as firmly as she should have.

"He doesn't need to know that. Tomorrow I shall make a fool of myself over you." He pantomimed a lover-like pose, thumping his hand to his chest. He'd better do more than that tomorrow and the next day—he looked like an imbecile.

She raised an eyebrow. "I hope that won't be too much of a hardship."

"Fishing for compliments, Miss Arden? You won't get any until they count. I'll be moonstruck enough in front of the guests at the hotel. All will believe I've fallen hopelessly in love."

Aunt Mim coughed. "If I might make another suggestion, Lord Raeburn. No one in their right mind would believe you to be a man who falls in love easily. In lust, yes. You have had that reputation since you were in short pants—or no pants, as the case may be."

Mary slapped her hand over her mouth. Aunt Mim always got to the heart of the matter.

"Dr. Bauer will be much easier to play if you involve him in a wager—which one of you can breach Miss Arden's defenses first? That will give you an excuse to find yourself in her company without attracting his suspicion. There need be no talk of love—you are still in mourning, are you not?"

Lord Raeburn was so still Mary wondered if he was breathing. Was he insulted about the reference to his rakish reputation? Angry at the mention of his dead wife?

And then he laughed. She'd seen him do so once before, when she'd admonished him as they walked into the dining room. He'd stopped himself then, but now he sat, like a merry bear, roaring and snuffling until tears leaked from his dark brown eyes. He was completely overset, and Mary had a moment of panic. What if the man was unbalanced?

What if he really had murdered his wife?

Oliver handed him another brandy when he stopped for air, which he swallowed in its entirety. When he caught his breath, he winked at Mary, then turned to Aunt Mim. "I was told you were a miracle worker, but no one said how very blunt you are, Mrs. Evensong. You are absolutely correct. I will not be falling in love with Miss Arden or anyone else— I'm past all that nonsense, and no doubt Bauer knows that. So, fine. I shall play the great lecher to egg Bauer on. That is a role I know how to play, as you pointed out."

A role he'd been playing all through dinner, Mary thought. He had taken flirtation to greater heights—and depths. It had been all she could do to ignore his "accidental" touches and outré remarks.

Mary Arden was supposed to be a naïve spinster, but Mary Evensong—spinster that she might be—was not really naïve anymore. Had she ever been? Wrapping up legs of lamb and dispensing bottles of Oxo had cured her of any romantic flights of fancy she had harbored as a schoolgirl. Treading between up and downstairs folks these past four years had nearly soured her on the human race altogether. Drunken footmen and dissipated dukes were two sides of the same coin. Most people did not know enough to get out of their own way, and it annoyed her that she was often hired to solve problems that were simply beneath her considerable skills.

Not this time. Lord Raeburn's difficulties would not be solved even when Dr. Bauer was exposed. What he needed was not hers to give.

Mary couldn't give him physical comfort. And anyway, he had enough of that sort of thing from his chorines. She was not at all in charity with the late Lady Edith Raeburn, who'd made him frustrated enough to betray his marriage vows, and now engage in this absurd game to avenge her death.

One didn't usually fall out of one's own bedroom window. Had she been pushed?

Or did she jump?

Mary wouldn't ask. She wasn't quite as blunt as Aunt Mim.

"Well, now that we have our stories straight, I propose to meet you after my examination tomorrow so you may begin to work your charm on me. Shall we have elevenses on the veranda?"

"Tomorrow morning canna come soon enough." Lord Raeburn stood, his color ruddy. "Please excuse my behavior this evening at dinner. I didna realize—"

"That I'm a respectable woman? I took no real offense, my lord. In fact, it was good practice for me. Dr. Bauer's blandishments can appear to go straight over my head. At least until Saturday."

"I have a feeling nothing much gets by you, Miss Arden. Goodnight, Mrs. Evensong. Oliver."

"Pleasant dreams," Aunt Mim said, smiling up at him. Even after the sitting room door closed, her aunt was still smiling.

"I like him."

Mary rolled her eyes. "You've only just met him, Aunt Mim."

"He doesn't know that. Handsome devil. Tortured soul."

"I like him, too," Oliver piped up.

He would. Oliver had a fatal weakness for a handsome face. His wealthy father had tossed him out of his house when he discovered Oliver in the arms of the household's dapper French chef. The French chef was still employed, for how could Mr. Palmer forego the man's fabulous foie gras terrine? But Oliver, as the youngest of six sons, was entirely expendable.

If he wasn't careful, he'd wind up just like poor Mr. Wilde. Mary could not bear to see that happen; she had come to look on Oliver as a real younger brother. He certainly was much more amusing and loyal than Albert, and deserved his happiness wherever he could find it.

She made a pretense of yawning and stretching. "I'm so tired! I'm sure as soon as my head hits the pillow, I'll be out. Come, Oliver, be a good brother and escort me down the hall."

"Yes, Mrs. Evensong. I mean Mary."

Aunt Mim chuckled. "Poor boy. Things just aren't what they seem, are they? Better to get used to that."

Chapter

6

Friday, June 10, 1904

Mary had played dumb. Dumber than dumb. She made no objection when Dr. Bauer dismissed his nurse, and pretended not to notice that his fingers strayed from his stethoscope to her left breast for a few seconds longer than absolutely necessary. She concentrated on keeping her eyes wide, yet unseeing, willing herself to blush.

It was one of her few feminine skills—she had practiced blushing with the other girls at Miss Ambrose's Academy for Young Ladies before Albert removed her to work the new cash register. Mary had several particular things she thought of to bring the color to her cheeks, and now that she'd made Lord Raeburn's acquaintance, he was being incorporated into her system. It was not difficult to think naughty thoughts about him—in fact, it was difficult not to think about him all the time. The man seemed to preoccupy her far more than her other clients.

Every question was answered in shy, breathless syllables.

The symptoms she recited to Bauer were nonsensical. If he had been a proper doctor, he would have told her she was just suffering from "nerves" and sent her packing. Instead, he nodded sympathetically and smoothed his hands all over her white-gowned body. He prescribed scented baths and his own elixir. Mary was fairly certain after one whiff the alcohol content in it was high—really, the hotel should just give up the temperance ghost and let its guests get drunk the old-fashioned way.

He scheduled her for an herbal bath and massage in the afternoon. Unfortunately, he said, he would be seeing patients and unable to perform the task personally. Mary was relieved. The man had touched her quite enough for one day. She had to give him some credit, though. He was gentle. Tender. His blue eyes were guileless, his blond curls cherubic. Satan came in many forms, she reminded herself.

So now she sat in a padded wicker chair, waiting to "bump into" Lord Raeburn. A little white china teapot sat in front of her with a plate of iced biscuits. She'd been too nervous to eat much breakfast before her appointment with Dr. Bauer, so she bit into one of them just as Alec Raeburn came up behind her and tapped her on the shoulder. Her entire body grew warm from just his fingertip.

"May I join you, Miss Arden?"

Mary nodded, swallowing hastily. Her tongue swept over her mouth to clean up any crumbs. There was nothing worse than being caught with something in one's teeth. "G-good morning, my lord."

Lord Raeburn dragged a chair closer and waved at one of the young aproned waitresses to order his own pot of tea. "Well, how was it?" he asked leaning forward so his knees almost touched hers.

She thought for a moment. Bauer had been smooth, yet his very smoothness set off all the alarms she'd learned about at Miss Ambrose's. "I can see why a woman might succumb."

"But not you."

Mary shook her head. "Oh, no. Even if I didn't believe your charges against Dr. Bauer, he's not my type at all. I do not care for beards."

Lord Raeburn's hand flew to his jaw. "Really?"

Had she offended him? She couldn't help it; she was honest to a fault, when she wasn't lying for a good cause. "It is a quirk of mine. I do not even like mustaches."

"The king has a beard. It does not seem to prevent his success with the ladies," Lord Raeburn said, looking affronted.

"That may be true, but it has no bearing on my feelings." Edward was notorious for his string of mistresses. Poor Alexandra—Mary would never put up with infidelity from her husband, even if he was a king. Not that she was likely to have a husband. In a few days she'd be back in London slaving over her files and the adventure at Forsyth Palace Hotel would be just a distant memory. She picked up a biscuit and snapped it in half with some violence.

The waitress delivered another little tray of tea for the baron. A light luncheon would be served in two hours, here in the glassed veranda or under tented tables on the lawn. The afternoon meal was much less formal than the night's dinner. Many of the guests had picnic baskets packed by the hotel kitchen so they could explore the property's trails or get back quickly to stand in their gaiters in the river. If lunch was inadequate, they wouldn't be hungry long—an elaborate tea was set for four o'clock. Mary would have to let out her new dresses if she had to stay for the full week.

She watched Lord Raeburn bite into his biscuit. Despite her hunger, she was suddenly shy to do the same and put both her pieces back on her plate.

He glared at her. His eyes were the darkest brown, nearly black, fringed with long thick lashes. "Why are you staring at me? Do I have food stuck in my horrible beard?" he asked.

"I was not staring." And his beard wasn't so horrible, really.

"You were."

"I wasn't. Well, I mean, you're right here next to me. Where else am I to look?" Mary asked reasonably, not feeling reasonable at all.

Lord Raeburn pointed toward the window with one long finger. "The view is generally conceded to be the attraction here."

"Fine." Mary turned her head, unmoved by the grandeur of the mountains. She'd rather look at the man in front of her, but she kept her eyes fixed to a faraway peak.

"So, what did he do?"

Was that an eagle? No matter. If she wanted to see an eagle, she could go to a zoo. Or America. "Who?"

Lord Raeburn sighed. "Bauer, Miss Arden. Did he remove all your clothes and make advances?"

She would not look at him. Would not. "I wore a hospital gown that covered me from neck to ankle. If the man is overly fond of bare toes, he showed no evidence of it."

"Did he promise to see you again?"

"He arranged for a hydropathic treatment this afternoon, but one of the attendants will do it. He is, as you know, sitting with me tonight at dinner." Mary was not looking forward to it, but she had to earn the generous fee somehow.

"I'll be there, too."

"I cannot stop you from eating, but I implore you to keep your distance."

She heard him take a sip of his tea. He did not slurp.

"I sent him a note this morning as Mrs. Evensong suggested."

She couldn't help herself. She turned her head a fraction and saw the spark of mischief in his dark eyes. "And what did you say in it, my lord?"

"Only that I'd decided to best him at his own game. That I had intentions of introducing you to the pleasures of the flesh as quickly as possible. That the best man would win."

Mary's mouth was dry, so she took her own sip of now tepid tea. "Indeed. And has he replied?"

"He has. I don't expect him to play fair, so be on your guard."

"Wh-what do you mean?" Was Bauer going to lurk in the corridors and snatch her away to some dark private room? The hotel was vast, a rabbit warren just as Lord Raeburn said. She'd never be found. Mary might have to resort to using her hatpin, another thing she'd practiced at Miss Ambrose's. Her school days were so far behind her, she hoped she remembered how.

"Expect a roomful of roses from the hotel's hothouse, or something equally banal. Bauer doesn't have much imagination."

"There's nothing wrong with roses," Mary said with relief. Receiving roses was preferable to being kidnapped.

Lord Raeburn simply snorted, then ate the rest of his biscuit.

"When is your treatment?" he asked once he'd fingered his beard for any errant bits.

She should never have said anything about his beard. Aunt Mim would lecture her. The clients were always right, even when it was clear they were wrong. It was none of Mary's business if Lord Raeburn had a beard down to his bottom.

Well, that was anatomically impossible. It would go down his front, right to—

"Miss Arden, I am speaking to you."

"I beg your pardon. The treatment is scheduled for two. I'm not sure what to expect."

"I believe they make you soak in a tub until your skin prunes up, then rub you down with some sort of muck. Edith would come here for the day. She said the baths relaxed her, but now I know more than hot water was involved." Lord Raeburn spoke lightly, but Mary wasn't fooled.

"I can meet you again for tea and tell you all about it," Mary said, feeling bold.

"That would suit me—that way the busybodies will see us together twice. Word will get back to Bauer. What is Oliver up to today?"

"He's playing golf. He hopes to strike up the acquaintance

of some gentlemen to join him for cards tomorrow night. You were generous to offer your supply of liquor. Not everyone remembers to bring their own libation and find the hotel's rules against alcohol most troublesome. I understand Raeburn's Special Reserve is the big draw. "

"The family business, don't you know. Or at least my brother Evan's. It's one of the smallest distilleries in these parts, but also the best. I'm sorry to say I have nothing to do with the enterprise except drink its product on occasion."

"Sorry? You mean you'd sully your hands in trade?"

"There's nothing wrong with honest work. I'm not one to sit on my arse and wait for the coins to roll in. I manage my estates to the best of my abilities, sometimes even working with my tenants. Are you surprised?"

Mary saw him in a field, stripped to the waist, his broad chest glistening with manly sweat from manual labor. She felt the tell-tale tingle on her cheeks. "Um, no. Very little surprises me, I'm afraid."

"And yet you are an innocent."

"One can still be a virgin without being vacuous, my lord." She felt heat spread beneath the tight lace collar of her shirtwaist.

"Indeed. There is something very pert about you, Miss Arden. May I call you Mary?"

"That wouldn't be proper."

"All the more reason to bedevil Bauer. You must call me Alec, of course."

Alec. Fancy being on a first-name basis with a peer of the realm. Even when she'd stopped Cristobel Burke's elopement, Lord Burke had not asked her to call him Percival.

"Very well. Alec." She liked the way her tongue rolled about her mouth when she said his name. "You said you had two brothers. Evan runs the distillery. Is your other brother involved with that as well?"

"Nick? Och, no. I'm not quite sure where he is at the moment. He's a traveler, our Nick is. An artist, or trying to be. Seems to think Raeburn Court is the dullest place on earth and can't find his inspiration. And he didn't much care for Edith, so I couldn't keep him home."

Mary met his eyes. "Can you tell me a little about her, or is it too painful?"

He did not avoid her scrutiny, and stared right back at her. "There is not a lot to tell. I married her when she was seventeen. Aye, she was much too young for me—I was almost twice her age. But she was a beauty, and I had to have her. Who would dream she'd go before me?" He looked down at his large hands, hands that looked very capable of tossing a frail young woman out a window.

"How did you meet?"

"Mary Arden, I didn't hire you to investigate *me*. It doesn't matter—I made a fool of myself and am still paying for it." He sounded more exasperated than angry.

"I'm sorry if I pried. I do tend to ask too many questions." And for some reason, most people answered them, at least when she was in her elderly woman guise. Alec Raeburn was not aware he'd told her his marriage had not been consummated—that surprising confession went to Mrs. Evensong. What a blow that must have been to him. He exuded male vigor—the air on the veranda practically crackled with it.

Or maybe it was just because she was so close, so aware of his size, his scent. He had, if she was not mistaken, taken a nip of Raeburn's Special Reserve already. He wasn't impaired, not by any means. And there were other aromas— warm wool, Blenheim Bouquet, a faint trace of cigar. But it was early in the day to be drinking. Men did such things out of boredom or despair.

He stood abruptly, snatching her hand from the tea table. "I'll take my leave now, my dear Mary." He bent and kissed each fingertip. "Until this afternoon." His ungloved hand cupped her cheek and he gazed down at her in a lover-like manner.

Mary sat, her mouth agape as he maneuvered between

the wicker chairs and table. And then she realized the reason for his display. Dr. Bauer had entered the room and was heading straight for her.

She didn't have to make herself blush—she was sure she looked as if she'd been set on fire.

"Miss Arden. We meet again." The doctor sat in the vacated chair without invitation. "I do hope you don't think I'm overstepping my bounds, but I warned you last night about Lord Raeburn's reputation. It does you no good to be seen in his company."

"W-we met here quite by chance."

The doctor frowned at the second teapot on the table. "Has he tried to make an assignation with you?"

"An a-a-assignation? What do you mean?" Mary stuttered, sliding into her dim innocent routine.

"He is a brute with women. I will be frank—someone with your tender sensibilities cannot be expected to understand his motives. You know, don't you, that he killed his wife?"

"No!" Mary breathed.

"The local authorities are a bunch of bumblers. The man should have swung by now. I feel a responsibility to my patients, Miss Arden, and I cannot allow that man to make you his next victim. You must be protected."

Oh, he did this well, the moral outrage. The devoted concern. Mary's hand got grabbed again. It was getting more attention in one day than it had in twenty-nine years.

"Surely you must be mistaken, Dr. Bauer. He seems so . . . nice."

"*Gott in Himmel!* Nice! The man is a menace. I forbid you to see him again. He will distress your delicate heart and injure your health, perhaps irreparably."

"My goodness. You seem so passionate about this, Dr. Bauer."

"I am passionate! There is nothing that means more to me than the care of my patients. I will do everything in my power, Miss Arden—everything—to make you well again."

Mary bit her lip to prevent her from laughing at his outburst. She had a fair idea what "everything" entailed.

"Th-thank you, Dr. Bauer. I will try to be more careful in the future. If I see Lord Raeburn again, I shall try to cut him."

"There is no try, Miss Arden, there is only do. If he makes himself a nuisance, come to me. I shall have him ejected from the hotel. Why Prescott lets him stay here I do not understand."

"The baron lives nearby, isn't that right? He says he's making improvements to his house and everything is at sixes and sevens."

"Bah! Let him sleep in his stables and keep him away from innocent girls such as yourself."

"I-I am not precisely a girl, Dr. Bauer," Mary said, fishing to see how he'd compliment her.

"You are young, fresh, and lovely. A vision. Do not throw yourself away on that Scottish clod."

Nor will I throw myself away on an Austrian clod, Mary vowed.

If Lord Raeburn—Alec—had not come to her, would she have seen through Bauer's gallantry if she had met him in the ordinary course of events? Perhaps not. His smoothness might have been a welcome diversion and not set off any alarms at all.

What if she'd brought Aunt Mim up here when the hotel opened? Mary had been feeling somewhat mournful over her spinster state over the last year, especially after seeing Charles Cooper and Louisa Stratton fall in love. Was she ripe for the picking? Susceptible to flattery and attention? Alec Raeburn made her feel dizzy and he was not even trying.

Maybe she was being just as silly over Alec Raeburn as Edith Raeburn had been over Josef Bauer.

No. Edith had been barely twenty-one when she met her fate. Mary liked to think her advanced years had given her some sense, and her sense was telling her that she could trust Alec. But she was not about to embark on an affair with him. That would be unprofessional, and Mary Evensong was nothing if not professional.

Damn it.

Chapter

7

Alec was less than impressed with the Forsyth Palace Hotel. Yes, the building was magnificent, the food fresh, delivered daily, and well-prepared, the beds angel-soft. The spa staff, however, left a great deal to be desired, and it was not only Josef Bauer who concerned him.

It had not taken much to bribe the beefy bath attendant. Good Lord, he could be anyone come to murder Mary Arden. His reputation should have given the masseuse pause, but his pound notes overcame her scruples. Alec should not be where he was right now, in a windowless room lit only by a fragrant candle, the door shut and locked. He should not be anywhere near Mary, who lay facedown, naked, and helpless on a treatment table. True, most of her was wrapped in a warmed linen sheet, her back still pink from its scalding bath. Her auburn hair was swept up, damp ringlets clinging to her slender neck, and it was all Alec could do not to bend over and bite her like a vampire.

She'd sent him a message this afternoon that Bauer had "forbidden" her to see him, so their tea date was canceled. It was unnecessary—she was fairly sure she could arrange a rendezvous with the doctor tomorrow night without provoking his jealousy over Alec.

Alec was sure she could, too. What man could resist her blushes and sighs, her wide hazel eyes, her plush little figure? While she was not a conventional beauty like Edith—nothing like Edith—he was drawn in despite his good intentions. For heaven's sake, she wasn't even really an actress, just a grocery clerk! A shop girl.

And not really a girl either, he reminded himself. She must be close to thirty. But maybe it was time for him to leave flighty young things behind. He was getting long in the tooth for meaningless dalliance. What he needed was a mature mistress, someone he could talk to. Better yet, someone he could be quiet with.

Mary Arden was a respectable middle-class woman. Alec doubted she'd jump at the offer to become his mistress when this was all over, no matter how much money and comfort he might offer her. Her tongue was a trifle too sharp for the job anyway.

So this might be the only time he ever had to see her in such a pose. Even in the dimness, he noted her shoulders were kissed by a scattering of freckles, and that her ankle was well-turned.

Alec had meant to speak to her about tomorrow, but he didn't want to frighten her. She was expecting a rubdown with smelly goo, not a conversation. The longer he stood near the door, the harder it was to gather up his wits. Perhaps he'd been unwise to sneak into the spa—he could have sent her a note back, or visited Mrs. Evensong's rooms after dinner.

But some maggot in his head kept muttering about her treatment at two o'clock, and the maggot was insistent. What if Bauer changed his plans and decided to deal with her himself? Mary would be at the man's mercy. Alec was only protecting her from assault from that smarmy foreign bastard.

Mary breathed deeply, and he snapped to.

"Are you going to begin?" she asked, her words muffled by the circular pillow she lay on. "I confess I've never felt so relaxed. I can't imagine what I'll feel like after the massage."

Alec felt his tongue thicken. This is when he should speak in his gentlest voice before she started to scream, explain that he'd come to keep her safe today and talk to her about tomorrow. He found he couldn't utter a word.

He took a step, then another. A bottle of ointment sat on a tray table. Alec uncapped it and poured some on his palm, then rubbed his hands together to warm the fluid. It smelled strongly of roses and he fought back a sneeze.

What the hell was he thinking?

The truth was, he was not thinking at all.

He placed his hands on her shoulders, his thumbs circling the base of her neck. He heard a little cracking sound, and wondered if his touch was too rough. All his life he'd fought against his size, feeling like a brute even when his intentions were innocent. He was not exactly innocent now, however.

Mary didn't seem to mind—in fact she stretched like a kitten which had been rubbed behind its ears. His fingers pressed into her shoulders, kneading inexpertly. Sometimes his paramours had touched him this way to ease his tension, and he tried to remember their technique.

Alec realized he'd always been on the receiving end, and while he prided himself on giving pleasure to women, his pleasure was always paramount. That's what he'd paid the girls for, after all. He'd been a selfish bastard, living an empty life. Marriage was supposed to change that, but it hadn't.

Mary groaned. He drew his hands back at once.

"No, no. I meant that groan in the best possible way. Your hands are magic," she mumbled into the pillow. "I have been very tense. The stress of my job—I mean my life, you know. It's a job to cater to my grumpy aunt, and my brother is a constant trial. My health has suffered."

Good save on her part. She wasn't supposed to have a job, just be an aimless heiress with a touch of hypochondria.

Probably Bauer expected his staff to report everything they learned about the patients. Alec said nothing, just resumed the rubbing, concentrating on where her wings would be if she were an angel. She gave a twitch and happy sigh, but blessedly ceased talking. She expected a female attendant, and Alec did not want to attempt to raise his voice several octaves and make the situation even more fraudulent than it was.

He was not going to lift the sheet and slip his big paws beneath it. He was not. This would be the speediest massage on record, because he knew now he could not possibly explain at this point why he had come into this room and was touching her so intimately when he'd merely meant to talk to her in private.

She would eviscerate him if she discovered who he was, and rightly so. Alec was as bad as Bauer, taking advantage of an unsuspecting woman. He would give Mary's exposed feet a few tweaks and leave the way he came.

Flee.

What an ass he was. His brain was scrambled. If anyone was tense, it was he—the last year had been hell and had obviously unhinged him.

After Saturday night he would go back to Raeburn Court and try to pick up the pieces of his life. Bauer would be disgraced, and that would have to be enough. Alec would have his brothers for company—if Nick could be unearthed from whatever international bordello he resided in—and hope that one of them married and had an heir to the barony. He'd be an indulgent uncle and try to find a hobby. Massaging women was definitely off-limits.

Alec squeezed his eyes shut as his hands passed over the sheet. Knowing she was nude beneath it dried his mouth. How silly he was—he'd spent quality time with a great many nude women before. But imagining what Mary Arden looked like unwrapped made his inconvenient manhood swell.

Feet. He'd concentrate on her feet. Alec had no foot fetish that he was aware of; he'd always been a breast man. Large or small, it didn't matter—breasts were marvelously soft and responsive. He was fond of the way a woman's waist curved into her hip as well. A rounded bottom was a lovely thing, too. Mary's looked tempting beneath the sheet.

Ah, hell. Think of her feet.

Her soles were clean, and he poured a bit more oil on his hands and held one foot between them. It was a small foot, a dainty foot for a small woman. But even though Mary was not tall, she exuded command and control.

Yes, she would kill him, probably brandishing a parasol. He would take his beating, for God knows he deserved one. He pressed her foot between his palms, smoothing over her heel, tugging at her toes. Massaging her back and shoulders had been much easier—there were a lot of damn bones in one's foot and they all seemed to be crunching a bit under his ministrations. Alec hoped she wouldn't be crippled afterward.

He dropped her foot to the table abruptly and took a step backward, then another, bumping into a chair.

The room was dark and dead silent. Mary wasn't asleep, was she? No such luck.

"Aren't you going to do the other foot? That felt lovely."

No, he was not going to do the other foot. He was about to use his own to race out of the room.

But then the doorknob rattled with considerable violence.

"Unlock this door at once!"

It was the bad doctor. Alec's luck had definitely run out. Bauer sounded enraged, his Viennese accent more pronounced than usual.

Mary stirred from the table.

"Don't move," Alec whispered.

Her head whipped around, her face pink with wrinkles from the pillow. "What? What's happening?" Damn, she rolled to the side and sat up awkwardly, clutching the sheet to her bosom. Her mouth opened when she spotted him edged flat against the wall, but she had the good sense not to scream.

"I can explain," Alec said, pushing his hair back with oily fingers.

"I seriously doubt it." She glanced around the candlelit room. "No windows. Only one door. I'd say you're trapped."

Bauer banged outside, hollering for someone to bring him keys.

"I told you not to follow me around, didn't I? And now look at the pickle you've gotten us into. Get under the treatment table," she snapped.

"Are you mad? I'll never fit under there!"

"It's your only hope. Unless you want to spoil everything."

Alec was fresh out of ideas himself. He dropped down and crawled under the padded table, finding himself covered by a draped sheet. Which meant—

He peeked from under the hem of it just in time to see Mary blow out the candle. A naked Mary, lit all too briefly. But lit long enough.

Mother of God. She was lovely.

She went to the door, struggling with the bolt, then opened it a crack. Alec dropped the sheet in the interest of sanity and self-preservation.

"Oh, Dr. Bauer. I'm so sorry. I must have fallen asleep. The scented bath was simply divine."

"Where is he?" Bauer sounded absolutely enraged.

"Where is who?" Mary asked, yawning. "Oh, no. You can't come in. I haven't a stitch on."

"I am a doctor, Miss Arden—I have seen many naked women before," Bauer sputtered.

"But not me, sir. It wouldn't be proper without your nurse present, would it? I was just a little surprised when you dismissed her this morning."

The cur. Alec made himself stay still, but it was a near thing not to leap from under the table and grab Bauer's throat.

"Never mind that. Where is Raeburn?"

"L-Lord Raeburn? Why would you think that horrible man is here?"

Horrible man? Alec supposed she had a point.

"He bribed Hedwig—your masseuse—to take her place. Naturally, she refused the money and came straight to me."

So Hedwig was a thief *and* a liar. And rather slow, when it came right down to it. Alec had had plenty of time to compromise Mary Arden.

"How ridiculous! There is no one here with me, Dr. Bauer. I waited and waited, and then I guess I fell asleep. If you hadn't made all that racket, I'd still be asleep. For the first time in months, I was finally relaxed, and now—now you tell me there is a madman after me and bribing people to have his wicked way with me!" She burst into noisy tears.

"Miss Arden, Miss Arden, calm yourself."

"Don't try to touch me!" Mary shrieked. "Someone get me my clothes. What kind of a health spa are you running here, Dr. Bauer? I shall need some prayer and quiet reflection before I go back to my room. Oh, my nerves!" She slammed the door.

"Are we still on for dinner, Miss Arden?" the doctor asked through the shut door.

"Yes. No. I cannot think. I am much too overset. Imagine if that dastard Raeburn had found me, naked and alone in this little room. Vulnerable. No way out. I might have been—oh! It's too ghastly to contemplate." Mary whacked the table hard and a metal bar dug into Alec's head. "I am too embarrassed to be seen by anyone. I cannot face you just yet." Alec heard a bottle smash, and the scent of roses cloaked the room. Damn it, he was going to sneeze—

"Um. Miss Arden. There is a little door hidden behind the instruments cabinet. It leads to the servants' ramp. You may leave with utter privacy. I shall communicate with the staff to vacate the area for—shall we say ten minutes after we get your clothing to you? Does that give you enough time to get to your room?"

Something else hit the wall and rolled by the table. The candle, Alec thought.

"Oh, you are too kind, Dr. Bauer! I am sorry I am breaking things. My temper, you know. Most of the t-time I am m-meek and m-mild, but when I am cr-crossed, Oliver says I am a regular termagant. Imagine that rotter Raeburn thinking to take advantage of me! If he were here, I might kill him with my bare hands! Choke the life out of him! Watch his black eyes pop right out of his head!"

Alec shut them, not that he could see anything anyway. He believed her.

"I shall see that no further harm comes to you, Miss Arden. You may rely upon me."

"Thank you, Dr. Bauer. Josef. May I call you Josef? And please fetch my clothing. Just leave them outside the door."

"Yes, my dear. Yes to the clothes, yes to the Josef. I trust I may call you Mary."

"Of course. I think we shall be great friends, once I calm down."

"I have ways to calm you, Mary. Leave it to me. Hedwig! Miss Arden's clothes, if you please."

Mary gave a vicious kick under the table with one of her adorable little feet. The sheet was snatched from the table, and in an instant she was wrapped up again.

There was a knock at the door. "Your clothes, miss. Do you want me to assist you in the dressing?"

"No thank you, Hedwig. Just leave them."

"Yes, miss. Very good, miss. You watch out for that man, now."

"Dr. Bauer?"

"No, miss. The black-bearded fellow. He is hard to resist."

"Oh, I believe I can resist him with no difficulty whatsoever. I loathe beards. Thank you, Hedwig. That will be all."

Mary waited a beat, then opened the door, grabbed her clothes, and locked them in again.

"You were magnificent," Alec whispered from under the table, somewhat afraid to come out. The room was pitch black, but he was pretty sure Mary Arden was glaring at him.

"Make yourself useful and do up my laces."

Alec was a bit more familiar undoing laces in the dark, but he managed to cinch Mary into her long corset, her stiff back radiating anger. There was a rustle of clothing where he heard mumblings, with perhaps a few curses included. Once her head was free of the fabric, she said, "What the hell were you thinking?"

Hadn't he asked himself that very question?

It seemed he didn't have to answer it. Her little fist punched his chest with each word. "I cannot believe you would be so brazen to come in here and—fondle me like some lecher. You, Lord Raeburn, are disgusting! Did you think you'd get away with it?"

Yes. Yes, he had. He'd almost made his escape. His boot heels hit the cabinet as she pounded him backward, and he shoved it out of the way. It was on wheels, and it crashed into the corner. He felt around the wall behind it, and found a door fit for Snow White's dwarfs. Alec pulled the door open, and a spill of electric light fell into the room.

"Ladies first."

Mary Arden looked more beautiful in anger than he'd ever seen her, even if her shirtwaist was misbuttoned. "You had better remember I *am* a lady, not one of your London tarts. I have half a mind to tell Aunt Mim—Mrs. Evensong, that is—I'm finished with this job. If she learns what you've done, you're a dead man."

"I meant no harm," Alec said, ducking under the doorframe and not quite clearing it. That would leave a mark. "I only came in to talk, but there you were, all comfortable. I didn't want to alarm you, and then you asked me to begin, and I—and I—"

"Oh, just shut up," Mary said, sprinting up the ramp. Alec noted the other small doors along the wall, convenient for the staff to supply rooms without being seen. They climbed until they came to swinging double doors that were marked Third Floor, where Mary's rooms were located. He followed her meekly to her door as she fished the key out of her reticule. Fortunately no other guests saw them as she pulled him into her bedroom. To his astonishment, she sat on a chair, removed her six-button boot, and tugged down her stocking.

"On your knees and finish the foot massage," she snapped.

Alec didn't have to think twice.

Chapter

8

It was very bad of her, she knew. No one had ever touched her feet before except a shoemaker, and her mother, she supposed, as she played "this little piggy" when Mary was an infant. Once Lord Raeburn was finished, she planned to kick him in the snout and then quit this job.

No, she couldn't quit. Exposing Dr. Bauer was just a day away. Her pride was not as important as making sure he didn't compromise any more innocent women.

But Mary was compromised. How much had wretched Raeburn seen? She'd been lucky she had been able to keep Bauer from barging in. A sheet was hardly a barrier to discovery, and it was the only thing at hand to conceal Lord Raeburn's bulk. She had no choice but to fling it over the man and hope for the best.

How comical he'd looked under the table, folded into himself like a telescope. How comical he looked now, like a dazed Prince Charming on his knees without a glass slipper.

"Oh, do get up. I just wanted to see how sorry you were."

"If you had a dozen feet, I would rub them all," Alec said, his face dusky with embarrassment. He stumbled up onto a chair and hung his head, the perfect portrait of penitence.

"If I had a dozen feet, I would kick you to kingdom come," Mary replied with asperity. "How could you do such a thing? I was *naked*. You, sir, are no gentleman."

"I canna argue there. All I can say is that things got out of hand."

Out of hand. Out of foot. Out of everywhere. His broad bare hands had touched her bare shoulders and back. Her left foot. Mary never had indulged herself with a massage before, but everything felt quite lovely when she thought Hedwig was over her, those magic hands circling her skin.

Mary tugged her collar up, though she already felt as if she were strangling. "We were fortunate I was able to hold Bauer off."

"You were truly amazing. You may say you are not an actress, Mary, but your performance was equal to anything I've seen on the Strand. You know I'm a devotee of the theater—you were more convincing than any woman I've ever—" He cleared his throat. She knew his reputation; it was rumored he'd bedded half the actresses on the London stage. Her eyes narrowed, and he had the grace to look even more embarrassed.

"All that shouting and throwing," he said with admiration. "It was quite a show. I'll have to have a bath myself to get rid of the smell of attar of roses."

Mary sniffed. The man was drenched in scent, as was she. It hadn't been wise to fling things, but she'd been very angry.

She was *still* angry, but there was no point in wallowing further. Cool heads always prevailed. She'd gotten them out of their predicament, and had furthered her cause with Dr. Bauer. Josef. They were on a first-name basis now and he thought she was unhinged. How much easier it would be for him to think he could seduce her.

Mary hoped she hadn't overdone it. If he thought she was truly mad, he might think she'd publicly denounce him in a fit of temper. She'd have to be especially tongue-tied this evening and apologize for her uncharacteristic fit of fury. Mary would place the blame all on Lord Raeburn.

Where it belonged.

"From here on in, you must stay away from me. *Far* away. If I see you, expect me to faint into Dr. Bauer's arms. You are now the villain of this piece, which should work in our favor. Let us hope he doesn't manage to get you thrown out of the hotel before tomorrow night. Bribing the masseuse," she huffed.

"Just to talk to you," Alec repeated. "I wasn't sure I'd get another opportunity."

"A fat lot of talking you did."

"I was worried about you, you know. What if Bauer rearranged his appointments with patients and came into the room, with you all naked and alone?"

"Like you did?" Mary asked, raising her eyebrow.

The baron soldiered on. "He could have molested you and you'd never have known."

"*Exactly* like you did."

"'Twasn't molestation, and well you know it, Mary. I barely touched you."

Ha! What would his touches be like if he put some effort into them? She had been more than satisfied. Her neck hadn't felt this limber in years.

"Let's agree not to discuss it further. I must admit I'm annoyed—all the other massage sessions are booked up through Monday. I'll never know what a proper treatment is like now."

"I'll—I'll make it up to you. Get you a thorough massage in London when this is all over. Get someone who isn't susceptible to bribery and lying. That Hedwig looks like a man, anyhow. I wouldn't trust her as far as I could throw her, which wouldn't be far."

Mary's lip quirked. She envisioned Hedwig tied to a caber, Lord Raeburn pitching her across a field.

No more imagining Alec Raeburn and his physical prowess. "You've got to leave. Make sure no one sees you."

"When will I see you again?"

"I'll report to Mrs. Evensong after dinner. I always—that is, since this job began, we've been sharing a brandy at the end of the day in her suite."

Alec rose, towering over her. "How did you come to work for her?"

"Oh, you know, the usual way." Mary shrugged. "I wanted a bit of an adventure after the grocery store."

"You seem very comfortable with her, almost as if you've been working with her for years. She's a frightening old lady, you know. Sees right into your soul."

Mary decided to feel flattered. She'd always been called old-headed, and following in Aunt Mim's footsteps had been relatively easy.

"You look a bit like her. Minus the wrinkles, of course," Alec went on, staring down at her.

She could tell him part of the truth, couldn't she?

"She actually *is* my Aunt Mim. My father's sister."

"Och, that explains it. No wonder she came along to watch you like a great black hawk. My Lord, she will kill me, won't she, if she finds out about this afternoon."

Mary had no intention of telling her aunt—or worse yet, Oliver—what had transpired in the treatment room. Perhaps someday, when this job was firmly behind them and they could have a good laugh over it.

Oliver could be invited upstairs now that he knew their secret. Between Aunt Mim and herself, they could keep him out of trouble.

"You won't tell her, will you?"

Imagine, a great big bear of a man like Alec Raeburn being frightened of Aunt Mim—or really *her*. This dual— no, triple—identity of Mary's was becoming confusing.

"As you said, she's an old lady. I would not want to distress her," Mary evaded.

"Until later then." He hesitated at the door. "Don't let that blackguard Bauer get too familiar tonight."

"I assure you my virtue is safe." For now. Mary couldn't swear to remain pure if Alec touched her toes again.

He opened the door a fraction, decided the coast was clear, and left her standing on one boot on her carpet.

She needed to sit down. Looking up all that way at him made her disoriented.

What a day so far! She was certainly earning every penny for the agency. Mary caught a glimpse of herself in the long mirror on the wardrobe door and she looked far too healthy—her cheeks were rosy, her eyes sparkled, and even her hair looked curlier. She would have to do something about that before she went downstairs for dinner.

Mary ran her own bath. That was a little redundant after being scrubbed so vigorously by Hedwig, but the rose oil was giving her a tickle in the back of her throat. She imagined Alec was doing the very same thing, lowering his long body into the short copper tub in his suite.

Each set of rooms had its own bathroom consisting of a Crapper, tub, and pedestal sink. Water for plumbing one hundred en suite bathrooms was plentiful in the Highlands—all that snow melted into the underground rivers and lakes, easily plumbed into the modern building.

The hotel closed in the winter months since the roads were impassable, though. To live up here year-round must be a challenge. How had Lady Edith Raeburn managed before the hotel was built and she sought her dangerous liaison? As far as Mary knew, Alec's young wife didn't even go down to Edinburgh, but stayed immured at Raeburn Court like Rapunzel in her tower.

Mary wondered if Alec and his brothers planned to spend their winter at Raeburn Court wrapped in the Raeburn tartan staring gloomily into the fire now that she was dead. It seemed Edith had driven the men out of their own home.

She sank into the steaming water, far from relaxed, her mind spinning, only to jump when Oliver knocked some ten minutes later.

"What ho, Mrs. Evensong?" he asked behind the door.

"Hush, Oliver. The walls probably have ears." She scrambled out of the tub, wrapping herself in a bath sheet. "I'll be right out."

"Reporting in, I am."

"Hold your horses." It didn't really matter if Oliver saw her in dishabille—he wasn't likely to feel any non-brotherly yearning. She dried off quickly and belted her robe. Oliver was in her bedroom, his feet up on her dressing table. It appeared from the bright pink of his forefinger he'd been messing with her rouge pot.

"Absolutely not," Mary said, sweeping the glass container out of his reach. "Not even for fun. How did you spend your day?"

"Do you know how very boring golf is? All that whacking at a little white ball to get it into a little brown hole. And for what? Bragging rights? At least my caddie was a handsome laddie."

"Oliver!" Mary warned.

"Oh, don't worry. I won't disgrace the mission. I've rounded up five fellows for cards tomorrow, and cream of the crop they are. Judge Whitley, who suffers from arthritis. Poor fellow kept dropping his club and I can't imagine what he'll do with the pasteboards. Stern old fellow, wrath of God in the courtroom. Big believer in right and wrong. I didn't dare to cheat," Oliver said, ticking off each guest on his fingers. "His friend barrister Richard Hurst, whose beloved young daughter is here for her asthma. Protector of the innocent and all that rot. Lord Peter Brantley, whose wife suffers from 'nerves.' Isn't that your complaint, sis? But when she isn't nervous, the woman is one of the biggest gossips in England and Brantley is not too far behind. Sir Jacob Rycroft, owner of *The London Ledger* and his brother Amos, both here for the fishing and a bit of brotherly bonding. *The Ledger*, you know, will print anything and worry about the truth later. I think we should be able to convince Bauer for the good of the hotel, which he owns shares in, he should resign and go back to yodeling in the Tyrol."

"I believe they yodel in Switzerland, not Austria," Mary said, grinning. "Excellent work, Oliver. You have been wasted at the reception desk all these months. When we get back, I'll talk to Harriet. She has been mumbling about a vacation for ages, but we've been so busy. Between the two of us, we can train you to take her place for a little while, and then promote you to junior assistant if all goes well. The agency workload warrants it."

Oliver leaped up, spinning Mary around so fast she thought she would get sick.

"Capital! I won't let you down, I promise!"

"Well, for a start, you can *put* me down," Mary said, breathless. "Won't these upstanding gentlemen object to playing with Lord Raeburn?"

Oliver shook his head. "Not everyone believes the rumors. Raeburn went to school with the Rycroft brothers. *The Ledger* was the one paper that didn't toss him in the mud when they could have. Brantley will want to fish around for the dirt. The London legal men are interested in Raeburn's Special Reserve. It's hard to get down south."

"What time is your card game?"

"Nine o'clock sharp. I've arranged for a card table and extra chairs to be delivered and my furniture rearranged."

"You do think of everything." Mary was impressed with the meticulous care Oliver had exhibited so far. "So if I invite Bauer to my room at ten?"

"We shall all be well-lubricated and ready to rescue you. Leave the connecting door unlocked."

Mary nodded. Tomorrow night was in train. Now she only had to get through tonight.

Chapter

9

*I*t was not hard to feel pale and nervous. Mary entered the dining room quite alone, after another put-up public row with Oliver in the lobby. There were a few sympathetic glances, but she had doomed herself socially by appearing twice with Alec and was now under suspicion and worthy of her brother's scorn.

She knew her dinner gown was exquisite, a glove-tight column of ecru satin dipped low and accented with spangled bows at her cleavage and shoulders. A bib of cobweb-fine ecru lace stitched to the bodice reached to and ruffled her throat, covering her freckles yet projecting an air of nudity. She had paste yellow diamond clips in her hair, and a mother-of-pearl fan, which she used to fend off the heat from equally elegantly dressed bodies in the room. Mary looked like an heiress, and only she knew she'd purchased the dress at a secondhand clothing shop. The train had been stained, but it had been a matter of minutes to chop it off and hem it.

Tomorrow night's dress was even better. Likely she would not be wearing the fourth dinner gown she'd brought—she'd be on a train on Sunday, heading back to black territory.

Now that she had her Mary Arden trousseau, she wanted to find a use for it. Perhaps Oliver could be persuaded to escort her to concerts and plays. He was good company when he wasn't being paid to fight with her.

She took a seat near the end of a table, placing her fan on the charger next to her, saving the seat for Dr. Bauer, if he didn't think she was a Bedlamite and kept their tryst. She drooped her shoulders and stared moodily into the flickering candle on the table. The room echoed with laughter and conversation, making her feel truly left out. She kept her gloved hands on her lap so she wouldn't be tempted to touch her hot cheeks and remove any of the white makeup she'd used to appear delicate.

The young waiters began streaming from the kitchen with the first course, and still Mary sat in isolation. Bauer wasn't coming after all. She'd overplayed her hand—Bauer must think she was off her onion and not worth the effort. She'd failed Lord Raeburn—she, who prided herself on performing the impossible, just as the agency motto boasted.

A waiter took pity on her and dropped a platter of prawns with Marie Rose sauce in front of her. As she reached for the serving spoon, a hand came down on hers.

"Let me, Miss Arden. Mary."

Mary looked up into a completely unfamiliar face. Pale blue eyes. Blunt nose. Sensual lips. His lightly accented words gave him away, however.

"D-Dr. Bauer?"

"It is I, Mary." He gave her hand a predatory squeeze. "Do you recognize me?"

"What happened to your beard?"

"A little birdie told me that you did not care for them. To win you over, I would do anything. You are the Delilah to my Sampson."

She must not laugh. Men did not like to be laughed at, even when they knew themselves to be ridiculous. Bauer did have an anxious look about him, as well he should, since his cheeks were scraped baby-pink and his chin appeared less than chiseled.

"Oh! How romantic for you to do that for little old m-me. I do hope you don't think I am the sort of female who wants to rob a man of his power. A m-man is s-superior in every way above a woman," she choked, crossing her fingers in her lap. "Except, of course, for my brother."

Bauer nodded, his chest puffing. "He is a toad," he agreed. "I see he has left you to fend for yourself again. May I join you?"

"Of course. As we arranged. I thought you had f-forgotten."

"How could I forget a girl like you, Mary? So sweet? So spirited?" He removed her fan from the plate and sat down. "I have decided to ignore everyone else this evening except you." He gave her what he probably thought was a smoldering look.

It was hard for ice-blue eyes to smolder. Now dark eyes, eyes belonging to Scottish noblemen, smoldered very nicely indeed.

"Your other patients will be jealous," Mary simpered.

"And they will have reason to be. I cannot think of anyone but you, Mary. Please say that my interest is returned."

Mary took an unladylike slug of water, wishing it were something much stronger, then drank the entire glass. Her mouth was dry. Flirting did not come naturally to her. In fact, it had been over a decade since she'd used her feminine wiles, when she'd had hopes of attracting Miles Stanhope, a solicitor's clerk whose office was across the street from her family's corner shop. Miles had not noticed her friendly waves as he passed and had married the solicitor's daughter. Mary had admired him for his ambition and chalked the episode up to experience. It was hard to be flirtatious behind the hanging sausages and skinned rabbits in the store window anyhow.

There had been no more clerks, ambitious or otherwise. And Dr. Bauer didn't really *like* her—he was simply adding her to his conquests, thwarting Alec Raeburn in the process.

Damn it. What was wrong with her? She might not be a

diamond of the first water, but her figure was good, especially when Hamblen laced her, and her face not a complete fright. She'd been teased about her wide forehead, and had cut some curls accordingly to soften the effect.

Mary shivered. She'd never been touched—with the exception of Alec Raeburn's extraordinary cheek this afternoon—or even courted. The stores and her nephews had taken up all her time when she was a young woman. Damn, but her youth was gone as if it had never been. She was coming on thirty, a spinster who was married to her job.

Alec Raeburn was only a client, no more, no less. She had a fiduciary responsibility to him.

Ha. She'd pay *him* if he rubbed her shoulders again.

"*Liebling*, you are not answering. Or even eating. Are you still of a nervous disposition? Let me add a little of my special tonic to your glass." Bauer reached into his jacket and pulled out a silver flask.

"That d-doesn't look like medicine," Mary said.

He chuckled. "I cannot go rattling about the hotel with glass bottles in my pockets." He tipped the flask. The liquid that spilled from it was as clear as water.

He would have to hold a gun to her head to make her drink it. Mary had heard of drugs that gentlemen gave ladies to make them insensate. She was not going to be tricked twice today, although Alec's tricking had turned out to be very relaxing.

She stabbed a shrimp and popped it in her mouth, tasting nothing. "Y-you make me a little nervous, Josef. I am unused to m-male company."

"This I cannot believe. Why, you are a beautiful woman. Are all men in England blind? I should not let an angel like you slip through my grasp."

It was all Mary could do not to roll her eyes. Really, Bauer was so predictable. Banal. Mary knew she was not beautiful. There was nothing freakish about her—she was comely enough, but her face was not apt to launch a thousand ships.

"I b-believe you are trying to turn my head."

His hand fell gently on her thigh. "Am I succeeding? I would so like to succeed."

Mary pitied the poor lonely women that had fallen for this rubbish. She plucked his hand off and smoothed out her skirt. "This is m-much too fast for me. I do not know how I feel. I b-barely know you."

"Let us become better acquainted then. We shall have a walk in the moonlight after dinner. The grounds have been planted with night-blooming flowers. Perhaps you too will bloom for me."

Not in this lifetime, no matter how much of an old maid she might be. "Oh, not tonight. I have promised to read to my aunt."

"Pah! Give the old biddy some of my medicine and she will never know you are not there."

Just as she suspected. Mary pushed her glass out of reach. "Oh, I couldn't. Aunt Mim depends on me. Oliver thinks of nothing but his own pleasure and she has no one else."

"You must not sacrifice your happiness for the whims of an old woman, Mary."

He couldn't know how right he was. Once she got back to London, things were going to change.

"Tonight is out of the question," she said firmly.

"Tomorrow then."

"I told Aunt Mim I'd dine in her room. She gets so lonely, you see, and it's hard for her to get around with her gouty foot. But perhaps after—" She let the words hum between them.

His determined hand landed back on her thigh. "Where can I meet you?"

Mary looked down at his hand, wondering if she should smack it away. Stab it with the butter knife. What would a confused virgin do?

She stumbled up from her chair. "I f-feel rather faint. You are making my head spin."

He rose, too. "Let me escort you to your room."

"Oh no! Everyone will see us leave together and get the wrong idea."

"The right idea, Mary. We belong together."

She took a deep breath and plunged into the abyss. "T-tomorrow night. In-in my r-room. Shall we say ten o'clock? My brother is planning a card party and he will never hear us."

"Mary! You have made me the happiest of men!"

Bauer did look happy. Smug. He was in for a rude awakening.

Mary walked through the dining room, head held high. The lobby was deserted, except for the uniformed elevator operator.

"Are you all right, miss?"

Mary nodded, not trusting herself from erupting in laughter. She held up three fingers for her floor as if she were a mute. Just as the operator was about to close the gate, a tall man in evening dress hurried in.

"Your floor, sir?"

"Three, please."

Mary looked up. Way up. Alec Raeburn winked at her.

A clean-shaven Alec Raeburn. His curly black beard was a thing of the past. He was more handsome now than she could have dreamed, and she *had* dreamed.

Good heavens. Who knew her words had such power over men? She might try "Peace on earth" or "Pie for everyone" next.

The elevator creaked up. When it stopped, Mary turned left toward her room, and Alec right for the benefit of the operator. As soon as the conveyance disappeared downward, he thundered down the hall after her.

Mary didn't bother to try to argue. She fished the key out of her reticule and opened the door.

"You've made me miss my dinner, you know," Alec rumbled, dropping into a chair. He loosened his necktie. Good heavens, he wasn't going to disrobe here, was he? Though if he did, it would only be fair. Tit for tat, so to speak. "Why did you leave?"

"I invited Bauer to my room at ten o'clock tomorrow night. There was nothing else to say. The thought of being pawed through the rest of the meal was not conducive to eating."

"The bastard!"

"Now, Alec, it's what we've worked for, isn't it? My thigh will survive."

Now *this* was smoldering. Without the mask of his beard, his dark eyes became her focal point. They were large, too long-lashed for a man, and glittering even in the dusky light of her bedroom.

"I can see why he couldn't keep his hands off you."

Mary took out a handkerchief and wiped her cheeks. "Is that supposed to be a compliment?"

"I don't dare to compliment you. You'll slice my tongue off. But that dress is very fetching. You look very— virginal."

Mary sat down in the club chair opposite. Right now her high lace collar seemed to be squeezing her head off. Perhaps she should unfasten one of the tiny diamanté buttons. She tugged off her gloves instead and folded them across her lap.

"Are you hungry?" Alec asked.

"Not really."

"You should eat. We can get a tray up from the kitchen."

"We?"

"No one needs to know I'm here." He bounced off his chair and picked up the telephone that rested on her dressing table. It was a closed circuit, with round-the-clock telephone girls in a little room behind the reception desk to fulfill the guests' every need. "Go on, order something. We'll share it."

Mary sighed. The job was proving to be more complicated with every passing hour. And how could she swallow dinner with her tight collar and Alec Raeburn so near?

Chapter

10

Room service had come and gone. Alec had stepped into Oliver's room when they delivered the trolley of food, and he was making do with the knife and spoon while Mary wielded the single fork. She had asked for a small sampling of the dinner menu, and refused the waiter's assistance when he volunteered to remain to serve her.

Alec had been amused when she ate her half of the dessert first, a wild strawberry and hazelnut meringue. She picked at the cutlets and skipped the trout altogether, shuddering as its eye condemned her from its plate. Alec had no scruples and wolfed down everything that was before him, washing it all down with a jug of ice-cold spring water.

"Delicious," he pronounced, wiping his mouth on his handkerchief. Mary was folding up the napkin like one of those Japanese paper things. She had barely spoken all through dinner. "You seem unsettled."

"I am, a bit. Why did you shave off your beard?"

His hand went to his naked chin. Well, not naked. Already there were bristles invading the virgin planes. That was the devil of it—he'd be obliged to shave twice a day now if he meant to keep civilized company. "Well, you said you loathed them."

"So?"

"What do you mean *so*?"

"My opinion should not matter to you, my lord. You've faced the strictures of society this past year without batting an eye or altering your behavior in any way. Music hall dancers, actresses, all while your wife was not yet room temperature in her grave. Why care about what anybody thinks now?"

Blast, but this female was annoying. And here he thought to impress her for a day or two. "Perhaps I grew tired of it." Alec had been rather appalled when his man began to lop it all off this afternoon. His cheeks had not seen the light of day since he was in his twenties and he was worried he'd look like a harlequin. Fortunately the new growth was covering the pale lower half of his face so he didn't look entirely ridiculous. A few rounds of golf and a wade in the stream and he'd look all one color again.

"I suppose Dr. Bauer got tired of his beard today, too. Really, men," Mary mumbled, pulling at the ruffle around her throat.

"What about us? Not that I like you lumping me in with that bastard."

"You think with one grand gesture you can worm your way into our hearts."

"Grand gesture? I assure you it was just a shave. And no one said anything about hearts."

"Exactly!" Mary looked somewhat martial.

"I have no designs upon you," Alec lied.

"Then why are you always underfoot, when you know discovery will ruin our plans? What if I'd been unable to keep Bauer or Hildegard or whatever her name is out of the treatment room? What if they'd found you cowering under the table?"

"I was not cowering! And it all would have played into the scheme of making Bauer jealous."

"And what if Bauer finds out we're eating in my room? My bedroom!"

"I paid you enough to get a full suite like your auntie's. It's not my fault you economized."

"That's not the point!" Mary tossed her napkin to the floor, where it burst forth like a dowager that had been too tightly laced.

Alec was annoyed. "What *is* the point?"

"My virtue is the drawing card. If Bauer thinks it's been compromised, he'll look for someone else to debauch."

Yes, this was familiar territory. Alec felt slightly ashamed, but only slightly. "I haven't touched you."

She lifted a bronze eyebrow. "Oh, haven't you?"

"Not really." Her skin had been like velvet as she arched and wriggled beneath him. Well, beneath his hands anyway. "It was a simple misunderstanding," he said, shifting in his chair. "A massage is not really *touching.*"

She snorted. He supposed he was coming on a bit Jesuitical. "I thought we settled this earlier. I've apologized. I meant well."

"The road to hell is paved with good intentions."

" 'Hell is full of good meanings, but heaven is full of good works,' " he quoted back to her. "If we manage to dislodge Bauer from his perch of wickedness, we can rest on our laurels for the indefinite future."

"I don't rest on my laurels. There is always something new that requires my attention."

Alec smiled. "At the grocery shop? Aye, you must have to deal with the weight of the world there, or at least the weight of a leg of lamb."

Her face darkened. "And now you mock my employment and my background. One cannot always be born with a silver spoon in one's mouth, Lord Raeburn."

No more Alec. Och, he was making a mess of the evening. Mary Arden was a redhead, after all, and bound to have a temper. Wasn't his own mother a volcano when his father hadn't turned her up sweet? His younger brothers had inherited her hair and her attitude, no matter how hard they tried to tame themselves. 'Twas a good thing Evan had his successful distillery to tend, else the family would be hiding the breakables. What havoc Nicholas was wreaking on the Continent was unimaginable.

"I fear I've put my foot in my mouth, possibly both of them, Miss Arden. I meant no disrespect toward you."

"You can't help yourself, can you? You are so used to getting your own way, you don't know what to do if you don't."

She didn't know what the hell she was talking about. "My own way! I'll have you know I had four miserable years of not getting my own way! Don't you dare tell me I don't understand what life is all about." It wasn't manly to complain, but Edith had given him plenty of reason.

"But you never sacrificed any of your pleasures, did you? Carousing all over the kingdom. That's why people could believe the worst about you."

"I don't give a good goddamn what people believe, Miss Arden. I canna live my life based on what someone else thinks is right. *I* know what's right. And I'll not live like a monk just because—" He stopped himself from going further. He'd been a fool to confide in Mrs. Evensong. Had the woman told her niece about his failed marriage and his shame? Damn it. Double damn it.

"It seems we are at an impasse, Lord Raeburn. Good night."

"You're kicking me out just because we're having a little disagreement?"

She snorted. "I wouldn't call it little. Nothing about you is little."

And he'd like to prove that to her. She was right—he was not a gentleman. It hadn't helped when he'd tried to be. No matter how carefully he'd treated Edith, she'd shied away.

And the worst—she hadn't trusted him to help her in the end.

He stood up, crashing into the cart. The coffeepot toppled, splashing his trousers with scalding liquid, and he sat right back down.

Holy mother of God. His thighs were on fire.

"Oh, dear," Mary Arden said. "Are you all right?"

No, he bloody well was not. "Clumsy," he ground out, then bit his tongue to keep from howling.

"I believe you should remove your pants."

He stared at her, not believing his ears.

"For relief. You can bathe your skin with cool water. I expect you are in pain."

What gave her that impression? He was not screaming, still just biting his tongue to keep himself from doing so. Alec tasted blood.

"Come, Lord Raeburn, don't stand on ceremony. I'm sure many women have seen you without your pants on. What's one more?"

Alec lurched off the chair and stumbled into the bathroom, slamming the door behind him. He tore at his falls and his pants dropped ignominiously to his ankles. His upper thighs were stained a livid pink—if the spill had occurred a few inches further up, he'd truly be howling, as he wasn't wearing smallclothes. He ran the tap and soaked a linen hand towel in the cold water, then pressed it to his legs. Agony.

There was a knock at the door. "May I come in?"

"No, you canna. Leave a man his dignity."

"I have a salve which might be beneficial."

Of course she did. She probably wanted to apply it herself just to pay him back for this afternoon.

Alec stared at his unfamiliar reflection in the mirror over the pedestal sink. He was as white as the porcelain. Fine. Let her do her Florence Nightingale impersonation. He'd prostrate himself upon her solitary bed and let her have at it. It might prove amusing to one of them. "I'm coming out."

He clutched up his pants without refastening them and walked gingerly back into her bedroom. She looked up at him with sympathetic concern, a tin of something in her small hand. "Why don't you lie down on my bed, Lord Raeburn?"

"I thought you'd never ask," he sniped.

"We'll have none of your sauciness, sir. If I'm any judge, you're not up to your usual strength. I feel quite safe."

"You shouldn't." Alec eased onto the plain white counterpane.

"Lift your bottom so I may lower your trousers."

She sounded just like his old nanny, all businesslike. Alec made sure his starched shirt still covered his privates and closed his eyes.

She gave a little gasp. "Oh, my. I wonder if we should call a doctor."

"What an excellent idea. Let's get Bauer in to consult."

"Don't be silly. But the burns look serious. Are you in very much pain?"

Enough so that his cock was barely stirring even though Mary Arden's sweet little hand was only inches away. "I'm fine. Rub the damn muck in and I'll be on my way."

Her touch was tentative. Alec grit his teeth as she gently dabbed the ointment on his skin. He felt cooler immediately, the sting abating.

"You can take the salve with you and have your man reapply it in the morning, or as needed. I have another tin in my trunk."

"You came prepared for anything, didn't you?"

She smiled down on him. "I do try. My aunt has trained me well. We're in the wilds of Scotland, you know."

"I'm sorry if I was dismissive of your experiences earlier. I imagine you get to know a lot working with the public every day in that store of yours."

"You would be very surprised." There was a gleam in her hazel-green eyes he didn't understand.

Alec struggled up to a sitting position, pulling his pants up over his raw skin. "I'd like to show you the wilds of Scotland, Mary, or at least my part of them. When this is over, why don't you and Oliver and Mrs. Evensong come to Raeburn Court before you go back to dirty old London? I can consult with your aunt about my staffing needs. If I'm going to live here year-round, I'll need more servants. I lost more than a few when Edith died. The rumors scared them off—we all know what a black-hearted villain I can be."

"I don't think you're a black-hearted villain. You're just—" She stared off into a corner. "—a little careless, I think."

So careless he hadn't a clue what his wife was going through.

"Talk to your aunt about coming. That's where you'll be heading now, yes?"

"I suppose. Once I get rid of you and the remains of our supper."

"I'm going, I'm going." He fumbled with his buttons, sorry to be leaving her. He would drink his own whiskey in his own suite instead of Mrs. Evensong's—a lot of it to dull the memories of this humiliating day.

Maybe there was something he could salvage of it. He got off the bed. "Thank you, Mary. For everything." He bent to kiss her cheek, just a chaste kiss, one friend to another. But he'd startled her and she turned, her lush lips open in surprise. Lips that somehow found his.

She didn't pull away, scream, or slap his face. Alec tasted strawberries, hazelnuts, and curiosity. It was clear to him she hadn't been kissed much—imagine, he'd thought her an experienced "actress" only yesterday when he'd said all those naughty things to her and ogled her bosoms. He could teach her, show her how it was done—she was an innocent, just as she was supposed to be for the role she played. Too innocent for him, but he wasn't about to let this kiss go to waste.

Alec was too tall for her, however—he was too tall for most women unless they were under or on top of him, and this standing kiss was not as comfortable as it could be. He gathered her to him, aware of the stiff corset that curved her so alluringly beneath her satin gown. Angling his leg around her—pain be damned—he slid them down to the mattress, where they were now sitting, much more equal. He opened his eyes to see her staring right at him. Disconcerting, it was, as if she were studying a bug under a microscope. She didn't look horrified, so he must be a nice bug, even if he was going cross-eyed. He shut his eyes and felt her hand on his jaw. The simple touch sent a violent tremor throughout his body. Gad, he'd never realized a bare jaw was a pleasure point—she may as well be touching his cock for the sheer joy he felt. But he had to make this kiss right for her. Make it special. Make her feel what he was feeling.

He'd kissed dozens—or scores—of women hundreds—or thousands—of times. He'd never kept track, though it was no doubt too many. He'd been at this man business for twenty years. But nothing had prepared him for this particular parting of lips, exchange of tongues, sharing of breaths. Alec slid his fingers into her hair and held her still, savoring the softness of her mouth and the shy dexterity of her tongue.

Perhaps she was teaching him something instead—her artlessness would bring him to his knees if he were standing. If he unleashed his beast, he would tip her backward and cover her body with his, claw through her satin and whalebone, steal much more than a kiss. It would be wrong, but feel unerringly right.

No, not tonight. Perhaps not ever. Mary Arden was not a wanton woman, and deserved more than the likes of him. She needed a man with a future, a man who'd made fewer mistakes than he had in his thirty-five years.

He'd never promise another woman to love, honor, and cherish her again.

Chapter

11

$\mathcal{M}$ary could feel his loneliness, though he was so close, the heat of his kiss inflaming her cheeks and dampening her in places she didn't want to think about. He kissed her as if he was afraid she would shatter, his fingertips barely touching her scalp. She supposed he was used to people being afraid of him because of his size, but she wasn't made of spun sugar, and he didn't need to be so careful. She cupped his jaw tighter, its strong edge digging into her palm.

He had a lovely chin, with just a hint of a dimple. No wonder he'd wanted to cover it—it made him look vulnerable. Between his lashes and the dimple, he was doomed to make women fall in love with him.

But not his child bride, and there was the crux of the problem.

Mary had never been kissed like this, but instinctively she knew there was more. Something deeper. Something darker. Something that would sweep her away and make her forget to say no. To say stop.

She was close to pulling away now, but she might never get a chance like this again. He was a baron. Barons didn't go around kissing women like her. He hadn't even meant to until she'd turned into his innocent kiss, the uncle-like peck on the cheek he had intended. She was not his niece, and she'd seen his bare thighs, so why not go one step further?

She hadn't seen male thighs except for her little nephews', and they hadn't been dusted with dark hair or looked like tree trunks. She'd smelled the starch of his shirt and the cologne he wore, and yes, a hint of lemon when she'd smoothed the salve on his blistered skin. Things were already so very improper between them that one little kiss could not make it worse.

Proper. Proper. Proper. Mary heard her late mother, Miss Ambrose, her sister-in-law, Phyllis, her Aunt Mim. Her whole life had been bound by warnings and duty.

Damn the warnings and the duty. Damn propriety.

She gave a little sigh and leaned forward, earning an anguished groan from Alec Raeburn. He seemed to like what she was doing with her mouth, so she did more of it. Mary was uncertain of her womanly skills, but Alec probably had enough manly skills for both of them. She let him lead, sweeping his tongue softly across hers, returning each parry and thrust with expectance. Mary was rewarded by his arm encircling her, bringing her so close to his broad chest one could not have fitted a calling card between them. Her breasts felt odd and tingly, and she couldn't get quite enough air in her lungs to prevent her from feeling light-headed.

This was not simply the result of tight-lacing. This was epic! Worlds and tongues and teeth were colliding. Now Mary understood what all those silly romance books Harriet loaned her meant when they used their ellipses. Mary dot-dot-dotted, her hands on Alec's shoulders, her eyes fluttering shut. She didn't need to watch him anymore, only feel his mastery over her as he overcame his scruples and kissed her like she was the only woman in the world. The idea was ridiculous—Mary was sure he'd had better, more confident kisses—but who was she to argue? She could not think straight, or even crooked.

Hot. Hard. Wet, which implied something less than

wonderful, but she did not have another word for it. Smooth. Rough. No more words. Her vocabulary was entirely insufficient. She fell back onto her bed and he was beside her, one big hand cupping her satin-covered breast, the other buried in her hair. She'd have to redo her coiffeur before she saw Aunt Mim—

Oh, she didn't want to see anyone or go anywhere. Ever. This was so . . .

Her lips quirked. So . . . unprofessional. Misguided. Marvelous.

But perhaps Alec heard the first two words and not the last, for he rolled away and uttered a word she had never dared to use or even think of.

He was flat on his back, staring at the ceiling, looking both fierce and flummoxed. Mary noted he clutched a pillow over his privates. She sat up and straightened her bodice. She would have loved to unhook the itchy lace insert, but Alec looked miserable enough as it was. She should not tempt him—or herself—further.

"There's no need to apologize, my lord," she said briskly. "That was very pleasant. My fault entirely. I tricked you into it, you see." More like she'd tricked herself—when he'd angled down she did the first thing that came to her and opened her mouth. It had seemed so natural. So right, although of course it was anything but.

His mouth opened, but no sound came out.

"When you meant to kiss me on my cheek. I turned my face. You couldn't help it. Please excuse my feeble attempt at seduction. Well, not seduction, precisely. I only wanted a proper"—*or improper*—"kiss, not all the rest of it." She waved vaguely at the pillow that was still being clutched as if it were a life preserver and Alec were about to drown. "You must know that with my background, my experiences have been somewhat limited. And after today and all the odd occurrences, I thought, what's the harm? It is only a kiss." To be fair, there really had not been much thinking involved.

"Only a kiss," he muttered, looking fiercer and less flummoxed.

"I am almost thirty. Call this day my swan song. After all, it is unlikely any of the events will be repeated. I was naked in a room with you—"

"It was dark and I couldn't see," Alec interrupted.

"—when you touched me most intimately, and then I had you remove your pants so I could touch *you*. Tell me, which is worse? The kiss or the touching?"

He made a growling noise. "It's all horrible. It must never happen again, Miss Arden."

Mary stiffened. Was she really that awkward and unappealing? "Of course not, Lord Raeburn. My curiosity has been satisfied."

"Curiosity killed the cat."

"You would never harm me, Lord Raeburn. I'm considered a good judge of character, and I would stake my life on that," Mary said with total seriousness. The man had suffered from society's suspicion enough. If more people had kissed him, they would soon be disabused of the fact that he was a murderer. He was the gentlest of giants. He had been most respectful during their interlude. Damn it.

Of course he couldn't go around kissing everybody, although he'd made a valiant stab at kissing females, according to his reputation. Good Lord, but her thought processes were somewhat mangled. She felt like an electric circuit that had tripped a wire.

He didn't move from the bed. "You're not going to tell your aunt, are you?"

"About our silly kiss? Do you think I am a tattletale? You are not the only one afraid of Aunt Mim." Oliver might appreciate the story, but Mary didn't want to give him any inspiration. The boy might get into trouble up here if he decided to kiss whom he pleased.

Mary could not be sorry that she'd pleased. No, it had been a worthwhile experiment. She brushed her lips with a finger to see if they were still there.

"I should get up." Alec made no effort to move.

"Yes. Yes, you should."

"I don't think I can quite yet." His knuckles on the pillow were quite white.

"I must look a fright." Mary managed to walk across the room and sit down at the dressing table, giving him a chance to shift whatever needed to be shifted. The pad she used to make her pompadour rise to outstanding heights was sticking out of her head like a small loaf of bread. Her lips were swollen as if she'd been stung by a hive of bees. There was no disguising what she'd been up to.

Or down to. She had lain down with a man on a bed, even if her corset was still laced as tightly as ever. It was all rather shocking and thrilling.

She was being as silly as a schoolgirl. "Drat." Mary pulled the pins from her hair and tossed the pad on the table. She had as much hair as the next woman, but sometimes it was hard to rat it up high enough without a maid to help her. Hamblen had enough to do tending to Aunt Mim and was not always available. Mary picked up her brush, preparing to untangle the red mess.

She heard a moan behind her. "Are you in pain, Lord Raeburn?"

"Aye, lass, that I am. I'd be better off blind."

"I know I'm not in looks, sir," she said crossly. "That's your doing."

"You will be the death of me yet. God give me strength," he muttered.

"God should give you strength to get off my bed! You must leave before the guests return from the dining room. You should not be caught on this floor."

Her brush snagged on a knot and she stopped herself from uttering the very same naughty word Lord Raeburn had recently used. He was a very bad influence. Until she had met him, she had never dreamed of removing trousers or lying down on a bed or kissing anyone, and if she had, that was all it was—a dream. Mary spent most of her life fully awake, practical and full of purpose. "What if the elevator operator recognized you and tells Bauer we came up together?"

"That horse has left the barn, my dear. And I could be visiting anyone. I'm so popular, you know."

Did he feel sorry for himself? At least he had his brothers.

"You must be more discreet tomorrow. Actually, it would be best if you didn't see me at all until Oliver rescues me tomorrow night. Nothing must upset the applecart."

"The applecart is already upset, Eve."

Now what did he mean by that? Her hair crackled under the hairbrush as she methodically counted her strokes. She could pretend he wasn't there, taking up so much space on her bed, in her room, in her h—

Mary Arden Evensong, she said to herself, *do not be so foolish. It was* just *a kiss.* Just because her life had been bereft of kisses so far, it meant nothing in the wider scheme of things. Lord Raeburn was a rake and a reprobate, and she was a ridiculous old maid who was too nosy for her own good.

Well, she'd satisfied one question—kisses were much nicer in practice than theory. Mary had always wondered how two people could enjoy smashing noses and swapping spit, but now it wasn't so incomprehensible. Actual lovemaking was probably equally enjoyable, if one could get over the embarrassment and body odor. Lord Raeburn smelled quite wonderful, actually.

She whacked her head with the hairbrush in an attempt to beat some sense into it.

She heard the bed creak. "Are you still here?" she asked with annoyance.

He was sitting up now, his dark hair disordered. "You have beautiful hair. Like a sunset."

Mary rolled her eyes. "It is just hair."

"My mother had hair like yours, all fire."

"I remind you of your mother?" Mary felt unexpectedly peevish.

"Aye. I mean, nae. You are nothing like her at all. She

was tall, a regular Valkyrie. Bruising rider. My brother Evan takes after her. You will meet him when you come to Rae-burn Court."

Mary turned to face him. "I really don't think that's such a good idea, my lord. I'm sure your housekeeper and your butler have an idea of the staffing needs of your home. They can convey that by letter to the Evensong Agency and we—I mean, Aunt Mim will do her best to get suitable employees."

"Ha, that's where you are wrong. They're both gone."

"They deserted you?"

His hand raked through his hair, disordering it even more. "In a manner of speaking. Old Elphinstone dropped dead last month, right in the front hallway where he'd sat for fifty years. Mrs. Spotwood retired shortly thereafter, saying the house was unlucky. I think it was just too big to keep after, being so short-staffed, and she had to do the cooking, too. The local girls would rather go down to be typists in Edinburgh now than swing mops and make oatcakes. So aside from the temporary workmen, we are in a bit of a jam. I drive over every day to keep an eye on the renovations, but I've always spent more time in my London house than here in the Highlands. My mistake. Evan doesn't have time to get it all sorted out, and since I intend to hibernate up here from now on, it falls to me. As it should."

The hairbrush almost slipped from her fingers. "Y-you are giving up your London life?"

"Aye. It's about time, don't you think? I've sown my wild oats. And it's damned unpleasant to walk into my clubs and have that silence fall. I'll be better off here with my brothers. One canna run away from one's past or one's heritage forever."

But he *would* be running away, hiding up here and licking his wounds. "I see. I'll talk to Aunt Mim. The visit may be too much for her, though."

"She seemed in excellent health when I met her on Mount Street. What happened?"

Lord, but this double life was hard to maintain. "Oh! Just

a little indisposition. It does not affect her business sense one iota. I would not want you or anyone else to think that the agency suffers from lack of leadership."

"No, its reputation is why I came to you in the first place. I have a friend—one of the few left—who's looking for a wife. He tells me your aunt does some matchmaking, too."

"On occasion. The fee for that sort of service is rather exorbitant, though."

"Don't worry. I'll not be availing myself of it. One disastrous marriage was enough."

Despite his assurance that he wouldn't marry again, Mary couldn't help but imagine which of her clients was suitable to be the next Baroness Raeburn. Then she shook the thought right out of her head. It was of no concern to her. Unfortunately, something else popped right in.

Chapter

12

Could this infernal day get any worse? Endless cold showers. Icy streams. Snowbanks. Blizzards. The North Sea in January. Alec thought of all the frigid places he knew, and some he didn't—like the North Pole—but nothing seemed to subdue his inconvenient erection.

He had touched her smooth freckled shoulders. Kissed her soft pink lips. Palmed a perfect breast. Now she was luring him with a curtain of copper and bronze that fell to her plush bottom.

He was only a man, prone to temptation as everyone and their mothers knew. He'd never been a saint, except for the brief period when he thought to cajole skittish Edith into his bed.

It was unfair—little Mary Arden had made sure he kissed her. Tasted her. And now he was supposed to slink away as if nothing happened.

All this nonsense about her having a "swan song!" He could show her all the swans and songs she could ever hope for, but they were talking about her aunt's agency now, of which she seemed to know a great deal for a grocery shop girl on holiday. Maybe her old aunt was grooming her to take over the business. He snorted. As if anyone could place their future in the hands of this pocket Venus. Alec didn't care how old she was—she looked like an innocent girl.

Not so innocent, the minx. She had stolen a kiss from *him*!

He rubbed his mouth, happy to find it still in place. His beard seemed to be sprouting right back, too. He'd let it grow again. What was he thinking to shave it off anyhow? He felt naked without it.

Ha. Naked. Ice floes. Eskimo. Robert Peary all rigged out in sealskin. Sled dogs. Snowmen. Snowballs.

Oh, *balls*.

It was useless. He'd have to crabwalk out of the room and hope he could find his way upstairs without attracting any attention. Perhaps Alec could take the fringed pillow with him.

"You don't intend to marry again?"

"Who would have me? Some poor girl would be avoiding all the windows at Raeburn Court when I'd be home, and let me tell you, there are a lot of windows. Mrs. Spotwood used to complain about cleaning all of them."

"Well, of course you wouldn't marry someone who thought the worst of you."

"My dear Miss Arden, the only people who believe I'm not guilty of my wife's death besides a handful of friends are my brothers—and I'm not even sure about Nick. He's not come home since it happened."

Mary smacked the hairbrush against her hand. "It's so unfair."

Yes, wasn't he just thinking that? "I should go. Your aunt is expecting you." He met her eyes in the mirror, and her lashes dropped. Did she feel guilty for what she'd done to him? Good.

And then she turned around to face him again, her hazel eyes dark as a forest. "Could I prevail upon you to help me out of this dress before you go? It's most uncomfortable."

Alec said a word he shouldn't. Again. "You want me to undress you?"

"Just the buttons in the back."

"*Just* the buttons. *Just* a kiss. Miss Arden, I don't believe you know what the meaning of *just* is. If I undo your buttons, I'll see your laces. If I see your laces, I will be tempted to tear them. With my teeth if necessary, if my hands are trembling too hard. And then we'll be down to sheer shift and skin. You cannot expect me to act like a gentleman, because I am not one at the moment. You should know this by now."

"Oh."

Her blush owed nothing to paint. Damn, why was he even trying to talk sense to her? Wasn't she offering what he'd wanted ever since he saw her in the lobby of the Forsyth Palace Hotel?

She was not exactly beautiful, he reminded himself. She was better than beautiful, though. Intelligent. Spirited. Her loose hair was a molten river, her body luscious.

But something about Mary made him *want* to be a gentleman, damn it.

"Stand up," he growled.

The buttons were shiny and minuscule. Perhaps he was getting old enough for reading glasses. His clumsy fingers slipped and slid and he uttered that oath again. Mary stood as still as a statue, her hair slung over her right shoulder. Alec was getting a crick in his neck again—they really were the most mismatched couple.

Hell, they weren't a couple—they'd only kissed once.

But what a kiss.

He stepped back. "There. I trust you can take it from here."

"Y-yes."

She seemed a little dazed, maybe from the warm breaths he blew on the back of her neck or the way his hands brushed her bare skin when it was revealed between the folds of fabric. He was a cur, and had only increased the discomfort in his aching nether regions.

Alec smoothed his hair down and returned his tie to strangulation mode so he could get upstairs without attracting attention. Putting his ear to the door, he heard a steady stream of footsteps in the corridor. Laughter. Doors opening and closing.

"I may have to stay here for a few more minutes. Dinner must be over."

She bit a lip and nodded. Was it so awful to be in his presence?

"Or I could go out Oliver's door. People might think I was visiting him," he said, gruffly.

Mary shook her head. "He hasn't come back yet. You might be taken for a thief. Someone might have seen him still downstairs and put two and two together."

Alec would like to put at least two together, but it was unlikely to happen as Mary Arden clutched the bodice of her satin dress. The lace bib had unfurled and her neck looked very kissable. He could see faint pink lines around her throat where the high-banded collar had pinched. Damn fool women and their fashions.

"Lord Raeburn—"

"Miss Arden—"

They had both spoken at the same time. Alec wasn't even sure what he'd been planning to say, but the silence in the room had been a little onerous. "You first."

"Um." She didn't meet his eyes. "If we come to Raeburn Court, I have a favor to ask of you."

Alec had paid her aunt a fortune, and hoped Mary would get a generous cut of it for her performance. But he had a soft spot for her, and was willing to give her something of her own. Within reason, of course. He wasn't made of money, though he had more than he'd ever need in his lifetime now that he wasn't going to dress a wife in the latest styles from Paris and furnish a nursery.

He tried to smile at her. "If you manage to ruin Bauer's reputation, you can have anything you want."

"You don't know what I want. At least I *think* I want it," she mumbled. She was shifting nervously from one silk-shod foot to the other as if she had to relieve herself. Damn it. He should *go*.

He sat back down on the bed. "Out with it, my girl. You intrigue me."

"Oh, I do hope I do. As you know, Lord Raeburn, I've led a rather quiet life. I'd like . . . something more."

"A trip to Paris, perhaps? I warn you, Frenchmen smell of garlic," he teased.

"No, not Paris. We were talking of Raeburn Court."

"So we were. My house and what servants are left will be at your disposal."

She looked straight at him, her hazel eyes wide and innocent. "I don't need your servants. I only need you."

"And what can I do for you?" Alec smiled for real now, frankly curious.

The hallway activity continued to rumble as Mary struggled for words. Odd. She usually had plenty to say to him, and not all of it kind.

She took a very deep breath. "I would like to experience one night of passion."

His vision was going, and now his hearing seemed deficient. "I beg your pardon?"

She looked up at the ceiling. "Oh, don't make me say it again."

He felt very stupid. "Say what?"

"Damn you. Never mind."

He sprang up from the bed. "No, no! Wait! I didn't quite hear you—I mean, you've been beating me off with a stick except for that aberrant kiss. Not that it wasn't lovely. In fact, it was about the loveliest thing—" Good grief. He was babbling. "You aren't saying what I think you're saying, are you?"

She folded her arms around her glorious décolletage, still holding up the dress. "I might be."

He sat down again before he fell. "Me? You want me to relieve you of—"

"My virginity. Yes, I believe so. I might change my mind tomorrow. But really, it's not as though I'm going to have many more opportunities in my line of work to meet an eligible man. Men like you don't come along every day."

That was true. Alec had never been in a grocery store in his life, although now that Mrs. Spotwood had left he might have to go shopping. "Have you considered my reputation?"

"That's precisely why this is a good idea. You have years of extensive interaction with females. I presume you know what to do."

"I should hope so," Alec said faintly. He thought of all the pliant courtesans, actresses, wives and widows he'd bedded. Well, not *all* of them—his memory was going the way of his eyesight and hearing. He'd never fielded any complaints, although some of his ladies were too well paid not to do anything but praise him.

Alec got a knot in his stomach. What if he was not the competent Casanova Mary thought him to be?

Her blushes had ceased and she was looking quite rational, even businesslike, somehow braiding her hair without benefit of the mirror and still keeping her dress up. "As I said, I'm almost thirty. I don't expect to ever marry and I don't particularly want to die a virgin. Not that I want any sort of complicated affair—I don't have time for that. I have enough secrets—I mean, it would be difficult to keep a secret, and if my aunt found out, she wouldn't much like it. But a night—or two—in the Highlands might suit me very well. Then I could go back to London with knowledge that might help me with my work."

What sort of grocery store was her family running that required carnal knowledge from its cashiers? "I thought you said the stores were in Oxfordshire."

"We might be branching out," she said vaguely. "Anyway, it's time *I* branched out. I haven't had any fun in years."

Fun? *Fun?* No decent woman of his acquaintance thought sexual congress was fun, more's the pity. That's why he spent so much time with indecent ones.

"You might be disappointed," Alec said, feeling considerable pressure.

Mary Arden eyed him with a speculative gleam in her hazel eyes. "I doubt it. You are a very fine figure of a man. I enjoyed the kiss. What could go wrong?"

"Your aunt—that Oliver fellow—"

"Oh, we'll be discreet. Raeburn Court is huge, is it not?"

"Aye."

"We'll just find a quiet place away from them. It's to our benefit your house is not well-staffed at the moment. No servants' gossip. Not that anyone will ever know who I really am."

She was a candidate for Bedlam, that's who.

"I think you should sleep on this idea, Miss Arden. If you still feel this way in the morning, we will discuss the subject again."

She looked stricken. "Oh! You don't want me. I understand. I've been much too forward. You probably flirt with and kiss everyone."

"I do not!" Alec lied. "And I do. Want you, that is. You are very . . . different. In a good way," he said quickly, watching her face fall. "In a very good way. You must forgive me. It's I that usually do the propositioning. I have not had an offer like yours since I left school. A randy young woman, but you don't need to know the details." Lord, would this night never end?

"Was she a virgin, too?"

"Gad, no. Grace slept with ev—that is, I should be frank with you, Miss Arden. To the best of my knowledge, I have never deflowered a virgin, not even when I was one myself." He remembered Dory, the saucy housemaid who decided to work her way through all three Raeburn boys when they came to stay at the London townhouse. He took a deep breath. "Your aunt must have told you—not even my wife. We never consummated our marriage. She was afraid of me."

"I'm not afraid of you."

"You should be! What if you fall pregnant after this one night of abandon?" Lord, why was he borrowing trouble? He should leap at this chance to do exactly what he'd wanted to do to—with—Miss Arden from the second he saw her.

"I expect you know how to prevent that."

"Nothing is foolproof." To the best of his knowledge, he

hadn't littered the countryside with his by-blows, which was a bit of a miracle, really.

Maybe he was sterile. Now there was a daunting thought. But Evan was his heir, and Nick after him in case Evan fell in a vat of Raeburn's Special Reserve.

The corridor was quiet. Alec staggered to his feet. "I'm going now. As I said, Miss Arden, we needn't make a decision tonight. I may not be the man for you. What about Oliver? He's a handsome boy."

Mary bit her lip again. "I'm afraid not."

The lass had probably approached the lad already, being as they had only a thin connecting door separating them. Ah, well. Alec was still flattered, more or less.

And somewhat terrified.

Chapter

13

$\mathcal{M}$ary couldn't blame anything on alcoholic spirits, because she'd had nothing but tea and good Scottish water. What had come over her?

Alec Raeburn. Technically he'd been beside her, but it wouldn't have taken much to get him to roll on top of her tonight. And she had wanted him to.

Where was her vaunted good sense? Not in the Highlands, that's for sure.

But really, was it so wrong for her to want the forbidden at her advanced age? Ever since the man had rubbed her bare shoulders—and her feet!—this afternoon, she had the oddest sensations bubbling in her blood and mind. It was as if Alec Raeburn had opened a tap and liquid insanity was pouring out by the bucketloads.

Mary had resolutely ignored her physical self all her life, apart from keeping her body reasonably clean and covered properly. For the past four years, her body had been covered *too* properly—all that black bombazine and hideous hats and gloves and glasses. That awful, awful wig.

No one had ever told her that her hair was pretty before. No one had ever kissed her as Alec Raeburn had.

If he agreed to her proposal, he would kiss her again.

And do much more.

Mary shivered. The poor man looked terribly anxious to leave her bedroom. She had shocked him. Well, join the club, Lord Raeburn, for she had shocked herself and it felt *wonderful*.

Before she'd left school, she'd heard stories in the dormitory. Harriet's books had been somewhat helpful. Acting as her aunt, she'd been privy to a lot of conversations that were completely inappropriate for an unmarried young woman to hear. Her knowledge was spotty at best. It was time she remedied that.

"I don't need a day to reconsider. Once I make my mind up about something, I carry on to the finish." Aunt Mim called her as stubborn as she herself was. "I trust you don't have any diseases?"

Lord Raeburn's pale face suffused with color. "What?"

"I may be a virgin, but I'm not entirely innocent. Do you know it is rumored that Isabella Beeton's husband infected her with syphilis? That's hardly household management in my book. Any number of historic personages have died from gentlemen's diseases. I should hate to break out in rashes or lose my hair or go mad."

The baron's lips twitched. "You are mad already, Miss Arden."

She tied the end of her braid with a ribbon, her dress nearly dropping to the floor. She wasn't ready for Lord Raeburn to see her yet, although he'd probably gotten an eyeful already. Was she mad? She was very much afraid she was.

She was infected with something—lust. Mary could see why females were so carefully chaperoned around men like Alec Raeburn. A few days in his presence and she'd tossed away years of self-control.

Well, why not? Who would ever find out? If she didn't seize this opportunity, nothing like it would ever come along again and she would be doomed to thwarted curiosity for the rest of her days.

She smiled at Alec in what she hoped was a perfectly sane way.

"Perhaps you'd like me to get a health certificate from Dr. Bauer," he snapped.

"That won't be necessary. I'll take your word as a gentleman."

Alec's nostrils flared. "I'm not a gentleman, remember? But I'm not diseased, either. Really, this conversation is extraordinary."

"Don't you usually have this discussion with your paramours? I would think they'd want to know, and so would you. One can never be too careful."

"What kind of a virgin *are* you?" Alec spluttered.

"My inexperience does not preclude my intelligence, Lord Raeburn. Alec. It seems silly to call you by your title when we are about to fornicate."

"Miss Arden—*Mary*—you are making all this sound much too cold-blooded for my taste."

"I'm surprised. I was under the impression that most of your liaisons were business arrangements. I did not take you for a romantic."

"I'm not a damned romantic! But this—you—it isn't proper!" He was adorably rumpled, his hair standing on end as he practically ripped it out. Mary had never suspected she could have such an effect upon a man.

"Exactly. I am somewhat tired of being proper. And I'm sorry if you think I'm being too forward. I realize women are supposed to wait for a man's overtures. But I'd say you made enough overtures today, wouldn't you? I am simply returning them."

"In spades," he muttered. "All right. If everything goes as planned with Bauer, we should be able to leave the hotel on Sunday. The Lord's day, Miss Arden, so I think you'll want to wait until Monday to conduct this harebrained experiment. I myself will be in Raeburn Chapel on my knees all day Sunday asking for forgiveness. And strength."

Mary wondered if he'd be in his kilt, the stones digging into his knees. "Better to ask forgiveness than permission."

"I really should rescind my invitation. You know the house is not finished," Alec reminded her. "The work crew will be at it for at least another week."

"Then we will have to be creative finding a spot for our rendezvous."

"I prefer a good, old-fashioned bed, Miss Arden. I'm getting too long in the tooth for acrobatics."

Mary doubted that. Alec Raeburn was fit, well-muscled, radiating physicality. She imagined he would be up to pretty much anything.

But she didn't want an exotic encounter, just the basic shag. No hanging from chandeliers. Mary would have enough to do preserving each sensation for future reference without worrying about pulling a muscle in her back.

"Very well. Let's shake on our agreement," Mary said.

"Don't you want to put it in writing? You remind me very much of your aunt. She's a canny, cunning woman. I almost wish I hadn't consulted her." Alec sounded deuced gloomy.

That wouldn't do. Mary did not want to think of herself as a duty, someone to be tolerated until the unpleasant task was accomplished. She was not a complete antidote, after all.

"Should you have misgivings, my lord, you can change your mind at any time." She held out a hand.

He looked at it with contempt. "A handshake to seal this kind of bargain? I think not." He grabbed her fingers and tugged her forward until she was flush against his body. Or would have been, if the arm holding up her dress had not been in the way. He glared down, and Mary felt misgivings of her own.

She shut her eyes as his face loomed closer, each bristle on his dark cheek looking quite deadly. His mouth covered hers in ownership, his tongue thrusting deep. This was not the kiss from before. There was no playful tenderness or gentle exploration. This kiss was pure possession, confirming Mary's hope to be swept away. She was bobbing on a sea of wicked waves right now, barely able to stand upright. He held her tight, each fingertip scorching the bare flesh of her back.

The disparity in their heights was an issue, and she stumbled toward the bed as he steered her sideways. A small voice inside her said, *Not yet*, but she could not have spoken even if her lips were free. How far would he go? How far would she let him?

He pushed her arm away and peeled back her bodice, answering one question. And then he nibbled his way down, attending an earlobe, her throat, the blade of her collarbone, searing her with expertise. While he kissed her, one hand was unhooking the front of her corset, pushing her chemise away, capturing a breast. His mouth followed his nimble fingers, and Mary gasped as he took her nipple in his mouth and sucked. She felt a string inside her snap and her legs fell apart as if she were a broken marionette.

But Alec confined himself to her breasts, her neck, her mouth again, his hands and teeth and tongue working together to leave her wanting more. And she would get it three long nights from now.

One should always be careful what one wished for. Mary felt way over her head, her arms lying uselessly at her side while Alec plundered. She didn't know what a man wanted. What a man needed. She'd have to find out before Monday night.

What if Aunt Mim didn't want to visit Raeburn Court? Mary would have to convince her without arousing her aunt's alarm. The journey to Scotland had tired her, so perhaps Mary could promise a few extra days of rest before they returned to reality and London.

She herself would need a lifetime to recover from the kisses and caresses of Lord Alec Raeburn. This—whatever it was—was so much lovelier than she'd expected, yet not enough. Mary's nose was becoming unaccountably numb, and there was a rushing in her ears. Her scalp tingled. Could one faint from pleasure? The spacious room had shrunk to the bed and the bodies on it, and she was glad she was safe in Alec's arms.

Safe. Ha. Not the right word.

Alec shuddered and inched away, pulling up her dress as

he did so. She stifled her urge to pull it back down. Leaning up on one elbow, he gave a ragged breath and stared down at her, his eyes dark.

"Are you frightened yet, Miss Arden?"

Frightened was not the right word either. Whatever she felt was a word that was nonexistent in her vocabulary. She really had to expand it.

"I don't think so," she said carefully, happy to find her tongue still worked for ordinary speech.

"This is not right."

She would try to overcome her ignorance. Should she ask Oliver? How different could his encounters be? "I'm sure I'll learn quickly."

An odd look passed over his face. "I mean, it's not *right*. Not proper."

Mary nodded. "I know. That's why I want to do it."

"You are playing with fire and you don't even know it. What am I to do with you?" He fell onto his back again. This time there was no strategically placed pillow and Mary got quite an eyeful when she looked.

"Just what you've been doing, only more of it."

There was a rumble, then a roar of laughter. Mary tapped him on his chest. "Be quiet! My neighbors will hear you!"

"Maybe they'll think I'm young Oliver," Alec said, wiping his face. "Where is he anyway? He should be bursting in here to save you from *me*."

Mary bunched up her dress and stood on wobbly legs. "He enjoys meeting new people. He's probably blowing a cloud in the gentlemen's smoking tower. You should go. I'm sure the hallway is empty now."

"Give me a minute."

"Does it—your condition—hurt if you do not find relief?"

"Don't ever fall for that old chestnut. You are not to mention my current difficulty. A lady isna supposed to notice such things."

"Well, it's very noticeable. I couldn't help you with it, could I?"

Alec shot up off the bed. "That's quite enough for one

night, Miss Arden. I'm going to shoot myself if you utter one more word about my unfortunate problem, and then you'll have to find a new man to torment. I canna believe this."

His Scottish burr became more pronounced when he was agitated. Mary thought it charming. It would always be easy to gauge his emotions.

Not that she would see him after Tuesday, when she bid him farewell after one night of bliss. Or Wednesday, after two nights. There was no future for Lord Alec Raeburn and Miss Mary Arden Evensong.

Chapter

14

Saturday, June 11, 1904

*H*ell and the devil. Alec woke up with a pounding headache, and he had only himself to blame. Certainly Raeburn's Special Reserve played its small part, but no one had made him lift his glass so many times. And then, he'd tipped back the bottle to get the last drops—

He had given his work crew Saturday off, so there was no need for the hotel stable boys to saddle his horse for the daily ride to Raeburn Court to inspect the progress. He had nothing to do all day but stay in this blasted place and avoid running into that blasted woman.

He groaned. What had possessed him to make such a deal with her? And how was he going to wait until Monday?

"Good morning, my lord." His valet Mackenzie drew open the drapes and Alec threw his arm across his face at the hideous beam of sunshine. "Like that, is it? I'll fix up my specialty." Mac tsked as he bent to retrieve the empty bottle at the bedside.

"Lock up all the liquor. I never want to see one ounce of it again."

"I was under the impression you needed it for tonight, my lord. For the card party that young Mr. Arden arranged. In fact, I suggest you ask Mr. Evan for another case just in case."

"I drank only one bottle, Mac. There are at least a dozen left."

The valet sniffed. "You know how gentlemen are when they are deprived of their usual amusements—they'll be thirsty tonight. I do not understand how the Forsyth Palace Hotel can turn a profit without offering spirits to their guests. It is unnatural for an establishment in Scotland."

Usually the temperance movement seemed highly misguided to Alec, but this morning he wondered if all those old biddies had a point.

"Do what you think best, Mac. I won't be going to Raeburn Court today, so you can take the car over yourself if you want to." Besides his horse, he'd brought his Pegasus motor car to the hotel's new garage, although right now it sat in splendid shiny isolation. Most of the hotel's guests continued to arrive by train or carriage. The roads were vertiginous, but the Pegasus could climb like a dream.

His valet blanched. "The car! I shan't be doing any such thing."

"Don't be a sissy, Mac. It's only two miles, and I've shown you how to drive. The road's not bad."

The valet folded his arms across a spindly chest. "I shall rent one of the hotel's carriages."

"Suit yourself. You'll be dragged into the twentieth century someday."

"But not today, my lord. Shall I ring for a breakfast tray to be delivered?"

Alec shook his head, which nearly killed him. "No. Just your concoction. Don't worry about staying to help me bathe and dress. I'm sure I can manage on my own."

Mac looked doubtful but was too wise to say anything. He disappeared into the sitting room and came back with a cloudy drink.

It was as repellant as Alec remembered, but he dutifully swallowed it all. Mac had had numerous occasions to mix up the vile brew in recent months. For all that society thought Alec was a heartless murderer and philanderer, he'd taken Edith's death hard, and had drunk himself into too many stupors to count.

Perhaps that was why his brain had disintegrated and he'd agreed to service Mary Arden like some kind of stud animal. What was her excuse? Quite frankly, he couldn't understand why she was still unmarried. Were there no men in Oxfordshire? She was a lovely armful, attractive, intelligent, though a bit of a challenge. In an age when women were meant to be cosseted and protected, Alec thought Mary would not be happy relegated to the hearth stitching an improving sampler. She would want her say—hell, she probably wanted her vote as well.

Alec stuck a foot out from under the covers.

"May I help you up, my lord?"

As if his scrawny valet could support Alec's weight. "Don't be absurd. I told you I'd be all right. Stop hovering. Go on to Raeburn Court, and give Evan my best."

Evan did not live in the grand house that nearly rivaled the Forsyth Palace Hotel for rooms, but in the dower house on the property. Edith had not wanted either of Alec's brothers underfoot. She hadn't wanted him underfoot either, hence all the time he'd spent in London. He'd depended on Evan lately to help manage the estate for him, but it was time to resume his responsibilities. Evan had enough to do with the distillery.

What a damn fool Alec had been, marrying an innocent girl half his age and expecting to find happiness. Edith had been the deb of the Edinburgh season, sought after by every man who saw her pale blond perfection. That she'd settled on Alec—or her parents did—had seemed a dream come true. But soon everyone involved woke up.

Bah. This was no way to start the day. Alec climbed out of bed, his head throbbing at the altitude. The damned sun was shining, the river sparkling, the golf course green velvet.

Alec had no interest in communing with guests, however, since his presence dried up most conversation. He looked forward to playing cards with the Rycroft brothers tonight, though. At least they had stood by him even when their newspaper sales could have skyrocketed dishing his dirt.

Should he shave? Likely he would cut his own throat. He'd have Mac do it when he returned. But he could dress himself for a tramp on the manicured paths that gave the guests the false idea that they were experiencing "nature." The fresh air would do him good, clear his head.

As penance, he took the stairs down instead of the elevator, his head throbbing dully at every tread. Clusters of people were lounging in the lobby and taking breakfast in the glassed-in veranda. A jitney waited at the hotel steps for a party of fishermen. Alec liked to fish as well as the next fellow, but preferred to be solitary and out before sunrise. One could hear the quiet, watch the world unfold. There was something holy about the Highlands, not that he'd had much reason to believe in God lately.

There were several groomed trails through the forest, one that led right to his border and stopped at a gate he'd built with his own hands. Alec picked that one and whistled tunelessly as he clomped down the twisty path, his head shattering at every step. Somehow with this torture he'd teach himself not to indulge in the family's finest. He was getting too old, and his head and stomach were not as impervious as they once were.

Photography had taken off since the Kodak Brownie had made the equipment so portable, and he expected to come upon an amateur photographer filming the wonders of a Scottish leaf or a startled fox. As long as they didn't try to film him with his raging hangover and sell the picture to the yellow press, to each his own. One needed a hobby. Now that he'd ruled out drink and loose women for the foreseeable future, he wondered what to take up himself.

As a boy he'd roamed these woods with his brothers; as a young man he'd hunted when invited by Lord Northcott. Financial reverses had led the man to sell off the land to the consortium that built the Forsyth Palace Hotel, and now, naturally, hunting on the grounds was forbidden. It wouldn't do to have the inexperienced guests go home in coffins when they'd come for their health. Consequently the wildlife had prospered, and Alec fielded complaints from his tenant farmers. Maybe he'd organize a hunt in the fall, if he could get anyone to come.

He sat down on a convenient rustic bench made of a fallen log, shut his eyes to the beauty around him, and squeezed his forehead to change the pain from one kind to another. And that is how Mary Arden found him.

"Good morning, my lord."

Alec was too surprised to stand. She was lovely in the dappled shade, a vision in a white shirtwaist. Well, mostly white. The hem of her skirt was damp and stained. A smart straw boater trimmed with black velvet ribbon sat slightly askew on her head. Nevertheless, his heart hitched. "What are you doing here?"

There was no trace of embarrassment on her rosy face, as if last night had never happened and they hadn't done what they did or talked about what they would do. "Why, the same thing as you, I imagine. I rose early and went for a walk to the falls. Do you know them?"

"Aye." They were almost two miles ahead, not far from his own boundary. "You shouldn't have gone all that way alone."

"I don't know about the alone part, but I agree it was a long walk," Mary said ruefully. "I think I swallowed a bug, and my boots feel much too tight."

Alec knew it was the current custom to wear footwear one or two sizes too small to appear dainty, but he'd seen Mary's feet, and they were perfectly proportioned. "You're not one of those girls who's a slave to fashion, are you?"

"If you are asking if my boots fit me properly, they do. It's just I'm unused to walking any great distances, and these are brand new boots. It all seemed a grand idea near dawn, but in practice it was a bit taxing. Do you think you can scoot over on that log and let me sit down?"

Alec stood up instead, realizing he should have done so in the presence of a lady as soon as he opened his eyes. "It's not very comfortable. They must have cut corners on expenses and used deadfalls instead of buying real benches. There are probably all sorts of insects inside."

"It will do, ants and all. I sat on a boulder a ways back and this is a vast improvement." She gave a happy sigh as she arranged her wrinkled skirts. "They haven't cut many corners here though, have they? The hotel is absolutely magnificent."

Alec glanced backward. The open towers and turrets were just visible over the trees. One could see the hotel on its perch from miles around. "It should be. It cost over one hundred thousand pounds to build."

"Heavens! Where did Bauer get the money?"

"He has partners, but I believe you know how he financed his share. One might even say I own a part of it myself," he said ruefully.

"He blackmailed your wife?"

Alec shook his head. "Not until the very end. I sent him money to pay for her 'treatments,' of course. A lot of it. She was here almost every day for one thing or another." He was almost sure delicate Edith would not have walked on this path to get to the hotel, though if she had, a guest might have thought he'd encountered a fairy sprite. Her silver-blond hair, her pale eyes, her slender body had been, to the uninformed, entrancing.

"Oh, Alec."

He didn't like the sympathy in her voice. "Yes, I was doubly a fool. But I would have paid any amount to have Edith's health improve. She was nervous. Volatile."

Mary looked straight into his eyes. "She sounds awfully spoiled to me."

He knew that now. But originally he'd been stunned by her fey beauty and wanted her just like all the other men that met her under the careful chaperonage of her parents.

Her parents must have known she was difficult, but they

blamed Alec anyway for what happened. He blamed himself as well.

Alec had to look away from Mary's bright hazel eyes. There were times when he thought she saw altogether too much. "Spilt milk, Miss Arden. Suppose you let me unbutton those boots."

"What? Here in the woods! You haven't got a buttonhook on you, have you?"

"Don't need one. I've gotten all sorts of women in and out of clothing for twenty years." She already knew the worst about him—everyone did.

She blushed. "You shouldn't brag about something like that."

"Why not? Isn't that why you picked me for your adventure?" He waggled an eyebrow and she turned pinker.

"Shh! Someone might hear!"

Alec looked up and down the path. There was birdsong, but no sound of footsteps or chatter. "I think we are safe. For now. There are half a dozen other paths. But we mustn't be discovered together. I believe that was one of your rules."

"Then you must let me go."

"Not until I've seen to your injuries." He sat back down on the log.

"I'm not injured! I'll just go back up to my room and put some salve on my feet."

"Ah, your famous salve. You'll be happy to know it was quite effective." He'd slapped the stuff on before he drank himself silly last night, and again before his walk this morning.

"Good." She looked like she was struggling with a difficult problem, then sighed and thrust a small foot on his lap.

"These boots are made for city walking, my girl. You're in the Highlands now. We'll need to get you a proper pair of brogues."

"I won't be here long enough for new shoes," she reminded him.

"Pity," Alec said, unfastening the buttons and tossing the

boot to the ground. Her stockinged foot was damp but smelled, remarkably, of citrus. Blenheim Bouquet, if he wasn't mistaken. She always smelled good to him, but that was because she wore his own brand of cologne! A gentleman's cologne at that. Miss Arden was an unusual gentlewoman.

"I don't suppose you'd let me roll down your stocking."

Her arms crossed her ample bosom, a much nicer sight of stubbornness than his valet Mac's earlier display. "Absolutely not."

"Then I'll just have to go by touch. Where does it hurt? Here?"

Mary winced.

"Blisters, I'll wager. No dancing for you."

She shrugged. "I don't dance."

"What! Never?"

"Not since Miss Ambrose's Academy for Young Ladies. We had a dancing master, but I left before I learned very much. My brother wanted me at the store when our parents died."

He heard her regret. "I'll teach you to dance at Raeburn Court." He could hum a waltz if he put his mind to it. There was even a ballroom, unused for decades. He'd get someone to sweep the floor clean. He'd sweep it himself if he had to for the pleasure of having Mary Arden in his arms.

"I'm too old to dance."

Alec thumbed the sole of her foot, earning an involuntary flex from her. He'd never given women's feet much thought, but Mary did seem awfully fond of a foot rub. "One is never too old to dance."

"I don't want to waste our time there. I'm not apt to be invited to any balls anyway."

"You never know." Alec remembered his youth, spent in the company of the idle rich. He'd attended too many balls over the years in Edinburgh and London, carefully avoiding that third dance with suitable young ladies. Until Edith. Before that, he'd been interested in strictly unsuitable young ladies.

Meanwhile poor Mary was toiling in her family's grocery store, no flirting or fripperies for her. Alec wanted to give her a bit of fun now, something that went beyond sexual congress. He gave her toes a squeeze. "Other foot, Miss Arden."

"What if I can't get my boots back on?"

He grinned down at her. "Why, then I'd have to carry you back to the hotel. I'd be the knight to your damsel in distress."

Mary delivered her other foot into his cupped hands. "That would never do and well you know it! We cannot be seen together, remember?"

"Don't be such a grump," Alec said, removing the boot. "If you're not going to relax and devote yourself to enjoying this, I'll stop." He began to knead briskly, and Mary closed her eyes *and* her mouth.

Her response to his touch was very gratifying. She didn't make him feel freakish or clumsy, even though she was so much smaller than he. She didn't seem to be afraid of him or what he might do to her when they consummated their odd friendship, either. She had literally entrusted herself into his hands.

Mary Arden was a most unusual woman. She deserved to dance.

Her lashes were several shades darker than her hair, tipped with gold, and they flicked every time he circled the center of her foot. Her lips parted, but she raised no further objections as one hand smoothed up her calf to circle that, too. Alec stroked as far as her garter. Above it was soft bare flesh which he didn't dare to touch. Not yet.

He watched her turn liquid under his care, her body swaying until she nearly toppled backward off the makeshift bench. He pulled her onto his lap, unashamed of his erection and oblivious to the tender skin on his thighs.

He needed to kiss her again, but the brim of her hat was in the way. Though Alec tugged, the hatpin held fast. Mary was too dazed to help him, so he managed to duck under and plunder. He had no time for finesse—someone could come upon them at any moment.

So the kiss was quick, yet searing. Alec felt it to his own covered toes, and hoped he wouldn't fall off the bench himself.

Chapter

15

rat. It was happening again, and she couldn't possibly say no or try to stop him. Mary was making up for a kissless lifetime all in the space of two days.

She was pretty sure he was a master kisser, if her traitorous body had any opinion on the matter. She was alternately hot and cold and quivering like someone who was ill but in an absolutely delicious way. No doctors in white coats were required here in the hushed woods. No ether either to knock her out—she was almost unconscious already, lost in the bliss of his kiss. He had tucked her securely against his body, tipped her face upward, and was commanding her compliance. Mary closed her eyes, opened her mouth and gave in, licking and nibbling him right back.

She simply didn't have the proper vocabulary—licking and nibbling did not sound at all attractive, biting even less so, yet he'd nipped her lip in the gentlest way that caused a paroxysm of sensation. Mary wanted to tear her own confining clothes off well ahead of Monday, which was a corkbrained idea if there ever was one. Here she was, barefoot and bereft of her common sense, cavorting with a known seducer in the middle of nature. Exposed. Exhilarated. Insane.

One of them had to disengage, but Mary was very much afraid it wasn't going to be her. In fact, she was working on the buttons of his coat. She was more or less trapped in his bearlike hug, and had no objection. She was comfortable, except for the annoying twinges in her feet. But some tiny ray of awareness penetrated the fog of her lust, and she punched Alec's chest.

He drew back and looked down, his eyes clouded. "What was that for?"

"Someone's coming! Can't you hear? It's like a herd of elephants."

"Bloody hell."

Mary found herself abandoned on the tree trunk as Alec sprinted through the woods. Goodness, he was as nimble as a buck in flight, his unbuttoned hacking jacket flying back behind him. He disappeared around the curve in the path just as two children and their governess came in sight.

"G-good morning," Mary said, trying to smile.

The children, a very ruddy little boy and a pale older girl, smiled back. The nanny looked at Mary from her crooked hat to her dirty hem to her stockinged feet with undisguised horror. "I say, miss, are you all right?"

"No, I'm not. These da—uh, devilish boots. New, you know. I thought if I took them off I'd feel some relief, but now I'm not sure how I'll get them back on."

The young woman nodded. "I have just the thing. One never knows what one will need with these two." She gave her charges a dark look and Mary felt instant sympathy for them. Out of a capacious reticule, a buttonhook was produced and put to good use. Mary's feet were encased in agony, but at least she wouldn't return to her room in shredded stockings. She stood up unsteadily.

"Thank you so much. Enjoy your walk."

"Do you want us to accompany you back to the hotel? People might get the wrong idea if they see you," the governess said.

Mary faltered. "What do you mean?"

"Penny, Jon, go look for some interesting rocks. Skip

twenty paces, Jon, and Penny, you may take giant steps but no running." The woman lowered her voice as the children ambled down the path, Jon shrieking with abandon. "You look ravished, miss, and that's a fact. Has a man tried to interfere with you?"

"Why, no!" Suddenly Mary saw an avenue for getting tonight's ball rolling. She dropped her eyes. "It wasn't just any man, but Dr. Bauer. My doctor. He probably meant nothing by it, but he came upon me and . . . and . . . kissed me! Does it show?" She fingered her swollen lips, trying to look ashamed.

The nanny frowned. "Your doctor? The one who runs this place? That's not right."

"He left to go get some salve for my poor feet. Perhaps he was just overcome with the forces of nature. The woods, you know. Do you suppose there are banshees and brownies here? Supernatural creatures that make one misbehave quite against one's will? I've read some folktales."

"Nonsense. And don't speak like that in front of the children or I'll never get any sleep tonight. Time's up!" she shouted.

Penny and Jon returned with a few pebbles, one of which Jon tried to put in his mouth before his sister slapped it away.

"We'll walk back with you. Just in case. I am Eliza Lawrence, and this is Miss Penelope Hurst and her brother, Jonathan."

"How do you do?" Mary said, bending to shake each grubby hand. "Is your papa the famous barrister?"

Penny nodded. This was the daughter with asthma that Oliver spoke of, poor thing. She looked a bit pinched but was not wheezing. The pure mountain air was alleged to be good for those with her condition.

It must be a challenge for Miss Lawrence to find suitable activities for two children with such obviously different needs. Jon Hurst looked like he needed a keeper all his own. He was disheveled from head to toe, and exuded the energy of a wayward puppy. No wonder the nanny carried buttonhooks and who knew what else in that big bag of hers.

The children scrambled ahead, and Miss Lawrence clutched Mary's hand. "Penny isn't in danger from the man, is she? She has an appointment to see him on Monday."

"I shouldn't think so." Alec had said nothing about Bauer trying to debauch prepubescent girls, though there were plenty of men whose tastes ran in that dreadful direction. "Just make sure either you or her mother is present." With any luck, Bauer would be gone by Monday.

"Penny's mother is dead. It's just me, I'm afraid."

"Well then, *you* had better watch out. I think Bauer tries to take advantage of unmarried young women."

"Well, he won't take advantage of me." Eliza Lawrence pulled a wicked-looking hatpin from her bag and waved it in the air.

"Are you happy in your position, Miss Lawrence?" Mary asked, reverting to what she knew best.

"Not really. I would be if it was just Penny—she's a lamb when she's not sick. But Jonathan needs a firmer hand than mine. I like children well enough, but I'd rather work in an office, to tell you the truth. I took a secretarial course, and am a whiz at filing and organizing things. In fact I was one of Mr. Hurst's typists until he needed an 'emergency' governess. I've been at it for a year now and he seems disinclined to replace me."

Mary didn't wonder. Miss Lawrence was blond and very pretty, too much of a distraction for the clerks in a law office but lovely to look at over the breakfast table. "Why do you stay?"

The young woman shrugged. "I need the position. My mother is unwell, and the pay is generous. But if Mr. Hurst thinks of marrying again, I'm sure I'll be out on the street. No wife will want me under her roof, for all that Mr. Hurst has been a perfect gentleman. I don't even think he knows what I look like, his head is so filled with torts and briefs."

The man must be married to his job or myopic. Mary reached into her own reticule and fished out her card. "When you get back to London, go to the Evensong Agency. Mrs. Evensong will find the ideal job for you. She always does."

Eliza Lawrence added the card to the detritus in her bag. "Why thank you, miss. I don't even know your name!"

"I'm sorry. It's Mary Arden. I'm here with my aunt and my brother."

"Oh! I believe Mr. Hurst is playing cards with your brother tonight."

"Is he? Oliver did tell me that he had something planned."

They passed through the last of the trees to the rolling lawn. A game of croquet was in progress, and the thwack of tennis balls could be heard coming from the tennis courts below. Mary was not much of a sportswoman—apparently she could not even *walk*—and had no interest in taking advantage of the activities provided for the guests. Miss Lawrence excused herself to chase after Jonathan, and Mary contemplated how she could spend the rest of the day.

If she were home, how would she be spending her Saturday? Behind her desk, sifting through letters and bills. The office was open six days a week, and she frequently interviewed prospective clients and applicants on Saturdays. When had she given herself the day off to go to a museum, or even shop? All work and no play was making Mary a very dull girl.

She walked through the crowded enclosed veranda where the waitstaff was serving tea and crumpets. She'd eaten a filling breakfast, which had inspired her to go on her unlucky walk to work it off, and was not tempted to stop. The scenery had been lovely, but the view from above was the real draw. Mary took the lift to the top floor, climbing the last few steps to the Ladies' Tower. It was empty of hotel guests, which suited Mary's mood.

From the four sides of the open tower she could see for miles. The river glinted in the distance, tiny men standing in it and casting their lures to tinier fish. A puff of smoke heralded the arrival of the morning train to the village station, bringing more guests. Closer to hand, wagons carrying fresh produce were lined up at the trade entrance, and maids and footmen scurried about. The hotel was a vast enterprise, a boost to the local economy, and Mary hoped Bauer's exposure would not doom its success. Surely another doctor could be found, someone who wouldn't ruin vulnerable women.

Mary took a deep breath of fresh air. Who wouldn't want to live up here for half the year? The hotel closed for the winter, though sometimes that meant October when it snowed early. There was a nip in the air even now for a sunny June morning.

Mary leaned over the balustrade, a gust of wind warring with her hat. She really should go down to her room and fix herself—she remembered Eliza Lawrence's look of dismay. But she was searching for someone in all the beauty and activity below.

And then she saw him step out of the woods, straightening his jacket and pulling his plaid cap from a pocket. How far had he run down the trail before he deemed it safe to come back? Did he get as far as the falls, which were, in Mary's opinion, breathtaking? Almost worth her blistered feet. He'd probably seen them hundreds of times growing up here; his land bordered the hotel's. Did he take all this scenery for granted? He was a man of privilege, accustomed to the finer things in life. Perhaps trees and mountains and rivers meant nothing to him.

She raised a hand. Of course he didn't see her. Mary was used to not being seen, but today she wished that Lord Alec Raeburn would look up and know someone was watching over him.

Chapter

16

$\mathcal{M}$ary really was suffering from nerves now. If Dr. Bauer had listened to her heartbeat, he'd likely want to hospitalize her. She'd been much too nervous to visit with Aunt Mim last night, sure that her aunt would take one look at Mary and know what she'd been up to with Alec Raeburn. Mary probably wasn't much better this afternoon even after washing up and changing her muddy dress. There was something too sparkly in her eyes, her cheeks were too pink, and her lips looked chapped from kisses despite the all-purpose salve. Mary felt as if the ends of her hair were on fire. She may as well have been wearing a sign that said, "In the Process of Being Seduced."

And that is what she needed to talk to Aunt Mim about. She rapped on her door, hoping she was not napping. Mary knew her aunt had booked a hydrotherapy treatment this morning and just how relaxing it could be.

Until Alec had sneaked in, touched her, and turned her world upside down.

Hamblen let her in. "I'm glad you're here, Miss Mary. Your aunt missed you last night."

"I—I had such a busy day that I was exhausted. How is she feeling?"

The maid grinned. "Feisty, I'd say, after this morning's news. Quite like her old self. Go see."

Oh, dear. Could her aunt have discovered her assignations with Alec? Mary wasn't sure she could explain. At least this morning's had been by chance.

She found her aunt sitting in a Bath chair by her bedroom window. Aunt Mim was not enjoying the view, but writing something on hotel stationery. A train schedule was on the table, and her trunk lay open on the floor. The closet had been emptied, and black dresses and the contents of the dresser lay on the counterpane, ready to be wrapped in tissue paper.

"What's all this?" Mary asked.

"We had a marconigram from Harriet this morning," Aunt Mim said without looking up from her furious scribbling. "Or from Harriet's poor father I should say. I could barely make heads or tails of it, he's that frantic. She is in hospital. Something about peri—perisomething."

"Peritonitis? That's awful!" The king's own coronation had been delayed by his bout of appendicitis.

"That's it. She's made it through surgery but will not be able to come into the office for ages. I've got to get back. The afternoon train, I should think. I can sleep for most of the trip, and I'll be perfectly refreshed by Monday morning."

"But—"

Her aunt raised an ink-stained finger. "No buts. You still have your job to do here, and Oliver can see to getting you home once it's done. You'll have to do without Hamblen, I'm afraid."

Mary had done without a maid for the first twenty-five years of her life. "Will you be able to manage?"

"The trip or my business? I should say so! This holiday, short as it's been, has done me a world of good. Traveling without too much discomfort. Being with people. It's about time I got back downstairs to the agency again. So what if clients see me with a cane or in a Bath chair? I'm an old woman, but not dead yet. I've got plenty of juice still in me! Maybe we'll even put a lift in the building. We've got plenty of money in the bank, thanks to you."

Mary swallowed hard at this surprising turn of events. "You're not going to fire me, are you?"

Aunt Mim looked up. "Fire you? Don't be ridiculous. You've been invaluable the past four years. Indispensable. Game for most anything. Why, you remind me of myself, and not just because you have the Evensong looks. You'll inherit the agency once I'm gone, you know, not your brother, Albert. You wouldn't want to go back to Oxfordshire and work for him again, would you?"

What an atrocious thought. "Absolutely not."

"Well, then, we'll figure out a way to introduce you to the clients. My office is big enough for a partners desk. You can sit in on the appointments. When people see that I trust you implicitly, they'll come around and disregard your youth. We'll figure it out next week when you get back."

"About that, Aunt Mim. Lord Raeburn has invited us all to Raeburn Court to assess his staff. He wants the agency to supply him with new employees. But now I suppose I shouldn't go." Mary tried hard to be brave about the whole thing. You couldn't miss what you'd never known, could you?

Aunt Mim returned to her writing. "Don't be silly. Of course you should go. You and Oliver are perfectly capable of taking care of all that without me. Spend an extra few days if you like. You'll know what he needs."

Mary knew what *she* needed. But her worry for her aunt was real. "I'll get back as soon as I can."

Her aunt waved her away. "Don't worry about me. You deserve a proper vacation. And it's lovely up here. It's too bad you cannot honor our hotel reservations, but I imagine after tonight your reputation will be in tatters. People can be so cruel. That whole Eve myth—it's always the woman's fault. Lilith. Salome. Delilah. Don't get me started. Yes, it's best if you go straight to Raeburn Court after this Bauer business is done. Enjoy yourself. You aren't too worried about tonight, are you? I've made some notes."

Aunt Mim handed her the list she'd been working on. It appeared to have instructions as to the ways she could incapacitate Dr. Bauer if her rescue was in any way delayed. There were even illustrations.

"I gave the same advice to all the duke's daughters. They said I should write a book, you know. And they're all happily married at last." The Evensong Agency had found a third husband for the youngest and wildest of them just last year. By all accounts, everyone was happy at last.

"You deserve the credit for that," Mary said loyally. She'd heard all the stories about the duke's five difficult daughters.

"I do. The duchess was hopeless, poor thing. Trying for a boy simply wore her out, and when he finally arrived was very disappointing, as you know. My instincts have always been good, Mary, and I believe you've inherited them. You could not have accomplished all you have the past few years without having an innate understanding of people."

Mary hoped her aunt was right. She was entrusting Alec Raeburn with her carnal education. She didn't want her heart broken in the process.

"Th-thank you, Aunt Mim. That's the nicest thing anyone's ever said to me."

"And isn't that a shame? A girl your age should be hearing compliments from people other than her old aunt. Now do me a favor and ring down to the front desk to make sure they have a carriage available to take us to the station. I've called twice already, but it never hurts to check on the details. I've taught you that, haven't I? Your list should have a list. And get Hamblen back in here to finish packing."

Mary did as she was told, happy to see her aunt so energized. It was true she still hobbled when she rose from her Bath chair, and her bad foot would never fit into a regular shoe, but she was stepping livelier than Mary had witnessed in four years. They hadn't been in Scotland long enough for all the spa's alleged miracle cures to have taken hold, so something else had shifted within her aunt. The fresh air? The spring water? Whatever it was, Mary was grateful. She might have a chance for a more normal life after all.

If that was the case, should she go through with this agreement with Alec Raeburn? She could have more free time in the future to meet a gentleman to court her. Some worthy dull fellow . . .

No. Her social life was apt to be as limited as it always had been. Alec Raeburn was her one chance.

Mary kissed her aunt good-bye and went to her own room. It was hours and hours until her assignation with Dr. Bauer. Mary picked up a book she'd brought with her, but put it right down again when the words made no sense at all to her troubled brain. She stared out the window and counted mountain peaks. She rubbed salve on her bare feet, and washed her hands. She thought about ordering tea or a sandwich, but her stomach did a little flip.

Mary was not used to being idle, but enjoying the amenities of the hotel seemed beyond her today. So here she sat, clean hands folded in her lap and stomach fluttering, doing absolutely nothing. It was almost painful, and her mind tripped from one frightening thought to the next, with nothing to distract her, nowhere to go, nothing to do until the grand show later. Eventually, she'd have to order another tray up to her room before she starved—she didn't dare go to the dining room for dinner. Contrary to what she'd said, it would be nearly impossible for her to get into one of her new evening dresses without Hamblen.

Her lips twitched. She could ask Alec to serve as maid, though undressing was more of his specialty. Oliver would probably lend a safer hand, but he'd be busy getting himself and his room ready for the card party.

Speak of the devil. There was a rap on the connecting door, and Oliver sauntered in, looking blindingly white in his tennis togs. He was a most welcome sight, although for a second she wished for her smoke-gray spectacles. Oliver was so very dazzling, too handsome for his own good. He threw his lanky body down in one of her chairs and frowned at her.

"Hey, sis. What's this I hear about Aunt Mim leaving? As a gentleman, should I volunteer to go with the old dear?"

Oliver had made himself quite comfortable in his false

family. It must be excruciating to be disowned by his own. Her brother, Albert, and his wife, Phyllis, might annoy her, but they were still *there*. Oliver couldn't go home. How had he spent last Christmas? Mary would make sure he spent it with her and Aunt Mim this year.

"She'd better not catch you calling her an 'old dear.' Yes, it's true, and no, you shouldn't. Harriet had to have her appendix removed and will be laid up for who knows how long. Someone had to go back to London, and it can't be me. Or you. Have you forgotten about the card party?"

"Not bloody likely. The hotel people are upending my room even as we speak. I'll have to hang out here for a while if you don't mind."

Mary heard thunking and sliding next door. "Not at all."

Oliver lowered his voice so he wouldn't be heard, not that it was likely with all the noise. "Raeburn could run the show for me if you're worried about your aunt, you know. Half the guests are his friends."

"No, that won't do. You're supposed to profess brotherly outrage and convince the men I'm much too innocent to have lured Bauer by myself. Aunt Mim will have Hamblen. She's a sensible girl, and the train's direct. I don't know what's gotten into my aunt—she's taken a new lease on life and wants to go back into the office!"

"I hope it's not due to one of those quack medicines they pass out at the spa. They're all alcohol, you know. No wonder the hotel doesn't serve liquor—the guests pay a fortune for it in their little brown bottles."

"Ha! Is that the secret? And here I thought it was the fresh air and wholesome food."

"Yes, the food is excellent. Almost as good as Antoine's." He sighed.

Poor Oliver. Antoine was his first love. The French chef was still employed in the Palmer household, although as far as Mary knew their affair had ended. When she got back to London, she'd have to look for a discreet young gentleman for Oliver. The Evensong Agency's matchmaking skills were renowned even for the most unconventional of clients.

"I'm not going downstairs for dinner tonight, so we won't have to have one of our fights. I'm much too nervous to eat much anyway."

"You have to have something or you'll faint dead away as soon as Bauer lays a hand on you. I'll order up a tea tray for us right now. I'm always hungry. We'll have a jolly little party, just us two."

Since Oliver had discovered she wasn't a formidable old woman, he treated her with a familiarity she really couldn't mind. The boy was lonely, and so was she. Mary had been too busy to find friends in London or keep them in Oxford. Goodness, but her life had been boring until she met Alec Raeburn.

No, that wasn't true. She'd had some adventures, but all on behalf of the agency's clients. It was her turn now.

Oliver finished talking on the telephone and flopped back into the chair. "Where did you go this morning? I knocked earlier but nobody answered."

"Oh, just for a walk in the woods."

"Like Little Red Riding Hood?"

There had been a Big Bad Wolf, but she wasn't going to tell Oliver. "Actually, I met a governess who might be the perfect replacement for you when we promote you. Now that Harriet will be recuperating, we'll have an even greater need of changes at the office."

"Have you spoken to your aunt about it yet?"

Oliver seemed very eager, and Mary was stricken. She'd been so busy with Alec, she'd forgotten. "Not yet, but I'm sure she'll have no objection. She likes you very much, Oliver."

"Oh, people always like me. They just don't want to employ me. If she's coming downstairs again, there may be too many cooks in the kitchen."

"Nonsense! You know what our workload's been like. It would be one thing if we were strictly an employment agency, but people come to us for so many other reasons. Speaking of which, Lord Raeburn has invited us to Raeburn Court once our little masquerade is over. He lost most of his staff over the past year. I gather the locals are not keen on working there, so we'll have to inspect the property and determine his needs."

"*I* know what the man needs, but I doubt he'd be interested." Oliver gave her a wicked wink.

Mary's face grew warm. "You cannot flirt with the male clients, Oliver, or I'll put you back at the reception desk."

"Don't worry—you know I'm well-behaved in public if I have to be. But it's just us now."

"One should act in private exactly as one does in public." Not that she had lately.

"Really? How dull. But I'm sure you're right. You always are."

Was she? She was beginning to doubt it.

Chapter

17

$\mathscr{A}$lec took a cold bath once he returned to his suite. He was too old to be seducing women in public places and then running through the woods to escape discovery. Actually, the public aspect of seduction had never much bothered him—people could draw their own conclusions about his lack of morals as he nibbled necks in theater boxes or green rooms. He was a patron of the arts, wasn't he, although his patronage was devoted solely to supporting actresses, music hall dancers, and artists' models. The girls gave themselves to him freely, and he returned their favor with generous financial aid and glittering trinkets. Everyone knew the rules, and everyone was happy. Even Edith had been relieved when he'd given up on her and gone to London for amusement.

But he didn't want to bring disgrace to Mary, and not only because of the game they were running with Bauer. She truly was an innocent, despite her outlandish proposal. He should never have invited her to Raeburn Court. He couldn't renege now; her feelings would be hurt. And Alec didn't *want* to reject her—he wanted her in his bed, her light auburn hair spread out on his pillow, her lush body under his, her white skin hot and flushed.

Gah. He'd have to take another bath if he kept thinking of her.

He went downstairs for a late lunch. The veranda was sparse of company, which suited him. He skimmed the newspapers that had come on the morning train. Yesterday's news, but no good ever came of being too up-to-date. Most problems solved themselves with sufficient time—there was no reason to concern himself about things over which he had no control. He'd done his bit in Parliament, and a more frustrating endeavor he'd never participated in, especially regarding the Boer Wars debacle. Alec's decision to spend most of the year in Scotland would be good for his mental health, even if he did have to live like a monk again.

He'd have his fling with Mary Arden. The memory of it would have to keep him warm this winter, and damn but Scottish winters were long and cold. But somehow his brother Evan managed to survive them. So could he.

Alec ate his lunch and returned to his room, pacing much of the next hour away in anticipation. Tonight, Edith would be avenged, and he'd pick up whatever scraps of honor remained to him.

The walls of his capacious suite seemed to be closing in on him, so he climbed the stairs to the gentlemen's tower to blow a cloud or two to break the monotony. The hotel's wagonette was on the circular drive, ready to take departing guests to the afternoon train. He took his silver match safe from his pocket and nearly dropped it over the balustrade as he saw Mrs. Evensong being helped into the vehicle by her maid. She was leaving? Were Mary and Oliver already seated under the canopy? By God, they were leaving him in the lurch after bleeding him of a fortune!

All thoughts of cigars gone, Alec raced down the stairs and practically bowled Mary Arden over in the lobby. Her eyes slid to the side in warning—Josef Bauer was bidding a patient good-bye near the hotel entrance.

"Pardon me, Miss Arden," Alec said, his voice gruff.

"Please leave me alone," she said, loud enough for everyone in the vicinity to hear.

Alec took a step backward, but was too late to escape Bauer's notice. "Raeburn! You heard the lady. Your attentions are unwelcome."

The insufferable snot. "I wasn't paying attention to anyone in my hurry, that was the problem. I—I thought someone I knew was leaving and I wanted to speak to her before she left."

"One of your *chères amies*? You see, Miss Arden, how inconstant the baron is."

"You have saved me from his wicked predations, Dr. Bauer. I'm ever so grateful."

The little witch batted her gilt-edged eyelashes, and Alec held back a chuckle. She could make a mint on the stage. Some artfully applied maquillage to enhance her pale, even features, and she might even be considered a beauty.

But he didn't want to change her in any significant way. Now that he'd seen her at close quarters, she was lovely just as she was.

"Still here with us, Raeburn? I must speak to the hotel manager."

"I've paid for another week, Bauer. Prescott has no reason to get rid of me. I'm as well-behaved—why, as *you* are."

Alec was pleased to see the doctor flush with anger. Now that he was beardless, his face looked like a bland boiled egg.

"Come, Miss Arden, let us leave this fellow behind. Will you join me for dinner later?"

Mary twisted her hands. She was not wearing gloves and her fingers were short and plump, much like the rest of her. Alec wanted to kiss each fingertip, and would soon enough.

"Oh! I cannot. Helping my aunt pack was qu-quite exhausting."

"I understand. Perhaps another time." Bauer winked at Mary to show her he'd not forgotten their ten o'clock appointment. Mary blushed—how did she do that on cue?— and nodded.

The three of them stood in uncomfortable silence staring out the open doors as the wagonette left. Mrs. Evensong waved a handkerchief and gave Alec a very pointed frown before turning away.

"It is a pity your aunt was called away, Miss Arden," Alec said.

"Yes. An emergency. But my br-brother is here to protect me."

"And I as well," Bauer said, daring to throw an arm around Mary. Alec bit his tongue, clenched his fists, and made for the staircase before he did anything rash. Of course he was relieved to find Mary and Oliver still here, but he wondered why Mrs. Evensong had to leave so unexpectedly.

He found out a quarter of an hour later when a tap at his door made him put down a glass of Raeburn's Special Reserve. He had changed his clothes, and so had Mary. She was at the door, veiled and covered entirely in black. She reminded him very much of her aunt, but he'd never tell her so. Comparing her to a seventy-odd-year-old woman would likely result in a kick to his shins.

He knew he was grinning at her like an idiot, but even swathed in black she was a joy to behold. "To what do I owe the honor? And aren't you hot?"

"Stifling." Mary threw back the veil and looked around his sitting room. It was larger and more luxurious than her aunt's, and she whistled her approval. "Very nice. I am incognita, but I thought we should have an actual talk before tonight. A talk, Lord Raeburn. No kissing or anything else of that nature. And my shoes shall remain on my feet for the duration." She sounded wistful about the latter.

"I pledge to be on my best behavior. May I offer you a wee dram of Raeburn's Special Reserve? My man Mackenzie is fetching another case. I expect him back any minute."

"He is actually downstairs with Oliver setting up the bar right now. All of Oliver's guests have confirmed they're coming. Mr. Mackenzie has agreed to serve—he's a very nice young chap, isn't he?"

"Mac? Yes, I suppose he is." The young valet had stuck by him when others had not.

"He isn't married or walking out with anyone, is he?"

Alec snorted. "I'm afraid he's not in the petticoat line. Any housemaids your aunt hires for me will be quite safe."

Alec had his suspicions about Mackenzie, but was not going to gossip about the fellow. Mac had never been less than professional, and if he wanted Alec to wear more colorful waistcoats, what was the harm? "About that drink?"

"Oh, yes. That would be lovely. I'd like to see what all the fuss is about."

Alec's great-grandfather had started the distillery over a hundred years ago. At first, it was for the family's sole use, but it would have been criminal not to share. Now its reputation was known worldwide, and most of its product was imported to the United States at considerable profit. He poured a scant finger of the rich amber liquid into a glass, thinking it nearly matched Mary Arden's hair, and handed it to her.

She looked at the tumbler. "It's true. You Scots are stingy."

"That will be quite enough for a wee lass such as yourself. And you may not like it anyhow."

Mary took a sniff. "It smells wonderful. Strong, but wonderful." She tilted the glass to her lips. "Oh, my."

He could not have asked for a more radiant expression of her appreciation on her face. "I'll tell Evan you approve."

"I do. Oh, indeed I do. Aunt Mim would love it, too."

"I'll send her a case for your evening ritual. That is, if you'll be staying in London with her."

"I—I think I will be. She wants to bring me into the business."

"*You?*"

Mary bristled beneath her outlandish black hat. "What do you mean 'you'? Is it so hard to believe I could manage to sort out people's problems? I'll have you know I'm quite competent!"

Alec had stepped in it somehow. He couldn't picture her chained to a desk on Mount Street. But then he couldn't see her behind the counter in a grocery shop, either. In fact, the only place he could see her was in his bedroom at Raeburn Court.

What the hell? She'd only be in it a day, or a few at the

most if he could persuade her to stay longer. And after that it was a life of penance and self-abnegation for him.

Wasn't it?

"I meant nothing insulting by it, Mary. It's just that you're so—" What was she precisely? Petite? Young? No, she really wasn't young, but in his experience a gentleman did not remind a lady of that fact.

"—spirited. I find it hard to see you shut up in an office."

"Maybe my aunt will assign me to more undercover work. I think it suits me."

She had been an effective actress, much more skilled than Alec's usual theatrical acquaintances.

"I will write you a positive recommendation if you need it. Where did your aunt go?"

"My—I mean *her* assistant had a medical emergency. Appendicitis. I gather she's lucky they caught it when they did. She'll be in hospital for a while, and then recuperating at home. There was no one to run the agency in her absence, so Aunt Mim left."

"No wonder she'll want you to help her. It's quite an operation, isn't it? The building was buzzing when I visited."

Mary nodded. "There are six full-time employees. With Oliver still here, Aunt Mim will have her hands full. The girl stenographers need a steady hand."

She seemed to know a good deal about the business already, so perhaps it was a good fit. "The Evensong Agency has an excellent reputation. I'm sure you'll add to it. Now, what did you want to talk about?"

She looked down at the feet she wanted to keep covered. "Just how far do you want me to let Dr. Bauer progress tonight before we are discovered?"

"Progress!" Alec didn't want Bauer "progressing" at all. He'd wanted to cut the man's arm off when he put it around Mary's shoulder in the lobby. "Don't let the bastard touch you. It should be enough that he's discovered in your room at such a late hour."

"I've been thinking about that," Mary said. "He can always say that I was unwell and rang for him."

She was right. "Blast."

"So I think I'll need to go a bit further than I—that is, my aunt—agreed to."

Alec felt a wave of revulsion sweep through him. "You're not suggesting—"

"Of course not." He didn't have to finish the sentence. Mary's face was scarlet, but she went on. "Just a touch of dishabille. My hair down. That sort of thing."

"You'll have to scream, too."

"I can do that. I actually practiced at the waterfall this morning. The water was so noisy I didn't think I'd alarm anyone."

Alec pictured Mary exercising her lungs near dawn. "You must have scared the squirrels."

"I must have." She cleared her throat. "I think we'll need to be on the bed."

"Pardon me?"

"Bauer and I. That way the implication will be clear."

When the honey trap Alec had envisioned was set with some nameless actress, it was one thing. What had once seemed like a brilliant idea was now rather horrific. "I suppose you're right."

"And you must let Oliver do all the talking. We are strangers, after all."

"Wait a moment. People have seen us together. It would be only natural for me to defend a lady in peril, even if I hadn't taken tea with her."

She gave him a stern look. "There will be no bloodshed, Lord Raeburn."

"I don't see why not," Alec said, feeling stubborn. He'd been itching to pummel Bauer into the ground for months. Below the ground, straight to everlasting hell.

"If anyone is to do any hitting, let it be Oliver. It will be good for him."

"I can't promise anything." He was seeing red already, imagining Mary in Bauer's arms.

"Look, Alec, it must not appear we're in collusion. If Bauer catches wind of that, your money will be wasted. And he might have grounds to sue you for . . . something. I'm not as well-versed in the law as I should be."

He could see her point, but the desire to eviscerate Bauer would not disappear anytime soon. "I'll do my best to remain a disinterested party. Let's drink on it." Alec raised his glass and tapped it to hers.

"To tonight's success," Mary said.

They were still standing, which was very odd. He watched as she took a swallow, her clear hazel eyes lifted to his. Some nameless thread tightened between them, stitch by stitch. His head felt woozy, and it was not due to the faultlessly blended liquor.

He was simply tired, that was all. And sexually frustrated. He could do something about that.

"Let's sit. Your feet must still be tender."

"I should go."

"There are hours yet before you have anything to do. Do you want to dine here with me?"

"Have you listened to a word I've said?" She sat down anyway, too far away on a chair near the window. The panoramic view was breathtaking, but he only had eyes for her.

"I take it your answer is no." He sat on the sofa, bringing the bottle of Raeburn's Special Reserve with him. "Would you care for more?"

Mary shook her head. "I daren't. You're right—it's quite potent. I wouldn't want to fall asleep and forget to open the door to Dr. Bauer."

"Maybe we should practice."

Mary looked at him blankly.

"You know. I can pretend to be Bauer. You invite me in. And so forth."

"Practice." She licked her lips and Alec thought he'd expire with lust. She would taste of Raeburn's Special Reserve and her own particular sweetness.

He cleared his throat and his mind. "Yes. Like a dress rehearsal."

"As they do in the theater. I suppose you'd know all about that."

He rubbed his face, surprised again at encountering bristles rather than fur. "You know my reputation. I can't deny it. I've misspent my youth and my middle age. But I mean to change that. No more chorines or aspiring thespians. I am a reformed man."

"What shall you do for entertainment, my lord?"

"I'll find something to keep me busy."

"Or someone," she said a bit tartly.

"Not here in the Highlands. They think I'm the devil. No decent—or indecent—woman will be seen in my company. I might toss her out a window, you know."

He couldn't keep the bitterness from his voice. Really, was this the way to get Mary Arden to frolic on his bed for a few minutes before she screamed her head off? Silently, to be sure. She'd have to mime that last part.

Yes, it seemed to be. She set her empty glass down and stood up. "All right. Go knock on your own door, and we'll see how to set the trap properly."

There would be nothing proper about it.

Chapter

18

Mary had run through various scenarios in her head already. Why not prepare in a more practical way? Hands-on experience, as it were.

Dr. Bauer had already touched her as her doctor. Tonight he was planning to touch her again. Mary wished she'd brought her aunt's notes with her so she could remember how to shift her body to deflect attention. She was afraid of being overpowered for however brief a time before Oliver ran in. Mary truly didn't think she had it in her to poke her fingers into Bauer's eyeballs—she had trouble removing a loose eyelash out of her own.

She lifted her knee experimentally, and Alec looked somewhat nervous.

Mary pushed him toward the door. "Go on. We'll start from the beginning."

Her room was much smaller, and had a bed in it. She reconsidered. "Wait a minute. There's no point in you going out to the hallway. I'll go into your bedroom and you can knock on that door."

"What are you wearing?" Alec blurted.

"You can see, can't you?" One of her dreadful Mary

Evensong black gowns. She'd almost left them all behind in London. But Mary prided herself on being ready for any occasion, and if she had to slip into her seventy-year-old self, she would be ready with this one dress.

"No, I mean tonight. You won't be in your nightclothes, will you?"

It might look suspicious to the other gentlemen if she let Bauer in wearing her white nightgown, not that it was at all enticing, with ruffles up to her chin and down to her knuckles. Nothing showed except her very ordinary face and toes. It was hardly an ensemble meant to tempt a gentleman. But as she needed to appear as innocent as possible, she probably should remain fully dressed.

"One of my day gowns, I suppose."

"Good. Don't let him touch any buttons or hooks."

"I shall endeavor not to. Now, are you ready?" She sat on a chair and folded her hands.

Alec looked as if he wanted to say something else. Instead, he shut the door and rapped an insistent tattoo behind it.

"Who is it?" Mary asked.

"It is I, Chosef Bauer."

She bit back her laughter—it was odd to hear a Scotsman try to speak English as a Viennese would. She stood and smoothed out her black skirts, counting to ten.

"Let me in, *liebchen*. Or should it be *liebling*?"

"I didn't realize you spoke German," Mary said.

"You vould be surprised how facile I am vit da langviches."

Mary expected Alec knew how to proposition women in any number of them. "One moment, Al—Dr. Bauer."

How foolish—her heart began to hammer as she walked slowly to the door. It was all she could do to turn the knob and open it.

Alec was a much larger man than Josef Bauer, but his size didn't intimidate her, and it was rather enjoyable to see him standing there in his shirtsleeves. He'd removed his waistcoat, tie, and linen collar, too, before she'd come and the column of his throat was intriguing.

"*Guten abend*, Fräulein Arden." He leered at her as if he were in some third-rate melodrama. He was only missing a mustache to twirl.

"Don't overdo it, Alec. Remember, you are a practiced seducer. You're used to getting your way with nervous females. If I were a nervous female, I'd run from that particular look. Or laugh."

"There is novhere to run, Miss Arden. You knew vhen you invited me what vass to happen." He didn't break character, his accent heavier than ever. She'd better get into the spirit of the thing, hadn't she?

"Oh, Dr. Bauer," she said breathlessly, "I wasn't sure you'd come." She stumbled backward to the chair she'd been sitting in. Although Alec's bedroom was larger than hers, they had similar amenities. A pair of tufted chairs sat before the window, and she gestured to the other. "Won't you sit down?"

"Miss Arden—Mary—I should so much like to do someting else. Shall ve dance?"

"What?" She was pretty sure Josef Bauer would not want to waltz with her.

"*Tantzen, ja?*" Alec held up his arms and winked at her.

"This is not a useful exercise, Alec. You are being silly."

"Who knows vhat a man might ask for, my dear? The vays of the mind are mysterious. Vun must be prepared."

"I am not prepared to dance now. My feet hurt, as you know."

"Ach. I am a doctor. Let me haff a look."

Mary was torn between annoyance and amusement. "You are not a doctor—well, I suppose you are for the purpose of practice, but I cannot imagine Bauer asking me to take my shoes off."

"Vy not? Ve men vant all the ladies to disrobe. Vun must start somewhere."

"I have no intention of removing my shoes. I told you that when I arrived."

Alec sighed. "Fine. I am inconsolable, but I persevere. Fräulein Arden, I haff never met anyone so shy and luffley. Please say dat you return my admiration."

"I—I suppose so. Y-you are very nice."

"Say it like you mean it or I am apt to get up and leaf, and you vill not have a chance to yell your *kopf* off."

"Blast it, Alec! I am no flirt! And you're you, not Bauer. I am sure I'll do much better tonight when it matters." Mary had had no difficulty stringing Bauer along the several times they'd conversed, but now her mind was devoid of any repartee, witty or otherwise. This was Alec—who seemed to make her vitless vitout even trying.

He looked skeptical. "You know vhy I haff come. Let's not beat around da bushes. I am going to pick you up now and toss you to da bed."

Mary's stomach flipped. "You most certainly are not!"

"*Ja*, I am."

Alec leaped up and dumped her on the bed before she could think about his eyeballs or his groin. Her hat flew off despite the hatpins, and she tried to scramble off the bed with no luck. Before she knew it he was perched over her, a manic gleam in his eye.

"You vant me. You know you do."

The trouble was, he was right. But if it was beastly Bauer behaving so barbarically—Lord, how could she think in such alliterative fashion when her virtue was being compromised?—surely she should do something to get rid of him. Mary gave a feeble push.

"Dat's all you haff got?"

"I don't want to hurt you."

The wretched man laughed, a delicious rumbly sound. With his mouth open at such close range, she observed his teeth were excellent.

Suddenly he rolled away, leaving an unsettling vacuum. He lay flat on his back and reached for her hand to prevent her from rising. She was still wearing her black kidskin gloves, but could feel the warmth of his fingers as they traced circles into her palm.

"You see, my dear Miss Arden, how easily you were manipulated. You should have hit me or screamed." All trace of the Viennese villain was gone.

"Well, of course I would have screamed if you were really Bauer, but you're not," she said, cross. "I don't think this dress rehearsal was worthwhile at all."

"You gave no indication of even *wanting* to scream."

Damn his smug, stubbled face. He was right. His nearness did something inside her and turned her brain to oatmeal. "I assure you, I know how to scream, and I shall do so when the occasion calls for it. And I'm quite sure Bauer will not be heaving me around like a rag doll tonight. Is this how you treated all your mistresses? All brawn and no finesse?"

Alec glared at her. My, he was fierce, even without his beard. "I have as much finesse as the next fellow."

"Prove it." The words flew out of her mouth without any of her usual caution.

"I don't need to pr—oh, hell. All right. You'll get what you've asked for, you impossible woman. Lie still, and don't say a word." He moved alarmingly closer.

"I didn't mean doing anything right *now*."

"Too late for second thoughts. I've been challenged, and I always rise to a challenge." He drew her gloved hand to the front of his trousers.

Oh my.

"You're not—you don't mean to—"

"Hush. I said no talking. But there may be a little screaming at the end."

He pulled her closer, the heat of all the clothes between them tropical. Then he tugged up her skirt and petticoats, exposing her thighs to the cool mountain breeze that wafted in from his open window.

"Alec!" She croaked like a frog.

"Shh. Let me pleasure you. With finesse. I won't do anything permanent—we haven't time."

A finger snaked beneath the suspenders that attached her corset to the tops of her stockings, but he made no attempt to remove them. Her feet would be safe, but the rest of her definitely would not. His hand moved up to the slit in her short combination and she forgot to breathe.

"You are wearing Blenheim Bouquet."

Mary blushed. She splashed it everywhere, even if it was a gentleman's cologne.

"I'm going to kiss you now, and touch you while I do. I have your permission?"

He sounded so serious. Mary nodded. She couldn't have stuck her tongue on the roof of her mouth to say no if her life depended on it. She closed her eyes, waiting for his kiss, and felt the mattress shift.

The location of his kiss came as a total surprise. It was not at all where she expected it. He parted the lace-trimmed silk, her womanly folds, and the tip of his tongue touched a knot of sudden need inside her. She did scream, just a little. It was more out of surprise than anything else, and he stopped stroking her instantly.

"May I continue?"

"Oh, do stop talking," Mary muttered, refusing to look at his upturned face. She shouldn't want to be complicit, but she was. She'd seen pictures of just this very thing in Lord Harwood's library while she waited for the man. She hadn't been snooping—the Chinese pillow book lay open right on his desk. It had been difficult for her to keep a straight face as he shyly discussed his need for an innocent young wife for procreational purposes to carry on the Harwood name. She suspected his wife might be very happy in the end if he was following the book's illustrations.

"I am at your service, my dear Miss Arden." She imagined Alec's wolfish grin, a man secure in his sexual confidence, a man who'd done this many times before to his helpless, happy victims. He returned to glide his tongue and gentle fingers around areas Mary didn't know existed. She was remarkably stupid, but had always been a fast learner. She did not need much practice to allow herself to experience this exquisite assault upon her senses.

She grew hot, the blood wild beneath the surface of her skin, even making her face feel tingly. One trembling hand clenched the rucked fabric of her dress, the other encouraging Alec's dark head to remain in place and continue his wicked kiss. His black hair was coarse beneath her fingers, but his tongue was smooth and supple as pulled taffy, contorting itself around her center with ease. He held her in place, too, one finger now stationed inside her passage. He had entered so gently that Mary felt nothing but liquid heat and the softest of pressure. She was tight and stretched—how would he accomplish anything more delicious on Monday?

As to that, could she wait that long? She was on the cusp of something now, a simultaneous loosening and tightening, which confused her. Mary now wished her boots weren't on. She wanted to arch her feet and curl her toes and flex from her lower back to her soles. She was mummified by her corset and clothes, gasping for air and reaching for an elusive something just at the edge of her clouded mind.

Alec intensified his suckling, encapsulating her swollen bud in his mouth with swift precision. A thumb pressed against her pubic bone at the exact same time and she fell and flew over that edge, incapable of any thought at all. She made an embarrassing noise wholly unfamiliar to her, which caused Alec to chuckle against her wet flesh and delve deeper within her. Stars flashed behind her eyelids and her skin flamed and froze.

This was torment. This was heaven. Mary could readily see why such activity was restricted, secret, even forbidden, for why would anyone ever want to get out of bed again? The world would stop and civilization would be in utter ruin.

Mary was not entirely ignorant. Posing as her aunt for four years had opened her eyes to the many vagaries and varieties in society. People thought she was an older woman, aware of the world. She'd heard confessions she wished she could close her ears to from both males and females seeking her help to find happiness. Everything then had been abstract, but now she understood all too well.

Mary was sated and splayed open, contractions rippling through her like receding waves as Alec withdrew his hands and mouth. She did not complain. In truth, she could not have born much more of his wickedness if she ever wanted to find her good sense again. He covered her with her crumpled skirts and slid up the bed, his face as flushed as hers must be, a mischievous smile on his twitching lips.

"Enough finesse for you, Miss Arden, or would you like another try? I'm at your service."

He was proud of himself, as well he should be. She felt boneless. Mary had never dreamed of such luscious languor. The thought of returning to her room—the thought of walking—seemed most impractical if not impossible.

He brushed a tear from her cheek. Odd. She didn't even know she had cried. Mary was not, in general, a crier. She didn't have time to be. Tears were useless—it was one of her firmly held beliefs. What on earth had happened to her?

"Wh-what was that?"

He misunderstood. "Just a French trick I learned on my Grand Tour. Did you like it?"

"Of course I did, you insufferable man. How could one not?" She'd read the words. *Cunnilingis. Gamahuche.* Harsh syllables that bore no resemblance to the actual thing.

He cupped her damp cheek and stared down at her. "I didn't hurt you?"

From the frying pan into the fire.

"No. No, it was lovely. Will you do it all over again on Monday?"

Chapter

19

Mary Arden was extraordinary in her wrinkled dress, a small package of brazen innocence. Her pale copper hair had come loose from its pins and lay in disarray upon his pillow, her topknot a misnomer, no longer on top. Her eyes were bright with tears—happy ones, he presumed—and her cheeks pink. He wished he could see if the flush extended to the skin beneath the pleated black fabric, but he'd have to wait. It wouldn't be too much longer.

"Until Monday then," he replied, his voice rough. "I picked up a few other things on my travels as well." And he would be privileged to try all his techniques on this vixenish virgin.

Alec tucked a silky strand of hair behind her ear. She would need considerable setting to rights before she left his suite, even if she was wearing a veiled hat. It would be fatal for their plan for her to be recognized. She was right—they'd been pushing limits every time they saw each other. Alec had been unable to stay away, to rein himself in. He was behaving like the veriest love-struck fool.

Blast! He was not in love. Would never be again. But he was feeling something damned inconvenient.

"I should go back to my room."

He didn't want her to. Alec felt as if he were sending her into danger. What if Bauer overpowered her as easily as he had?

He'd be right next door with Oliver and the others, he reminded himself. Even his weedy valet Mac was stronger than he looked.

"Let me help you." He rolled off the bed with reluctance and picked her black straw bonnet up from the floor. Its brim had taken a beating and he smoothed it out with his clumsy hands.

It looked familiar. Alec paid attention to women's clothes, as so often he had paid for them and wanted to see if he was getting his money's worth. He'd seen this grim hat before, minus the veil, on Mrs. Evensong's gray head when he went to engage her services.

Perhaps aunt and niece shared clothes. Mary was too young to be encased in black, though. He found mourning clothes to be needlessly depressing—what good did it do the dead to have their female relatives mope about like a murder of crows? It was easier for gentlemen; he'd worn his black armband for Edith, of course. It was the least he could do, after failing her so badly.

Mary sat up and tried to make some progress with her hair.

"Here. Let me." Alec went to the shaving stand and picked up his silver-backed brush. Mac could clean the reddish hairs out of it and taunt him later. He slid the hairpins from her hair and placed them on the pillow. "Sit still and turn a little."

Alec knelt down behind her and ran the hairbrush through the glory of her hair. She tensed over a knot, and he placed a hand on her shoulder. "Sorry. Believe it or not, I'm not used to doing this."

Once he got the hang of it, it was comforting to perform such a domestic chore. Her hair rippled beneath the brush, threads of bronze and amber and gold shining bright. The plain three-letter word *red* did it injustice—her hair was the color of a painted medieval Madonna he'd seen on the same Grand Tour where he'd learned some distinctly sinful things.

Alec knew he had to send her on her way before he was tempted any further. He gathered up the rose-gold river of hair and wrapped it into a clump, then set to restoring the pins. Her hat would cover the mess he was making, and she could ready herself her own way for Bauer's visit.

"There. Good as new."

She rose and went to the angled mirror of the shaving stand, adjusting it to her much smaller height. "You'll never make a good lady's maid, I'm afraid." She smiled into the mirror, meeting his eyes.

He grinned back. "Then it's a good thing I'm a baron, isn't it?"

"What does a baron do? Tramp around the hills in a kilt and play the bagpipes all day?"

He hadn't noticed the little crease on her left cheek when she smiled before. What else was he going to discover? "Hardly. I'd scare the sheep on those hills, and the sheepdogs would howl and bite me for certain. It's beautiful scenery to tramp through, though—you'll see when you come to Raeburn Court."

He stood and passed her the ugly hat. "I have the usual dependents and properties and investments to look after." Which he'd neglected too long.

Mary tucked the messy bun into its crown and dropped her veil. "I'll see you later."

"Wait." He lifted the veil and touched her cheek, looking for the dimple. "A kiss for luck."

"Alec. We shouldn't. You've done quite enough today to bring me luck." Her eyes dropped in sudden shyness. A few minutes ago, the most private part of her was open to him.

"I can never do enough." He bent and kissed her cool wide forehead, then skimmed her nose to touch her objecting lips with his own. She shivered as he covered her mouth.

He intended to be simple—a quick brush of his lips against hers. But the kiss turned complex almost at once, their tongues tangling with near desperation. Her arms were wound around his neck, pulling him down to her level. He'd have to get her to stand on a footstool in the future.

Could she taste herself? His head was still full of the citrusy tang of her pleasure. She'd been so responsive, like a candle in flame. There were things he could do, things he could teach her in their time together so that she would never forget him.

Was that fair to her? She should marry, not slave for her aunt in a crabbed little office. Of course, the Evensong Agency was not crabbed at all—its rooms on Mount Street were spacious and well-appointed, clear to all clients that the concern was a prosperous one.

What was he doing thinking of work and office space? He had a lovely warm woman in his arms who should drive all rational, troublesome thought from his head. That's what women were good for—to divert, to ease, to tease. But Mary Arden made him examine his feckless past and made him want to be something he was not.

He was heading into dangerous territory, a place he'd been before with disastrous results. He'd thought to build a new life before with Edith, and marriage had only driven him back deeper into deviltry. Not that he'd done anything dozens of his peers did not do—he had plenty of company as a stage-door Johnny. His tastes weren't peculiar and didn't run to underage girls. In fact, he was about as dull a devil sinning as he could imagine.

He smiled as he kissed her, feeling the fool. Strange how a perfect innocent should be teaching him to examine the error of his ways.

Alec didn't want to think too far ahead. Getting through tonight would be enough for now. Shaming Bauer would go some way to eradicating his own shame. And then, he had bedding Mary Arden to look forward to.

Her lips were as soft as the rest of her, and his senses were clouded with her fragrance. Alec could get used to holding her, kissing her, teaching her to respond to his touch. How could she have escaped sensual experience all these years?

He thanked God for it. She was ripe for him. Hell, this had all been her idea! But he wasn't familiar with virgins—he'd have to be careful, more careful than he'd been with Edith. He'd frightened her to disgust, and he couldn't bear to do that with Mary.

She wasn't disgusted now. Her plump little fingers were feathering through his hair, giving him chills straight down the back of his neck to the base of his spine. But he was fully clothed. What would she do when she saw his manhood rising to impale her?

A man of his station had custom clothes and footwear made as a matter of course, but if he'd been a regular chap, he'd be doomed if he had to buy off the rack. He was simply too big. Everywhere. His usual flirts were always complimentary when they saw him in undress, although they hid their initial look of alarm quickly—they were actresses, after all.

He'd never hurt a woman, had trained himself to give as much pleasure as he got. His *chères amours* received more than jewels and trinkets in his keeping. But Mary Arden was not a voluptuary.

Could she tell he was nervous? It was as if twenty years had dropped away and he was a gawky youth. She pressed her sweet form against him as if to assure him she was confident of his abilities. He himself was not so certain, though the kiss promised all the heaven to come. He did not know whether the promise originated from Mary or him, and didn't care.

For once he didn't feel under suspicion. These last months, his wealth had bought companionship, if not peace. True, he'd paid Mary's aunt an exorbitant sum, but Mary was in his arms because she wanted to be.

Alec wanted her back on the bed, out of the dreadful dress, white legs splayed again, breathless, liquid, lush. He would center his cock over her neat copper nether hair and make her his in a gentle, achingly slow thrust.

Mary had a different idea, her hands now between them, pushing him away as the kiss turned to a series of frantic, ragged nibbles. He wasn't insulted. He could not mistake what she needed, yet had no time for. So this must stop, wind down somehow. He had to find a modicum of sense—Mac could come in at any minute. Tomorrow they'd have more time to explore the electricity between them.

He drew back and held her at arms' length. Her hat was tipsy again, her cheeks and lips red. Mary wore the dazed expression Alec so rarely saw in his paid lovers. One couldn't fake such a look, and it made his cock swell with impossible pride. He adjusted her hat and dropped the veil so no one else would recognize the signs of her submission.

"Do not let that vile lecher lay a finger on you or I'll have to kill him. You are *mine.*"

Her laughter was strained. "You sound very fierce, my lord. I suppose I'm yours for a little while at least. I begin to wonder if I've bitten off more than I can chew."

He pictured her swollen lips around his cock, minus any biting, and was swept with longing. Alec needed to let her go and get ready, and he needed a good stiff drink and a cold bath.

He led her from his bedroom to the parlor. "Let me look out into the hallway. If anyone does see you, they'll probably think you are your aunt. Hopefully they won't be aware that she left this afternoon." Alec opened the door. The carpeted hallway was empty. "All clear, my dear. I will see that you are safe tonight. Do not worry."

"Worrying is one of my specialties, but I trust you and Oliver." She gave him a little wave and hurried down the hall toward the stairs.

His rooms were much duller without her presence. Alec poured himself a drink and gazed out the window with disinterest. He had almost the same view at home, just from a different angle. Raeburn Court had been built into these hills far longer than the Forsyth Palace Hotel, but they were similar in architectural style. They both sported stone towers and odd metal decorations along the roof. It seemed the London architects had based their plans on his ancestral home, only doubling the size of it. Imitation was a form of flattery, but it had galled his brothers that their territory could be invaded by the public. He'd put up the barriers on the connecting path himself.

Raeburn Court was a wilder place, lacking the groomed trails through the forest that might attract trespassers. It was a real castle, as opposed to this trumped-up version, though Alec wouldn't mind importing some of the plumbing and electricity. All that was on his list this winter as he modernized the generations-old family seat. Future Raeburns would be grateful, although neither of his brothers seemed in any hurry to reproduce. Perhaps old Mrs. Evensong would put her matchmaking skills to work to ensure the succession. He pictured Evan's scowl at being introduced to a suitable girl. Nick would simply laugh and book another train ticket to some exotic place.

Alec rubbed his jaw, heavy with his afternoon beard. This trying to please Mary Arden was arduous, he thought with a rueful grin. Should he wait for Mac to return or just swipe his razor over his face?

To his shame, he'd seen the rosy rash on her white thighs from his earlier attentions. The poor girl now had something tangible to remember him by, and that couldn't be pleasant, although she did have her salve. He'd have to do better at Raeburn Court next week, even if he had to shave five times a day.

Chapter

20

For the past hour, Mary had jumped at every thump, shout, and knock from next door. The card party was lively, the waft of cigar smoke burrowing in under the connecting door between her room and Oliver's. They also shared a bathroom, and Mary felt herself go scarlet every time one of Oliver's guests relieved himself.

Apparently men could continue conversations as they pissed, which seemed very scandalous to Mary's way of thinking. She was simply unused to being in such close proximity to men and their rude behavior. When she had lived with her brother, Albert, and his family, she'd been stuck up in the attic with the servants, having been turned out of her own girlhood room above the store when the twins arrived. She was still living over the store so to speak, but males of any age were entirely absent upstairs on Mount Street. Hamblen lived in, as did Mrs. Norris, their housekeeper-cook. Mrs. Norris had begun her career as Norine de la Rue, and of the streets she had been until Aunt Mim took her in. Aunt Mim was an exacting but fair employer, Norine had proved a better cook than courtesan, and Mary's home life had been comfortable these last four years.

Would she remain comfortable now that Aunt Mim was reclaiming her authority? Only time would tell.

She checked her watch for the hundredth time, listening for Alec's rumbling laughter next door. At least one of them was having a good time. She had never been more anxious.

Her hair was down, tied at the nape with a blush-pink ribbon that matched the tea gown she'd decided on. Pink was a fragile color, girlish. Having red hair, Mary had not worn much pink in her life, as it was against some unwritten feminine rule. She thought she looked quite nice in it, however, and decided to canvas more secondhand shops for some wardrobe improvement when she returned to town. She couldn't wear pink in the office if she expected to be taken seriously—brown and gray and navy blue it would be—but she might have more time to have some sort of social life.

And she would have it in pink dresses.

It was just past ten o'clock. Was she imagining things, or had Oliver's room quieted some? She poured a glass from the carafe of springwater that had been delivered to her room and took a nervous sip. She had not requested it, but the Forsyth Palace Hotel had every amenity, including a turn-down service. Ha. As if she was incapable of folding over the white coverlet and fluffing her pillows by herself. The tray the maid had brought had come with a crystal dish of bonbons, too, but Mary had been too wound up to eat any. With her luck, she'd smear chocolate on her dress and get some stuck to her teeth.

Mary paced, then drank more water, wishing it was Raeburn's Special Reserve. Where was Bauer? Did he have a medical emergency that prevented him from keeping their appointment? So much depended upon his prompt arrival. Mary knew card games could last all night, but she couldn't—she was suddenly exhausted by the startling events of her day and wanted to do nothing but crawl under that turned-down coverlet and fall asleep.

She yawned, her mouth opening so wide her jaw cracked.

Goodness. If Bauer didn't come soon, she might miss his knock altogether. She sat down in one of the armchairs and closed her eyes. Just for a moment.

She did not hear him as he entered, or feel his fingers as he nimbly unbuttoned the front of her dress. It was the click of his Brownie camera that woke her.

She clutched at her gaping bodice, her head swimming. "D-Dr. Bauer! How long have you been here?"

Mary's room was blazing with lights. She had been aiming for a "romantic" atmosphere earlier, but every electric lamp had been turned on. She blinked and tried to shake herself awake. Her arms and legs felt leaden.

"Not too long, my dear. I knocked but you didn't answer. I thought, no wonder with all the noise in the next room. But then I find you sleeping like a fairy princess in your throne. So *schön*." His fingers stroked her cheek and Mary sank deeper into her chair.

"H-how did you get in?" She was quite sure her door had been locked.

He chuckled. "With a passkey, my love. So convenient, yes? I had wondered if I might find you in bed waiting for me. I confess I am a little sorry to find you still dressed."

And decided to help her out of her dress while she was asleep and then photograph her in dishabille. Dr. Bauer was even creepier than she had imagined.

But he must keep evidence to use against his conquests—pictures and letters to make them pay up. Mary glanced down to see if her corset was still firmly hooked. It was, thank God.

"I—I thought we w-would talk first," she said, stuttering without even trying to.

He pulled her up from the chair with alarming strength. "We shall be much too busy to talk, Fräulein Arden. I am taking you to heaven while your silly brother plays his games."

Mary untangled herself from his embrace. "I am horribly thirsty. Do you want some water?"

Bauer gave her an odd look. "No thank you, my love. But

water is good for the body. Adam's ale, I believe you English call it. Drink it—drink it all up." He tipped the carafe and splashed more water into her goblet. She swallowed a huge mouthful and then remembered last night and his little flask of clear liquid. Had he arranged to have her water drugged? Perhaps the chocolates were poisoned, too. He expected her to be too weak to fight him off.

She dropped the glass, where it rolled harmlessly away on the thick carpet.

"Oh dear. I am so clumsy. And I don't feel quite the thing." She really was woozy and warm. Mary needed to do something, but when? She felt mired in molasses, unable to form a plan.

"Ha! Then it is perfect that I, a doctor, am here. Let me help you out of these confining clothes. You women and your corsets. If you are not careful you will ruin your organs with all this tight-lacing."

Mary couldn't work up the energy to stop him. He spun her around and she heard the snipping sound of her corset strings being cut. Probably with surgical scissors, the fiend. The compression on her waist and abdomen relaxed, yet she held the front of the corset up with a trembling hand. This was not supposed to be happening this way.

He was tipping her backward on the bed now, covering her exposed throat with wet kisses. Mary shuddered and closed her eyes to stop the room from spinning. His hands were everywhere. She heard the corset clatter to the floor, felt her combination slide down and heard Bauer's grunt of satisfaction. Her nipples hardened in the cool evening air and then inside Bauer's mouth. She flailed ineffectually at his back, but was unable to beat him off.

He chuckled above her, his long fingers caressing her breast. "We shall take a photograph now, yes? Before and after. Before, you are worried a little. Silly girl. After, I make you a woman and you have a big smile on your face. No more nerves."

He arranged her body on the pillows. Mary was as

helpless as a rag doll, unable to stop him from tearing away fabric and ribbons. She watched with blurred vision as he picked up his camera and shot his six pictures, then reloaded the film.

"Now we get down to the business of lovemaking. But perhaps I should put something over your mouth. We don't want your brother hearing our fun." He glanced around the room for a handy gag and Mary clawed her way out of her lethargy.

"Alec! Oliver! Help! Help me!"

Her words sounded faint to her own ears, but they must have done the trick. Oliver burst through the connecting door, his guests hot on his heels.

"Jesus Christ! What is the meaning of this, Bauer? What have you done to my sister?"

The doctor stood frozen, his necktie slipping from his fingers. Alec pushed past Oliver and covered Mary with his coat. "You fuck your patients, Bauer? Isn't that against some sort of oath?"

"She—she invited me here. It meant nothing."

"Nothing?" Oliver sputtered. "My sister's virginity is nothing to you? You swine!" Oliver lunged for Bauer and grabbed him by the collar.

"Are you all right, Miss Arden?" Alec asked, his face white with rage.

"Dr-drugged. He put something in the water so he could . . . you know." Her eyes filled with tears. Another minute or two and it would have been too late for her. For them.

"I'll never forgive myself for this," Alec said, and he knocked Bauer to the carpet with one crunching blow as Oliver let him fall.

"Here now." The elderly judge—Mary couldn't remember his name—placed a hand on Alec's shoulder. "Don't trouble yourself with this foreign bit of rubbish. We'll report him to the manager."

"He's part owner of the hotel," one of the other gentlemen

said. "I bet he's been doing this kind of trick ever since it opened."

Mary nodded. "He t-told me he would cure my nerves like he c-cured the others." Her lips felt numb. It was a struggle to get the words out.

Another stranger loomed over her. "He didn't—"

"N-no. Thank you for coming to rescue me." The dam had burst and Mary was sobbing for real now. One of the men went for the pitcher of water.

"No! It has something in it. I can barely move."

That was enough for Alec. He kicked Bauer even though the doctor was still cowering on the floor. "Get up, you blackguard. And get out."

"You! You orchestrated this." Bauer glared up at Alec, wiping the blood from his mouth.

"What on earth are you talking about?" Oliver interjected. "Get out of my sister's room before I call the authorities."

"You'd best leave the premises before word gets out of your proclivities. No one will come here to take your kind of 'cure,'" one of the men said. "I have the power to shut down the hotel. One word in my newspaper of what I've witnessed here and the place is finished."

The newspaperman. Alec's school friend. Mary had a piercing pain at her temple. She wished everyone would leave. "The pictures," she said groggily.

Oliver picked up the camera. "You took pictures of Mary in this state?" Mary thought he might pitch the camera at Bauer's head, but instead he threw it out the window, where it smashed below.

"We'll go down to talk to Prescott. He'll find another doctor if he knows what's good for his paycheck. Don't worry, Arden. Our lips are sealed. Your sister is the victim here. No one would believe she lured Bauer up here—she isn't the type."

Mary was too exhausted to be insulted. So she didn't appear attractive enough half-undressed and wrapped in

Alec's jacket, her hair every which way? Fine. She didn't want to be pawed or slobbered over ever again.

"I'll go down and make sure Bauer packs up," Alec said. "Oliver, take care of Ma—Miss Arden. Order her some tea and put a dash of Raeburn's Special Reserve in it to settle her."

"If I didn't know better, Raeburn, I'd think this was all an elaborate hoax so I couldn't recoup my losses," a mustachioed fellow said. "Quite an evening, quite an evening. Let's go speak to Prescott, gentlemen, and give Miss Arden the privacy she needs."

Alec dragged Bauer up from the floor and pushed him out the door, followed by the other men. Oliver raked a hand through his blond curls and looked down at her. "By Jove, that was a close thing. I'm so sorry, Mary. I kept wandering over to the door all night. Even went into to the bathroom half a dozen times. I hardly heard you when you finally called."

"Sit down. I'm seeing two of you." When she and Alec had "practiced," she'd never expected drugs to be involved. How lucky that she'd had only a few sips of the water. "We should have that water tested to see what he used. I wonder if he drugged everyone to get his way with them."

"I suppose we'll never know. No wonder it was easy for him to blackmail the girls. He had photographic proof. What a bastard."

"Th-thank you, Oliver." She reached for his hand.

"I didn't do half enough. Raeburn got his licks in, though."

Mary pulled up the coat. It smelled of cigars and Blenheim Bouquet and Alec. "I hope that won't seem odd to the witnesses."

"It was all so confusing when we came in, I doubt they paid much attention. All eyes were on you—Raeburn's jacket doesn't quite cover everything."

Mary realized her useless bare legs were still splayed on the bed. "Get me a blanket, Oliver, would you? I really can't move."

"What have I been thinking?" he cried. He dashed into his room and came back with his own white coverlet, tucking it tenderly around her quaking body. "Do you want me to call room service for tea?"

"No. Just fetch a glass of liquor for me. If there's any left."

"I probably drank more than I ought to have, I was so edgy. I'll be right back."

Mary shut her eyes. So much for best-laid plans. But at least Bauer was gone and couldn't assault any more young women here.

What if he got another position and tried the same thing? Mary's head hurt too much to think of it. Perhaps Oliver's guests could spread the truth somehow and prevent Bauer from repeating his repellent behavior.

Mary felt filthy. His hands and mouth had been on her, leaving an invisible trail of slug slime. What she wanted was her drink and a hot bath and several nights' sleep. She sipped the spirits that Oliver handed her and asked him to run her a bath. She couldn't trust the maids at the hotel to come up and help her. For all she knew they were in Bauer's thrall. The girl who had brought the tray this evening had such an innocent freckled face.

Looks could be deceiving. She knew that firsthand after masquerading as her aunt these past four years.

Oliver emerged from the bathroom. "It's ready when you are, Mary. I'll make sure you're not disturbed."

"We're leaving first thing tomorrow morning," Mary said, sitting up on the bed holding up the bits and pieces that covered her.

"I think that's wise. We'll go directly to Raeburn Court, yes?"

Mary paused. Was that where she wanted to go? Was it not safer to take an express straight back to London and put all of this misbegotten adventure behind her?

She had come close to being robbed of her most sacred self. She once had thought to offer that part of her to Alec

Raeburn, but did she really want to go through with it? What if his touch was every bit as disgusting as Bauer's had been?

"I don't know, Oliver. I'm going to have to sleep on it."

If she *could* sleep.

Chapter

21

Alec had argued—quietly, so as not to upset Mary—with Oliver, but the boy was obdurate. No way was he going to permit Alec to see Mary tonight, and that was final. The door had not been slammed in his face due to the late hour, but it may as well have been.

It had taken Alec some time to get Bauer packed up and sent on his way, wherever that might be. Alec didn't care where the doctor wound up as long as the hotel driver he'd roused ferried him far enough from Mary Arden. It was now after one o'clock, and Alec's bruised knuckles stung. Bauer had not gone without a tussle.

But he had gone without his hotel skeleton key. Alec had confiscated all the photographs and letters hidden in the man's sock drawer and turned his pockets out just in case he'd missed anything else incriminating. The key had elicited a gleam in Bauer's eyes, which boded ill for the safety of any future guest. Alec was determined to detach Bauer legally from the consortium. In the meantime, he'd see to it the doctor could not sneak into anyone else's room.

The cold key burned into Alec's palm. Dare he disturb

Mary and incur Oliver's wrath? He had a near virulent need to see that she was well and safe.

And a need to apologize. He'd subjected her to the predations of a monster. No paycheck was worth what she had gone through tonight, and Alec vowed to make it up to her somehow. Thank God her aunt had left else he'd be wearing his guts for garters.

Edith had written nothing of being drugged in her diary. Perhaps Bauer did not do that to every victim—some must have been more of a sure conquest than others. But Alec should have suspected what Bauer was capable of.

Alec sagged against the hallway wall. He should go to bed and try to put the past behind him for just one night. Maybe Edith would not come to him in a panic in his dreams, and if she did, he would listen this time. Vengeance was cold comfort when he was failing another woman in his care. Mary Arden had made a narrow escape, and it was his fault for underestimating Josef Bauer.

He had to see her, even if it meant just watching her sleep. Alec fitted the master key in the lock and turned the handle. A brass lamp was still lit at her bedside, making his job easier. She looked terribly small in her bed, her face as white as the coverlet. There was a groove between her brows, as if her dream were a puzzle she had to solve, and her braid looked darker. Alec reached out to touch the end that curled on the pillowcase—it was damp. She must have bathed after he left, to wash the stain of Josef Bauer from her skin, even from her hair. His heart contracted with pity.

Alec wondered if she always slept with a light on, or if the evening's events had frightened her so she saw danger in the shadows. Another burden on his doorstep.

Well, he'd seen her and would have to be satisfied for now. He took a step backward to leave and stumbled over something soft. A pillow. Its harmlessness did not prevent him from uttering a quick curse. His whispered oath had the unfortunate result of waking Mary, and she sat straight up in bed, eyes wide.

Blast. No quick escape, and from the look on her face,

he was about to receive a well-deserved set-down. "It's only I, Mary. Dinna fash yourself. I'll just be going."

She blinked. "Wh-what are you doing here?"

She had the sense to whisper. Oliver would be in here like a shot if the connecting door was still unlocked. Alec didn't want to hurt the boy if he had to defend himself. Mary might rise up and bash him, too.

"I came to see if you were all right. Are you?"

"I was. Go away." The groove on her forehead deepened.

"I canna. Not until I've said my piece. I am so sorry for what happened tonight. To have put you in danger as I did—I don't think I'll ever forgive myself." Could she hear his sincere shame?

"Is he gone?"

No need to ask whom she meant. "Aye. I put him in the wagon myself."

She glared at his hand. The silver key glowed in the lamplight. "And stole his key."

"To protect you, and anyone else." Alec dropped it on her bedside table. "I only used it because Oliver wouldn't let me in. He told me you were settled in for the night, but I had to see you for myself."

"It took me forever to fall asleep," Mary said, sounding grumpy.

"I'll sit with you until you do again." He could hold her, keep vigil.

Try to keep his hands still.

Mary lifted a gingery brow. "Oh, yes, that will be relaxing. A great hulking man like you at the end of my bed watching my every breath and twitch."

He couldn't even be angry at her description. He was a clumsy clod. "I swear I won't say a word."

"You won't have to. I'll *feel* you there." She pushed a loose strand of wet hair behind her ear. "I suppose we should talk anyway. About Monday."

Alec's heart lurched. He'd already worked it out in his head—she wouldn't be ready to engage in an affair with him or anyone by Monday, if ever. "We don't have to do anything. I promise not to even touch you, unless you ask, and I don't expect you to. After your ordeal here, I don't imagine you have much faith in men."

Her mouth formed a perfect o. "How did you know what I was thinking?"

"I'm not a complete dunce. If I were in your shoes, I'd be throwing breakable objects at my head for dragging you into this. But you deserve a holiday after what happened. We may not be fully staffed, but I shall see to your comfort personally."

"You want to be a lady's maid." She almost smiled.

"Not just any lady, Mary. Yours." And damn, if he didn't mean it. Her current fragility appealed to his honor, though he well knew her boldness was lurking in abeyance.

She wore a very prim and proper white lawn nightgown that was buttoned up to her chin. Alec thought it was the most alluring thing possible, and cursed himself for it. If he wanted her to trust him, he'd have to get control of his primal urges.

She'd nearly been raped. Of course she didn't want to go to Raeburn Court and carry out her crackpot idea. He sat down gingerly at the edge of her bed, trying hard not to hulk. "It will be all right, Mary. A few days in the mountain air, some good food—"

"I thought your housekeeper left."

Blast. He really would be offering her potluck. Maybe he could kidnap one of the cooks from the hotel for a week. "We'll manage. There's a girl. Katie. And my man Mackenzie is a dab hand in the kitchen, a regular jack-of-all-trades. The only thing he doesn't want to do is drive."

"You have a car?" There was definite interest in her voice.

"To be sure. Two, in fact. I keep one in town and one up here. My two-seater Pegasus is in the hotel garage at the moment. I thought we'd drive over to Raeburn Court in it tomorrow. We can send a carriage back for Oliver and Mac. I haven't lost anyone from my stable yet." He had a passel of young grooms who were eating more than his horses.

Her frown deepened. How he'd like to erase it with a

thumb. "I don't know if that's wise. It might look like collusion."

"What could be more natural than me offering the Arden family a respite from their ruined stay at the Forsyth Palace Hotel? It would be the least I can do as a hospitable Highlander. You cannot want to stay here."

"Well, no, naturally not." She shifted back against the pillows. "Actually, I was thinking of returning to work. To London, that is."

That was an insupportable idea. Alec took her hand firmly in his. "I won't hear of it, Mary. You need to rest."

"I seem to recall I was finally doing that before you barged in." There was no sting in her words, though, and she made no effort to pull her hand away.

He looked down at it, plump and white and ringless. It was a capable little hand, safe in his palm. Holding it made him feel safe, too. "I didn't mean to frighten you."

"You didn't actually. You don't scare me at all."

"You are a brave woman, Miss Arden. I—I admire you."

"Thank you, Lord Raeburn. The feeling is mutual. You have stopped a vicious predator, and the hotel management should be grateful."

He'd send off his letters to the members of the consortium on Monday. Gossiping tongues could be unleashed and the trust Bauer had from society would be in tatters. The threat of exposure from Rycroft's newspaper and possible legal action from Judge Whitley and his barrister friend should be enough to detach Bauer from the business.

And Edith's secret was still safe.

"I understand why you want to put all this behind you, but I wish you'd consider staying with me for a little while."

Alec could practically see her thinking, the little gears whirring behind her forehead. He gave her hand a squeeze. "I'm sorry. I'm being a nuisance, aren't I? I've got no right to badger you about anything after what you've been through. Forget I said anything. Forget I came." He started to stand, but she didn't let go.

"Shh. Don't go off in a wave of nobility. Did you mean it when you said you'd stay with me until I fell asleep?"

"Aye."

She scooted over. The bed was narrow and he was not. "If I could put my head on your shoulder . . ."

"My shoulder would be honored." Between them they arranged the pillows and blankets.

"You should take your tie off."

So he should. It had blood spatters on it anyhow. His jacket and shoes followed, but he sensed that was all he would be permitted. He angled himself, not quite sitting, not quite lying down. Mary nestled against him in the crook of his arm and sighed.

And that was all. There was no banter or chatter or kissing, and certainly nothing else of a warmer nature. Alec had never spent the night with a woman in such a chaste, almost brotherly way, and chuckled to himself. Pray God she couldn't feel his erection or the erratic beat of his heart.

He listened for her steady breathing, which was not long in coming. How Alec envied her being able to fall asleep again after the night they'd had. He reached over with his free arm and extinguished the bedside lamp, plunging the room into murky grayness. It would not be too many hours before the sun climbed over the mountains and the new day began. Alec looked forward to driving Mary on the winding road that led to Raeburn Court. He was proud of his home, from the miniature castle gatehouses at its entrances to the acres of slate roof he'd played on as a boy, much to his nanny's displeasure. He and Evan and Nick had been wild little things, and were not really so evolved now.

Well, Alec was trying to be less wild. He had a young woman in his arms and had not even unfastened a button or stolen a kiss. Mary trusted him to keep her safe, and he would do anything to earn her regard.

He shut his eyes and concentrated on the dark around him. He smelled Blenheim Bouquet and laundry soap. Heard soft little snorts. Felt Mary quake against him. He held her tighter and rested his chin on the top of her head, counting sheep and clouds and blades of grass. Nothing set his mind at rest, and his body burned for what could not be his yet. Perhaps never, and it was entirely his fault. Women were sensitive creatures—look how they acted when they saw a harmless mouse. Leaping up on chairs and screaming. Mary had been Bauer's helpless victim, unable to leap and scream. She might not ever get over her fears.

Edith had never gotten over her fright of Alec, even when he'd bent over backward to give her everything he thought she wanted. Maybe he was doomed when it came to the weaker sex.

Ha. He imagined Mary Arden's sharp elbow in his gut. She might be small, but she was not weak. Tomorrow they could start fresh and put Bauer and the Forsyth Palace Hotel out of mind.

Chapter

22

Sunday, June 12, 1904

*M*ary woke from a jumbled dream, awash in perspiration. Someone had turned off the light. The blanket
was stifling, and so heavy it must be made of lead. She
couldn't seem to push it off either.

Then the blanket snored. Of course. She was squashed
halfway under her knight errant, Lord Alec Raeburn, and
too damp to enjoy it properly.

He'd offered to stay with her until she fell asleep, but they
both had been in the arms of Morpheus these past few hours.
Mary wasn't sure when his shoulder had given way to the
lace-edged pillow or when his large hand landed on her left
breast, but apart from the heat she was quite comfortable.
His breaths tickled her scalp, and it seemed a shame to
wake him.

She didn't really want to. How cozy this was, spooning in
her single bed. All panicky thoughts of Josef Bauer had disappeared, at least for the time being. Mary was not going to
permit herself to fall into fear. Bauer had not managed to really

harm her last night, and she wouldn't let his bogey do the job now. Alec had promised to keep her safe, and while they'd both underestimated Bauer's vileness, she was still intact.

Did she wish to remain that way? That was the question. Alec Raeburn was nothing like the doctor. While he probably had more female conquests, his women had been willing—nay, eager if rumors were to be believed.

It was only Edith who had thrown herself away on Dr. Bauer, and then out a window.

Mary should feel more pity for the girl, but if she was honest with herself, what she felt was anger. Edith Raeburn had hurt her husband in a fundamental way. She had to know her death would blight his life forever.

But Edith hadn't cared. She'd chosen Josef Bauer over Alec, which only proved the girl must have been mad.

Mary burrowed a bit deeper into the haven of Alec's long body. A woman could get used to this warm strength beside her. Alec was solid everywhere. Hard. His only sign of softness was the adorable dimple in his chin.

Mary squinted at the crack between the drapes. It was not yet dawn, but she felt refreshed. Where would she go today, and who would she go with? Oliver was game for anything, he'd said as he tucked her in last night. He'd been just like a real brother to her—no, better, because she'd never live long enough to see such a kind expression on her real brother Albert's face. Now if she'd been a mis-shelved tin of biscuits or an aging loin of pork, Albert might concern himself with her. To him, she was just an extra pair of hands in the store and at home with his boys.

Well, that was one thing settled—Mary would not be going back to Oxfordshire.

To London? Revitalized Aunt Mim would have everything shipshape by Monday morning. She could terrorize the giggling typists as Mary had never been able to do. Before she left the hotel, Mary would write a note to encourage that governess she met in the woods yesterday to apply for Oliver's position. The girl seemed competent enough to run the entire Evensong enterprise in five years' time.

So, that left Raeburn Court. Mary could go there and go through with her scandalous proposal. Or not. Alec had assured her she could merely rest for a few days to get the taste of Josef Bauer out of her mouth.

Alec wouldn't touch her. He had promised.

He was touching her right now, though. True, he was unconscious, but his fingers were definitely surrounding her nipple and his hips were cradling her derriere. He was, if she was not mistaken, rather harder in one spot on his body than the rest. If the man were awake, he'd know he'd miscalculated by several inches, thrusting dreamily against the small of her back with a gentleness that was quite at odds with what Mary suspected he was capable of. But she enjoyed his tentative touch. Even in his sleep, Alec Raeburn was a desirable man.

She had nothing to worry about. There were layers of clothing and some bed linen still between them. Mary did not have to decide right this minute how far she'd let Alec go when he woke up. She didn't know yet, but had decided the Pegasus alone was enough motivation to get her to Raeburn Court. She owned shares in the motor car company, and had a keen interest in seeing how the automobile handled the primitive Highland roads.

And if Alec permitted her to drive it, all the better. She hadn't dared to do anything but be a passenger the few times George Alexander took her for a spin before she invested in his company. He'd been surprised at the amount she had handed over to him, but she'd always been careful with her money. Mary had had little leisure time in which to spend it these past four years, and the Evensong Agency fees were rather exorbitant. Aunt Mim always said rich people were suspicious if they weren't asked to pay enough, so Mary asked, and asked a lot. Most were happy to pay, and frequently they forked over a bonus if Mary had been able to accomplish what had originally looked like an impossible task.

Nothing was impossible. Well, of course Mary couldn't flap her arms and fly, but she was sure one day a proper flying machine would be built. Just a few months ago two

American brothers were reported to have had sustained periods of flight in a glider until a gust of wind smashed it up.

Mary was interested in the modern age. Science. Engineering. Things a mere woman was supposed to be ignorant of. She'd spoken at length to the lift operator at the hotel, wondering if such a device could be installed in Mount Street. Why shouldn't she learn about things that would make life more convenient? One never knew when such information should prove useful.

Mary had an inquisitive, generally tidy mind, much like a set of file drawers where everything was put in its place for future reference. She wasn't sure where she'd put Alec Raeburn, however. He would not fit in any drawer, and it wasn't because of his size.

He grumbled and stirred behind her, his hand pressing more firmly on her bosom. Mary hoped he wouldn't be embarrassed when he woke up to find that he'd so thoroughly immobilized her. Not that she wanted to jump out of bed—Alec's closeness made her feel protected. Cherished.

But she probably should try to extricate herself and go to the toilet. Brush her teeth and make some semblance of order to her hair. Call room service for some coffee and sweet rolls, maybe even eggs. She was famished.

Send Alec back to his room.

She flattened herself in an attempt to slide out from under his arm with no success. His grip grew tighter, and he moaned in a rather intriguing way. There was nothing to be done but wriggle against him and give him a shove.

The result was not what she expected. Alec flipped her on her back and nuzzled her neck. His breath was hot, and sent chills straight to her toes. That did not make any sort of scientific sense at all.

"Be still, you naughty wench. It's too early," he mumbled, giving some attention to her right breast now.

Mary was many things, but a naughty wench was not one of them. Did he even know who she was?

"Lord Raeburn, unhand me." The sharpness of her voice could have cut diamonds.

His face was close enough to hers to see his brow furrow, his eyes blink beneath their lids but not open. She put a hand on his rough cheek and pinched him.

He reared backward and nearly fell off the bed. "Ow! What's that for then?"

"You are taking liberties," Mary said, feeling somewhat out of charity with him.

"Liberties! Don't be daft. You didn't complain when I—" She knew the moment he was fully awake; his body was in full retreat, scrambling to the edge of the bed.

"Holy hell. Forgive me, Miss Arden."

"I think you might as well call me Mary again. You did sleep in my bed."

"And that's all I did, if I remember correctly. I've still got most of my clothes on, don't I?" He tried to smooth his wild hair down to no avail. "I'm sorry if I frightened you. I was having a dream and got carried away."

"And thought I was someone else."

If there had been more light in the room, she could have seen whether he had the grace to blush. He probably found himself waking up in a woman's bed on a regular basis. Mary had not had a male in her bed save for the time her nephew Eddie had the chicken pox and she was supposed to keep him from scratching all night long.

Alec sat up and pulled the lamp cord. His hair was even worse than she thought, his face shadowed by black bristles. He looked dangerous and, if she were honest, decidedly delectable in a shipwrecked pirate sort of way.

"I am sorry. I promised to keep watch over you and I've failed." He sounded contrite.

She shrugged. "I never expected you to stay awake looking at me. That would have been silly."

"Nevertheless. You put up with enough pawing last night without me adding to it this morning."

Mary did not want to talk about Bauer. Not this morning, possibly not ever. She had made a miraculous escape and was not one to look a gift horse in the mouth. What good would it do to dwell on the terror she had felt, her limbs useless, her voice hard to find? She'd been encased in drugging amber.

"Enough," she said briskly. "*Bauer* may not be a four-letter word, but for our purposes it will become one, not to be uttered unless one wants one's mouth washed out with soap. I have no wish to relive last night and be tormented with your remorse. It will be I who will have to keep assuring you that it's all right, and my bravery may falter. I don't want to be brave. I don't want to think about what could have happened. I want to be normal. I am just fine."

Alec raised a dark eyebrow. "No tears and recriminations?"

What was the point? Is that how Edith behaved? Mary was not Edith. "None. I knew there were risks when I— when Aunt Mim proposed the job to me. I wanted a bit of travel and adventure."

"And got a little more than you bargained for."

Her mind was made up. There was to be no more foot-dragging or hand-wringing. She wasn't getting any younger. "I do hope so."

Now both brows were raised. "Are you saying what I think you're saying?"

Mary gave him what she hoped was a naughty wench smile. "I might be. Let's just take all of this one day at a time. After breakfast I will pack and you can drive me to Raeburn Court. We'll see what happens."

Alec picked her hand up from the counterpane and kissed her fingertips. "I shall endeavor to give you all the travel and adventure you can bear. I presume young Oliver will be accompanying us?"

"Yes." Oliver had spent some time at her bedside, ultimately confessing he had been flirting with Alec's valet. Mary wondered why the boy was always attracted to the help, but decided it was none of her business. Oliver could have his own travel and adventure, as long as he was careful about it. She wouldn't want Alec to fire his servant—he had precious few of them as it was.

"Capital. I guess I'd better sneak off before the corridors become crowded. I'll meet you in the lobby. Can you be ready by ten o'clock?"

She could be ready now if Alec wanted her in a damp, clinging nightgown.

Before she had the chance to agree, an unearthly howl sounded in the hallway and bells began to ring.

"Fire!" Alec scooped her out of the bed and ran to the door.

Mary sniffed. "I don't even smell smoke!" She put a hand to the wood but it was simply room temperature. "You should put me down. Go wake Oliver."

That proved unnecessary. Oliver burst through the connecting door, wearing a handsome Chinese robe and nothing else. He stumbled to a stop at the sight of Alec in his wrinkled evening clothes, Mary in his arms. "I say. Good morning. Let's evacuate, what? But I think you should let me carry Mary. I'm her brother and all. Or supposed to be."

Mary rolled her eyes. "Nobody needs to carry me. Alec, put me down. Oliver, fetch me my slippers. They're under the bed."

Suitably shod, she followed the men at a run down the staircase. Alec had a death grip on one hand and Oliver the other. The shrill alarm and endless bells had done their job. Other scantily clothed guests, some with suitcases, tumbled down the stairs after them. Bleary-eyed hotel staffers directed all of them out the double doors to the sloping front lawn of the hotel.

Once they were outside, everything appeared completely normal in the misty morning light. Flames were not leaping behind windows, smoke was not billowing. Of far more interest than the building to Mary were her fellow guests, who in their state of dishabille did not look like titans of society and industry. Several ladies and gentlemen were missing their wigs and teeth, and, in one case, eyebrows.

Some were wrapped in sheets only. Mary thought it a very good thing that there were no Brownie cameras to be seen in the crowd.

"What's happening?" Alec asked a young waiter who seemed to be assigned to their section of lawn.

"One of the maids spotted a fire outside a tower suite. Nothing damaged but a bit of carpet and a scorched door, but old Prescott thought he'd better sound the alarm just in case. They put it out quick enough, but every corner's being checked. There will be hell to pay today. You lot don't like to have your peace cut up."

"At these rates, who could blame us? But I don't expect you get your fair share," Alec said in sympathy.

The waiter snorted. "Prescott's a pinch-penny, that's for sure. I have me mum and sisters to support, and there's little enough work in these parts."

"What about Raeburn Court?" Mary asked.

"Work for that murderer? I should say not. Funny thing— he's staying with us temporarily, and 'twas his suite that had the fire. The Lord's work, for sure. Bolt of lightning, I bet."

Mary put her hand on a stunned Alec's arm. "You didn't take all his keys."

Chapter

23

*T*he devil. When Alec was allowed back into the building, his stocking feet soaked in dew, he went directly to his rooms with the hotel manager. Not only was the varnish burned off the door and the rug in front of it in scorched ruins, but another fire had been set at the interior ramp door that served as the hotel staff's service entry. Both egresses from the suite would have been blocked, and Alec didn't much fancy his chance of survival if he'd been there to jump from his top floor window. Prescott tripped all over himself in apology. After the contretemps last night, it was clear to both of them what had happened.

Mac had not been sleeping in the dressing room, either, thank God. Alec had seen him safe and sound on the lawn, wearing a bedspread wrapped like a Roman toga. He decided he didn't care whose bed Mac had slept in—it was a mercy they were both still alive.

"I shall of course move you to another suite, even if it means rearranging some other guests," Prescott said, rubbing his hands nervously.

"That won't be necessary—the Ardens and I are leaving this morning. And it wouldn't do much for the hotel's reputation to inconvenience anyone more than they've already been inconvenienced. You were lucky someone caught the fire in time. I'd like to speak to her, if I may."

"Of course, of course. One of our girls was on her way up with an early breakfast tray. The staff is well-trained to respond in case of emergency. She did everything right."

Including removing the tray she must have dropped when she put out most of the fire with a bucket of sand in the hallway. There were only a few grains remaining on the wet rug to show anything had ever been there.

Alec fished for his room key. The doorknob was still warm to the touch. The sitting room was just as he'd left it before the card party, an unfinished glass of Raeburn's Special Reserve on the table. Mac had been buttling the party and must not have come back to clean up before he sought his own adventure.

"Notify the hotel garage to ready my car and bring it to the entrance at ten. We'll need a carriage for the luggage and my manservant and Miss Arden's brother as well. My Pegasus only seats two, and I don't want them here any longer than necessary."

"Of course, my lord."

"You will tell me if Bauer turns up to make more trouble."

Prescott nodded vigorously. "We'll bar him from the grounds. I don't want any difficulties with the authorities, Lord Raeburn. This fire is bad enough to unsettle the clientele. We've taken every precaution so that our guests feel safe. I don't know what's come over the man to do something like this."

"This is the least of it. He's been compromising his female patients since the hotel opened, probably before that, too. A bit of burnt wood is nothing to the ruination of a woman's reputation. He preyed upon his victims, then blackmailed them to keep silent. You know he drugged Miss Arden to get her to be cooperative. I'll see him stripped of his medical license if I can."

"Just as you should, just as you should," Prescott said,

radiating obsequiousness. "But if you can avoid implicating the hotel—I had no knowledge of his activities, I swear. The hydrotherapy end of the operation was entirely in his hands. I don't know where we'll get another physician on such short notice. The nurses can act in his absence, I suppose. They know the procedures."

"I don't give a damn how you solve your staffing problem," Alec replied. "Now if you'll excuse me? Send that maid up so I can reward her. A breakfast tray, too, please. And make sure Miss Arden and her brother get something to eat before they go."

Prescott hurried off. The fellow looked like he was coming down with a splitting headache. His day would probably not get better with more than one hundred excitable and sleep-deprived guests to placate. Society was fickle and spoiled and expected first-class treatment at a first-class resort. June was just the beginning of the hotel's season and if word got out of any difficulties, an avalanche of canceled reservations would result. The consortium wouldn't like that after their massive investment.

Mac returned in his toga, looking sheepish, and got straight to packing them up. A tentative knock on the door brought the heroine maid and his breakfast tray. Alec handed over a fistful of his winnings and made an offer of employment, which she blushingly refused. She'd heard he was a murderer, too.

Alec shared some of his breakfast with his valet, feeling just a touch nervous about the next couple of days. At a quarter to ten, the porter arrived for his belongings. He'd traveled lightly, being only two miles away, and visiting his house almost daily to get whatever he'd forgotten. The refurbishment was still ongoing, and Alec resigned himself to the sound of hammers and piles of sawdust.

He'd sent no word of Mary's arrival, for he really had no one to send word to. One of the remaining kitchen maids was ostensibly in charge of feeding the rest of the servants, and might be persuaded to expand her repertoire. The bedrooms were mostly shut up—if he had to, he'd remove the

Holland covers and prepare them himself. He'd promised Mary respite, and he didn't think she'd want to be saddled with a broom and bucket.

Maybe he could borrow his brother Evan's housekeeper. She didn't hold him in too much aversion and had a rather easy job looking after his little brother. Evan was so consumed with the distillery he was hardly ever home, and never noticed what was put in front of him as long as it was hot.

The phone rang. Mac picked up the receiver before Alec had a chance to move.

"That was Prescott himself. You've put the fear of God into him, I reckon. The car's downstairs, and the hotel carriage is loaded and ready for Mr. Arden and myself. Shall we go, my lord?"

Alec looked around the handsomely appointed room. He wouldn't miss it. "Yes. I did what I came to do. We're meeting the Ardens downstairs."

Mac wrapped his arms around his too-narrow chest in a pose that was nevertheless intimidating. Alec sighed. "What is it?"

"If that doctor fellow tried to burn us out up here, what's to stop him from coming to Raeburn Court?"

Alec felt a sudden chill. "He wouldn't dare."

"Oh, wouldn't he? You've got the woman he wanted. You've wrecked his career. What's he got to lose?"

Damn. Mac was right. There were too many doors into Raeburn Court, and, God knows, too many windows and too few men on the estate to protect them all twenty-four hours a day. The nearest magistrate was in Pitcarran. Alec would have to go talk to him once Mary was settled. No doubt Bauer had friends at the hotel who could help him hide. He didn't trust Prescott an inch.

He should have gone with Bauer last night to make sure he left the area. Driven him down to Edinburgh himself. But he'd wanted to get back to Mary.

"You make a good point. What do you suggest?"

"Take Miss Arden somewhere else."

"Where?" Paris might be lovely this time of year, but he didn't think Mary would agree to be his public mistress.

Mac clapped his hands. "What about the north gatehouse? No one lives there."

"And hasn't in donkeys' years. The place must be encrusted in dust. And it's so *small*." Alec had been looking forward to showing Mary his house. Even in its partly renovated state, it was imposing. The gatehouse was its exact replica, save for the fact it was a tiny fraction of its size.

"I could take care of that for you. No one would think to look for you there. We can put it about that you're still at Raeburn Court until Bauer is caught. I'm sure Mr. Arden would be game."

So that was where the wind blew. Alec had suspected his valet was attracted to Oliver at the card party. There had been a few smoldering gazes, which fortunately the other gentlemen present had overlooked. "Are you now?"

Mac blushed. "He seems like a fine fellow."

"And you look good in his bedspread."

"Och!" Mac was scarlet now. "You can fire me if you want."

"Now why would I want to do that? As long as you remain professional with me—such as you are, you cheeky devil—I have no objection to what you do in your off hours. But I fancy myself a modern man. There's no telling what other people might think. Or do," Alec warned. He'd been made to read his Bible along with his brothers and been to public school. Society was not in the habit of forgiveness when it came to transgressions of a sexual nature. Alec was probably going to Hell himself for the variations he'd enjoyed as a young cub.

Mac looked at his feet and spoke softly. "Don't you think I know that? I've had to hide my true self all my life."

"I'm sorry for it. But be careful with Oliver. He's younger than you are, and a bit impetuous. Miss Arden wouldn't want any harm to befall him, that I'm sure of."

"Yes, my lord." Mac gave him a wobbly smile.

He had been with Alec since before his marriage. Not a

lifetime, but the valet had served him well and knew his likes and dislikes. This morning's confession had not really come as a surprise, but it might make things awkward with Mary. Oliver might be her pretend brother, but there was real affection and concern between them.

But maybe she already knew. She did seem to know everything. Mary Arden had a wise head for someone as young as she was, almost as if she'd traded places with her elderly aunt.

He and Mac chose the stairs instead of the elevator. Oliver was pacing across the lobby floor while Mary sat serenely in one of the plush chintz-covered chairs, the picture of a late spring day. One would never know to look at her that she'd been drugged, attacked, and evacuated from a burning building in the space of twenty-four hours. She was in one of her demure white dresses, a straw bonnet pinned with pink roses atop her pale red hair. A gloved hand rested upon a white lace parasol.

"Ah! There you are, Lord Raeburn. How kind of you to run me down to the station for my return to London," Mary said in a carrying voice. A few heads turned in their direction.

Alec extended his arm. "Are you worried that Bauer will come looking for us at Raeburn Court?" he asked softly. "Mac is."

"I confess it crossed my mind. He shouldn't suspect me, but I fear you must be careful if he's still in the vicinity. The fire business wasn't well-planned, but he'll have time to get more creative."

"I should have had him arrested," Alec said as he led her down the steps to the waiting car. "In fact, I'm going to Pitcarran later today to lay charges, at least for the arson, even if I don't have proof. I'll try not to involve you in anything."

"I don't mind being involved. What he did was—was—was most ungentlemanly."

"That's a bit of an understatement." He tipped the mechanic and settled Mary in the passenger seat, giving her white dress a long look. "I'm afraid you're going to get dirty.

The road to Raeburn Court is not oiled. Hang on a minute."
He rummaged around in the storage box and came up with
his duster and a two pairs of goggles.

"Here, put these on."

The coat swam comically around Mary's petite figure.
"Should I take off my hat?" she asked, as she rolled back
the sleeves.

"If you value it at all."

Mary removed her hat, tucked it under her feet, and
pulled a silk scarf from her handbag. She tied it under her
stubborn little chin, looking oddly fetching, something like
a Russian orphan with her wide forehead and high cheek-
bones. "I've ridden before, you know. George—I mean, an
acquaintance of my aunt's is the owner of the Pegasus Motor
Company." She strapped on the goggles, still managing to
look adorable.

George, was it? A hot flush of jealousy swept through
Alec. "Have you? I shall endeavor to drive as well as he."
Alec turned on the petrol, switched on the ignition, checked
the commutator and lubricator. The engine started up with
a satisfying blast. He moved the speed lever from the
out-of-gear notch, and they were off down the long hotel
drive in a cloud of dust.

Goerge. Alec racked his brain, trying to remember the
man's last name. Some sort of industrialist who had his
fingers in a lot of pies. Surely he was too old for Mary, even
if he was rich as Croesus and forward-thinking. The automobile was the wave of the future. Drivers might be considered hobbyists now, but eventually motorcars would be
available to everyone. Alec was thinking of investing in the
company himself. He owned two models already. His car
in Town had room for more passengers, but he was glad to
be private with Mary now.

She said something, but he couldn't hear her over the roar
of the engine. He released his pressure on the driving pedal
and slowed. "Pardon?"

"I said," shouted Mary, "do you think you could give me
driving lessons?"

Driving lessons? A woman behind the wheel? He knew all about Dorothy Levitt, that madcap motorina who was busy breaking records in boats and automobiles, and he couldn't approve. Next the woman would be taking up aeroplanes. Even if she were instructing the Queen and her daughters, a woman wasn't meant to drive—it was unnatural. Mary Arden probably didn't know the difference between a pair of gas pliers and a pair of cutting pliers. There was much more to driving than holding the steering wheel and going forward. It was a dirty, dangerous, complicated business.

But Alec looked at the sparkle in her huge hazel eyes behind the goggle lenses and said, "We'll see." He hoped he could distract her in bed so she wouldn't think of anything with wheels for a week.

Chapter

24

This was thrilling! Rather like flying except from the comfort of a plump leather seat and no arm flapping required. Mary kept her hat still on the floor beneath the tip of her parasol, and lifted her face to the sun, freckles be damned. The profusion of late spring leaves shaded the road sufficiently so she wasn't afraid of sunburn.

The scent of fir trees and petrol exhaust made for an odd aphrodisiac, but Mary could not have been more aware of Alec Raeburn's physical presence. His hair blew backward in the wind, revealing his splendid profile, chiseled chin and formidable nose. He handled all the controls and levers with familiar aplomb, his feet dancing on the pedals on the floor.

The road they were on was not really designed for auto-mobile travel—in fact, it was not much better than a shep-herd's path—but Alec cruised effortlessly, avoiding bumps when he could and giving her a solicitous look when he couldn't. Conversation was more or less impossible over the noise, and that was fine. She'd have a day or two to talk to Alec Raeburn until her tongue was tired.

What else would she do with her tongue? The thought of

his kisses warmed her cheeks and other regions she was not supposed to think about.

After a blissful interval, they broke through the hedgerows. A snaking stone wall lined the road, leading to a charming gatehouse with miniature conical turrets. No one came out to greet them. Alec rolled the car to a stop, leaped from the vehicle, and pushed the wrought iron gates open.

"No more gatekeeper, I'm afraid." He shrugged. "Another defector. All the country mice think there are more opportunities in the city. And some of the boys went to war and didn't come back."

"I cannot imagine leaving such a place, for any reason," Mary said. Not even duty to King and country would pry her from these hills if she lived here. She could see Raeburn Court down the straight shot of the long driveway, a monumental Scots Baronial pile smaller but grander even than the Forsyth Palace Hotel. The grass on either side of the drive was a hayfield. He needed a flock of sheep to set it to rights if he couldn't hire some mowers.

"One gets bored, I do assure you. And you have not seen a Scottish winter." He tinkered with the car and they headed for the stone courtyard ahead. A large fountain, completely dry, stood in the middle of the cobbles. Alec pulled the car in front of the steps and cut the engine.

No one came out to greet them here, either. Mary picked up her slightly crumpled hat and waited for Alec to come around to her side of the car.

He waved a hand toward the empty entrance. "You can see why I need your aunt's services. Who knows how long we'd have to stand out here before someone came to the door? Money is not the issue—I've pots of it, more than I'll ever need."

Mary knew his financial circumstances. She always investigated her clients thoroughly. She took his hand and stepped out of the automobile. "The house was fully staffed when your wife lived here?"

Alec studied his feet. "Edith was not the easiest of mistresses, and we are rather isolated up here. It's always been difficult to run Raeburn Court, even in my mother's day—she had very exacting standards. Problems with the staff began back then and haven't improved much. After Edith passed away, they got much worse."

"I shall write to Aunt Mim at once. There are many anxious, hardworking applicants in our—I mean, in her files. A bit of snow and some silly rumors should not affect their enthusiasm for a good-paying job in a fine country home."

Alec raised a skeptical eyebrow. "I wish I could believe you. I'll get you settled and you can write to your heart's content. I'm going to ride down to Pitcarran and speak to the magistrate about Bauer. Get the local constables on their toes."

He had mentioned it before, but Mary had hoped he wouldn't leave her alone just yet. "On a Sunday?"

"There's no time to waste. Who knows what the man has in mind next? And we may discover that he's already on a train to Edinburgh, which would be a vast relief. I'll give you the grand tour of the house when I get back. But don't get too comfortable. Mac thinks it best if we decamp to the gatehouse."

"The building we passed on the way in?"

"No, the one on my northern boundary, through the home wood. It's more private, and we'll be out of the workmen's mess. The building looks just the same, though. My ancestors were keen on symmetry."

The gatehouse Mary had seen was like a child's castle. Staying in a place like that with Alec would be much cozier than in this stone fortress. They entered a hushed medieval-inspired hallway, replete with dusty suits of armor and weaponry on every wall. The massive fireplace was full of ashes. She heard the steady thud of a hammer down the hall. Goodness, the men were working on a *Sunday*. Alec must pay very well indeed.

He led her up the broad oak staircase to an enormous well-used library, leaded stained glass windows casting colorful patterns across the faded carpets. There were more books than Mary had ever seen in one place, and cracked leather sofas and chairs on which to read them.

"This is my territory, and my father's before me. I wouldn't let Edith disturb this room or the entry hall—somehow that seemed sacrilegious to the Raeburn clan. You can use my desk to write your letter, and wander about as you see fit. There is a modern washroom just next door."

He seemed proud of this homely space, and so he should be. It was an entirely masculine room, with scattered ancient Turkish carpets on parquet floors and enough hunting prints on the walls to choke a horse. Mary felt quite dwarfed beneath the high timbered ceiling.

"I'll let whoever I can find know that you're here so they can bring up a luncheon tray," Alec continued. "Fair warning, though, it might not be much. Mac is passable in the kitchen, but he's volunteered to get the gatehouse ready for us, and I believe your brother—that is, Oliver—might be roped in to help him. I will find someone to station outside the library door so you won't be all alone."

Mary examined an ancient globe in its circular stand. The room was filled with treasures, and she had to admit to herself she was not averse to doing a little snooping. "Surely that won't be necessary. We don't expect Bauer to jump out from behind a curtain, do we?"

"He'd be sneezing his head off from the dust if he tried," Alec said. "But I'd rather have you safe until I get back. One of the workmen might like a break. They had the day off yesterday for a wedding, and agreed to come today." He put his hands on her shoulders and stared down into her face.

Goodness, she must look a fright, with her scarf knotted under her chin and road dirt on her face. Alec had a smudge himself on one cheek. She lifted a gloved hand to smooth it away and he bent to kiss her palm. She could feel the heat of his mouth through the thin kidskin.

"I couldn't bear it if something happened to you," he said, his voice barely audible.

"N-nothing's going to happen to me." Except for one thing. Mary was afraid she was pitching headlong into the abyss of love and had no idea how she'd ever be able to climb out.

There was supposed to be a no-nonsense business arrangement between them. She would have her curiosity satisfied, and go about her future a little wiser. Her long-held innocence had become an inconvenience. But standing so close to Alec, it was hard to remember that they barely knew each other, had nothing in common, and soon would go back to their lives as if nothing had happened.

She was close enough to count his eyelashes if she tried. He'd shaved this morning, but inexpertly, and she could count his bristles, too. But instead of counting, she closed her eyes in artless invitation, and felt him come even nearer. His warm lips touched hers.

Kiss. The word was a sigh itself, starting with strength and trailing off to soft abandon. His fingertips pressed into her shoulders as his mouth pressed into hers, and Mary stretched up on her toes. Alec maneuvered her to the arm of a sofa, which she slid over and he soon followed. It all would have been so much more orderly if they started the kiss from scratch, but Mary didn't mind the tangle of limbs and clothes as long as Alec kept doing whatever it was he was doing. She was in his lap now, firmly in his arms, his tongue toying with hers, his teeth nibbling.

Mary had never given much thought to kisses before. She'd endured the sloppy wet ones from her little nephews and would only confess under penalty of death that the girls had practiced with each other in the dark dormitory at Miss Ambrose's Academy for Young Ladies. Alec was certainly superior to any of those people.

And then there was the comfort of being held against his large body. She felt sheltered. Protected. Treasured.

Mary wished she could kiss him forever. But they both had things to do. And very soon, there would be other expressions of affection that would involve more risk and fewer clothes.

But just a few more seconds of languor alternating with electricity. Mary was on an amusement ride with no rules. For a woman who valued organization, she was sadly disorganized and almost completely at the mercy of Lord Alec Raeburn.

True, this had all been her idea to start. But Alec seemed suitably enthusiastic. The rigidity of his lap was proof of that. How odd it must be to be a male. One's body served as a visual barometer of arousal, while a woman kept her secretions a secret. Except for—oh!—a peaked nipple that brought itself to attention and received the benefits of Alec's nimble fingers. Mary's head tipped back and Alec delved deeper. Her scalp tingled as a wave of heat crept over her body. She must be as red as the shredded curtains hanging at the mullioned windows.

It was time to push away, much as she didn't want to. She didn't want to lose her virginity on an old leather sofa in the middle of the day. His chest was broad and hard, and it cost her to rap a fist against it.

He pulled back, shaking his dark head to clear it. "Too much, or not enough?"

"Both," said Mary, noting the dangerous glitter in his eyes. "You have to go see the magistrate, and I have to write my letter."

He cupped her cheek, his thumb idling over the corner of her mouth. "I find I don't want to go anywhere at present."

"And I don't want you to, in all honesty," Mary replied. "But it's not Monday."

"Monday? What the devil does Monday have to do with it?"

She could feel her face growing hotter. "We agreed to Monday. T-to do the thing on Monday."

"'The thing'?" Alec's face split into a smile. "My dear Miss Arden, I am an impatient man. I feel we haven't a minute to lose, and I certainly am *not* going to wait until Monday to do 'the thing,' as you so inadequately put it, and make you mine."

Mary would never be his, not in any sense it counted. Their worlds were too disparate, their philosophies at odds. Gracious, he didn't even know her full name.

"We can talk about it later when you come back," she said, sliding off his lap. The leather crackled beneath her bottom, adding another aspect to her embarrassment.

"Talk, eh? Vastly overrated. But," he said, suddenly looking serious, "if that's all you can bear after last night's debacle, talk it will be."

Mary had almost forgotten Bauer and his attack. He was in one of the neatly organized file drawers of her mind, safely locked away. She would *not* allow him to pop out with his beardless pink face and come between her and Alec. The man could not be allowed to spoil her one chance.

"Thanks for understanding." The disappointment on Alec's face was gratifying. It wasn't because of Bauer she wished to delay their intimacy until Monday. She wanted things to be perfect. For one thing she did not want to have a scarf strangling her neck and such butterflies in her stomach. She'd be better prepared Monday night—in one of her new negligees, clean hair rippling down her back, her body perfumed.

"I'll leave you, then. Someone will be up here before too long."

"There's no hurry," Mary said. She wanted to use the washroom to get soothed and smoothed out.

Alec stood up and walked to the open door. Anyone might have seen their embrace. They'd have to be more careful. But if they were to be sequestered in the gatehouse, there would be more freedom for both of them.

Free to explore. Free to make the best kind of mistake.

Chapter

25

Mary decided the letter could wait. She was much too curious about Alec's home to sit docilely in the library. She wouldn't interrupt the workmen downstairs, whose efforts made enough noise to wake the dead. Before anyone could be summoned to come upstairs and stop her, she opened doors along the long corridor. Most of the rooms were swathed in Holland covers, drapes drawn. There were a good many bedrooms, but none looked occupied. Perhaps Alec bedded down on the crackling couch in his library when he was home.

She climbed a curved staircase, holding on to the rope railing. Raeburn Court felt very much like a castle, and she could easily imagine a swordfight up and down the broad steps. She could play Rapunzel once she got all the way up. Survey Alec's domain and see if she could catch a glimpse of the Forsyth Palace Hotel across the wooded valley.

Somewhat out of breath, she encountered a locked door at the top of the stairs. Locked doors were not particularly a problem. Mary had once been given a professional courtesy lesson from a private inquiry agent she'd hired to help her with a certain difficult client. Sometimes she couldn't do everything herself, though not often.

Mary pulled a hairpin from her hair and got to work. There was a welcome click and she turned the knob.

And then stood stock-still, trying to get her bearings. She was in Lady Edith Raeburn's tower bedroom. The scene of the possible crime. Edith still reigned, in a portrait that was larger than life. Mary had the uncomfortable feeling that the baroness's cold eyes stared straight at her, and tried to shake off the chill.

Mary didn't believe in ghosts or curses. In her experience, there was always a practical explanation for odd events. Alec's remaining staff may have fallen under some superstitious Scottish spell, but Mary was sure Edith Raeburn was not walking at midnight or howling like a banshee. In a dwelling this old, noises were to be expected. Mortar crumbled; stones became loose and fell. Wind whistled through loose panes of glass. And unlimited access to Raeburn's Special Reserve could not help but induce hallucinations for those with overactive imaginations.

The gilt furniture in Edith's room was so dazzling Mary wanted to reach for her old gray spectacles to dim the glamor. It was a place fit for a fairy princess, quite at odds with the rough stonework and timbered splendor of the Raeburn Court below. The downstairs rooms were being restored to their masculine origins, but this space was an exclusively feminine room, somehow frigid in its pretty perfection. Pastel floral tapestries covered most of the walls. The bed hangings were picked with metallic thread, too sheer to ward off the chill of a Scottish winter. Not one chair looked strong enough to support a normal human being, never mind a man of Alec's size.

Mary looked up at the massive painting between the two curved window seats. Its subject would have seen it first thing when rising from her bed. Edith Raeburn's hair had been the color of champagne, her eyes more silver than blue, her skin translucent save for the faintest flush of pink the artist had brushed onto her cheeks. The image of a fictional snow queen came to mind, painted as she was in white furs, a little white dog at her feet. Quite a lot to live up to with sandmen still in one's eyes and one's hair every which way from sleep. But perhaps Edith's hair didn't tangle like Mary's.

Mary could see why Alec—why any man—would have been enthralled by her ethereal looks. There was something otherworldly about Edith, something frail and fey.

Mary tried to feel sympathy for her, but failed. She was a jealous cow. Edith posed no threat to her—the poor girl was dead and had made Alec's life a misery. But anyone might feel unequal to her beauty, even if one were not a short, plump, middle-aged, middle-class person with no fortune or fame.

Edith had been the daughter of a viscount. Mary was the daughter of a grocer. Whatever social graces she'd picked up since her schooldays had been self-taught. Alec might haunt the Gaiety Theatre green room for fun, but for the serious business of choosing a life companion, he would want someone with a background similar to his own. And he *would* marry again—it would be criminal not to. He was a handsome, hot-blooded man, too potent to let his birthright pass to his brothers.

Oh Lord. Mary should not be here, snooping and feeling sorry for herself. Alec would certainly never ask her to marry him, and she would certainly not accept a proposal if he did. She had the business to run. Her aunt was not well, no matter how energetic she felt at the moment, and past retirement age besides. The Evensong Agency was too important to too many people to give it up.

Mary stuck her tongue out at the painted Edith and felt no better. She walked to the circular window seat and looked out through the leaded glass. Ben-y-Vrackie was wreathed in clouds in the distance. Closer to home, Alec's sheep were scattered on the hills below. Mary could just catch a glimpse of the turrets of the Forsyth Palace Hotel over the trees. How strange it must have been for the Raeburns to watch the interloper rise across the way.

She made a deliberate decision not to look down on the stone courtyard where Lady Edith Raeburn met her end.

Mary had never been afraid of heights, but then she'd never been up so high before. She would not try to imagine the state of Edith's mind before she climbed up on the satin cushions and opened the window.

It seemed pretty clear that Edith had not accidentally stepped out her window into the void. Somehow Mary couldn't see a disgruntled servant pushing her, no matter how demanding she'd been. Alec would have moved heaven and earth to discover the culprit who was responsible.

And he had settled on Bauer.

To Mary's way of thinking, suicide was the most selfish of acts. Alec was still tortured by his wife's death, even though he hadn't loved her at the end. He would forever question what he could have done to prevent her from taking her life. By choosing to end it in such a rebuke to him, Edith had made sure he'd never love anyone else again. How could he ever trust a woman with his heart when he'd been so definitively rejected?

Why had she done it? Out of unrequited love for that blighter Bauer? It was hard to imagine.

Mary felt a shiver that owed nothing to the cold stone walls around her. She felt a bit like Pandora—she'd opened the damned box and now was inundated with unpleasant thoughts and images. Mary would have been better off sticking to the library and writing her letter.

"You win," she whispered to Edith, and closed the door behind her. Before she could take one step, there was a scrabbling sound and furious growling on the stairs below. Someone had discovered her trespass. Not a banshee or a ghostie, but a dirty ball of fluff rounded the staircase and hurled itself at her. The vicious little beast tore at her skirt when it didn't yap, and Mary backed against Edith's door.

"Good doggie," she said faintly. A lie to be sure, but it had an effect. Its button eyes blinked, then the animal continued to chew on the hem of her skirt with unbridled relish.

"Down."

The dog sat on the step but continued its assault.

"No! No biting or chewing!" What was Gaelic for *stop*?

Mary gave a tug and a strip of lace was left in the little dog's mouth.

"Damn it. I guess I'm getting what I deserve. Protecting your mistress's quarters, are you?" This was the dog in the painting, no longer looking like the snow queen's pampered consort. "You're not very white now, are you, little fellow?" Mary cooed to the creature, hoping it would be satisfied with her skirt trim and not decide to remove her fingers. She bent to scratch between its lopsided ears. The dog gave a muffled bark through the fabric.

"All right now, we'll just go downstairs, shall we? Nice and slow. See? I'm harmless." Mary hung on to the rope railing and took a tentative step around the dog. After a second, he bounded down the stairs in front of her, then doubled back, herding her all the way back to the library.

Oliver was there. He leaped up from a chair, looking guilty. "There you are! I've been searching all over for you!"

"Not very hard, or you would have found me," Mary retorted. "What's that you've got in your hand?"

"N-nothing. Just an old book. Raeburn said I was to keep an eye on you until he returns from Pitcarran. Someone's bringing us up a lunch tray."

The dog growled but kept its distance. "Sit." Both the dog and Oliver obeyed. "Oliver Palmer. You are the most awful liar. What have you been doing?"

"It takes one to know one, doesn't it? You've been pulling the wool over everyone's eyes for four years!" Oliver objected.

"Never mind about me. Confess. I hear it's good for the soul."

"I didn't do anything you wouldn't have done, had you the chance, Mary, and that's a fact. You're a veritable terrier when it comes to digging for information. Like that wretched thing at your feet." The grimy little dog cocked its head but didn't bark. "Raeburn said you were going to write a letter, and all I did was try to get things ready for you. Paper, pen, ink, just the way you like things lined up on your desk at the office."

"Very enterprising of you. And?"

Oliver looked at the slim volume in his hand. "And I found this. In a drawer."

Mary felt the blood drain from her face. "You went through Lord Raeburn's private things?" Alec would have every right to boot them both out.

"Not everything. I stopped when I found this." Oliver leaned forward and passed her the hand-tooled leather diary.

Alec had mentioned a diary the first day she had met him. Edith had kept one, and that's how Alec discovered her infidelity.

"Put it back!" she snapped.

"But, Mary, don't you want to read it first?"

Of course she did, but not with Oliver perched like a vulture on the chair. The dog, too. He—for it was a male, now that she had seen him roll on the carpet in ecstasy with the strip of lace in his mouth—gave her a look of disgust and snorted, dropping the material in a wet ball.

"It is completely inappropriate," Mary said stiffly.

"But didn't you swipe that viscount's diary to help his wife get a legal separation?" Oliver asked.

"That was an entirely different matter. Lady Cary had every right to defend herself against such a vile abuser." Some might have called what Mary did blackmail, but Lady Cary was now happy in the Cary mansion in Mayfair while her husband tried his luck on an Australian cattle ranch. If there was a merciful God, the man would be gored by one of his prize bulls.

"All right. I'll put it back," Oliver said, looking abashed. "It's in the bottom left-hand drawer if you change your mind."

"I thought you were going to the gatehouse."

"Mac—that is to say Mackenzie—drafted one of the young grooms to help him. I told him I didn't mind doing a bit of cleaning—my brothers always stuck me with their chores. But he didn't want me to 'lower' myself, as he put it." Oliver's family had servants, of course, but his martinet father did not believe in coddling any of his sons. He had risen up by his own bootstraps, and his sons would, too.

"Is he nice?"

"Who?"

"Don't be coy, Oliver. Mac. The valet."

Oliver slammed the drawer shut. "Are you going to forbid me from his friendship? He's not exactly a client, Mary."

She sighed. Poor Oliver's life was a complicated affair. "Of course not. Just be careful. I don't want to see you hurt."

"Mac couldn't hurt a fly. He's a quarter of the size of his master."

"I'm not talking about how big or strong he is, Oliver, and you know it."

"Well, you be careful, too. I've seen the way Lord Raeburn looks at you, like he could eat you up without a spoon."

Really? Mary felt absurdly pleased. "He just feels guilty for subjecting me to Bauer and wants to give me a little holiday."

"I think it's more than that. And why would he put you up in that gatehouse? If he's so worried about the bad doctor coming after you, he should send you back to London."

There was a certain logic in Oliver's thinking. "We're here on business, too, remember. I'll depend upon you to get the lay of the land here. As a matter of fact, this will be your first big project for the Evensong Agency. Lord Raeburn needs new servants to run a place this size. Determine how many. *You* can write the letter to Aunt Mim. Then when we get back, you can do most of the interviewing."

Oliver lit up. "I say, Mary, that's capital! But what are *you* going to do while you're here?"

He really didn't need to know the truth now, did he? "Rest. Walk. The usual country pursuits. If Lord Raeburn agrees, I want to learn how to drive."

Oliver whistled, startling the dog to attention. "Clear the decks."

"You're getting your transportation metaphors mixed. Why shouldn't I learn how to drive?" asked Mary, irritated.

"Well, for one thing, it's a rich man's hobby."

"It won't remain a hobby for long. Automobiles are the

future." They'd better be. She'd invested most of her hard-earned money in the Pegasus Motor Company.

"You don't have the full rig, driving hat and all that rot."

"I'm sure something can be found." Mary only hoped it hadn't belonged to the golden Edith Raeburn.

Chapter

26

After their quick and very basic lunch of cheese, pickles, and bread, Mary sent Oliver to the bowels of Raeburn Court to interview its skeleton crew to assess just how many maids and footmen might be required to give polish to the place. She wondered when Alec would return. He had taken his horse instead of the car, which was still parked below in the courtyard, gleaming in the sunshine. It was tempting her to go down and do some assessing of her own, but mindful of her limited time, she shut the library door, wrote a brief letter to Aunt Mim telling her to expect more details from Oliver, and opened up the bottom desk drawer.

Mary knew it was wrong. It was one thing to break some rules gently on behalf of her clients—a white lie, a judicious omission—but this time she was abusing Alec's trust. He'd left her in his library, his favorite room in the house. He did not expect her to go mining into his past.

The perfect painted image of Edith Raeburn taunted Mary; the mystery of her death intrigued her. She avoided the dog's censorious eyes as she sat at Alec's desk and opened the journal.

And then she blinked. It appeared to be nothing but a long list—an inventory of Edith's possessions in elegant copperplate script. Perhaps this was not the diary after all. Fox stoles, diamond clips, Worth gowns. Thirty-one in all, if Mary counted correctly. Thirty-one Worth gowns! They must have cost a fortune.

Worth was not the only fashion house that was well-represented in Edith's closet. There were a host of other French designers, including Doucet and Poiret. Several of Monsieur Poiret's controversial kimonos had been purchased just before Edith's untimely death. The list went on for at least thirty double-sided pages, with the dates of each newly acquired bit of frippery, starting from just before Edith married Alec. He had showered her with engagement gifts, and had not seemed to stop once she was his wife. Almost all the entries had been marked "from Alec."

Mary felt a sour stab of jealousy—he had been inordinately generous to his young bride, even when he was in London with all his demimondaines. His wife had been in his thoughts while he was in bed with other women. Had it been guilt that inspired such expensive gifts, or something else?

She fanned through a few blank pages, ready to return the journal to its dark hiding place when fresh writing appeared.

> *Today I visited the new spa hotel with Mummy. It was their Grand Opening, and some of her friends are staying there. What a bore. Nothing but old sick people and fishermen, and I am bored enough at home. But we met the handsome doctor in charge, and he gave us a tour. He tells me the special baths are ideal for people who live on their nerves as I do. Mummy says I should give the place a try, and since it is so close, I just might. I am so tired of her lecturing me about my duty.*

Mary warred with herself. She should shut the book right this instant. But instead, she skimmed Edith's beautiful writing.

That is to say, her penmanship was elegant. What she had to say in it was rather puerile. Mary reminded herself that Edith was barely twenty-one when she died, a veritable child. A spoiled child, from the paragraphs she penned, endlessly complaining about the servants, her parents, the weather, Alec's brothers, Alec himself.

Mary remembered herself at that age—she was busy working for her brother and sister-in-law and minding her nephews when she was not. She hadn't had time to keep a diary, and would have had nothing interesting to write down anyway.

She continued to read. It had taken precisely two weeks from their first meeting before Josef Bauer flirted with Edith and flattered her into bed.

Her golden bed in her golden bedroom right here at Raeburn Court, Mary discovered, the same bed she would not invite her husband into. And at the spa, in spare hotel rooms, once even on a blanket in a sheep meadow on the doctor's afternoon off. Mary became less impressed with Edith by each sentence.

Mary had to race through the gushing by the poor deluded girl. Knowing Bauer's proclivities now as she did, Edith hadn't stood a chance. But even so, it was jolting to read of her bad judgment, knowing the hurt it had caused Alec and the ultimate price she paid.

The little dog had been quietly sitting under the desk, but he suddenly ran out and started barking and spinning around in circles. Mary shut the book and shoved it into the desk drawer just in the nick of time.

"Alec!" she said brightly. "I didn't expect you back so soon."

"My horse cast a shoe and I had to walk him back at a snail's pace. I suppose the visit to the magistrate can wait until tomorrow." He looked disheveled and weary. "Down, Beowulf!" he said to the dog, swatting him away from his riding boots with his gloves. The little dog leaped to bite the leather fingers. Alec won the tug-of-war.

"Beowulf!" Mary giggled. "He hardly looks like a hero."

"I didn't name him. He looks like he's been rolling in an ash-heap again. No one's looked after him properly since Edith died. He was her baby." He gave the dog an absent pat.

Should she tell Alec she'd already seen their portrait together in Edith's room? He had invited her to look over the house, but probably did not expect her to pick a lock to gain entry.

"He seems very protective," Mary ventured.

"Aye. He thinks he owns the place. I can send him to the stables if he bothers you."

"Oh, no! I like dogs. We never had one, living over the shop." She clapped her hands, and Beowulf trotted over, wagging his tail. She scratched behind his lop-sided ears and he appeared in ecstasy.

"Did you write your letter? I can post it tomorrow when I go to Pitcarran."

"I did. Actually, I've turned over the hiring task to Oliver. He was raised in an upper-middle-class household, and is very suited to determining your staffing needs. His family is very well-to-do."

Alec raised an eyebrow. "Are they? Then why is Oliver working for your aunt?"

Mary did not want to betray Oliver's secrets. "He had an unfortunate falling-out with his father."

"I wager I know why."

Mary looked at him, startled.

"Do you think you're the only soft-hearted person in the world? I suspect my valet and your aunt's assistant have a great deal in common."

"And you approve?"

Alec shrugged. "Only God knows why people are made as they are. It's not up to me to sit in judgment—I have enough troubles of my own. Come, I promised you a tour of the house, and a tour you shall have."

Mary rose from the desk. "You don't have to, Alec. I'm sure you're tired."

"I may be tired, but you'll not deny me time spent in your delightful company, will you?"

He probably would not think her delightful at all if he knew she'd been reading his late wife's diary.

"All right."

Alec took her arm. "I'll show you where I would have put you were we staying here. You're likely to be very disappointed with the gatehouse—it's quite a comedown."

"You realize you are talking to a woman who was raised over a corner store. The gatehouse will be lovely. It wasn't until recently that my brother bought a house separate from the business."

"Doing well, is he?"

"I suppose. He doesn't tell me much."

"You are an observant young woman. You must know."

Heavens, Alec thought she was still employed in the shop and just on some sort of temporary working holiday with Aunt Mim. She should tell him the truth.

But the last thing Alec Raeburn needed was another woman who lied to him. Mary swallowed her conscience and made suitably appropriate comments as he showed her around. He took her by all the vacant bedrooms she'd already seen, then turned left at the end of the hall to another set of stairs.

Mary looked across the landing. "Where does that staircase opposite to this one lead?" She knew very well.

"That room is locked, and I don't have the key with me," Alec said, being vague.

Mary had forgotten to lock Edith's room after being caught out by Beowulf. If he went up there later, she hoped he'd think one of the workmen had neglected to secure it. She followed him up a short flight of stairs to another wing of bedrooms.

"Here," he said, throwing open a door, "our best guest room."

The wallpaper was fresh, an Arts and Crafts pattern that suited the dark woodwork. It was handsome but not overly luxurious.

"You are too polite to say so, but I can see you're not

impressed. What's best about it is that my room is right next door." Alec grinned.

"Oh." Mary knew she was blushing.

He tugged her through a connecting door to his own room, a masculine lair with a lingering aroma of Blenheim Bouquet and old books. No one had been up here to pick up after him for quite a while. There were papers and books strewn across a table by the window and stacked precariously at his bedside. "Mac isn't happy with me—I won't let him tidy up. He has to satisfy himself with organizing my dressing room."

"Was this your room when you were a child?" Mary asked.

"It was. I moved back here when things were at an impasse with Edith. She moved, too. Lord knows, the house is big enough to house a dozen unhappy married couples. Musical rooms, as it were. That guest room used to be my brother Evan's room. He lives in the dower house on the estate now."

Mary pictured two young boys slamming doors and giggling, up all hours making mischief. "What about your other brother?"

"Nick? We never let him come down from the nursery, so he decided to thumb his nose at us and just enjoy it up there. Said the light was good for his painting. But he's been away since I married. I worry about him."

"You should get him to come home. At least to London."

"Do you think I haven't tried?"

"He needs an inducement. Leave it to m—Mrs. Evensong's Agency. Aunt Mim will come up with some scheme to get him back here."

Alec laughed. "And what will that cost me?"

"Not a penny. I'll—we'll do it as a favor. After all, you're doing me a favor soon, aren't you?"

"Not soon enough," Alec murmured, and took her in his arms. Mary was aware of the large bed nearby and the insistent heat of Alec's body. He smelled of leather and horse and sweat, which should have been off-putting but wasn't. How could anyone's lips be both soft and firm, teasing yet steady? She forgot that she'd breached his trust by snooping, forgot that Monday was tomorrow. Mary wanted him, without layers of clothing and secrets between them. She tiptoed up to clasp her hands around his neck, her knees weakening with every brush of his tongue to hers.

She was near to slipping to the floor when he stopped kissing her and nuzzled her earlobe. "I don't want to wait, Mary." Alec searched her face for her answer. She'd washed the smudges off, but was certain he wouldn't care if she'd rolled in an ash-heap like Beowulf. Desire danced between them, etched with urgency. He wanted them to leave Raeburn Court, go to ground in case Bauer was still determined to make him pay.

"It's—it's daylight," Mary stuttered.

"All the more reason for us to do this now. I want to see what's under that boned collar and corset."

"I don't know if I'm ready."

Mary had been thinking of perfumed baths and loosened hair brushed one hundred strokes, but Alec misunderstood. "Of course. I'm a bloody idiot. I promised to give you time to get over your ordeal."

Mary put a finger over his mouth. "It's not that. I wanted to wear my best nightdress. Brush my teeth." Goodness, she'd eaten a pickled onion at lunch—how could he even bear kissing her?

"You little darling. You're pretty perfect just as you are." He strode to the doors and locked them. "The gatehouse won't be stocked and ready until later, and tomorrow morning I'll have to make another attempt to get to Pitcarran. Let's make good use of the hours we have."

He looked at her with such hopefulness, she simply could not say no.

Chapter

27

Alec did not know why it was so important for him to bring Mary Arden into his boyhood bed. It wasn't like him to be sentimental or so impatient. God knows, he'd spent enough of his youth's dark nights imagining a willing woman in his bed with a hand on his cock, but he hoped he'd outgrown that by now.

She was counting on him to introduce her to lovemaking—she depended on his alleged skill and experience. She trusted him. Alec wasn't used to such a misplaced honor. He wanted to fumble with his falls and push up her skirt like the imaginative boy he'd been.

Finesse, Alec, he reminded himself. *Seduction*. She was an innocent, for all their brief sensual encounters over the past couple of days. Apart from last night, he doubted any man had seen her naked save the doctor who delivered her.

He'd only seen bits and pieces of scented white skin, but he knew what she tasted like, how slight she felt in his arms, how her russet lashes fluttered as he kissed her. He wanted to unwrap her as a present to himself, something to ease the edge of the misery of these past months. He had thrown himself into the giddy theater crowd, and the actresses had not been the only ones pretending.

His clumsy fingers caught on a thread-covered hook. It was the devil to release it from its eye, and there were a half a dozen more to go before he even got to a decent-sized pearl button. Mary stood breathless as he worked his way down the back of her dress. How had she managed to get into it without a maid this morning? His Mary Arden was a resourceful woman.

Her dress dropped to her hips, and he spun her gently around. She must have fastened her corset from the front—more damned hooks—and he unfastened them with more difficulty. His hands betrayed him at every inch, shaking as they were. She wore a lacy shift, more white against the cream and gold of her skin. There were tiny freckles on her collarbone and across one shoulder, and Alec bent to kiss them.

She reached behind her back, tugging at her sash. Her batiste dress dropped to the floor, and she was left shivering in her petticoat and slip.

"Are you cold?" Alec asked.

"Just nervous. You are currently overdressed, my lord."

He wished her hands were upon him doing the same things as he did to her, but that was expecting a lot. "Get into the bed, sweetheart."

"With my shoes?" she asked impertinently.

"Sit," he ordered. Mary sidestepped to the bed and sat, her hands folded in her lap like an apt pupil. He was on his knees in an instant, taking her kid boots off. A stocking snagged on his rough hand as he detached it from the garter.

Damn. He was rough even when he was trying to be gentle. He unrolled the silk from her legs, smoothing his hands over the pale gold fuzz. She was absolutely still, her womanly scent washing over him. He was so close—why not? There would be time for the main event after a few well-pleasuring minutes.

Alec pulled her to the edge of the bed and worked his way up from her dainty toes to her thigh, dropping butterfly kisses on her fragrant skin. She guessed his intention, and opened herself to him.

Alec buried his tongue between her rosy folds. She grew even more rigid, a sharp cry escaping. He feasted until her nails dug into his shoulder blades and her thighs trembled. She was drenched in honey, almost ready for him.

But he was, as she'd pointed out, overdressed. He tore his clothes from his body as if they were on fire. In the meantime, she had shyly untied her petticoat and pulled her undergarments over her head and the pins from her glorious hair. She was pale and exquisite, her breasts full, apricot-tipped. He feasted there, too, tipping her back on his bed amidst the crumpled worn quilt.

Her breaths came faster as he brushed his fingertips across smooth skin, then silenced her with a solemn kiss. Did she hear his silent pledge to make this good for her? It was not really possible to wait much longer.

Her eyes were wide and questioning, the recent daze now absent.

He took her hands in his. "You're sure, Mary? There will be no going back."

She nodded once.

One finger sought her center, gently parting her. She was so tight—all of her was much too small, really. He was apt to crush her. And then it came to him. She had wanted to be taught, but perhaps she should take the lead, establish the pace. Last night, she had nearly been Bauer's helpless victim. He wouldn't do the same thing to her today. No woman should feel robbed of autonomy, unless that was what she wanted, of course. Somehow, Alec couldn't see Mary abandoning all control.

Mary was opinionated, and Alec wanted to discover all the things she craved. She probably didn't know yet herself, but he'd give her the opportunity to find out.

He rolled to his back and settled her plump body over his. Her hair tickled his chest and he held her tight.

"What are you doing?" she croaked, blushing at him.

Alec didn't want her to be embarrassed. He gave her what

he hoped was a most appreciative smile. "I'm turning the reins over to you, my love. We shall go as slowly as you wish. Or as fast, although I do hope we can savor our time. It's apt to hurt in the beginning." He guided his finger in again, then out, steady yet with the lightest of touches. She was not ready to be stretched any further, though his patient strokes seemed to be having a gratifying effect.

Mary groaned. "I want more."

"Not yet, my greedy girl. Relax."

"When people tell me to relax, it only makes me less so," Mary said crossly.

"But you must relax, else this will be uncomfortable. Do you feel how snug you are? We'll want another finger inside before we try anything else. Feel me, Mary. I'm a bit fatter than two fingers."

Her hand touched his cock. Even her inexpert contact gave him joy.

"Does one talk through this? That seems very odd." She curled her small hand around him and he prayed not to spill into it.

"One can talk. One can even laugh on occasion. Of course, the best times are when one is so swept away, one canna think."

That is how this afternoon should be unfolding—he should have kissed her senseless all over. There should have been champagne. Strawberries. Feathers, perhaps. Feathers were fun. Och but he was four kinds of a fool.

Mary's eyebrows knit. "How long will it take to improve me?"

"Hush. Ye need no improvement, my love. Rise up on your knees and straddle me, then sit back." *And stop thinking.*

He kept his hand fast at her center, circling her clitoris with his thumb and dipping his finger deeper inside her. He fisted his cock with the other. Her lovely bottom brushed against his thighs. She stared down to where their bodies met, her back straightening, her nipples hardening. She was flushed from her hairline to her navel.

Then her eyes moved up his torso to his face. "You're looking at me."

"Aye, and you're looking at me. At us. What a beauty you are, Miss Arden. Copper hair and pearl skin and emerald eyes. Do you know they've flecks of gold in them, too? You're like a jewel box come to life."

"You don't have to say such silly things." She gave him a nervous smile. Did she really not know how perfect she was?

"Do you doubt my sincerity? You shouldna. I don't know when I've seen a prettier sight. See what you've done to me? Nay, don't look away. This is for you." He spread the gleaming drop of fluid around the head of his penis. He was hard as stone.

Damn. He should have put a condom on. There were some in his trunk, but it would rather spoil the mood if he leaped up now. He'd just have to go carefully later, lift her away before—

Would it be so dreadful if there were consequences? Alec had not allowed himself to think of any sort of normal future in years.

A wife.

A family.

But he barely knew Mary, and she barely knew him. Maybe she wouldn't want to be saddled with a gorilla for a lifetime. He'd have to be happy with a few days of delicious sin.

A second finger slowly joined his first, and Mary shut those glittering green eyes.

"Does it hurt?"

"Not exactly. I just *feel* you."

"I should hope so." He looked at her arms, hanging idly at her side, and had an idea. "Where else do you want me to touch you?"

"I don't know."

"Your breasts look lonely."

Her lips twitched. "Don't be ridiculous. Breasts can't get lonely."

"Och, but they can. Why don't you touch them? I'd love to see that."

Mary's eyes snapped wide open. "M-me? That wouldn't be proper."

"Come now. I can't think of one proper thing about what we're doing, can you? You're watching me stroke myself as my fingers move inside you. I'd love another pair of hands right at the moment to get more accomplished, and guess who has two with nothing to do? Have you never touched yourself?" Alec knew he was being wicked.

Mary rolled her emerald eyes in exasperation. "Not with anyone watching me! You tell me to relax, but I don't see how I can!"

"So you *have* touched yourself."

"Alec," she said with fraying patience, "I am twenty-nine years old. A modern woman. My curiosity did not suddenly rise to the fore when you walked into my office. I've seen other men in kilts before, and you know the saying."

Her mouth dropped open in sudden dismay at her words, and he stilled his hands. "What? What do you mean?"

"Oh! Never mind. Keep on keeping on, please." In a frantic gesture, she grabbed her breasts and squeezed. It looked more painful than pleasurable.

It couldn't be. But she was so like her aunt, and knew so much about the Evensong Agency. They were about the same height. The same size. Hell, they even sounded alike. Had she played him for a fool all along? Taken advantage of *him*, after he confessed to the coldness of his marriage? Like an idiot, he'd poured his heart out to the old woman.

"Mary Arden, do you have something you want to tell me? Something important?"

"No. Nope." She shook her head and pinched a nipple halfheartedly.

Alec rolled her off his lap. "I canna stand dishonesty, Miss Arden. Even my mistresses know better than to lie to me. I pay them for truth. And it seems to me I've paid you, too. Quite a shocking sum for your services—or should I say your niece's services?"

"Blast," Mary muttered.

He waved an arm between them. "I don't understand this. Who are you really?"

"You know who I am! Mary Arden . . . Evensong."

The last was said on a whisper. Alec's hand went to the beard that wasn't there, then he slapped his own face.

"Say that again."

She studied her fingernails as though they were diamond-tipped, refusing to meet his eyes. "I—I didn't mean to deceive you in particular. I've been deceiving everyone. My aunt has been ill, and I stepped into her place."

Alec was dumbfounded. The Evensong Agency was known far and wide as the preeminent employment agency in the country. Of course, they solved other sorts of problems, too, but somehow he couldn't see shy little Mary Arden . . . Evensong doing all the things her crafty old aunt was reputed to do.

"For how long has this masquerade been going on?"

"F-four years."

Alec felt his eyebrows fly up. "Four years? Does that mean it was *you* who went to Viscount Burleigh's father-in-law and—"

Mary's face was scarlet, as it should be if she had been mixed up in *that* affair. The old man deserved whatever punishment she had meted out, and Lady Burleigh was safe at last. "Yes, yes! But the gun wasn't even loaded. Drat, I never divulge the exact nature of my arrangements with our clients. Some of them are not quite so tricky, you know."

"Tricky? I'll say it was tricky! Good Lord! And here you've convinced me you're pure as a Scottish snowstorm."

"I am! Or I was before I propositioned you. I've never wanted to bed a client before. It's not at all professional," she said with no apparent irony.

He was suddenly conscious that he was stark naked. Mary had had the good sense to wrestle a sheet over herself after her fingernails must have proved satisfactory.

"Four years. You've been pretending to be an old lady

for four years? I suppose the grocery store nonsense is all a myth."

"Oh, no! It's perfectly true. My brother runs the family business now, and I was trapped, and terribly, terribly bored, if you must know the state of my mind. When Aunt Mim suggested I come to London to help her, I jumped at the chance." Mary was sitting straight up now, her stubborn little chin jutting out. Her nipples, too, under the worn sheet.

Alec turned away. "Help her! The things you've seen and done . . ." He was quite overawed, if they were telling the truth to each other now.

"Well, I had to! Her business would have suffered irrevocably if word had gotten out she'd turned it over to her ignorant twenty-five-year-old niece. She has dealt with rather delicate matters since well before the turn of the century. I had the agency's mission to fulfill."

" 'Performing the impossible before breakfast,' " Alec quoted back to her. "I'll be damned. So it was you under that horrible hat all along. What a little actress."

"I never meant to lie to you. Well, of course I did, but I didn't expect to *not* want to lie to you. To lie *with* you, as it were."

"You're a wordsmith, too." He reached for his trousers.

"W-what are you doing?"

"Getting dressed. I suggest you do the same."

Mary's lip quivered. "You mean you won't finish what we started?"

"I don't believe I'm in the mood. Isn't that what you ladies say?" Alec asked, feeling inexplicably betrayed. Really, what did it matter to him if she'd dressed as a dwarf or in sackcloth and ashes these past four years? She had accomplished what he'd hired her for—Bauer was no longer employed at the spa and Edith was avenged.

"I wouldn't know. I'm not a lady, just a grocer's daughter." There was the chin again.

"And a liar, don't forget. A charlatan." A chameleon, who turned from doddering dowager to pocket Venus.

Mary's lips curled. "What makes me different from your

actress friends, then? Don't they lie with every word onstage? You don't seem to mind *them*. A dozen of them at least if the gossip rags are accurate."

Hoisted on his own petard. Damn her for throwing his reputation back in his face. "All the world is *not* a stage, contrary to that Shakespeare fellow, Miss Arden. Miss Evensong. Whoever," Alec replied, tangling his foot in the leg of his pants.

"You hired me to lie," Mary reminded him.

"But not to me."

"I've told you the truth now! But I won't beg you to come back to bed. No doubt I'm nothing like the women you're used to."

No, she jolly well was not. Alec let out an exasperated sigh, and not at his evident inability to get back into his own pants. "Are you trying to get me to compliment you?"

"Certainly not!" Mary huffed. "I would never want you to say or do anything that goes against your beliefs. It's clear you have a disgust of me." She clutched the sheet tighter. "This has all been a terrible mistake. You can get us to the evening train and we can forget about the whole affair. If you wish," she said with some brutality, "I shall give you a full refund."

"A full refund! I don't want my money back, you daft woman! I just don't like being used. You've played me for a fool, Mary Arden . . . Evensong. You might have told me at the beginning who you really were. All those blushes and stutters—by God, if they gave out acting awards, you'd be first in line to get one!"

"I haven't been acting with you!" Mary said hotly. "I just wanted a little experience. Is that such a crime? You have no idea—" She broke off, probably deciding he didn't have an idea and never would have.

"You know much more than I thought, if you could deal with the Burleigh mess."

"Anyone can read a book, Alec. One hears things at school, even over the grocery counter, if you can believe that. Aunt Mim was always around to give me advice, too.

I am every bit as innocent as you thought. Or I used to be," she reflected, reminding him of all the things they'd done together the past few days.

Wet things. Wicked things. Warm kisses on her sweet puckered mouth and warmer ones where they really counted.

"Innocent." Alec snorted, but he didn't try to stand up. By God, the woman was a witch.

"Innocent," Mary affirmed. "But perhaps there will be someone in London to relieve me of my unwanted virginity. Someone with fewer scruples than you have, if that's possible."

Alec felt the hot color wash over his face. "I'll show you scruples," he growled, and tugged his foot out of his pants.

Chapter

28

Oh dear, but he was angry. What had made her reveal her identity in such a careless fashion? Of course she had wondered what he wore beneath his black and yellow kilt the first day she'd met him—even Aunt Mim might have been curious if she had seen him in all his Highland glory.

And she *would* have told him who she really was.

Eventually.

Maybe.

After.

But she'd blurted it out before, and now it seemed things were going to be very odd indeed. A few minutes ago, she had been perched atop Alec's massive thighs, dripping an embarrassing amount of fluid onto his talented fingers, wondering exactly what he meant by giving her "the reins." Did he expect her to ride him while he looked up at her touching her breasts, his dark gaze so acute? She had felt somewhat mortified. Exposed. She didn't want to be in control—Mary really had no idea how this act was all supposed to be achieved, and that was precisely why she had sought Alec's assistance. He was a legendary lover, was he not?

At least with everyone except for his wife.

She might have seen and heard a shocking thing or two in the underbelly of the best of British society in her masquerade as Mrs. Evensong, but she was totally at sea now. Alec's anger did not seem to depress his ardor one whit as he slanted his mouth over hers. She gave a little yelp as his tongue burrowed into her mouth, hot and seeking. Gone was the gentle, teasing man who showed such hesitance and concern for her sensibilities. Mary was drowning in his corded arms, breathless, airless.

And somehow she wasn't tempted to clout him on the head to stop him. He was rather masterful, really, all muscle and masculine intent. She felt his erection against her belly and snaked a hand down to it. He'd seemed to like her touch before, and judging from the near-violent racking of his body now, he still did.

Alec growled into her mouth, nipping her tongue, pressing a big hand into her loosened hair, the other onto her mound. Mary wished he'd tuck his fingers inside her again to improve her, and soon he did. He must have telepathic capabilities, knowing exactly what a woman needed at any moment, for he was certainly—oh—doing a splendid job of it. His thumb pressed against the knot of flesh at her apex, driving it into her pubic bone—she *had* read books—and driving her wild.

She raised her hips up, ready to fly. So close, so close, just beyond the corner. He was steel velvet in her hand—one day she'd like to examine him thoroughly but right now her eyes were closed, tiny red sparks flashing beneath her lids. All the while, their kiss veered between playful and purposeful, and after a bit Mary just let the sensation wash over her like a warm wave. She was cradled beneath him, safe, his hand over hers now as he centered himself to breach her.

The discomfort wasn't so very bad, but she forgot to relax for a moment. She may even have cried out. Alec continued to kiss her, teasing his tongue over hers as he eased himself inside her and then stilled. Her eyes fluttered open to see his, dark as death above her.

He broke the kiss. "Are you all right?"

"Of course I'm all right. Do we have to talk right now?"

He chuckled, and she felt his cock twitch inside her, as if it were in on some joke. "Nay. What would you like to do, Miss Evensong?"

"Well, the—the usual, I suppose." Really, what was the man getting at? She was stretched to the limit and could not think.

Did not *want* to think. The lovely loose feeling she had was evaporating, and she wanted it back.

"Och. The usual, is it? Well then, wrap your legs around me, yes, just like that."

Mary thought he'd slipped in even deeper, if that were possible. Her every nerve was racing to her lower region. She felt swollen and lush, and yet still uncomfortable.

"Your arms, too. Make that one arm. Keep a hand between us and touch yourself as I was doing before. I'd do that myself but I don't want to crush you—you're such a little bit of a thing."

He was braced above her, and there was too much space between them. Mary wanted skin on skin, her breasts brushing his broad chest. She could see what he meant about having more hands. They'd be very useful about now, because she wished to pull his shadowed face back down for more kisses instead of this odd conversation. She angled her hips and dug her heels into his buttocks, hoping to distract him from the shy hand that sought her center. It was very wicked, but my, if felt wonderful. To be filled and touched at the same time, even by her own fingers.

And then she understood the reason for the distance, as he swooped down to capture a nipple in his mouth. The suckling tug went directly to her groin, and she may have made another noise again. He divided his time between her breasts, tongue swirling, teeth grazing, as she fingered herself more frantically. He was moving now, in and out, and she rose to meet him, hearing her arousal with every slippery slow thrust and teasing retreat.

The sound should have been embarrassing but was not. It became a kind of music, the tempo changing as she opened to him, the groan of the mattress adding bass notes. The cloud of unfamiliar male scent, the dampness, the roughness of his beard against her throat, the sweet and savage kisses, the satisfied grunts of possession—Mary allowed all of it to sweep her away. She had dreamed of this for years, and this was so much better than any dream. They were joined precisely where they needed to be and in moments she would fracture apart.

Alec knew before she did and acted accordingly. His fingers replaced hers and she really did scream now—there was no doubt about it. With one final elegant twist, Alec withdrew from her body and spilled onto the sheet as she shattered beside him. His face was a mask of blissful agony as he pumped his cock into the linen, and Mary wondered if she'd looked the same.

Wild. Primitive. Pure.

He had been watching her—she'd seen him through the slit of her eyelids just when she thought she could bear no more. His eyes had been black and glittering, his grin feral, like some proud, delicious demon.

He had every right to feel pride. The entire encounter had been beyond educational. Quite ethereal actually, especially toward the end. In fact, she wanted to do it all over again, as soon as possible, if he didn't remember to be angry with her about her deception.

Alec didn't look angry now. His face had smoothed and his lips were parted a fraction as he tried to draw breath. She touched a bristly cheek as gently as she knew how.

"Thank you, Alec," she whispered.

"I should be thanking you. Are you sure you're all right? Not too sore?"

"I'm fine. Truly." But now that the heavenly friction had disappeared, she could acknowledge she felt *something*.

There must have been uncertainty on her face. He sprang off the bed and went into his bathroom, returning with a glass full of warm water and a flannel. "Lie still and I'll take care of you."

"I told you I'm fine!" But when she looked down, she saw the streaks of blood on her thighs and felt a little light-headed. She'd bandaged her bleeding nephews often enough, and had seen enough butchered meat to last a lifetime. Why was the sight of her own loss of innocence a problem?

"Steady, now. My God, I'm sorry for this, Mary."

"D-don't be. It's—it's nothing."

He was so careful, swabbing and patting, parting her folds with extreme delicacy and wiping away the wet. There was a bleakness about him, though—guilt—and she wanted to smack him.

"I asked for this, Alec. And it was lovely. Really, *lovely* doesn't begin to cover it. I'll have to consult a thesaurus."

"I was a brute. Look at you, like a porcelain statue! And look at me—a bull in a china shop. I've hurt you."

"But you didn't! Well, maybe a little at first, but after that it was—oh goodness, now are *you* the one fishing for compliments? I have nothing to compare you to, but I assure you, I enjoyed myself very much. In fact, let's do it again right now." She plastered a smile on her face, avoiding looking at the bloody washcloth.

An eyebrow quirked. "Right now? You do think me a bull then. I'm afraid men take more than a minute to recover themselves. And I would never abuse you so soon after you've lost your maidenhead."

"I didn't *lose* it," Mary said. "You make it sound like a dropped handkerchief or a misplaced glove. It was just a bit of tissue, after all, completely pointless, like one's appendix."

Alec stared at her, then threw back his head and laughed. She loved to see him like this, the brooding Highlander disappearing. He should laugh more.

And Mary decided to make that her mission for the time that remained at Raeburn Court. They both could do with some levity in their lives, at least for a little while.

"No wonder you could pass as your aunt. You are old-headed, aren't you? A practical girl."

"*Practical* is my middle name. Well, actually, it's Arden, and you know that now. And I'm usually prepared, too. Thank you for not—" How could she frame her words? *Emitting* or *ejaculating* sounded so clinical. "Um, at the end . . . uh, thank you." She even possessed a German contraption, smuggled in out of curiosity, but it was buried in her stocking drawer back in London. Her hand had hovered over it as she was packing for Scotland, but she hadn't the nerve to bring it.

To bring it would have meant she'd already decided that Lord Alec Raeburn was the man for her, and that would have tempted fate. A grocery clerk and a baron? Ridiculous! But fate must have heard her yearning, for here she was in Alec's bed, being cosseted.

"Aye, I'm usually better prepared, too. I've no by-blows I'm aware of," Alec said, his cheeks reddening right along with hers. What a funny conversation to be having. Their passion spent, it was almost as if they were friends.

"There are condoms in my trunk," Alec continued. He folded the wet cloth and set it on the bedside table. It would leave a mark on the wood, but Mary didn't want to nag. "We'll take them to the gatehouse. If we go, that is. You will be staying a few more days, won't you?"

Mary tried to smile. "Do you want me to? I thought you were rather put out with me."

"Aye, so I was. I don't like a woman to be untruthful."

Like Edith. Alec had been almost mortally wounded by his wife.

"I promise to tell you everything from now on. Not about the agency, of course. Our work is confidential."

"I don't care about Burleigh or any of that. I've had enough problems of my own," Alec said, pulling the sheet back over her. "Well then, we've kissed and made up, so to speak. Are you cold? I could start a fire."

She was, even though it was June. The thick stone walls of Raeburn Court seemed to have trapped winter's chill inside them. "But we aren't staying here, are we?"

"Mac is still fussing over the gatehouse for us. I had some particular arrangements I wanted him to make. A surprise. He's not back yet."

"How do you know? He may have come back when we were—" Not *fornicating*, that sounded wretched.

But not *making love* either. That would attach far too much significance to what had just happened. Mary felt her heart wrinkle just a little.

"—otherwise occupied," Alec supplied. "No, he took the wagon, and I'd have heard it return. It's funny, we're so isolated up here—or were before the hotel was built—the least little noise was audible for miles. My little brother, Nick, claims he can hear a bird's feather drop over the loch. We always knew when our parents were returning from Edinburgh or London, and would be all lined up on the front step even before the carriage came through the gates. My mother thought we were touched."

He was relaxed, comfortable sitting on the edge of the bed in his own naked skin as he reminisced about his child-hood. Alec was, Mary thought, a rather magnificent crea-ture, almost larger than life, if that could be said about an actual living man. His shoulders were broad, his chest defined and dusted with dark silky hair. To her regret, one large hand had settled over his manhood. Mary gulped when she saw flecks of her blood on his thigh.

She grabbed the washcloth and made a hesitant swipe. He looked down and took the flannel from her.

"Hell. What have I been thinking? We should have a bath."

"T-together?" Why she should feel shy about it after what they'd just done was a mystery for the ages.

"Aren't you the saucy one? Nay, my love. My tub's not big enough for two—we'd get stuck and I don't think Evan would ever let me forget it. He's around here somewhere. You'll meet him. That is, if you want to. He's more or less a discreet fellow, which I canna say for Nick, wherever he may be. Wild as the day is long, that one."

He said it with affection. Alec loved his brothers. He was a nice man, too nice to go through life all alone up here with only their company, listening for feathers to drop into lakes.

Stop it. She pinched herself mentally. She mustn't confuse this afternoon's lust with love. What good would it do her to fall in love with Lord Alec Raeburn?

Chapter

29

Alec left Mary in the bath, dressed quickly, and went downstairs to the library. He was not going to dwell upon what had just happened, and what he hoped would happen again. And again.

And maybe again before he put her on the train Tuesday morning.

Or Wednesday.

He should be angry at Mary Evensong. Furious. She and her aunt had tricked him—hell, they'd tricked the entire ton for four years. Imagine, sending a little slip of a girl into the lion's den like the Burleigh house with an *unloaded* gun, washing society's dirty laundry as well as matching mistress with maid and bride with groom. The Evensong Agency did it all, and did it well.

And sweet blushing Mary had been at the heart of it all.

Well, perhaps she wasn't so sweet. Alec had felt the laceration of her tart tongue. But not, he reflected, quite where he wanted it now.

He threw himself on one of the cracked leather sofas and stared out the window. Ben-y-Vrackie stared back, blue and gloomy in the late afternoon sunshine. The house was quiet, his hired workmen no longer breaking the Sabbath rules. He was beginning to get hungry, but whatever edible items were in the larder had now been transferred to the gatehouse.

He was anxious and unsettled. He should feel relaxed. Triumphant. Bedding Mary had been a revelation. She had been so responsive that he'd almost forgotten to withdraw. He'd wanted to cover her with his body and crest together, as if they shared a common purpose. But that was ridiculous. He hadn't even known her true name until an hour ago.

Perhaps a drink would settle his nerves. He was about to rise when Evan strode into the room, his auburn hair a mass of dark wet curls. In fact, everything about him was damp, and rather ripe-smelling if Alec would be rude enough to mention it.

"Been swimming?" Alec asked.

"I have been feathering your love nest, you great daft idiot. Your man Mac waylaid me and ruined my Sunday. I must have moved every stick of furniture in the gatehouse and crawled on my belly like a reptile. There were desiccated rat carcasses everywhere. If I were ten again and she were still alive, we could have fun putting them in Miss McCorkle's bed."

Miss McCorkle had been one of their unfortunate governesses. She had been ancient, and the three lively Raeburn boys had not been easy charges. The boys hadn't killed her outright, but she'd retired from their household and died shortly afterward. Alec hoped the woman had forgiven them from wherever she was. As he recalled, she was Attila with a ruler, but she should have used a yardstick.

Evan headed for the drinks table without invitation and poured them both a staggering amount of Raeburn's Special Reserve. "So who is this woman you're so anxious to hide out with?"

"A . . . friend. Is everything ready? All the rats taken care of?"

Evan snorted. "I doona know why you need to bury your-self in that dusty little hole when you have all the Court to cavort in. We can take care of this Bauer fellow if he drops by."

"You'll be occupied at the distillery, and I don't expect you to stand as watchdog. You have your own house to sleep in. I'll just feel better if no one knows where Mary and I are. The man tried to rape her and set me on fire."

Evan gave a low whistle, waking Edith's dog, who had been sleeping on the other end of the sofa. Alec would probably pick up fleas from the mangy little beast. He twisted his face from eager little kisses and set the animal on the floor. Beowulf promptly jumped back on the sofa, curled himself back into a ball, and sighed.

"I knew that hotel would ruin the neighborhood. What can I do?"

Alec knew exactly what his brother might do for him, which meant he could spend the morning lingering in bed with Mary. "Are you going to the bank tomorrow?"

"It's Monday. I always go to the bank on Monday."

"Good. That will save me a trip into Pitcarran. I want you to find Sir John and tell him to put out a warrant for Bauer, or at least find out where he's gone. I'll put everything in writing."

"The magistrate? Isn't he an investor in the hotel?" Evan asked doubtfully.

"Aye, and if he knows what's good for business, he'll clap his pet doctor behind bars. I have witnesses, and that weasel Prescott will corroborate if he wants to collect a paycheck. I could shut the whole place down if I put my mind to it. Gah, you stink."

"You're welcome, brother." Evan swallowed his drink down and clinked the glass on a side table. "I'll just go upstairs to our old rooms and take a bath if I offend your delicate sensibilities so much."

"No!"

"No?"

"Mary's up there. Miss Arden. Miss Evensong," Alec amended.

"You have *three* women in your chamber? A regular

harem! By God, Alec, I'm proud of you! I thought you'd lost your touch when Edith died. We were all so worried about you."

"Damn it, Evan. Only Miss Evensong is up there, and you are to treat her with every courtesy." The thought of Evan catching a glimpse of Mary's fair freckled skin made his blood boil. He'd beaten Evan senseless before and could do it again. Evan smirked, and Alec felt his fingers curling into his palm as a matter of course.

"Who is this femme fatale? Is she related to that woman who runs the infamous Evensong Agency?"

Alec had confided his plans to Evan before he went back to London to hire Mrs. Evensong's services. Evan had thought the plan crazy; therefore he was confident of its success. Alec had always been the big thinker in the family, trying to be rational when it would have been so easy to let his temper and his size win the day.

But he wasn't feeling rational now. Mary Evensong made him feel . . . itchy. And not from Beowulf's fleas.

"She works for her aunt," Alec said, not wanting to go into the details. Evan would howl if he found out Alec had mistaken Mary for her aunt, no matter how convincing the wig and glasses had been, and he'd never live it down. Lord Alec Raeburn, consummate connoisseur of females from the age of fifteen, fooled? He could hear his brother's laugh now.

"When do I get to meet this paragon?"

"Not until you've made yourself presentable."

"You're not exactly top of the trees yourself at the moment. Your hair looks like it's been brushed with an egg beater, and you need a shave. A shave! Damn, what's happened to your beard? I knew there was something off about you."

"I was tired of it," Alec lied. Mary Evensong was some kind of Delilah.

"You are a hairy fellow. You'll be tired of shaving two or three times a day soon enough," Evan said, reminding him why he'd grown a beard in the first place.

"Mac can earn his keep. Did he come back with you?"

"He wasn't far behind, just putting the finishing touches on the old place. How long do you intend to live in the woods?"

"Just until the matter with Bauer is settled. If it turns out he's gone back to Edinburgh and the wife and kiddies, that might do." And then Mary would go, and he'd—

Just what the hell would he do all summer? Shear his sheep? Help his tenants with their harvests? Hang out in Evan's office all day and drink himself into numbness? Parliament would not be in session for months, and politics bored him silly to begin with. He'd spoken against the Boer Wars for years and what had that got him except accusations about his patriotism?

Maybe he should travel. Try to find Nick and drag him home.

Home to what? The beauty of the Highlands didn't make up for the emptiness inside Raeburn Court.

Maybe the emptiness wasn't inside his house, but inside him.

"Hang on while I write something up for Sir John. Then make yourself scarce. I don't want you frightening Miss Evensong." Alec went to his desk. Mary's letter to her aunt was in an envelope propped up against the inkwell. "You can take this, too, and mail it."

"Are you sure you don't want to come with me? It might come about better if you delivered your allegations in person."

"I don't want to leave Mary alone. Bauer could be lurking in the bushes right now."

Evan walked to the window. "No sign of him. How's your car running?"

"Like a dream. You should get yourself one," Alec replied, scribbling away the bare bones of what happened last night and early this morning.

"What, and drive from the dower house down the road to the distillery? It's not even half a mile, a waste of petrol when I've got perfectly good feet. A car would be useless in the winter, too."

"Someday cars and roads will be built for the elements, mark my words. All right, this should be enough to get the ball rolling. Tell Sir John I'll probably visit him on Wednesday if I take Mary to the station."

Evan raised a russet brow. "If? Never tell me you're going to ensconce your mistress here at Raeburn Court on a permanent basis."

"Mary isn't my mistress! She's a . . . friend who's had a great shock. She may not be ready to leave on Wednesday."

And Alec might not be ready for her to go, either.

Chapter

30

Mary was back in her embroidered white dress, its sash tied tight over a body that still felt boneless beneath her rigid corset, its high collar obscuring abrasions on her throat. Her hair was neatly repinned as though it had never suffered incursions from Alec's desperate fingers. She had soaked and scrubbed in the little bathing chamber that had been allotted to the Raeburn boys. It was not luxurious, but it had modern plumbing and copious amounts of hot running water, but not quite enough to wash away the sense of languor she had.

She would ask Alec to continue the tour of the house before they left—they really hadn't gotten beyond his room.

She wanted to see him inside Edith's golden chamber. Was she a glutton for punishment? Would he look rapturously at the portrait, or avoid it altogether?

Avoidance didn't mean he had no feelings left for his wife.

Mary tried to remember the correct turns in the halls, and eventually found Alec in the library, an empty tumbler beside him. He looked pleased to see her, so she must have acquitted herself well enough in his bedroom.

"You've just missed Evan. My brother."

"The one who runs the distillery."

"Aye. He was dragooned to help fix up our new quarters, and he's going to consult with the magistrate for me tomorrow. Are you ready?"

"Now that the workmen have left, I'd love to see what they've been doing," Mary said. "And—and I'd like to go up in the tower. The views must be spectacular."

Alec's face shuttered. "The views there are no better than what you saw at the Forsyth Palace Hotel."

She had to tell him—she'd promised to be honest. "I—I've already been up there today. It was Edith's room, wasn't it?"

"That room is locked!" Alec glared at her. "Let me guess. A locked door is nothing to the resourceful Mrs. Evensong."

"I'm afraid not. I was tutored by a private detective who was taught by a lock-picking expert. Actually, I think the expert was a criminal. I cannot crack a safe, but a simple lock poses no problem." It was just one of her many accomplishments, but she doubted Alec would appreciate most of them.

"If you've been up there once today, isn't that enough?"

"It should be. But it isn't."

"Explain yourself."

"I'm not sure I can. I just wonder as you're remodeling other rooms in the house, why you haven't touched hers."

Alec lurched up off the couch and poured more golden liquid into his glass. He didn't ask her to join him. He tossed off the entire glass and poured more.

Oh dear. She was driving him to drink when she wanted somehow to soothe his soul.

"D-don't you think it would be better for your house if you, um, exorcised your late wife from the premises? You might be happier here," Mary ventured.

If Alec was a regular client, she would have been much more forthright in tone. People paid her for her opinions, after all. They expected her to solve their problems whether they were domestic, professional, or personal.

Alec stopped mid-pour. "Exorcised? Are you saying my house is haunted?"

"Of course not!" Only his heart seemed to be.

Alec set the glass down untouched. He turned, his expression somber. "It seemed disrespectful somehow. To touch her things. Invade her space. But now that I've avenged her, perhaps you are right."

"I know I am." Mary tried to sound sure of herself. It was unnatural to have a virtual museum dedicated to a woman who had not loved him. The ghost of Lady Edith Raeburn might not walk along the cold stone floors of Raeburn Court, but her unhappiness lingered over her husband for certain.

"All right." Alec walked to the doorway. "We'll have a look then. I havena been up there since she—since she died."

Beowulf jumped off the sofa and followed his master down the corridor and up the stairs. Mary had difficulty keeping up with Alec's long strides. Once he'd made up his mind to do something, he seemed anxious to get on with it.

Up and up they went until they landed at the heavy oak door. He reached into a pocket and pulled out a ring of keys.

"Or would you prefer to do the honors? What did you use? A hairpin?"

"Yes." Mary resisted pulling one out of her bun. She didn't want to be a show-off. "I mean, no. It's not locked. You don't need the key."

The door creaked open on its unoiled hinges. The late afternoon sun slanted in the mullioned windows, making all the gleaming surfaces gleam even brighter. Alec took a step, then stopped. "After you."

Mary slipped by him. Beowulf raced in and jumped onto the bed, rooting around some tasseled pillows before he lay down with a happy snort.

"He misses her," Mary said.

"Aye, he's about the only one. Edith was not a very popular mistress. I should not speak ill of the dead. Imagine what folks will say about me when I'm gone. They talk about me enough now."

Mary had to do something to rehabilitate his reputation, but she couldn't think what. To be suspected of murder was a terrible thing to bear.

It was not like her to be idea-less. But standing so close to him, her wits had gone begging.

Alec did not once glance up at the giant portrait of Edith. His hands were stuffed in his pockets, and he looked somewhat pinched, as if he'd split if he moved too quickly. There was no place for a man his size to sit in this room anyway— the chairs were unequal to his weight. Beowulf did not look anxious to share the bed, either.

"Would Edith's parents like the painting?" Mary asked.

"I suppose. It doesn't do her justice, though."

Lord, could the woman have been even more beautiful? Mary's heart sank.

"I think you should offer it to them."

"You're probably right." His hands dug deeper in his pockets. They were barely standing a foot inside the room. Mary reminded herself it was her suggestion to come up, for all she wanted to flee.

"Unless you want it as a memento—"

"God, no! I told you I haven't been up here in months. Do you think I stand up here and worship at her altar after what she did?"

Alec was angry. She had pushed too far, but then she always did when she thought she was right about something. Which was probably much too often.

"Of course not. I didn't mean that at all. What about her clothing and personal things? Her mother might help you sort through them. Some items could be given away to charity. You could start a memorial fund."

"You snooped in the closets, too?"

"Alec," Mary said softly, "the wardrobe is standing open." Both doors were in fact wide open, as though Edith had gone hunting for something and hadn't found it yet. She seemed to favor white. Many of the silks and satins were in various shades—it was surprising how many colors "white" came in.

"A memorial fund, eh? That isn't such a bad idea. Her parents might like that. They don't talk much to me anymore, as you can imagine."

"Do they . . . think you . . ."

"Killed her?" Alec spat the words. "Aye. Or at least they hold me responsible. I couldn't tell them about Bauer. It would have broken their hearts. Edith was an only child, you see. Their pride and joy when it suited them."

"What do you mean?" Mary asked.

"I think they knew she was a bit of a handful, but to be critical of her meant they had to question themselves. How they raised her. I think they hoped for more than a lowly baron as a husband for her, but the fact I was filthy rich and Scottish helped. Edinburgh's nae so far away. They used to visit often."

Mary almost smiled. It was true a baron was not as grand as a duke, but if the baron was Alec Raeburn, how could one possibly have an objection?

"They shouldn't have married her off so young," Alec continued. "She wasn't ready. I failed her."

Mary laid a hand on his sleeve. "Stop thinking that way." Her cheeks grew hot, and her eyes dropped to the carpet. "I have a confession, Alec, another one, and it's almost as bad as the first two. Maybe even worse."

Alec sighed. "What now? I know who you are, and that you took it upon yourself to break and enter. Have you robbed a bank? Blackmailed a client? Do you have a husband stashed away somewhere you've never slept with? You wouldn't be the first." His laughter was hollow.

"I've promised not to lie to you again. And anyway, the lies I told were more lies of omission than commission."

"Don't go all Jesuitical on me, Miss Evensong. I've had my classical education. Let's just say you've been economical with the truth. Why, you could be a Scot yourself. We do mind our pence."

"I'm not very proud of myself." Mary took a breath. "I read quite a lot of Edith's diary before you came back this afternoon. I—I apologize."

She waited to be castigated. When Alec said nothing, she stumbled on. "Forgive me for saying so, but she seemed very silly and very young. You could not have known what she was thinking of—she barely knew herself."

He didn't raise his voice, but Mary shivered just the same. "What else have you done today, Miss Evensong? I leave you alone for an hour and you've invaded my desk drawers and locked rooms. Is there no end to your meddling?"

"You've paid me to meddle! That is, it's what I do. Usually people accept my suggestions."

"I didna ask you to do anything but expose Josef Bauer!" Alec said, each word leavened by a heavier Scottish accent. Mary had noted when his feelings were engaged, he lost his cut-glass public school accent. "I doona need you poking around my house and picking at scabs. You've done your part—more than your part if you count an hour ago. I thought we shared something, but if it was just a pity fuck—"

Mary felt a buzzing in her ears. "What on earth are you talking about?"

"You, trying to make me feel better with your ridiculous proposition. 'Relieve me from my virginity,' my arse. Well, I'm never going to feel better, Mary Arden Evensong. Not today. Not tomorrow, not in a hundred years."

He wasn't mad—just miserable. Mary suppressed the urge to claw down Edith's portrait and stomp it. Where had the devilish, teasing Alec Raeburn gone, the toast of back-stage corners and private balconies? Something was not right here. Not right at all.

"Why not, Alec? You have your whole life before you."

"Do I?" he asked bitterly. "Everywhere I go, there are whispers. My own brother won't come home. Do you really think some charity in Edith's name will stop the rumors?"

"It's a start. Perhaps if you enlisted Edith's parents' help—"

Mary reached out to touch him, willing him to look her in the face. If he did, he would see the truth, plain as day.

Chapter

31

$\mathcal{A}$ lec plucked Mary's plump fingers away and walked to the tower window. The flagstones below had been scrubbed and scrubbed, but he could swear he still saw the blood. He wasn't even really angry that she had snooped in the desk. It was his own fault—the diary was right there where anyone could find it. He should have destroyed it instead of torturing himself with it these past months.

He put a hand on the glass. One of his clumsy, useless paws that brought nothing but fear to most. "You don't understand anything."

"Then explain it to me."

The vista had calmed him all his life. The shadows and clouds on the mountains were as much a part of him as the air he breathed, but today he felt nothing.

How often had Edith stood in this very spot, feeling trapped?

"I left Edith alone up here in this tower when I shouldn't have. She was so young, a girl really, when we married. She objected to my mother's suite almost at once, perhaps because it was adjacent to my father's, therefore mine. She was afraid I would come in to bother her."

"Exerting your husbandly rights is not precisely bothering her. You didn't try to take her by force, did you?"

Alec felt the blood drain from his face. Even Mary doubted his honor.

He had been damned and doomed for his size and strength all his life. Only his brothers understood, for they were much the same dimensions as he. It was one thing to wrestle with them—he would never touch a woman without every effort to be gentle.

"Of course not," he said with resignation. If Mary didn't believe him, what did it matter? She would go back to London and her business and her secrets, and he'd be right here, alone, where he belonged. "I left her while I amused myself in London, and then even after I returned, we lived separate lives. She breakfasted by herself. Dined by herself. I'd stopped trying. We barely spoke, and when we did talk, it was to argue."

He ran a hand over his nonexistent beard. He missed it. Well, now he could grow it back since he wasn't trying to please Mary Arden anymore. "We could have managed in a white marriage. People do. People whose desires are kept under control. But I didn't have any self-control. I thought with my cock. I'd fuck anyone available. Maybe I'm still doing that."

He heard Mary's hiss of breath as she understood the insult. He didn't mean to hurt her, but after today, he was no longer sure of anything. Who was Mary, really? An innocent virgin or a conniving businesswoman? Certainly someone who uncovered his most closely guarded shame without much difficulty. He was unraveling before her eyes.

"Alec, she rejected you for all the years of your marriage. Made you feel like a—" He listened as she reached for words that would hurt *him*. He'd used them all on himself. *Beast. Lecher. Animal.*

"Yes, yes. Like some kind of brute. No matter how gentle I tried to be, she was repulsed. But I should have understood and tried harder. She was so afraid of me that she took her own life rather than tell me the truth."

"Perhaps she was afraid to tell you she'd broken her marriage vows."

He shook his head. If only it were that simple. "When I had more than a dozen times? You know my well-deserved reputation. No, it was worse than that. Much worse."

Alec needed to tell her if there was any future for them at all beyond today. He sat down on the window seat. Nine months ago, Edith had climbed up on this jacquard cushion to plunge to her death.

"Edith was pregnant with Bauer's child, Mary." He was proud his voice didn't break—he'd never uttered the words out loud. Not even Evan knew. "The good doctor offered to get rid of it for her, but apparently she couldn't go through with it. I gather you didn't get that far in her diary.

"She tried to tell me, but I didn't pay proper attention. We quarreled as usual over something stupid—can you believe I can't even remember what? I've tried and tried, and it's all a blur, just accusations and recriminations running together like a jerky movie reel. She ran away from me, came up here, and jumped."

He didn't dare look at Mary behind him, just focused on the stone courtyard below. "I would have cared for the child as my own, I swear, even if it had meant Evan not inheriting. I always wanted children—that's really why I married. It's ironic. I'll never have any of my own, and Edith's child is lost to me forever. She didn't trust me to raise it. To her, it was better to kill the baby and herself than depend upon me to do the right thing."

"Oh, Alec." He heard the swish of her skirts as she walked across the room and sat down beside him. He still couldn't face her, couldn't face his failure.

She didn't try to touch him, thank God. He thought he might shatter if she did. The quiet of the room had a sound of its own and Alec had never felt such bleakness. His confession had ended what was between them, whatever it was. It was just as well. But at least she would understand why he wasn't fit for anyone.

The minutes stretched between them. Why didn't she just

get up and go? He'd arrange to have them driven down to the railway station first thing tomorrow morning, if Oliver could be untangled from Mac.

"You cannot blame yourself. She was unbalanced." Her voice was soft. Reasonable. She spoke to him as if he was an injured child.

He turned to her, his anger growing. "Did you hear anything I said?"

"Every word. She did a horrible thing. *She* did it—it had nothing to do with you. You were patient with her for four years. Most men would have sought a legal separation or even a divorce. You gave her everything she wanted, and still she betrayed you."

Alec waved his arm at the overdecorated room. "I just gave her *things*. They mean nothing."

"They meant enough to her to write about them in her diary, pages and pages of descriptions of furniture and jewels and dresses. You were very generous."

"I tried to buy my way into her favor," he said, bitter. "It didn't work."

"And never would have! You are no manipulator, Alec. Not really. Yes, you go after what you want. But you are a good man at the heart of it. You would never have tried to seduce me. Remember, *I* asked *you*. If Bauer has any skill over you, it's that he sees weakness and takes advantage. I don't think—" She paused. "I don't think Edith could have been altogether in her right mind at the end. She was a perfect candidate for Bauer's spa—unworldly, high-strung, rich, and hysterical in the truest sense of the word. She was so awfully young. Immature for her years. Most twenty-one-year-old women are mothers. You told me yourself she had no friends, and her family was eager to hand her over to you. I know from what you said and from what I did manage to read in the journal, the servants that remained did not like her. I read her complaints in her own words."

"She was mercurial." At first he'd been charmed by her flights of fancy. She was so beautiful he thought he'd give and forgive her anything, but had not anticipated the cost.

"Listen to yourself, making excuses for the inexcusable. Now listen to *me*. You cannot blame yourself for what happened. You have protected her reputation throughout all this at the expense of your own."

"What good would it have done to tell the truth? No one would have believed me, and I'd only appear a bigger cad than I was already. I learned long ago that no one wins here, certainly not poor Edith. The fact is, she was desperate and I didn't help her."

"I am not going to sit here arguing with you. You are wrong, and I am right." Mary's face was set, and for a flash he could see the seventy-year-old woman she would become. No wonder she could fool people. Would she be around so he could see her grow into that old age every day? Be lectured by her, harassed and harangued? She touched something inside him he thought he never had to begin with.

Alec Raeburn had never expected to fall in love. People of his class did not. *Should* not. His father had, and look what that had gotten him. He'd fallen for his tenant farmer's daughter. Once the ardor between them inevitably cooled, their mismatch was a misery. His parents had been more or less civil, but Alec and his brothers had not been fooled. His mother's tempestuous rages were brought on by disgust at something his father had done, or didn't do. The old baron spent much of his marriage hiding out in London just as Alec had done. The man hadn't gone there for the views.

Men were expected to break their wedding vows, and Alec had. He had wanted Edith, for who had not the year she'd debuted? But they'd never enjoyed even a temporary warmth between them, a honeymoon phase he could look back at with gentle regret as he squired his latest mistress down Bond Street.

What would marriage be like to a woman who was not mercurial, but sensible? Level-headed. A woman whose wise advice had been accepted by valets and viscounts. A woman with russet hair and gold-flecked skin, a stubborn chin, and a bosom that could only be described as spectacular.

"You are right and I am wrong," he repeated. If only it were that easy.

She nodded. "Exactly."

What the hell. Maybe he could persuade himself not to think of anything unpleasant or meaningful for a few days. Just have a sensual interlude before the past came back to haunt him. He had the rest of his life to be guilty and unhappy.

Alec got on his feet. "Let's get out of here. That is, if you're still game to bunk down in the gatehouse for a day or two."

Mary looked up, smiling at him as though she had no reason whatever to be repulsed by him and the mess he'd made of everything. "You have promised me a holiday. I have no intention of leaving just yet."

"Even after what I've told you. You are a most peculiar woman."

"I shouldn't like to upset your valet and your brother if they've gone to all the trouble of fixing up the place for our use."

He wouldn't mention the rats.

Chapter

32

$\mathcal{M}$ary held on to her hat as Alec's Pegasus bumped through an old-growth forest. The estate trail to the north gatehouse was much worse than the public road they came in on. The canopy of trees arced above them, blocking out sunlight and mountains and sky. The air was fragrant with pine and ancient earth. Mary felt as though she were submerged beneath a green sea, its dim light somewhat oppressive.

"No one uses this path anymore," Alec shouted over the roar of the engine. "As you can tell." The car dipped into a rut and miraculously pulled out. He shifted gears and slowed down, wary of the darting creatures ahead. The car had awakened a squadron of red squirrels who chattered above them as they rolled onward.

They came at last to the stone lodge, a little smaller than the one at the front gates. Alec parked in the attached stable, throwing a tarp over the vehicle once he'd helped Mary out and gathered up their cases.

There were condoms in his trunk, and Mary was determined to put them to use. Alec needed connection—he needed *her*.

No wonder he had been so determined to bring Bauer down. She had been very careful not to show her horror when Alec revealed the truth about Edith's death, but she *was* horrified. To live under such a burden—no wonder Alec had lost himself in the fleshpots of London. Mary almost could not find it in her heart to sympathize with Edith, for what she had done had ruined three lives.

Would Alec ever be able to move forward, to find a normal woman to share a life with? He deserved to.

Mary had fallen, and fallen hard. Well, it was inevitable. She'd been so busy masterminding other peoples' relationships that it was only a matter of time before she got around to masterminding her own. However, she didn't really have a "relationship" with Alec. It had begun as a business arrangement, then transmuted into something she had no vocabulary for.

Lust factored into it, of course. It was hard to remain unmoved at the sight of Lord Alec Raeburn's magnificent body. But there was more. She enjoyed his company, his conversation, his teasing.

She enjoyed his touch. Oops, she was back to lust again, she thought ruefully.

Alec shouldered into the oak door, ducking his head as he entered the narrow hall. He set the stacked trunks on the clean-swept flagstone and turned to her. "Well, what do you think?"

The house smelled of lemons and lavender. Bunches of the latter were dangling from rough beams overhead. The staircase was roped off, discouraging exploration of the upper floor.

"What's up there?" Mary asked.

"A smallish bedroom with a lot of broken things, as far as I can gather. Mac and my brother stuck everything that wasn't functional up there. There are two bedrooms on the ground floor, so you can have your privacy if you wish it."

Mary had not thought of actually sleeping alongside Alec, although she had last night. She could decide about her accommodations later.

Really, it had been a long day and the sun was still over the mountains. The fire, the confessions, the intimacy—one of those alone should have her knackered to bits. Instead, she felt a surge of hope as Alec guided her around the little dwelling.

To the right of the staircase was the small kitchen, furnished with a simple wood table, two benches, and a sagging black range that had seen better days. Dented pots hung from hooks on the wall. Several baskets with foodstuffs and a blue bowl holding three apples were on the table.

"We'll be roughing it. Do you cook?" Alec asked.

"A little." But not really well enough to impress Alec or any man.

"We'll take turns, then. I burn toast better than Escoffier ever dreamed. Let's go into the parlor."

They crossed the hall to the other side of the house. The parlor, too, was small, but someone had put flowers in a glass bottle on the bare mantel. There was a dusty-looking sofa, one chair, some odd tables, and a threadbare rug. This was a very far cry from the grandeur of Raeburn Court, but it was charming in its way. The windows sparkled and a wildly overgrown perennial garden, the source of the flowers, was visible through the wavy glass. A painted door next to the fireplace led to a bedroom, which in turn led to another bedroom. Both quilted counterpanes and linens were frosty white, and had obviously been imported from the main house.

"Home sweet home," Alec said. "In all honesty I must point out the chamber pots under the beds. There is a privy in the back garden behind the kitchen. No one has lived here for at least a half a decade, so it shouldn't be too bad. Mac tells me he removed the spiderwebs from the seat personally. Ready to run screaming, or settle in?"

"It's adorable," Mary said truthfully. "I half-expect to see Snow White and a dwarf or two pop up."

"If the story is 'Jack and the Beanstalk,' I'm your giant. This isn't quite how I planned your holiday. If we get word that Bauer has been taken care of, we can go back to the

Court and listen to the hammers. Are you hungry? It must be past teatime by now."

"Starved, actually." Sex must act as a stimulant. The bread and cheese she'd had for lunch felt like eons ago.

Alec lit the old stove without too much difficulty, pumped some water into a copper kettle, and put it on to boil. Mary peeked into a basket—more bread and cheese, a tin of crumbled currant biscuits, a chunk of ham. She sliced and arranged while Alec dealt with the teapot.

The china on the shelf was mismatched but it made no difference. They sat at the table and ate.

"Mac will bring us more supplies. Being short-staffed means the larder up at the house is pretty bare."

"This is fine," Mary said. In fact, this reminded her of sitting up over the shop having tea with her parents when she was a little girl. Before her father's success, there had been plenty of broken biscuits and old cans filled with something mysterious that hadn't sold.

"I can make cheese toast later for supper."

Mary smiled. "But you said you burned toast. This is enough for me, but please yourself." A large man like Alec probably needed to eat frequently. Not that he was fat—he was simply solid everywhere.

"If you don't mind cleaning up, I'd like to get something ready for you," Alec said as he pushed himself away from the table.

Mary didn't mind. Conjuring Alec with his sleeves rolled up over a dishpan was impossible. Barons didn't wash up.

"Meet me in the back garden when you're done. There's still plenty of daylight left. I had thought originally we'd do it in the parlor, but I forgot how small it is."

Do it? Do *what*? By tacit agreement Mary had supposed there would be further sexual adventures between them, but exactly what kind of acrobatics did Alec expect from her? The sitting room couch was obviously too short—and lumpy—to be of much use, and Mary didn't fancy lying on the floor on the ancient rug, so she could see Alec's objection about the parlor. What was wrong with either of the bedrooms?

She didn't want to strip naked in the jungle of a garden! There must be bugs out there, and who knew what else? What if a shepherd or someone came upon them in their altogether, like an Adam and Eve who had strayed very far from Eden?

Although the Highlands were the closest Mary had ever come to heaven. Even the ramshackle gatehouse had its charms.

From the high window over the sink, Mary could see the top of Alec's head go by as he stomped around outside in the walled garden, whistling. She dried her hands on a towel mid-scrub, climbed on a bench, and peered out. He had taken his jacket, waistcoat, and tie off, had a scythe in his hand and was sweeping through the overgrown lawn with a vengeance. Tasseled grass fell over his feet and flew into the empty raised beds of what must once have held vegetables. He had cleared a large uneven rectangle—trapezoid? She'd been better at algebra than geometry—twice the size of the sitting room already in just the short time she'd been putting away leftovers and washing tea cups. There was a large wooden box against the open stable door and something atop it wrapped in an old quilt. Fascinated, she watched him enter the shed, come out with a rusty rake, and bundle all the grass to one side.

Coupling with Alec outside in the fading light should have shocked her, but instead she felt a frisson of interest. If he intended to take her on the lawn, she could always lay that quilt down before she picked up chiggers. Her skin tended to be sensitive, and there was no point in fighting against nature. Nature always won.

Mary hopped down and dried the dishes, her heart racing just a bit. She had broken a great many rules today—what was one more? Her vow of honesty to Alec applied to herself—she wanted him, inside or outside. She'd gone from being a respectable spinster to a harlot in just a matter of days, but she suspected Alec Raeburn had that effect on women without even trying. Now that she knew the nature of his wounds beneath the gruff exterior, she was even more smitten.

But she couldn't "fix" him with a frolic in the grass. It was only in novels that the love of a good woman worked magic by the last page. She had seen too much in her four years as Mrs. Evensong to expect Alec to shed his melancholy overnight. But Mary did have this night, and she meant to use it, perhaps not wisely but well.

Deciding to surprise—and shock—him, she kicked off her shoes, unhooked and unbuttoned herself down to her corset and shift, and pulled every pin from her hair. Mary would signal she was ready for anything he had in mind. Let him finish the job of undressing her.

No. Why waste precious time? Mary unlaced her corset, tore off her shift, and folded everything neatly on the kitchen table. Old habits died hard.

Taking a deep breath and tossing her hair back, she stepped out the kitchen door onto the cool, shorn grass. Alec's mouth dropped open and the handkerchief he was using to wipe his brow fell unnoticed to the toe of his boot.

"I'm finished," she said in a husky voice.

"Mother of God," Alec croaked. He made no move to come near her.

Had she made a mistake? Misunderstood his desire? Maybe he wanted to have nothing else to do with her after this afternoon, despite bringing her here. Suddenly feeling way too brazen, she lurched toward the box and lifted the edge of the quilt. She could wrap herself in it and spare herself further humiliation. Obviously she had misread the situation, which wasn't like her at all.

Her emotions were a jangled mess, and she felt her cheeks grow hot and the rest of her body freeze up. What had she been thinking? Clearly, she had not been thinking at all. But Alec had been so friendly over tea she had assumed his surprise was of a sexual nature. She tugged the quilt and the box pitched to one side.

"Careful!" Alec shouted, finally snapping out of his

torpor. He raced over to her and took the material from her numb fingers. "There's a phonograph under there. I had Mac bring it, and some wax cylinders, too. I was going to teach you how to waltz. But it seems you have other ideas, and I like yours much better."

"Wh-what?"

Alec cloaked Mary in the quilt. It had definitely not been stored in a linen closet with lavender and she wasn't sure eau de quilt was at all appealing. Glancing down, tufts of batting were sticking out where the stitches had disappeared. Tiny black specks lodged in the white cotton. Not bugs, but—

"You know. Dancing. One two three, one two three. You told me the other evening you had never been to a ball, and I thought—"

"Mice!" Mary shrieked, throwing the quilt at Alec and hopping up and down.

"Surely not," Alec said, shaking the quilt with vigor.

"Not now, but they have been nesting in it. And defecating! Ugh!" She brushed imaginary mouse droppings off her goose-pimpled skin.

Alec looked genuinely stricken. "Oh, dear. I'm afraid that's my fault. I grabbed the first thing at hand in the shed to cover up the phonograph so I could surprise you."

"I'm surprised, all right," Mary said, feeling foolish. And very naked.

"Do you want another bath? I'm sure I could fill up some buckets and heat them."

Three baths in one day. Such luxury. But she had seen the tin hip bath in the kitchen corner and was not much impressed. Besides, she'd only worn the quilt a few seconds at most.

"I'm all right. Just my pride is bruised. You must think me very forward, t-taking off all my clothes." May the earth open up and swallow her whole.

"I like you forward, Mary. And backward. Come here."

Chapter

33

The sun had dipped behind the mountain range, but the sky was bright enough for Alec to see every delicious inch of her. She stepped into his arms, and shivered. Alec smelled soap and grass and Mary, a heady combination.

When she'd opened the kitchen door, he thought his heart might forget to beat. For a short woman, she was very— commanding. Compelling. All that pale skin and tumbling red hair just begged to be touched.

It had only been a few hours since they'd argued. Less than that since they'd been tangled in each other's arms. Alec felt like a pendulum, swinging from one extreme to the other. Mary Evensong unsettled him.

But right now he felt steady, holding this naked woman against him in the lengthening shadows. She deserved a dance, and he was the man to teach her. Who said clothes were required? No strangling starched white tie, no tails or patent leather dancing shoes. Tonight, he would be tribal. Primeval.

He cupped a smooth cheek. "At the hotel, you said you were too old to learn how to dance. I'm going to prove you wrong."

Mary looked up uncertainly. "I have not danced since I was a girl at school."

"That's criminal, in my opinion. You were meant to dance." He put one hand on her waist and held her arm up, and bent to kiss her fingertips. "Just like this. But I think you are onto something, Miss Evensong. One's movements will be far less restricted if one is not encumbered by constricting clothing."

"Oh, I am so embarrassed," Mary mumbled into his shirt.

"Don't be! I think you are brilliant. Haven't you told me often enough that you are always right? 'You are wrong and I am right'—wasn't that how you put it?" Alec released her and quickly divested himself of his own garments. Mary looked everywhere about the garden but at him, her cheeks the color of the climbing roses at the kitchen door.

"Now then." He inserted his fingers inside a waxed cylinder and placed it onto the mandrel of the phonograph. "This will only play for two minutes. When you're at a real ball, of course a waltz lasts much longer—quite a treat for the young folks in the first flush of calf-love. Do you know, when peasants first waltzed, their faces touched? I'm afraid I'd have to pick you up to accomplish that."

When he was a youth, the prospect of spinning around the dance floor with a pretty girl had made him scandalously hard on more than one occasion. He was not far from that state now.

The cylinder was worn from frequent play, and the tinny sound was nothing like a live orchestra. Still, Mary's face was lit with joy as she drifted in his arms over the fresh-cut grass, her tantalizing body brushing against his. Alec held her too close, but that was the point, was it not?

It was inconvenient to pause every two minutes to replace the cylinder, so after a while, Alec abandoned the Edison Gold Moulded Records and simply whirled her around without music, counting softly, then not speaking at all.

The shadows deepened and the air cooled. This was the most extraordinary dusk of his life, alone with Mary in the abandoned garden, naked as they were born, bodies moving to inner music. They circled and swept and dipped, eyes meeting all the while. She had overcome her mortification and smiled up at him as if he were a prince.

He was not that. Would never be. But under Mary Evensong's artless gaze, he had never felt a better man.

Forget the past, she had told him. Perhaps it was possible if he had her in his arms.

"Are you cold?" he asked, a bit breathless.

"Only a little."

He should bring her ever closer, kiss her, cover her with his body to keep her warm. Fall to the grass and let nature take its course. But that would be taking advantage, and might prove to be uncomfortable besides.

"A little is too much. Come, we'll go inside and I'll start a fire in the parlor. We can have some wine." The temperature had dropped and he felt it himself, his own skin sheened with sweat.

Alec wrapped the phonograph in the ragged quilt and returned it to the corner where Mac had hidden it. Perhaps they'd dance again tomorrow.

"I'm going to get dressed," Mary said from the kitchen doorway.

Alec lifted a brow. "Why? You are lovely just as you are."

She was, all gold and ivory and copper in the waning light. He wished he could paint like his brother Nick—he'd immortalize her perfection this night so he could see her on other nights after she had gone.

She crossed her arms over her breasts. "You don't need to be kind."

"Kind! You overestimate me, madam. I'm no saint, just an observant fellow. You are beautiful."

"I've never been beautiful in my life, Alec. Or at least no one has ever told me so. Handsome, perhaps. Not a complete antidote."

She looked so grave he burst out laughing. "You have obviously been associating with the wrong gentlemen. I could look at you all night and never get tired." He ruffled her hair, which was in disarming disarray over one shoulder.

"Tell you what. If you will be more at ease, get into a dressing gown. I'll put together something from the kitchen and we can relax a little before bedtime. I'm ashamed to say I feel a little worn out after spinning you around. I'm out of shape."

"Tell me another. *You* are the beautiful one."

"Flattery will get you everywhere. Go on in and dress. I'll be with you in a moment."

The sky was turquoise and lavender, the mountains navy blue. Alec stood in the patch of grass breathing crisp Highland air. There was nothing like it anywhere. All those glittering months in London were not worth one gulp. This was his true home, and somehow he'd get things back to rights.

A moth fluttered over a line of rotten straw bee skeps in the far corner of the walled garden. Mr. Hamilton, the last gatekeeper here, had provided Raeburn Court with honey. The man had died years ago, but Alec still remembered the taste. Maybe he could become a beekeeper himself, kitted out with one of those suits—if he could find one to fit him. He barked out a laugh, imagining himself with smudge pots. Likely he'd be stung to death.

He would have to find a proper occupation up here. It was time for him to settle down.

Settled. Unsettled. His thoughts turned to the woman in the house behind him.

Somewhat reluctantly, he brushed off his clothes and put them back on. He'd missed his moment to take Mary under the single star that had appeared in the changing sky. It had almost been enough to hold her close, their bodies gliding together effortlessly, around and around until he barely felt his feet on the ground. She was easy to lead, responsive. Dancing with her was much less difficult than conversing, when she was apt to follow her own brand of music.

She had surprised him in so many ways today, some pleasant, some not. The past few days had been tumultuous—it was time for a glass of wine before the fire. An early night.

Alec entered the spotless kitchen. Add housewifery to Mary's list of assets. He rummaged through a basket and came upon some stale cheese straws and a bottle of burgundy. That would do.

He found Mary in the single chair, her nightgown buttoned and robe belted. She had plaited her glorious hair. A modest fire was already going. Just how long had he stared at that star?

She was efficient. Neat. He longed to muss her.

But it was too soon. She must be sore and tired.

"It's chilly for June," she said. "I hope you don't mind that I started the fire. It was all laid."

"Not at all. It can be a little nippy up here this time of year, certainly colder than down south. Summer is slow to come." Alec poured the wine into heavy lead glassware Mac had packed. "Here's to a Highland summer," he said, passing her a glass.

She held it but didn't drink.

"Would you prefer white wine? There's a German hock in one of the baskets, although it won't be properly chilled."

"Oh, no. It's the toast I object to."

"What have you got against summer? Sunny blue skies, puffy clouds, all those birds and butterflies and flowers."

"But I won't be here to see them," Mary said quietly.

You could be, he wanted to say. But he didn't.

"Here's to summer then, in London as well. I suppose you don't get away much, chained to your desk and all that," he babbled.

"Not generally, unless I'm needed to iron out something at a nobleman's country house. That has happened a time or two." She took a sip of wine.

"A busman's holiday, then."

"Yes."

He wouldn't ask her about those trips—she wouldn't tell him anyway. Her discretion was a good thing. No one would hear of the fool he'd made of himself over Edith.

Alec crunched into a cheese straw and admired the fire. The spit and crackle was the only sound in the room. Somehow the wordless understanding between them as they danced outside had not accompanied them indoors. Mary looked tense, clutching at her wineglass as if it was a life preserver.

Alec cleared his throat. "It was a lovely evening. You dance beautifully."

"I suppose it's like riding a bicycle. One remembers after a bit. You are a very good instructor."

All this politeness was driving him mad. He set his glass down with a clunk.

"Let's not beat about the bush. I want to take you to bed, Mary. Again, but if you can't bear it—"

"Of course I can bear it! I'm not made of spun sugar."

"You may as well be. You're a delicate little thing, and I've already—" Verbs tumbled about his head, none of them useful.

"Before, you said you needed time to recover, too. But you are able again now," Mary said.

"Oh, yes," he said with understatement. "But you might not be."

She stood up. "Let's see, shall we?"

Was it that easy? Alec didn't trust the happiness that swelled his heart. He followed her to the first bedroom, its simplicity at odds with his convoluted thoughts. She undressed with unromantic efficiency, while Alec's fingers fumbled at the button of his flies.

This was all wrong again, too cerebral. She had been right earlier—there should be no talking. He wanted to rob her of her calm acceptance as she lay passive underneath the lavender-scented bedclothes. Ravish her until she cried his name.

Alec tamped down his brutish desires and climbed into the bed. They both lay still, side by side, looking up at the ceiling. There was a damp patch very much resembling Africa—or possibly South America?—up there. He wondered if Mary noticed.

He was not about to start a discussion about geography with her now. He was not going to talk one word for the next . . . hm, he probably wouldn't last all that long. Mary Arden Evensong did something to him that wiped his years of experience and expertise quite clean.

Alec sat up and stripped them both of the coverlet and sheet. There must have been something on his face that prevented Mary from questioning. He parted her thighs—gratified by the slightest tremble—and buried his tongue inside her, no teasing preliminaries, just stark possession. Women loved this, and Alec did, too. The forbidden taste, the helpless acquiescence, and the musky scent unique to each recipient always brought him to a hardness that was near-agony.

To deny himself and bring pleasure became all-consuming. Mary's tart sweetness drove him to madness, and she was at her edge before he could finesse her vault into that brief infinity when everything was crystal clear.

It was a very good thing they were alone in the gatehouse, for her cries could have awakened poor dead Mr. Hamilton. Banshees had nothing on Mary when she reached her peak, and Alec smiled with pride as he took her over it again and again. To be responsible for unraveling practical, perfect Mary Evensong—here was the role he was born for.

Her braid was history, her eyes wild. Alec lifted himself over her and lost himself, hoping never to be found.

Chapter

34

*I*t was too much, and yet not enough. Mary held on to Alec, tumbling and twisting, vowing to finally be silent. It was impossible to be dignified, but she did not have to yell her head off—although Alec didn't seem to be startled. In fact, he was smiling when he wasn't ravishing her mouth with hot, reckless kisses. Sinking himself so deep inside her, both tongue and cock, that she felt as if they were one person.

Their dance had been the sweet appetizer, but this coupling defied description. Mary shut her eyes and lifted off the bed, toward South America on the ceiling, or was it a squashed Australia? One of the Poles? Her map skills were hazy at this point. Alec should do something about the damp patch before the ceiling crashed down on their heads. But not right now, please, God.

How would she be able to go back to London and continue with her celibate life? Now that she knew what she had been missing—

There were plenty of men in London, she reminded herself. But perhaps it wouldn't be the same with just any man. Alec was special, a very unique specimen.

She *loved* him.

Oh, dear. That wasn't supposed to happen. When she'd made her grand bargain with him, she had been looking for quite a different experience, something almost impersonal. This—whatever it was—was about as personal as it got.

With an anguished groan, Alec tore himself away from her and spilled into the sheet. So, he had enough presence of mind not to get her with child. That was the right thing for him to do, so Mary shouldn't resent him for it.

But she did.

He was only being honorable, watching out for her future. He was so damn full of honor she wanted to clout him on his dark head.

He could have solved his problems if he'd exposed Edith and Bauer in a much more traditional way. Let the magistrate read her diary, for example—he was on the consortium board as well as an officer of the law. The man could have removed Bauer with the flick of an eyelash.

But if Alec had revealed his wife's secrets, he might not be as appealing to Mary as he was. He had honored Edith's memory, even if she didn't deserve it.

Mary wished she didn't feel jealous. Wished she wasn't a second choice. Wished she wasn't an Evensong.

Alec had flopped on his back, chest heaving. He covered himself with one corner of the crumpled sheet and she did the same with the other.

"That was—" Alec began. "I canna describe it."

Her lips turned up. "I was thinking the same."

He rolled up on one elbow. His hair was damp and curling, making him look like a very naughty angel. "We are good together, aye?"

Mary nodded. "Aye." When in Scotland . . .

"When do you have to go?"

Never. "By Wednesday, I should think. That will give us a few more days to do . . . this again." Two more nights. Hell, two more days. Mary wouldn't wait until nightfall to find herself in Alec's arms again if she could help it.

He grinned down at her. "I have another surprise for you, too. An even better one than the dancing."

What could be better than waltzing at twilight? "Oh? What is it?"

"Not until tomorrow. You'll nae worm it out of me, no matter how you try."

Mary tapped his bicep. "I can worm with the best of them, my lord."

"I've no doubt you can. All those years working behind that desk—you must know too much for your own good."

Like a bell that couldn't be unrung, Mary's mind was filled with facts she'd gleaned from her various business dealings. People had poured their hearts out to her, thinking she was a wise old woman.

Right now, she felt most unwise.

"Maybe I shouldn't go back to Aunt Mim's office. There are lots of other jobs I can take."

Alec frowned. "You won't go back to those grocery stores."

He made it sound as if they were brothels or charnel houses. To a baron, they were probably just as bad—though with his history, Alec probably had no animus toward brothels.

"I don't know what I should do. Aunt Mim depends on me, no matter how wonderful she's feeling at the moment. I owe her everything. She's not strong, except for being strong-willed."

"Hm, so that's where you get it," Alec teased.

"She trained me well." If Mary was honest, she had been plenty stubborn and independent long before Mim brought her to London. That had been a constant source of friction between her and her brother and sister-in-law.

"I'm sure training you wasn't a difficult job. You're very bright, aren't you? Empathetic, too. You understand things."

She was uneasy with his praise. "What I understand, my lord, is that I'm exhausted, and you must be, too. We've had a trying twenty-four hours."

He shifted on the bed. "So we have. Do you want me to sleep in the other room?"

No, she did not. His body was warm and comforting. But what if he preferred to be alone?

"What do you want to do?" Her voice broke the tiniest bit.

"Do you really need to ask, Mary?"

"Some people sleep better undisturbed by a bed companion," she said lamely.

"And I'm usually one of them," Alec said. "But we managed just fine last night, didn't we? Unless you don't feel the need for my protection anymore."

She had never felt safer than when she'd been in his arms, waking or sleeping. "I'd like it if you stayed."

"Then that's settled. Do you want your nightgown? You might get cold."

Mary had no idea where it was, but then remembered she'd folded everything onto a chair. She started to sit up but Alec stopped her. "I'll get it. Get some water, too. I've a powerful thirst all of a sudden. All the hard work, you know. You are a slave driver." He gave her a wink.

Alec tossed her the nightgown and she watched him walk out the door, his bottom as handsome as the rest of him. He was very much at ease in the nude—all those years of experience, she reminded herself. Which is why she had picked him, wasn't it?

She would not start thinking of all the times he'd made love to other women. She was jealous enough of Edith.

Mary put on her nightgown, retrieved some pillows from the floor, and straightened the bedcovers. The scent of lavender was now joined by musk and Blenheim Bouquet. Last night he had slept by her side . . . and then on top of her, she recalled. It had not been an unpleasant sensation at all, even for a woman who was used to her privacy. Privacy, she decided, was overrated.

When Alec came back from the kitchen, he gave her a mug of water, too. It was crisp and cold, better than any wine. He was still gloriously naked, and the sip of water did nothing to assuage her dry throat at the sight of all that masculine muscle and might.

"Shall I walk you out to the privy? We can navigate by starlight, or I can light a lantern."

Perhaps privacy wasn't so overrated after all. It was one thing to share her body with him, but her bodily functions? She felt a blush sweep over her.

"I—I can go by myself."

"Unthinkable. There might be wolves about."

"Nonsense. Surely they've been hunted to extinction, like the poor bears." Men were always killing something.

"One never knows. And if you'd seen a bear, you wouldn't call it 'poor,' believe me. When I was in Canada—"

Mary perked up. "Canada? I've always wanted to go there. The United States, too. I have some friends who have moved there. To New York." Charles and Louisa Cooper might count themselves as friends—they would not have met without her.

"You should go. Wide-open spaces, and all that. Some parts of Nova Scotia remind me of the Highlands, in fact. I was only a boy when my father took me, but I remember a lot, especially the bear. My brothers were green with jealousy."

"Were you attacked?"

Alec laughed. "Nae. The bear was part of a traveling circus, missing most of his teeth and older than God. But in his prime he must have been a fearsome thing."

Mary did not approve of circuses. She'd had to take her nephews to too many of them.

"I'm sure it's perfectly safe to go outside—your bear is nowhere near here," Mary said, getting out of bed.

"I'm going with you anyway, and don't argue."

That was that. And to be truthful, Mary did not mind holding on to Alec's arm as they traversed over the freshly cut grass, the lantern bobbing the way. A great many stars twinkled overhead, and the air was as crisp and cold as the water had been. Mary took care of her needs, then waited for Alec to do the same, holding her hands over her ears to maintain the dignity between them. She was probably being missish, after fornicating twice with the man in one day.

Really, there should be a nicer word, something that sounded less stark on the tongue. If she couldn't find one, one would have to be invented.

They returned to the gatehouse, climbed into bed, and extinguished all the lights. Through the open door, the last flickering flames of the parlor fire were visible. Mary arranged herself in as small a space as possible—the bed was not large and Alec was. He pecked her forehead and they lay side by side in the dark silence. Mary had not brushed her teeth, but that seemed unimportant at the moment. He hadn't tried to kiss her goodnight properly, which was just as well. Who knew if she could stop at one kiss?

Sleep would not come, even after the day's events. By rights, she should be unconscious. But the mind was a peculiar thing, and hers skittered from this morning to this minute. Alec did not seem to share her reflective tendencies. His steady breathing was almost instantaneous, which was rather annoying. How could he ignore her when she was aware of every inch of him?

Mary had spent just four days in Alec's daily company. She would have two more, then leave. It had taken her less than a week to fall in love.

How many days would it take for her to forget him? She was afraid she knew the answer only too well.

Chapter

35

Monday, June 13, 1904

At some point, Mary must have fallen asleep, for here she was, waking. Which was good, for her dream had been filled with crowded city streets, noxious air, cars backfiring, horses whinnying desperately—worlds away from the peaceful stone house. London awaited, and judging from her jangled dream, she was not anxious to go back to the chaos.

She was alone, a dented pillow the only sign that Alec had ever been beside her. The bedclothes were pulled up and the curtain on the little window mostly drawn. There had been no hanky-panky in the night—Mary's nightgown was still buttoned up to her chin and her lips remained unkissed. She was as well-made as Alec's half of the bed.

She sat up and listened, hearing nothing but birdsong and the hiss and crackle of the parlor fire. It was chilly, and still early, the pale lemon light slanting through the wavy glass onto the bare wood floor. She sniffed, and did not detect the aromas of coffee or bacon.

Mary sensed Alec wasn't in the house—it was just too still. He must be in the privy, so she found the ironstone chamber pot under the bed, then washed her hands and face. Alec had brought in water while she slept, as well as started the fire. He had been so quiet she hadn't heard a thing, so maybe she *would* find him on the sofa, waiting for her to wake up.

But he was not. The parlor was empty, yet cozy from the fire. Mary resisted standing before it in her dressing gown, for there were things to do.

Alec had spoken of a surprise, but she could surprise him, too. Mary more or less knew her way around a kitchen, at least when it came to the basics, although she was very much out of practice. Mrs. Norris, her cook in Town was too fabulous to interfere with, but here was her chance. She would put together something from the hampers for their breakfast and do her part.

He'd thought to light the fire in the old range before he left, too, and she pumped water into a kettle for tea. The shelves were stocked with simple ironstone, and she set the table. She found the diminished ham, sliced it into a pan to fry. There did not seem to be any eggs, but there was bread and jam and cheese. Her stomach rumbled in an unladylike fashion, but she would wait for Alec to return.

The edges of the ham curled up, and still Alec did not come back. Mary moved the pan to a back burner, then took it off the stove altogether. The tea leaves had been steeping in the pot for quite a while, too.

Goodness, what if he was ill in the privy? Or worse, had gone for a morning constitutional and tripped over a root or something? She pictured Alec unconscious on a woodland path. She'd never be able to drag him home, even if she could find him. Raeburn Court was a vast estate, and the road to the main house miles away.

It was not like her to borrow trouble, but Mary had had enough practice at the Evensong Agency to anticipate possible problems and their solutions. *A stitch in time saves nine* and all that. She just couldn't remain at the table waiting. Surely it wouldn't hurt to step out into the garden and call for him? She didn't want to disturb his privacy, but if he needed her—

Mary didn't bother to find her slippers or comb her hair. Alec would have to take her as he found her, just as he'd have to consume the dry ham and stewed tea. The grass was wet beneath her feet, and she noted with some dismay clumps of it stuck to her as she walked toward the small outbuilding in the corner of the walled garden.

"Alec? Good morning!"

There was no response. She knocked on the blue-painted door, and it swung open, revealing the empty wooden seat and a neat stack of toilet paper beside it. There was a small book on the earth floor that Mary did not think had been there last night. She picked it up—Shakespeare's sonnets, unusual bathroom reading material, in her opinion—and tucked it into the pocket of her robe. It would be ruined if it remained on the damp ground. She really should have worn some shoes.

"Alec!" This time her voice was louder. Birds rustled in the bright green leaves, but Alec did not pop out from behind the bee skeps or scraggly rosebushes in the brick-walled garden.

He might be tinkering in the stable. The door was closed, so it was possible he hadn't heard her. She opened it and looked in. Alec's car was still covered with the tarp, but the sliding door to the estate road was open. He must have gone for a walk along the bumpy track. Determined now to eat her breakfast, she turned to leave.

And then something moved to her right.

"Don't move, Fräulein Arden."

Mary stood stock still. There was no question of who was in there with her.

What could she say that would sound calm and rational? Not, "What have you done with Alec, you bastard?"

She found that out soon enough. Bauer stepped out of the shadows and threw back the tarp with one hand, a remarkably shiny silver pistol in the other.

She would not scream. Would not. Alec lay crumpled on

the seat of the car, his shirtless torso pale as snow. There was matted blood in his hair, and his eyes were closed, but she thought she saw his chest rise.

Did she really, or was that wishful thinking?

Bauer was disheveled, as though he'd been sleeping rough. Gone was all trace of the smooth seducer. She had never found him attractive, but now she wanted to claw his pale blue eyes out.

"Why did you do this to me, Mary? Were you in his employ all along?"

"I d-don't know what you are talking about." Let him think she was witless. She scanned the stable for anything she might use against him. The rusty rake hung back on a wall, and a shovel lay next to the car. Bauer must have used it on Alec. She had no confidence she could reach either before he shot her.

"You set me up. Was it for money?"

"Wait just a minute! You set *me* up! You drugged me in order to rape me—I don't think you're in any position to cry foul. Just how many women did you trick that way? I suppose you had to—no one else would have you otherwise." Mary had let her temper get the better of her, but she enjoyed watching his mouth drop open.

Her enjoyment was brief. He stepped across the shed and slapped her face. She stumbled backward, tripping on the phonograph beneath the ratty quilt, and landed on her bottom. She couldn't very well beat him with the wax cylinders that rolled to the floor, but she clutched at the faded cotton fabric, thinking hard.

Her position was disadvantageous, to say the least. Bauer towered over her, the gun pointed at her head with an alarmingly steady hand.

"Why don't you just shoot me?" Mary asked. It really was a very good question, and she wanted to know the answer.

"That would be much too easy. No, my dear, your baron is going to shoot you, and he will go on trial for your murder as he did not do for his poor wife."

"Alec did not murder Edith," Mary said.

"That is just what he has told you, you stupid thing. He pushed her out the window."

Mary shook her head. "She jumped. She took her own life, because she was carrying your child, and the thought of any part of you inside her disgusted her."

Bauer turned purple. "You lie! She was in love with me, and wanted us to run off together like some idiotic romance."

"But you are married."

Bauer raised a brow. "You know a lot about me."

"I make it my business to know about people. You'll never get away with this. Alec would never shoot me."

"Who says I'll wait for him to do the job? It will only look as if he has. The gun will be found in his hand, your lifeless body beside it. It is his pistol, by the way. So easy to gain entrance to Raeburn Court with no staff about. If Raeburn awakes, let him explain *that* away. I will be long gone before you are discovered by that useless brother of yours. It is good you shall be dead, not having to live with the shame of his proclivities. He was kissing Raeburn's valet the last time I saw him."

Poor Oliver. To be held in contempt by such a piece of slime like Bauer was insupportable.

"How did you find us?"

"It wasn't hard to monitor the comings and goings, all the back and forth by the valet and the other brother. Evan, isn't it? Soon to be the baron. And I watched your little show last night. The naked dancing. It was—what is the word in English? *Touching*. You would have been better off to go home." He paused, giving her a wicked smile. "But then my plan might not be quite so entertaining. There is symmetry, no? First Raeburn tries to ruin me, and now I ruin him."

Bauer's words would not taint the beauty of what she and Alec had shared in the twilight. Mary's heart beat too fast. She took a breath, then tried to center herself. She was not at the feet of a madman, and Alec was not lying injured— possibly dying—in the car. She was Mary Evensong, clever fixer. Godmother to people much older than she was.

"He's rich. He can give you money to go away, to take

your whole family. To go back to Austria, or wherever you want to go. I can persuade him."

Bauer shook his head. "No, that won't do. My reputation is in tatters."

"You should have thought of that before you took advantage of so many young women."

"I admit I made a mistake with you. And you are not really that young now, are you?"

Why argue with him? He spoke the truth.

"Were you even a virgin?" he asked.

"I *was*." Mary looked up at him, defiant.

"Then Raeburn has a lot to answer for. The hypocrite."

"I gave myself to him willingly. Which no rational woman would ever do with you."

"Shut up!"

Mary's tongue was running away with her. It was really rather remarkable that the man had not shot her already and called it good. But she thought if she kept arguing with him, he could not resist trying to dominate her. Maybe by some miracle, Alec would wake up or she could throw dirt in Bauer's eyes or *something*.

The ground proved too well packed. Mary would die with dirty fingernails.

"Will you shoot me where I'm sitting, or may I stand?"

"What does it matter?"

"I've read about firing squads. Aren't the men lined up against a wall? So much easier to take proper aim for you."

Bauer shrugged. "If that is what you wish. You English are mad."

"Will you not give a hand like a gentleman to help me up?" Mary wasn't sure she could rise on her own. "It is the least you can do."

Another shrug. His left hand extended, the right still training the gun at her head.

She wouldn't have much time, and it was apt to be awkward. She had been working the quilt away from the phonograph since she'd tripped over it. One good tug, and it might get free.

And Bauer would provide the tug.

Mary imagined she was bowling a cricket game. The quilt arced in the air and landed over Bauer. She hoped his mouth was open in surprise and some mouse droppings landed inside.

"Scheiss!" Bauer screamed, batting at the blanket.

Precisely.

She stuck out a bare, grass-covered foot, which the temporarily blinded man stumbled over.

The gun went off as he fell, and Bauer hit the ground. For a few long seconds, he struggled under the quilt, then didn't move.

Mary raced to the wall and took down the rake. It looked much more lethal than the shovel, and she had no qualms whatsoever about using it.

Alec, Alec, please wake up, she prayed. She raised the rake over Bauer, flipping the tine side away at the very last moment, and brought it down with a satisfying swoosh. She didn't dare lift the blanket to see where he was injured. He was mercifully still—hopefully, he'd given himself a mortal wound and would be of no further threat.

Mary was shaking uncontrollably now, but held on to the rake as if it were a lifeline.

Then she hit Bauer with it again.

Perhaps she'd go to hell, for this and so many recent activities, but she hoped not.

"You've been busy, lass."

Alec's voice was faint, but audible. She turned to see him sitting up in the Pegasus, blood trickling from his scalp.

"Alec!" she cried.

"Not so loud. I've got a devil of a headache." He pointed toward Bauer. "The good doctor, I presume? I never saw who hit me. Is he dead?"

"I don't know. I daren't look. I hope so."

"Such savagery from a sweet little lady such as yourself. Help me get out of the car, Mary. Please."

Mary offered her arm and Alec nearly fell out. "Seeing double. There are two of you, but what a bonny sight. Sorry

I failed you." He was unsteady on his feet, leaning against the wing.

"You didn't fail me. Who could have imagined he'd come here?"

"I should have. We have to make sure he's dead, Mary. Give me the rake to lean on."

Mary wasn't certain she could release her grip on it—she was as unsteady as he was. Her fingers uncurled with reluctance and she passed it to him, wondering what would hold *her* up.

Alec was barefoot, too, clad only in trousers and blood. He stepped across the floor, leaning heavily on the rake.

"You're going to have to bend down and lift the corner of the quilt, Mary. I canna, or I'll fall down. Dizzy."

Mary swallowed, afraid of what she'd see. She shut her eyes, but could hear perfectly when the gun went off again.

Chapter

36

"This is not precisely how I intended to surprise you this morning," Alec gasped, clutching his shattered shoulder. The pain was so intense he saw spots dance across his eyes, and they were not gently waltzing. He closed them and tried to get his bearings and his breath.

It was only his left shoulder, not his heart. Bauer's aim had been mercifully off when it counted, and now the villain was dead. He had shot himself accidentally when Mary had tripped him, but didn't have the decency to die before he made more mischief.

There was blood. A lot of it. And Mary's face had lost all of hers as she tried to appear in control. Her hands gave her away as she wrapped his wound in the torn sheets she had fetched from the gatehouse, the blood soaking through as fast as she could cover his skin.

"What surprise would that be?" she asked, her voice reedy.

"Well, you said you wanted to learn to drive. This will be your chance."

"D-drive?" She said the word as if it were in a foreign language.

"It's miles through the wood to Raeburn Court. By the time you got there on foot, I might wind up like our friend over there."

Mary shuddered. Alec didn't think the hole in his shoulder was fatal, but one never knew. He'd forgotten whatever he'd learned at school of veins and arteries—the only thing he knew for certain was that the blood was flowing like a red river, he couldn't move his arm at all, his head was bursting, and he needed a doctor. He was braw enough, but not stupid.

"I'm sorry, Mary. It's the only way. I'll talk you through it. You'd better go get dressed."

"Dressed?" she asked stupidly. She seemed unaware that her dressing gown was soaked in blood and she was barefoot.

She was in shock. What she had done for him would probably haunt her all her days. Bauer had died from the wound to his gut, but not before Mary kicked away the gun and hit him again with the rake, tines down, this time with no ragged quilt to obscure his pain-twisted face. She was Alec's own Boudicca.

"At least put some shoes on. Your feet will slip off the pedals. I'll wait." Alec tried to smile.

She had been so brave. Alec had listened to her taunt Bauer from his painful perch in the car, struggling to come to and save the day. Well, it was Mary who'd saved it, but she wasn't done yet, poor girl.

"I don't want to leave you," she said.

"Don't worry, I'm not going anywhere. Off you go, lass." *And hurry.*

He sat against the wall and pondered his future. If he lived. Once the bullet was removed, things could still turn septic. He might even lose his arm. And then how was he to embrace Mary, waltz with her to a real orchestra, hold himself over her as he sank into her sublime depths?

She would have killed Bauer for him if the man was not already breathing his last. The malevolence in the doctor's eyes had been more deadly than the wild shot he fired. It was over. There would of course be some legal mumbo-jumbo, but Edith was avenged and Mary was safe.

Alec would ask her to marry him. He couldn't let a woman like Mary Arden Evensong get away.

If she could forgive him for placing her in such an untenable situation.

He'd make it up to her. Furs. Jewelry. A car of her own.

What was he thinking? Apart from the car, Mary's head would not be turned by trinkets. She was far above his touch in every way that mattered. He had never met a woman like her, and never would again. Raeburn men were not total idiots, even if they were attracted to unsuitable women across the centuries. They saw what they wanted, and went after it. His own father had spied his tenant's daughter riding across a field, and that had been that. Their love hadn't lasted, but then Alec's mother was nowhere near as sensible as Mary.

But you didn't tell a woman she was sensible and expect a reward. Sensible meant wearing plimsolls on the beach so you wouldn't cut your feet and carrying an umbrella at all times to ward off sun or rain or whatever nature threw at you. Keeping lists and sticking to them. Tick. Tick. Tick.

Alec wanted to walk barefoot on a beach with Mary, feel the sand and tide between his toes. To stand in the garden in a rainstorm and smother her with kisses. To toss the list away and do what felt right.

His cock stirred, and he chuckled. He might live after all.

He heard the kitchen door slam. Mary burst into the stable, wearing button-up boots and a dress that was *not* buttoned up. Her hair was still in its wild braid, and he reluctantly admitted he was glad she hadn't spent much time sprucing up.

He smiled up at her. "Ready for your adventure? What a lot of them you've had the past few days."

"Don't remind me. This entire affair screams, 'Be careful what you wish for.'"

Alec felt a stab of dismay. "Are you regretting accepting my job offer?"

"Of course not. Regrets are pointless, aren't they? One makes mistakes, learns from them, and moves on. Speaking of moving on, we don't have time for idle chatter, Alec. Can you get up on your own?"

"I'll never know until I try." Was he one of her mistakes, quickly to be forgotten? Alec hoped not. The shed swam around him as he lurched up. Just a few steps to the car. He could do that. Nothing to it. Perhaps he should try to bend over and pull the starting handle. No, not wise. Mary would have to do it.

He held on to the bonnet. "I already checked everything before Bauer knocked me out. The radiator's full, and the petrol cock is open. The hand brake is on—you'll have to release it so we can back out." Alec slid into the passenger seat and tried to steady himself without knocking into any levers.

"What should I do first?" Mary asked, looking anxious.

"You'll have to turn the crank a few times. Keep your thumb under the handle—we wouldn't want you to lose it if the car backfires. Then switch on the magneto." Mary looked at him blankly. His hand wavered in its general direction. "See? It's in the A position, which means it's off. As soon as the engine turns, move it to the M angle."

Mary made a few less-than-robust assaults on the starting handle. Miraculously, the engine sputtered to life, and she hopped into the car. Alec pointed to the various knobs and gauges, all the while sounding very much like he'd committed the driving manual to memory, which he had. Every car manufacturer did things their own way—there was no uniformity in the fledgling industry whatsoever. While Alec had mastered his Pegasus, other car models were complete mysteries to him.

"Ease back on the throttle . . . close the carburetor choke . . ." He went on, gently chiding her when she was too tentative. They had rolled backward out of the stable and were perilously close to smashing into the trees. "Brake!" He reached over and helped her shift gears, wincing.

"I can do it!"

"Of course you can." Her hands were riveted to the steering wheel. She was as white as parchment, each golden freckle standing out across the bridge of her nose. Maybe his best strategy was to pass out and wake up at Raeburn Court and not witness her terror, for her terror was contagious.

He hoped they wouldn't blow a tire on this rutted track, which was perfectly possible. Of all the parts on a modern automobile, tires were the least reliable. Alec didn't fancy trying to pump and patch one in his current condition.

He shut his eyes, not caring to see how fast they were going. Whatever the speed, it felt too damn fast. The Pegasus tipped with less regularity than other sorts of cars, which is why he had purchased one, but with his luck today, they'd wind up in a ditch. He lifted one eyelid to see Mary's grim profile, a martial light in her hazel eye. Against all odds, she seemed to have the vehicle in control.

"You're doing beautifully!" he shouted over the revolutions of the engine.

"I am, aren't I?" she shouted back, her eyes not leaving the road. "I've read some books, you know. On engines."

Of course she had. She'd probably read books on radio waves and X rays for amusement. He pressed his hand onto the lumpy bandage trying to stanch the flow of blood. He was light-headed, and every jarring bump on the road made him feel nauseous. At least he had no breakfast to vomit up—they'd never gotten around to it.

He'd hated to leave her at dawn. She'd been curled on her side, her face flushed, her braid a copper tangle. Alec had had every intention of coming back to bed and waking her up properly with loving attention, but getting the fires lit and relieving himself had taken priority.

And then he'd gone into the stable to check on the car for his little surprise.

Alec should have anticipated that Bauer would come after him, but he had honestly thought they'd be safe hidden away at the gatehouse. He'd counted on time alone with Mary. So much for best-laid plans.

Beneath the leaves and brightening sky, the day was really very fine, if he didn't think about Josef Bauer's body lying on the stable floor. Mary took the corners carefully, and it wasn't too long before they saw the stone turret of Raeburn Court peeking over the treetops. Emerging from the wood, they passed innumerable sheep that were kind enough not to trespass on the road, and eventually rolled into the cobblestone court near the converted stable where the Pegasus made her home.

Alec tried to sit up. "Slow down now, brake—that's it— and let down the sprag once the car comes to a full stop." There was little likelihood that the car would roll backward, but they had come this far and Alec did not want to crash into any outbuildings.

"You'd better honk the horn for help," Alec said, gritting his teeth. Now that they were at a standstill, the world still moved all around him. He was reminded of his sea voyage to the Americas when he was a boy, and for one brief moment wished his father were still here to take care of things.

Mary did as she was told, with the foot horn as well as the one connected to the steering wheel. The noise split Alec's head in two.

"I'm going inside," Mary said. "Don't move."

"Nae a chance o' that, I'm afraid," Alec said. His eyes rolled back and he slumped onto the dashboard.

He came to as he was carried to his own bed, jostled by Mac and Oliver Palmer. The two of them together were not up to carting a man his size up a flight of stairs, but with Mary barking orders at them, they had no choice.

Alec wondered where the workmen were. Fortunately he didn't hear hammers, which would have been the pièce de résistance to his headache. Perhaps it was still too early. He had no idea what time it was.

He was dropped into bed, every bone jarring. He recognized the girl who currently presided in the kitchen, standing mute as Mary told her what to do.

"I'm taking the car to Pitcarran to fetch the doctor," Mary said.

That woke Alec up. "You are *what*?"

"Oliver will come with me."

This was news to the young man. "I *will*?"

"Between Mac and Katie you will be in good hands," Mary said, ignoring Oliver. "Katie will fetch you some broth and tea and Mac will see to your dressing."

"What if the car breaks down?"

"Mac has already sent one of the grooms ahead. Dr. King will get here one way or another."

Alec envisioned the whiskery old doctor riding sanguinely next to Mary and failed. King did not hold with modern inventions, or modern "coddling" methods of medicine. Alec might die yet.

Dr. King had had no patience with Edith's megrims, which had made her ripe for Bauer's treatments. King had been loudly dismissive of the Forsyth Palace Hotel's facilities, and resentful of the new doctor in the area. But he should be able to dig a bullet out of a shoulder and prescribe some cod-liver oil, and be more than pleased his competition was dead.

"Are you sure you know how to drive, Mary?" Oliver asked, his voice quavering.

"I got here, didn't I? I just can't sit around waiting for the doctor to arrive."

"It's downhill all the way," Alec reminded her. "And when you come back up, if the car starts sliding, pull every knob you can see and put your foot on all the pedals. Something will work."

Oliver looked green.

"And if worse comes to worst, just jump out," Alec said, trying to be cheerful. The thought of Mary burning up in a wreck was not something he wanted to dwell on. King would probably pick them up in his carriage—he doubted the Pegasus had enough petrol to get all the way to town anyway, and he decided not to mention the extra can of fuel in the garage.

It would be better if she was out of the way—he was tired

of being brave. Like a wounded dog, he wanted to bite and howl and growl.

And he wanted Mac to get his mother's emerald ring out of the safe in his library. Alec had a proposal to make.

When he felt a little better.

Chapter

37

"You told me your father kept a whole fleet of cars in his garage," Mary grumbled. She brushed the dirt off her no-longer-white dress. Oliver was beyond brushing. He lay on his stomach peering at the engine under the front seat of the Pegasus. His hands were covered in oil. Even his golden curls were not exactly gold anymore.

"Well, he does, but we have a chauffeur, Mary! A mechanic who knows what he is doing. And I haven't lived at home in a year, remember? I was thrown out. Disinherited. Have I enough money to purchase a car of my own? No, I have not."

Poor Oliver. She should not be taking out her frustrations on him. "Well, you're getting a raise and a promotion."

"Not soon enough. What were you thinking to try to get to Pitcarran on your own?"

"I'm not on my own. I have you." In truth, Mary did not know what she had been thinking. She had been absolutely desperate to bring Dr. King back as quickly as possible. She couldn't bear to look at Alec's anguished face or see the bright red blood coursing from his shoulder. What if he bled to death?

She had—in simple terms—panicked. Fled, in the guise

of going for help. She'd been a complete coward. And now she was stuck on the side of a mountain, the car smoking, and loyal Oliver furious with her. She burst into tears.

Oliver scrambled up in a dust cloud and hugged her. "Hey, hey. None of that! Haven't you told me time and time again that tears are useless?"

"Wh-what if Alec dies? It will be my fault!"

"How can you say that? You got him back to Raeburn Court."

"But I sh-should have taken care of Bauer when I could. I was too afraid to look under the quilt to see if he was dead."

"And look what happened when you did take a peek. He could have shot *you.*"

"I never leave anything to chance. Never." Mary had been a planner all her life. How foolish of her to count on magic when she tripped Bauer in the stable. He might just as easily leaped up, more enraged than ever. It had been sheer luck that the gun had gone off as he batted at the quilt.

But not quite enough luck.

"Look, Mary, Bauer was a madman. You can't be expected to go around killing people with rakes. It just isn't in your nature."

"But I *wanted* to kill him. It was the most frightful feeling." She had raised the rake and brought it down. Twice. But each time, at the last minute, she had not given it her all.

Except for the third time.

She didn't know what was worse.

Oliver ruffled her hair. "Of course you wanted to kill him. He hurt the man you love."

Mary pulled the handkerchief from Oliver's coat pocket and blew her nose. "I do love him. But it's useless. Useless as tears."

"Why?"

"Because he's Alec Raeburn, and I'm Mary Evensong!"

"Well, it's good you haven't lost your marbles completely. You do know your name."

She shoved against him. "Be serious, Oliver. It will never work."

"Why not? Don't tell me you'll let class distinctions stop you. You are equal to anyone. You are starchy enough to be a duchess."

"I don't want to be a duchess. Maybe I can be his mistress," Mary said, sniffling.

"What rubbish. I'll have a talk with him when we get back," Oliver volunteered, his smile boyish and oh so naïve.

"You will not! Or I'll fire you. I mean it."

"You do not. But I won't say anything to Raeburn if you don't want me to. Just work your feminine wiles on him—he'll come around."

"I have no feminine wiles." Mary hiccoughed.

Oliver grabbed the handkerchief and wiped the mucus from Mary's upper lip. She must look a fright. "I admit, they wouldn't work on me, especially since you're all blotchy and wet, but don't sell yourself short, Mary. Now that you're not wearing a wig and those silly glasses and brandishing an umbrella, you're a very attractive woman."

"Now who's talking rubbish."

He shoved her back. "You'll have to give me an even bigger raise if you want me to keep complimenting you. Come on, Mary. Raeburn is crazy about you. At least that's what Mac says."

Mary's heart fluttered. My word, it really did—it just wasn't a literary convention. "He did? What did he say?"

"I can't remember exactly. But Mac said ever since Lord Raeburn met you, he's been much—how did he put it? Lighter. Although, let me tell you, carrying the man up those stairs wrenched my back. You will have to give me a vacation from this vacation once this is all over."

Mary threw her arms around Oliver, almost knocking him down. "You can have as much time as you like. Thank you for everything. I don't know what I would have done without you." She gave him a kiss on his cheek, which he wiped off at once, leaving a grease streak.

"I suppose we'd better leave the car and turn back. That doctor should be coming along any second."

Mary listened for the sound of any sort of activity below. "That's if we're on the right road. There was that fork—"

"You saw the signpost as well as I did. Pitcarran. Five miles."

"But what if someone turned it?"

"Oh, yes, because that's what Highlanders do for fun. Really, Mary . . ."

They bickered all the way back up the hill, until they came to the signpost in question. Mary's feet were killing her again, and she vowed if she ever lived a normal life in the future, she would do it barefoot. And if Alec's big gentle hands could massage her feet, so much the better.

After a brief argument where she wanted to turn left and Oliver right, he pointed. There, over a stand of trees, was a smidgeon of Raeburn Court's stone turret. On the right.

Edith's room.

Don't think about Edith, Mary said to herself. Don't think about Bauer. Don't think about Alec bleeding to death. Where in *hell* was that doctor?

The open front gate was in sight by the time they felt the hoofbeats on the road and heard the jingling of a harness. To Mary's dismay, Dr. King didn't slow down for a second and they had to leap into the culvert to avoid being run over.

"I say!" said Oliver, his fist shaking.

"It's much better he go straight to the house instead of stopping. Look at us—would you pick us up?" If Mary looked half as disheveled as Oliver, they must appear to the world as a couple of tinkers. Oliver had tossed his oil-stained jacket on a bush a mile back, saying he was hot, and Mary had no hat, black or otherwise. They were both drenched with perspiration and filthy. "Let's hurry," Mary said. What was one more blister?

*F*our hours later, Mary was at Alec's bedside, washed, wearing one of Katie's ill-fitting dresses, and frantic. Alec was still, his skin the color of fresh plaster. Dr. King had given him a sleeping draught, which was working only too well.

He didn't have to wake up for very long, just enough for Mary to tell him she loved him. He didn't have to love her back, but when he came to London, she would be available. Very available.

With the agency's help, he could get his household in order, and then he might have time for a few trips to Town. Mary didn't even mind that she might have to share him with an actress or two—

Oh, that was utter nonsense. She would want to scratch their eyes out.

Or pick up a rake.

This bloodthirstiness was a new emotion, and Mary was rather afraid of herself. She was supposed to be calm. Careful. Cautious. All those good *c* characteristics seemed to be absent at the moment.

Wake up wake up wake up. This was the second time today she prayed that Alec would return to consciousness. She didn't want to cause a setback to his recovery, but she really did want to speak to him.

And then she would go. Mac could get them to the evening train—in the estate's reliable carriage. Someone could send her belongings from the gatehouse when they got around to it. Mary didn't mind traveling back to London looking like a kitchen maid, minus the apron. It was sweet of Katie to offer her clean clothes after the awful way she'd harangued the poor girl over Alec's care.

She would run away, also for the second time today. She was still a coward.

She took Alec's cold hand in hers and gave it a squeeze.

He didn't squeeze back.

Dr. King said he should be just fine—the bullet had missed anything vital, and that with rest and rehabilitation, Alec's arm would be as good as ever. They were to watch for fever and signs of infection, as one would after any injury of this nature, but he was confident that Alec would pull through.

Mary had met Alec's brother Evan, a rangy redhead with a magnificent—if one liked such things—beard. He had come back from seeing the magistrate, and once Alec was patched up, went right back down the mountain to tell Sir John to call off the search and give him the latest grisly details. Presumably people were taking care of removing Bauer's body, but Mary had not bestirred herself to look out the window.

Alec would be in good hands. He had his brother. Mac. A skeleton staff that was loyal. A crusty old doctor who had cared for him since he was born.

He didn't need her underfoot.

"Alec," she whispered. "Please wake up before I have to go."

Chapter

38

Something warm and firm was on his hand, a pleasant diversion from the fire in his shoulder and the lead weight on his head. Alec needed to wake up to do something, but he couldn't quite remember what.

He shifted restlessly in his bed. He'd tried to wake up once before today, and had been much too late, to his shame. Mary had needed him, and he'd put her life in jeopardy. He would do better in the future. Take care of her.

If she would let him. She was an independent woman. Bossy. A bit like his mother, minus the tantrums.

But he wouldn't compare her to his mother. No woman liked to be compared to a man's mother. Alec knew enough about women to keep his compliments suitably vague in that regard. But he'd loved his mother for all her faults, and it grieved him that his parents' marriage had not been a happy one.

Was it possible to have a happy marriage? Not in his experience. But Mary was a different sort of girl—so sensible, not that he would tell her that, either, when he made his case for marriage.

That was it! He was going to propose to her.

"Alec, please wake up before I have to go."

What nonsense was this? Alec tried to lift his eyelids. They were weighted down with bricks but he managed to raise them nonetheless.

She sat at his bedside, wearing a rusty black dress fit for a funeral. Good Lord, he wasn't dead, was he? If he was, he'd much prefer to see Mary in the nude, her delicious curvy body dusted with freckles. How nice it would be to spend Eternity with her, dancing on clouds to angels' harps. He'd teach her to waltz properly—

But that would mean she'd have to be dead, too, and that was a dreadful concept.

He couldn't help but blurt it out. "Are you dead? Please say no."

"No. Of course I'm not dead, Alec, and neither are you. I'm afraid there's something wrong with your car, though. We had to leave it on the road."

"I'll buy another. One for you, too." He'd hire a chauffeur for hers, though. He'd been a little afraid of the gleam in her eye as she sat behind the wheel.

"Thank you, but a car would be a nuisance in London."

Had she said she was going there? He couldn't think.

"Is your aunt all right?"

"I suppose so. I've not had a marconigram to tell me otherwise."

"Then you're not going back to London," Alec said. He hoped he sounded firmer than he felt.

She took her lovely soft hand away. "But my aunt needs me."

"You just said she didn't. You can't go. *I* need you." Where had he put the damn ring? Not in his pajama pockets—he wasn't wearing any pajamas.

"I'll arrange for servants to be sent up from the agency. A round-the-clock nurse, if necessary."

"I don't want a nurse! I want you."

She lowered her eyes. "It's really not proper that I stay

here any longer. And there's no need—Bauer is dead and we are safe."

Alec wasn't feeling safe at all. His heart thudded. "You can't go. I have another job for you."

A job? Had Bauer blown his brains out as well as his shoulder? Alec was making a hash of this proposal business.

"I'm sure I can handle it from London. And when you visit, I should be more than happy to—entertain you when you come."

"The devil you will!" Alec tried to sit up. An unfortunate choice. "Mary, there will be no 'entertaining,' as you put it. You are staying right here."

"I have a business to run, Alec! Just because I hold you in some affection doesn't mean I can throw all my hard work away."

Alec fancied himself a modern man. He didn't want some decorative wife in a gilded cage—he'd had one of those, in a gilded tower, anyway—and he hit upon the perfect way to convince her to marry him. "I wouldn't expect you to give up your job entirely. I know your aunt depends on you. You can go down to London a few days every month. Longer if you have to. Don't you think the Evensong Agency will have even more cachet if one of its proprietors is a baroness?"

Mary's perfect rosy mouth dropped open.

"I'm asking you to marry me. Granted, I'm not going about it the right, romantic way, but honestly, if I have to get down on one knee, I'll nae get up. And I doona want to wait until I feel better."

"You—you've had a head injury today," Mary said faintly.

"Do you think my brains are so scrambled I doona know I love you? Nae, I know my mind, and I thank Bauer for making it crystal clear that I canna live my life without you. Say yes. I have my mother's emerald ring here somewhere. Ah! Under the pillow, I think. Grab it and put it on."

"I—I could be your mistress. You don't have to marry me."

Alec's head was pounding. What woman didn't want an emerald ring that would match her eyes? "Are you daft? Why wouldn't I want to marry you?"

"My father was a grocer."

"So?"

"So? Is that all you can say? You're a baron! We may live in the twentieth century, but it would be a scandal if you married me."

Alec laughed. "Scandal! Remember who you are talking to, my love. I've lived the past year under a black cloud. 'Twould be you who'd suffer, and doona tell me you're afraid of a bit of scandal. I can get Rycroft to tell our story in his paper—how brave you were through everything. How could any man resist marrying you, grocer's daughter or no?"

Mary blanched. "You mustn't mention the rake. I cannot get it out of my head."

"Och, you wee poor thing. Come here, my love." Alec forgot and tried to lift both arms to her. Another unfortunate choice.

She came anyway, and set her head on his good shoulder. "Are you sure you love me? You only met the real me on Thursday."

"I am sure. I confess I'd like to hear you accept—right now—but you have had a trying few days. If you want to wait . . ."

"I wasn't brave," Mary interrupted. "I'm not brave now. I don't know how to be a baroness."

"If you can pretend to be an old woman, you can pretend to be a baroness."

"You make it sound so easy," Mary said, nestling into the crook of his arm. He could tell she was coming around to appreciate his idea—she hadn't said no, even if she hadn't said yes.

"This time—and maybe only this time—I am right, and you are wrong."

"You're making fun of me."

"I would never do such a thing. I am in awe of you, Mary, and that's the truth. I wish I'd met you years ago, but we canna go back and change the past. We've only the future, and I want to spend it with you."

There, he was getting better at this proposing thing as the minutes ticked by.

"You really wouldn't mind me working?" Her words tickled the hairs on his chest. They could lie like this for the rest of their lives, tickling and talking. Touching. Kissing. Loving.

"Not at all. But when the children come, we can revisit the issue. But I expect with all your business connections we'll have the most fearsome nannies available. They'll be perfectly capable of caring for them, although if our children are anything like me and my brothers, they'll have their work cut out for them."

"Children." She said the word like she had said *drive* earlier today—had she never considered the possibility?

"Maybe just *a* child," Alec amended. He didn't want to frighten her. "I'll be happy with whatever comes along."

"Children!" Mary sat up, her eyes bright. "I didn't much care for my nephews, but your children might be altogether different."

"I should hope so. Really, Mary, do say yes. I'd find the ring myself but I'm not a contortionist."

She slid her hand under the pillow and pulled out the rather dazzling betrothal ring, her eyes widening.

I am right and you are wrong. Or was it *you are wrong and I am right?* They could take turns saying that to each other until they were both gray. Thanks to Mary's wig, he had an idea how lovely she would be as she grew older.

She held it in her palm but didn't put it on. "It's beautiful."

"My mother was the last to wear it. May I put it on your finger?"

Mary looked at him, her eyes brighter with tears. "You may."

Alec smoothed the ring over her knuckle. It was a little

loose, but nothing that couldn't be fixed by a jeweler. He vowed there would be nothing between them that couldn't be fixed, one way or another. "There. You belong to me. For better or worse."

"We belong to *each other*," Mary corrected.

She was right. As usual.

Her imagination ran wild—and ran away with her . . .

FROM NATIONAL BESTSELLING AUTHOR

VERONICA WOLFF

Devil's Own

A Clan MacAlpin Novel

After surviving slavery, Aidan MacAlpin has nothing but thoughts of vengeance. When his tutor, Elspeth, learns a secret to his past, it thrusts them both into a game of passion and deception that neither may survive.

PRAISE FOR VERONICA WOLFF AND HER NOVELS

"A poignant story . . . It explores family, friendship, revenge, obsession, and the power of love to heal deep wounds."
—*RT Book Reviews*

"Profoundly touching and emotionally searing."
—*Fresh Fiction*

"Wolff writes a story that will grab you from the first word and not let go."
—*Night Owl Reviews*

penguin.com

M1004T1011

DON'T MISS

Ladies Prefer Rogues

Janet Chapman, Sandra Hill, Veronica Wolff, and Trish Jensen

Out of time, out of place, but still searching for true love.

New York Times bestselling author **Janet Chapman** writes about a band of twenty-third-century warriors on a mission to save mankind . . .

USA Today bestselling author **Sandra Hill** plunges a woman back in time to post–Civil War Louisiana, where the poor Southern belle must make a living as a matchmaker . . .

National bestselling author Veronica Wolff tells of a seventeenth-century Scotsman who avenges the death of his greatest love . . .

USA Today bestselling author **Trish Jensen** spins a fetching fable about a woman from the Wild West who lands in modern-day Nevada . . .

penguin.com

Enter the rich world of historical romance with Berkley Books . . .

Madeline Hunter

Jennifer Ashley

Joanna Bourne

Lynn Kurland

Jodi Thomas

Anne Gracie

Love is timeless.